CW00833546

PRIMAL HEAT

Shifters of Darkness Falls

JASMIN QUINN

JEM MONDAY
PUBLISHING

Visit Jasmin's website at https://jasminquinn.com/

First Printing: 2021
Jem Monday Publishing Inc

Amazon Paperback ISBN: 9798714190469

❀ Created with Vellum

Cave-Right is the right of the Father——to hunt by
himself for his own.
He is freed of all calls to the Pack; he is judged by the
Council alone.

Rudyard Kipling
The Law for the Wolves
The Second Jungle Book (1895)

PROLOGUE

Ulrich needed a beer. Shit was coming to a head and first thing in the morning, he was set to head to Alberta. Almost 18 months for his team to catch a break and now all the pieces were set. It was going to be a long drive, but Ulrich didn't fly. It wasn't natural, not for shifters, humans, or even cats in carriers.

The good news he got this afternoon had his blood pumping even if his brain listed all the things that could go wrong. Every fucking thing was scrolling through his head like the credits after a long, dramatic movie. The operation had to be perfect with no spilling of blood, no loss of life. Too much was at stake.

He walked into Becker's Pub and immediately regretted his choice of watering hole. The fucking place was busy, no matter that it was the middle of the week. He would have turned around and left except that *her* car was in the lot, which, if he were being honest with himself, was the real reason he stopped by.

He sidled up to the bar and heaved his bulk onto a bar stool. A mug of beer magically appeared in front of him and

1

he nodded his thanks to the bartender, a human by the name of Harris Palmer. Ulrich tried to keep his expression neutral, but he fucking hated the dick, even if he was efficient. Too charming, too polished, too fucking good looking.

He shrugged off his irritation and swivelled in his seat, taking in the room. Jackson Hayes was sitting with Ren Ketkah, and Ulrich felt annoyed for some unfathomable reason.

Nah, he knew why.

Ren was an alpha, maybe the only alpha in this part of the world who had half a chance of bringing Ulrich down. Shit like that brought out the unreasonable beast in him – his wolf was always looking for a pissing contest. Best to stay as far as possible from the Mountain alpha, but he also knew that wouldn't be an option, not as his reason for being in Darkness Falls progressed.

And then there was the woman – human, small, crushable. Sitting among the shifter females like it was the most natural thing in the world. Maybe it was... for them. Not for him though.

Aubrey Powell. Middle-school teacher with a dead sister and the reason he was in town to begin with. Not her. The dead sister.

His fascination with Aubrey went far deeper than the case he was working on. He'd known the moment he saw her, months ago, when he walked into the RCMP station for a meeting. She'd strolled out of the precinct's conference room with Chief Jackson Hayes on her heels.

It was a lightning bolt moment – something he'd never experienced in his life with any other woman. Strange thing, this fated mate bullshit. All the stars had to align to find that one perfect match. And there she was, an underfed little waif in shabby clothes, worn shoes, and defeated posture. The woman was hurting, neglected, alone. He saw all this, and his wolf went wild.

He'd been in plenty of situations in his past where he'd had to restrain the inner beast, but that time, in the cop shop, he almost lost the battle.

What kept him from making a complete fool of himself was that, despite his immediate physical response to her scent, her voice, and her wide-eyed stare, he also wanted to bite her head off. He didn't have the time nor the inclination to be distracted by a human woman or any female for that matter. He'd already had his fill of domestic bullshit to last a couple of lifetimes.

He was never going to hook up with a woman for more than a simple roll between the sheets, fated mate or not.

Still, over the past several months, it had taken every ounce of willpower he possessed not to stalk this woman, hunt her down, make her his.

Which brought him back to the now.

He was at Becker's because she was there. He kept telling himself that it wasn't because she mattered to him, but because his wolf's instincts were driving him to be near.

Ulrich drank almost half his beer as he leashed his beast. It was good he was leaving town tomorrow, good that she was a secondary distraction to the bigger issues he was grappling with.

He set his mug on the bar top and dug in his pocket, pulling out a few bills and tossing them next to the glass.

Ulrich contemplated Aubrey's drinking companions. She was sharing the table with Cherime Montana, sister to the Lodge pack's beta and as far as he could tell, as high maintenance as women came. And the other shifter, the little one whose name escaped him, was at the table too, that crazy little bitch from the Dominant pack. Didn't make sense, these three women together, but then again this was Darkness Falls. Not much made sense.

Lowry Pattison, the barmaid or whatever the pc term was these days, was standing at the table talking to the three.

He was about to stand, get the hell out of the bar and away from the call of the human siren, when he heard Ren's name mentioned. Apparently so did Ren, because right on the heels of a fit of female giggles, he strode over, looking as pissed as a cat in a shower.

He brushed up against Lowry, and Ulrich scented the woman's desire, but Ren's focus was on Cherime. "I've been calling."

Ulrich almost grinned when he realized that Ren had it bad for Cherime. No, it was more than a case of boy meets girl. They were pair-bonded.

Cherime glanced down at the weird green drink she'd ordered. "I've been busy." She picked up the glass and raised it to her lips, but Ren deliberately bumped the bottom of it, causing it to spill down her chin and onto her sheer white blouse, soaking through to her tank and bra.

"You asshole!" Cherime exclaimed as she jerked to her feet, baring her teeth.

"Tabernacle," Lowry mumbled as she moved away.

"You broke Lowry's fucking heart, mountain man." The crazy one knelt up on her chair, so she was peering into his face. "The least you could do is not make a mess."

Yep. The little shifter was certifiable.

Aubrey stood too, sort of. She was swaying on her feet, trying to focus her eyes on Ren. "You're mean."

Shit. The woman was drunk, which made her reckless. Which might turn into a blood bath if Ren lost control. And Ulrich's wolf wasn't all that happy with her talking to another male, an alpha one at that.

"I did you a favour, didn't I?" Ren spat at Aubrey. Then to

Cherime, he said, "What the fuck are you doing hanging out with the human?"

Hold the fucking stagecoach! Nobody was going to talk about Aubrey that way, especially not a behemoth shifter who seemed to have a hate on for her. He got to his feet and stalked towards the little group, which was fast attracting the attention of the rest of the bar.

Ren caught Ulrich's approach. "Back the fuck off, asshole," he snarled.

Ulrich's wolf almost howled in glee. It had been spoiling for a good fight for months.

Jackson was on his feet too, moving fast to intervene before Ulrich reached Ren. "Nope. Not here," he said aggressively to Ulrich as he shoved himself between the two.

Ulrich humoured the cop while his wolf roared like a champion. "What the fuck do you mean, you did her a favour?" Ulrich snarled over Jackson's shoulder.

"No!" Jackson's voice reverberated through the bar as he pushed up against Ren. "Outside, all of you!"

"Fuck," the little brown-haired shifter moaned. "I hate when we have to go outside. Somebody always makes me go home."

"Time to go home anyway," Ren said to her. "You fucking trouble-maker."

She stood on her chair so she was taller than the mountain alpha. "This isn't my fault, you fucking alpha."

Holy shit! Ulrich was shocked speechless at the woman's aggressive disrespect. She was off her territorial land and seemingly without any other members of her pack. Not a good combination when facing down a bastard like Ren.

Ren seemed to think the exact same thing as his eyes turned amber at her disrespect.

Ulrich almost leaped between the two, but Cherime grabbed Ren's arm as Jackson snatched the little female around the waist and threw her over his shoulder, carrying her out of the building while she shouted her protests.

Ren stalked after them with Cherime in tow.

"Leah's high!" Cherime shouted at the Mountain alpha. "And she can say what she wants to you. You're not her alpha."

Leah, right.

Cherime glanced behind her as Ulrich wrapped his hand around Aubrey's arm, so thin he easily circled it with his grip. "Let her go!" she yelled at him.

Ulrich ignored the female shifter. The important thing was to get Aubrey out of the line of fire. Take her home where she could sober up.

"Fucking trouble, the whole lot of you!" Ren cursed as he stepped out of Becker's, Cherime in tow.

Cherime was fighting him every inch of the way, but in her ridiculous high heels, she wasn't much of an opponent. "Then why bother, Ren? If I'm so much goddamn trouble."

"Because you're a good lay," he snarled as he rounded on her, his temper overriding his good sense.

"You're such a shit." The she-wolf smacked him before he had a chance to stop her.

He grabbed her wrists and yanked her flush to his body. "Do that again, Cherime. I dare you."

Leah jumped on Ren's back, grabbing him by his hair and riding him like he was a wild horse. "Do not threaten Cherime, you fucking alpha!" She looked around Ren's bicep and said to Cherime. "Don't know why you're so mad. It sounded like a compliment."

Ren dropped his grip on Cherime, reached behind him, and grabbed Leah by the waist, hauling her over his head and thumping her ass-down on the ground in a puddle of water. "Go the fuck home, Leah!"

Leah crawled out of the mud, her teeth bared. "You don't tell me what to do, asshole! And you don't hurt my friends!"

Jackson pushed his way between Leah and Ren. "Go home, Leah, before I have you arrested for public intoxication."

"I'm not drunk!" Leah snarled.

"I don't know that!" Jackson returned her snarl and raised her a growl. "You got three seconds or I'm going to cuff you."

Leah peered at him, her eyes curious. "Maybe I want to be cuffed – last time was kind of fun."

"One—"

"She shouldn't be walking out here alone," Aubrey gabbled, staggering into Ulrich, who still had a grip on her arm. She tried to wrench it away with a weak jerk that almost knocked her on her ass.

Ulrich pulled her upright. "Stop wiggling." Each time she bumped up against, his body reacted like it was being tasered.

"Aubrey's right," Cherime agreed. "It's late, dark, and Leah's little."

Leah glared at Cherime. "Stop with the little shit!"

Cherime rolled her eyes. "I didn't call you a shit!"

Ulrich cursed under his breath. "I'll take them both home." Yep, he regretted the offer the instant in fell out of his mouth.

"I'm not going home with you," Leah bared her teeth at Ulrich.

Aubrey giggled as she staggered two steps towards Leah before Ulrich yanked her back. "I think he meant he'd drop us off at our homes." She stretched her head back as she looked up at Ulrich. "It's what you meant, right big guy? I'm not really into threesomes."

Leah widened her eyes. "Neither am I, you pervert. I'll find my own fucking way home."

"Christ," Jackson muttered as he scrubbed at the back of his head. "I'll drive you home, Leah."

Leah shook her head and stepped away from Jackson. "No, nope. No way am I arriving home in a cop car."

"We're leaving," Ren growled, pulling Cherime towards his truck.

Ulrich going to let Ren just waltz out of there without clearing the air. "Hold the fuck up!" he growled. "I'm not done talking to you."

Aubrey tried to straighten her back and stand still, but she was rocking like a boat on a stormy sea. "Yeah, and no one's taking Cherime unless she wants to go." She pointed an unsteady finger at Ren.

Jesus Christ. What was wrong with these women, talking that way to a sonofabitch alpha like Ren?

Jackson turned to Ren. "Aubrey's right. Cherime doesn't go with you unless she wants to."

"Who's gonna stop me?" he boomed. "This is shifter business, you fucking cop!"

Ulrich had to give Jackson credit for holding his ground. "Consider me off-duty, alpha. She's not fucking getting in your truck unless she wants to."

Ulrich stepped up next to Jackson. "I got your back on this one."

Cherime rolled her eyes. "Stop with the pissing contest. Let's agree you all have big dicks." She grinned at Ulrich and Jackson. "Thanks for being all gallant and shit, but I can take care of myself."

"Are we done here?" Ren snarled.

"Not done." Ulrich held a dangerous edge to his voice but kept his distance because Cherime was between them and despite her annoying personality, he wasn't going to be responsible for her getting hurt.

He handed Aubrey off to Jackson as Ren moved in front

of Cherime. "You got something to say, you motherfucker, get it said."

"Fuck," Jackson muttered as he shoved Aubrey towards Leah. They were practically the same size, but Leah staggered under Aubrey's drunken weight.

Ulrich ignored everyone but Ren. "I asked you a question inside that you didn't see fit to answer. What the fuck favour did you do for Aubrey?"

Ren bared his teeth. "Why the hell is that your business?"

Ulrich took a threatening step towards the fucker. "I'm making it my business. You have a hate on for humans, and you aren't going to make Aubrey a target for your bigotry."

Cherime wiggled out of Ren's grasp and pushed herself between the two Alphas. "Ren's not prejudiced against humans. Just Aubrey."

Ren tried in vain to yank Cherime behind her out of the line of fire. "Not really helping, Wolverine."

"For god sake's you guys!" Cherime exclaimed as she shrugged Ren off. "When the snowstorm hit, Aubrey and I got stranded on the mountain with some high school girls and took shelter in the Mountain's pack's community centre."

"Yeah," Aubrey added. "He didn't throw us out even though he wanted to."

Cherime glared at Aubrey. "I've got this covered, Aubrey."

Ren pulled Cherime behind him again. "I'm gonna say this once, you rogue shifter. What I do is none of your fucking business. Not now, not ever. You question me again and I'll turn you into fucking bear bait."

Ulrich inhaled deeply. "Go home to your mountain and stay there." The threat was clear in his underlying tone. He stalked over to Aubrey and Leah. "Let's go."

As they left, Leah did a 180 from difficult batshit crazy female to relaxed batshit crazy female. "Where're we going first?" she asked from the backseat of his crew cab.

"Taking you home."

"No," Aubrey protested, her voice sanding the edges off the sounds of the consonants. "Les's do somethin' fun." Her head was pressed against the back of the seat, her face tilted up, her eyes closed. She was on the verge of passing out.

"It's midnight, Cinderella."

Leah pouted. "I don't want to go home."

"I have no intention of taking you home." Ulrich doubted Leah was still high, if she ever was. "I'm dropping you off at the edge of your territory and you can walk."

Aubrey turned her head in Ulrich's direction, her big eyes drawing him in. "You're goin'a make her walk? Thas's not nice."

"I can't cross into her pack's territory," he muttered, feeling the need to defend his actions for some reason.

"And I don't need the hassle of you dropping me off at my house," Leah snarked, then shoved her pointer finger in his line of sight. "Drop me off there." She indicated a lone, ancient Western Hemlock. "I'll walk from here."

"Is's too far to walk, Leah," Aubrey complained, but Ulrich ignored her. He had no interest hauling around another pack's female any longer than he had to.

Leah flipped open the truck door and jumped out. "You keep your fucking hands off her," she rasped at Ulrich.

Aubrey belly-laughed at Leah. "Go home before you fall down."

"As if," Leah grumbled but she was already walking away.

Alone with Aubrey, Ulrich became hyperaware of her presence. It was the first time he'd been near her since that day in the cop shop. Pair-bond or not, there nothing compatible about them at all, but that didn't seem to matter to his wolf, who was holding a party in his gut.

Tempted as he was to pull over and spend some time with her, he drove directly to her home. He needed to drop her off and get the hell out of there because his fucking wolf was turning into an unreasonable snarling mess of desire and aggression.

Take her, now! Mate her, now!

Fuck the fuck off! The woman was dead drunk, and no way was he going to fuck around with her when the only thing currently keeping her upright was the seatbelt.

At her apartment building, he half-carried, half-dragged her inside, his wolf urging him to throw her over his shoulder and carry her off to bed.

Jesus Christ! he told his wolf. There was nothing remotely desirable about her in her current state.

You're full of shit!

Clearly, Aubrey thought so too, because as soon as they were at her door, she threw herself at him, standing on her tip-toes, arms circling his neck.

"Come inside," she slurred. "For *coffee*." She fluttered her eyelashes in an exaggerated manner that elicited a snort of laughter from Ulrich.

That seemed to encourage her, and she ran her hands over his chest, tracing the hardness of it with her fingers while she giggled. "You're amazing." She looked up at him, her big brown eyes filled with adoration.

Aubrey was pea-sized next to him. Thin with small, barely noticeable curves, tits that were scarcely a mouthful. Add to that her inherent shyness when she was sober, her mousy brown hair, her social awkwardness, and the fact that she was a fucking schoolteacher, and she shouldn't have appealed to him.

Yet, Ulrich's wolf was howling, pacing, ripping him apart from the inside out.

Ulrich grabbed her wrists, then hesitated. Not because of his fucking wolf – he'd managed to tune that needy prick out. No. It was all him, getting caught up in eyes too big for her face, the whiff of coconut on her silky skin, the lingering way she spoke, her tiny hands, her trusting gaze.

The thought of her soft, plump lips under his, her sweet-as-honey taste, her passionate cries as he fucked her, made him harder than he'd ever been in his life. Then she launched herself at him, her fingers grabbing his hair, yanking his head down to hers and mashing her lips against his.

The shock of the kiss almost razed him of all rational thought and his wolf roared inside him. This woman, his woman, he had to have her.

He grappled with his desire, his wolf's howls of excitement, and his need to take her, make her his in every way. But he couldn't, wouldn't do something in the inebriated state she was in.

He didn't kiss her back, but he didn't push her away. He let her have her way with him.

Then the door across the hall slammed open and a cantankerous croak from behind him shocked him out of his lust fog. "Take it the fuck inside and let the rest of us get some sleep!"

He yanked Aubrey off him as she giggled.

"Sorry," she slurred to the older woman, peeking past Ulrich's broad body. "We'll do juss that."

"No, we won't," Ulrich said to Aubrey as he turned towards the neighbour and glared. "You'll take it inside. I'm leaving."

Despite his size, the hostility in his tone, his glare, the woman across the hall didn't seem the least intimated. She threw Ulrich a knowing sneer, then disappeared back into her apartment, slamming her door.

"You don't have to leave," Aubrey whined as she went in for another kiss.

He'd had enough. He wasn't about to appease his asshole

wolf by fucking a drunk woman who would wake up in the morning hung-over and pissed-off.

"Get the fuck inside and lock the door behind you."

Aubrey pouted, narrowed her eyes, flared her nostrils, and yes, she even stamped her fucking little foot. "You're mean," she declared as she fished her keys from her purse. "It's because I'm ugly." Her face reddened as she blinked her eyes rapidly.

Shit, please don't fucking cry.

Tears started streaming down her face as she tried to fit the key into the lock.

"You're not ugly," Ulrich muttered as he took the keys from her and opened the door.

He shoved her inside and she turned, her big wet eyes looking up at him like adoring kittens. "Then why won't you stay?"

There was no reasoning with a drunk woman. "I'm leaving town first thing in the morning. Have an early start."

"Are you coming back?" she said in a hurt little girl voice.

Was he coming back? He shouldn't, not with her here, but his work in Darkness Falls wasn't done. And he liked the town, knew it was the best place for him, a good place to raise children.

"Yeah. I'm coming back." Before she could say anything more, he banged the door shut in her face. "Lock it!" he snapped.

He waited until he heard the click of the deadbolt, then stepped back, ignoring the lingering disappointment and the painful ache in his balls.

In the morning, she'd be full of her own regret and Ulrich was glad he wouldn't be around to witness it.

CHAPTER ONE

Aubrey sat on top of one of the desks, dead centre in her classroom, feet planted firmly on the seat of the desk in front, elbows resting on her knees, hands clasped together propping up her chin. All the surrounding desks were in neat rows like prisoners of war facing the firing squad... er... chalkboard.

Too soon to be jaded, she chided herself. This was her first official year of teaching under contract. No more substituting in another teacher's classroom. This was her classroom, and in a week, it would be filled with Grade 7 and 8 students. Twenty-seven of them to be exact, unless there were some late enrollers, which, according to Mr. Blake in the classroom next to hers, almost always happened.

Aubrey sighed. Mr. Blake was only a few years older but lorded his four years of teaching experience over her as if she were clueless about what she was doing. She was, but that didn't excuse his assumptions.

Last school term, when she was subbing, she'd made the mistake of calling him Clayton in the hall, and he corrected her in his stern teacher voice. "It's Mr. Blake, Ms. Powell.

Anytime students are around, in or out of school. These students must learn respect and if we don't model it, who's going to teach them?"

Maybe their parents? Aubrey thought but didn't say.

Mr. Clayton Blake. Middle name jerkturd. If the stick up your butt fits, wear it.

She'd drawn the short straw with the split 7/8 class. There was also a grade seven class and a grade eight class. Mr. Blake got the grade eight students because according to Mrs. Blake, the wife, who got the grade seven class, he was the only one who could handle the hormonal beasts.

Everyone in the school knew that was a load of bullcrap since Aubrey had her own set of grade eight students. Half as many maybe, but they were as much beasties as Mr. Blake's. The reality was that from grade six onward, it was one major hormonal shark infested pool, and it didn't matter who taught who.

There were too many students for single grade seven and eight classes, but not enough to justify smaller class sizes and more teachers. Putting the grades together meant teaching two curriculums with lesson plans that aligned so it seemed seamless to the students and their parents. It meant late nights and early mornings for Aubrey, but that was okay. Aubrey wasn't much of a sleeper anyway. Too many stupid dreams.

She wasn't complaining about drawing the short straw. She had a full-time job with a good paycheck for the first time in her life. And aside from Mr. Blake, the other teachers were approachable and seemed willing to overlook the fact that her arrival in Darkness Falls was related to the unsolved murder of her sister, Adrienne.

And she had friends now, the kind that were keepers. Crazy ones that scared her sometimes, but loyal and fierce, and would be there if she needed them.

Given that one of her friends was Leah Kavik, Aubrey already had plenty of practice at dealing with crazy. She'd wager none of her students had swallowed the family pet goldfish in an effort not to be wrong. The memory curved Aubrey's lips.

While the school year didn't officially start until after Labour Day, there was a ton of administrative stuff to do and everyone was prepping their classrooms and lesson plans for the year.

Grades seven and eight were transitional years for her students. They were becoming teenagers, on the cusp of puberty, highly sensitive to social positioning, and as squirrely as... well... as squirrels.

They'd talk nonstop, push back against convention, and try to be as individual as they could while still conforming to peer pressure. She hated that schools still had a pecking order, that some students were considered lesser beings than others – picked on for being different, being poorer, being smarter, being quieter.

She knew better than anyone because she'd been one of them, still was in some ways.

She sighed and returned her attention to the task at hand – setting up her classroom. Perhaps she should arrange the desks in a circle with a few empty ones in between. She liked to use her big teachers' desk when the class was empty or the students were working but preferred to sit among the students when she taught. It gave her an advantage and with 12- and 13-year-olds, she needed every advantage she could get.

A light rap at the open door drew her attention and she almost fell off the desk when Ulrich Calhoun's magnificent form entered her classroom, a young boy trailing behind him.

She bit her lip as her face heated in embarrassment. The last time she'd see Ulrich was when he'd given her drunken butt a ride home after a girl's night out with her friends, Cherime and Leah. Her dim recollection was that the evening almost ended in a brawl in the parking lot at Becker's.

Yeah, she'd been drunk, but unfortunately not so drunk that she didn't remember attacking Ulrich outside her apartment door. Yep, shy, demure Aubrey threw herself at the sexy giant. Kissed him. Flirted with him. Invited him inside.

Her stomach somersaulted when she recalled the aggressive way that she'd clutched his hair so she could drag his face down to hers. She might have been drunk, but she hadn't forgotten a second of the kiss – his lips against hers, his earthy taste as she'd slipped her tongue between his lips.

Over the summer, she'd managed to avoid any encounters with him, but today, her streak ended, because there he was, standing just inside her classroom, all freaking six feet and million inches of him, his wide shoulders and chest tapering to a honed waist and perfect hips.

He was outfitted appropriately for early September in an untucked black T-shirt and faded blue jeans that hugged him in all the right places. She willed herself not to let her eyes linger on the bulge at the apex of his strong thighs, or his biceps or his big hands or... or... or....

She glanced into his water-colour blue eyes and saw the storm in them. They were full of expectation and interest as they studied her.

Her stomach rolled like a ship in a hurricane as she stood, her shaky legs betraying her reaction to him. This had to be one of those karma moments.

Ulrich had been nothing but a gentleman that night, for which she was grateful when she woke the next morning with a pounding head and a raging thirst. He'd declined all her drunken advances, reassured her that her ugliness was not a factor in his refusal, and mumbled something about going out of town for a while.

Find your voice, teacher. This man isn't here to bring up the past. "Mr. Calhoun," she squeaked, then cleared her throat as she looked past him to the tall sandy-blonde haired boy he had in tow. The hair, the height, the eyes, the brow. They had to be related.

"Ms. Powell," Ulrich greeted in that deep rich baritone that made her think of the K-I-S-S-I-N-G song. *Ulrich and Aubrey sitting in a tree.* "I've been to the office to register Taggart for school and the secretary sent me this way."

"Tag," Taggart mumbled, his hands firmly in the pockets of his jeans while he studied the floor.

"Tag," Ulrich corrected. "Apparently, he's in your class for the year."

Aubrey dropped her jaw slightly as she gazed at Tag. "Awesome!" Not awesome. No, not a good idea at all. Not when this kid was... what? What was the relationship?

"Is he your...?"

"Son." Ulrich filled in the blank.

She opened her mouth to respond, then closed it again. *He's got a kid and a wife, and I threw myself at him like a hooker on BOGO day.* No wonder he left town.

Ulrich held her eyes as if waiting for her to say something.

Pretend he's any other parent, not the one you drunkenly pawed. "I didn't know you were married." Wow, Aubrey. That was as clever as it was transparent. She was sure that her face had turned permanently red.

His lips curled up in what might have been mistaken for a grin... or possibly a grimace. She couldn't tell. "Does that change things, Ms. Powell?"

She bit her lower lip trying to come up with something intelligent. "What things?" Yup, clever like a broomstick.

"Do you really want to go there? The last time we saw each other was—"

Seriously? "Don't. Please. I was obviously not myself." She

glanced at Tag as he wandered off, seemingly bored with the awkwardness between the adults.

"So your drinking problem—"

"I don't have a drinking problem." She glared at him, wondering why he was being an ass.

"That's good to hear. You know... for the safety of my son. I wouldn't want to find empty wine bottles outside your class-room window."

"Please stop." Aubrey's embarrassment had turned to annoyance. "That was a one-time thing."

"Which part? Drinking too much or throwing yourself at some random guy?" This time the curl to his lips was clearly a smirk.

She glanced at Tag who was tapping on the cage of Prince Charles, the class guinea pig that she had inherited from the outgoing teacher. "I don't do either." She lowered her voice. "I'm sorry if I offended you."

What she couldn't tell him was that he was not a random guy. Any other man, and she would have left him at the curb. But Ulrich Calhoun appealed to her on a primitive level. He was the only reason she would ever make a fool of herself.

He shrugged as he held her eyes. "Had the shoe been on the other foot, I would've gotten arrested for my behaviour."

Let it the heck go! "Double-standards. I know. Thank you for being a gentleman."

He glanced past her to Tag. "Hey kid, you want to go to the truck. I'll be just a minute or two."

"Thank god." Tag breathed his relief as he grabbed the set of keys dangling from his father's finger and fled the classroom.

Aubrey's stomach twisted at being alone with Ulrich. Something about this guy grabbed her attention and it went well beyond her physical attraction to him. Darkness Falls grew them big and sexy, but Ulrich did more for her than give her fantasy-rich alone time. In fact, she was almost certain they were fated mates, though she had no idea how to determine it. She wasn't about to ask her friends, Cherime or Eva, because she'd never live it down. And Leah... well, no. Just no.

Ulrich strode past her, across the front of the room, his bearing, stride, and stance the same as Tag's, but with far more confidence. They were definitely father and son. He stopped behind her desk and stared at a pinboard plastered with pictures of past Prime Ministers, his hands in pocket.

Aubrey let the silence linger, not sure what to say to this tall brooding man. After a moment, he moved on towards the back of the room near Prince Charles, then turned back to Aubrey. "I'm being an ass about that night. I'll move on, but I'm about to share some stuff with you about Tag and I want to be assured of your discretion."

"Of course." Aubrey held her expression bland. There were circumstances where she was required by law to report concerns about students to the authorities, but it wasn't worth noting for this discussion.

He nodded as he crossed his arms over his mighty chest, the bulge of his biceps exceeding the size of one of Aubrey's thighs. "Tag's mom and I are divorced. I've always had custody of him."

Aubrey nodded and refrained from asking where Tag had been the last year because he hadn't been attending Darkness Falls Middle School, at least not while she was subbing. She also shoved the unsolicited flair of jealousy down to her toes and willed it to stay there.

"Several months ago, my ex grabbed Tag and took off with him. My team located their whereabouts, but we had to sit on the information until it was safe to extract him. It's why I left town last June."

Aubrey tucked her lower lip between her teeth and nodded. Was he justifying his disappearance or was it part of

"Chief of Police. Can't go wrong there."

"And you."

Aubrey was shocked almost speechless. She managed to squeak out a, "Me?"

Ulrich contemplated the floor for a few seconds, then pinned her with his eyes. "I don't do relationships, Ms. Powell. Sibyl burned me bad and the few women I've let close to me since never really understood that Tag always comes first."

Aubrey wondered at his message as he groped for words. "As a shifter, he's on the cusp of manhood. Puberty is the point when a pup becomes a wolf. He has to master his wolf and he needs people around him that he can trust, that can handle him."

Aubrey shook her head as she felt a heavy weight of responsibility press down on her. "We don't know each other, Mr. Calhoun. Not really. Why would you include me?"

His blues eyes were serious. "I know what we are to each other – have since the day I first laid eyes on you. That means nothing in the big picture, understand me?"

Aubrey didn't understand him, not one single bit, but she nodded anyway.

"I know in here." He curled his fist and thumped it against his heart a couple of times. "That you're a good person. I can trust you. You'll do right by my son."

"How can you know? I don't even know." Did he think that her being a teacher made her special?

She should tell him that teaching hadn't been her calling and children weren't her salvation. She'd done what she needed to do as a foster kid who aged out of the system; she sought a practical career that would provide a steady income and allow her a safe place to hide from the cruelty of the world.

Ulrich knew nothing about who she was or her past. That

silly fragile thread of attraction was clouding his good sense. She was like any other human woman who was attracted to a man – jealous, possessive, and irrational. Not nurturing, or understanding, or even brave enough to protect a child.

Right now, she wanted to kill Tag's mother, but not because the woman had ripped a son from his father. Nope, Ulrich was the main reason for her dark thoughts. If Sibyl came to Darkness Falls, would Ulrich open his door to her again. Let her back into his life, and maybe even into his bed?

She dropped her eyes to her hands to steady herself. Who was Ulrich anyway? A man clearly on his own in the world if he was reaching out to an almost stranger to help him with his boy. And why? Because theirs was something more than a simple attraction? Or because he mistakenly thought Aubrey was more than the battered child inside her?

CHAPTER TWO

Ulrich saw the self-doubt on Aubrey's face and the disappointment in her eyes when she realized he was offering her nothing but his trust. It was a heavy burden and he sensed that the woman in front of him struggled with her self-worth. He wanted to help her with her burden as much as he wanted to take her to his bed, but he resisted both inclinations.

The timing was wrong. The months spent with his mother's pack had royally fucked up his son, who was celebrating the reunion with his father while at the same time mourning the loss of his mother.

Again.

Because that's what it had been for Tag his entire life. Sibyl made promises she never kept; couldn't see past her narcissism to recognize the damage she had done... was still doing to him. And to Ulrich. He and Sibyl could have been happy, could have had the life they'd talked about when they first met.

He didn't hate her; he felt nothing for her. Not anymore.

"You okay with me using you as an emergency contact?"

The hesitation was there, on her face, in her eyes, in the way she crossed her arms over her chest. "Is she a shifter?"

He nodded.

"Unstable?"

He wasn't about to lie to her. "As a fucking car with a flat tire."

She bit her lip. "Okay...."

He waited for her to add the 'but'.

She didn't. Instead, she walked to her desk and picked up her cell phone, unlocking it, then handing it to him. "We need to swap information, right? So I can contact you if she shows. We have no shifters on staff here, so it would be difficult to take her on should she show up here and become violent."

That made sense but violence by Sibyl was a worse-case scenario. "She's never gotten physical, but she's highly manipulative." He added his information to her contact list, then texted himself so he had her phone number. "If she shows, you call me, and if I'm not answering, Jackson."

"No problem." Her eyes dulled and her voice deflated. "Your expectations of me are too high. I'm not heroic."

Ulrich's wolf didn't like weakness and Ulrich could feel the mutt pacing inside him, impatient with her mood. He talked over it. "You're stronger than you think. Inside, where it counts." What a stupid fucking thing to say. Now was not the time to offer her anything but his thanks. Maybe the right time would never come.

Apparently, she thought it was a stupid fucking thing to say too because she quickly switched topics to Tag. "I don't know your son. I have close to 30 students in the class this year, so there's going to be little one-on-one with him or any other student." She pursed her lips.

The soft plumpness distracted Ulrich and he had to pinch himself to refocus on her words.

"He has to understand that I'm the authority if his mom shows up. If I can't get his cooperation, I can't help you."

Ulrich liked the tone behind her words; she carried a hidden strength in her core. "I'll talk with him. Maybe the three of us can spend sometime together so he can get to know you better."

Her cheeks bloomed pink as she dropped her eyes to the floor. "I don't think that's a good idea," she mumbled.

Ulrich thought about pushing her to see how quickly she'd fold, but this wasn't about him or her. It was about his kid. "How about we take it day to day. The odds of Sibyl showing her face in the next month are practically nil."

"How can you know that?"

"I know my wife."

Aubrey winced at his choice of words but nodded. "Okay." She offered her hand to Ulrich. "It was nice to see you again, Mr. Calhoun."

He took her hand, small, smooth, silky, and felt goose-bumps rise on his arms. "It's Ulrich. Let's not pretend, Aubrey."

She pursed her lips and gave a small nod as she took back her hand and wrapped it around her waist.

ON THEIR WAY HOME, Ulrich and Tag stopped off at Rozi's Café for a bite to eat. They'd been reunited several weeks now, spending the summer camping and moving from place to place to cover their tracks as they headed north.

Tag was nursing anger and hurt, and the father-son alone time had helped repair some of the damage. But September came too soon, and he'd had to return to Darkness Falls, for Tag, because school was about to start, and for Ulrich, because his job demanded it of him.

During the months that Tag and Ulrich were separated, the kid had sprouted up like a weed. No one had to ask to know that Tag was a shifter. The evidence was out there for all the world to see. He was already taller, heavier, bigger than most other kids his age. Angry though, because of what happened, because he was caught in the middle of a war between his parents, one Ulrich vowed would never impact Tag.

That had been naive and foolish on Ulrich's part and it was apparent that Tag was struggling to understand his place in the world.

There were so many things he should have told Aubrey, would have to tell her once Tag settled into his new school. The angry kid was on the cusp of puberty. A boy today, a full-blown shifter with a wolf he couldn't control, tomorrow. It was a case of lighter meeting fuse. It wouldn't take much to set Tag off.

"How're you doing, kid?" he asked his boy after they settled at a table and ordered their food.

Tag shrugged as his attention wandered everywhere to avoid looking at Ulrich. "Okay. How long will we be in Darkness Falls?"

Strange question. "Where would we go?"

Tag furrowed his brow in a way that reminded Ulrich of Sibyl. They looked so much alike in their expressions that it killed him. "You're here on a job, aren't you? When that's over, what happens?"

Ulrich's mind flashed to Aubrey as he shrugged. There couldn't be anything between them, but at the same time, the idea of leaving her behind seemed untenable. "Maybe we stay. You need stability, kid."

Tag seemed to be set on arguing. "How do you know what I need? I need a mother too, but that doesn't seem likely since you've basically dragged me up here and hidden me away."

Ulrich raised his eyebrows. The reunion with Tag had been a happy one and even though Tag was messed up, he had seemed to easily slip back into life as he knew it before Sibyl disrupted it. But now he was changing his tune. Ulrich could chalk it up to the exhaustion of the hard travel the past couple of days, but he suspected that there was more to it than that. "You had your mother for the past year. How'd that work for you?"

"Maybe if you tried harder, Dad. Maybe if you—"

He was cut off by the arrival of the waitress with their drinks – coffee for Ulrich, coke for the Tag. After she left, Ulrich shut down Tag. "I'm not going to mess around telling you what you already know. Not sure what's going on inside that head of yours, but you got something to say, say it plain and simple. Don't pussyfoot around."

Tag wrapped his hands around his coke glass and pulled it towards him so he could take a drink through the straw. After he swallowed, he locked eyes with Ulrich. It was shocking to Ulrich, like looking in a mirror, seeing the future. This boy was going to become an alpha and that was a bigger problem than the current one, because Ulrich had no pack to offer Tag and without one, shifter instinct would send Tag out looking for one. The boy would either kill or get killed in his quest.

"There's something between you and that teacher. I can feel it."

Shit. Sensitive little jerk. "There's nothing between the two of us. We know each other. She's attractive." Unlike humans, shifters weren't uncomfortable in their skin nor did they suppress their natural instincts. It's what made them passionate – in love and war. It's what made them savage and blunt.

Tag shook his head. "You can't f— sleep with my teacher. That would be a death blow for me at school."

His son's lecture made Ulrich grumpy. "We're friends." *They weren't.* "Not lovers, not anything else." He hoped Tag wouldn't see through his lies.

"Doesn't matter and you know that."

Ulrich hated that the kid was right, hated that he'd missed out on months of watching Tag change from a pup to a boy on the cusp of manhood. Hated all the possibilities that would never be.

Tag was on the verge of shifting for the first time and there was no pack to support Ulrich through the aggressiveness that his emerging wolf would bring about. No one but Ulrich to teach Tag how to master his instincts.

"You know what's coming, don't you?"

Tag furrowed his forehead. "Uh, yeah. I read. And mom's pack was prepping me."

Self-doubt crept through Ulrich. "Should I have left you there?"

Tag held his father's eyes, a sea of emotion clashing in a storm. "No." This time he didn't hold back. "I want nothing to do with that fucking pack."

After lunch, the two stopped for groceries and then returned to Ulrich's house. It was nice enough – a two story mid-90s house with a basement and reasonable rent. When Ulrich first came to Darkness Falls, he hadn't planned to stay for more than a month or two, but that had stretched into a year now, and the town was starting to feel like home, especially with Tag back.

The main floor of the house had an office, two full baths, and three bedrooms, and the finished basement was almost like a suite unto itself. Tag elected to set up downstairs, and when they arrived home, after they brought in the groceries, he disappeared to the lower level. Ten minutes later, Ulrich could hear the blaring of the TV.

Ulrich put the groceries away, then opened a beer and wandered to the office. He'd have to get a lock for the door now that Tag was home. Case files were scattered over the surface of his desk, evidence boxes were piled haphazardly in corners, and gruesome photos were pinned to the walls.

He walked up to the photos of Adrienne Powell, before and after her death. Aubrey and the murdered woman shared some physical similarities, but not many. No one would guess that were sisters. Half-sisters, he corrected himself. Different fathers, same last name because their fucked-up mama had some brains.

He took a swallow of his beer as stared into the dead woman's eyes. Since the moment Aubrey arrived in town, he'd had nightmares about her sharing the same fate as her sister. Raped, marked, throat torn out by a shifter. Because of Adrienne's murder, he knew everything about Aubrey and her upbringing. More than he was comfortable with because it almost felt like a betrayal of Aubrey's privacy.

The only reason he felt that way was because she was his fated mate. He hadn't expected the explosion of primacy and savagery inside him the first time he saw her. How could he have known? The universe was stingy in its doling out of pair-bonds and many never crossed paths, no matter how much fate tried to intervene.

He turned from the wall of horror and thumped heavily down in his desk chair. Without a serial killer drawing Ulrich to Darkness Falls, without the murder of Adrienne Powell, he and Aubrey might not have met. He never thought much of the concept of fate, but he knew that it was as evil as it was good. And the painful circumstances that had to happen to bring him and Aubrey together cast a shadow on their future.

If they had one.

Because in another twist of fate, he got his son back and Aubrey was the kid's teacher. In some ways it was good. He didn't do relationships with women anyway – Sibyl had destroyed most of his trust in women, and the few relationships he'd had since finished it off.

He and Tag were a package deal and though the women he'd dated pretended they were okay with it, they weren't, not really. They didn't understand the responsibilities of being a parent and because they were attracted to Ulrich's size and heritage, the relationships were shallow – about the sex and bragging rights.

Maybe that was meant to be, too, so that he didn't fuck up again before he met his fated mate.

He snorted his cynicism as he recalled his words to her. *You're a good person. I can trust you. You'll do right by my son.*

His speech was a naïve wish that Aubrey could be everything other women weren't. It was bullshit, but as much as he wanted to vanquish her from his thoughts, he knew it was impossible. Would always be.

He dug his cell phone from his pocket and stared at it, thinking he should call or text her, make sure she made it home from school. It was his instincts talking to him and he snorted.

Even if Tag weren't a factor, one of the common denominators in the attacks on the victims was that they had all been in serious relationships with shifter males, but not yet marked.

Better no one knew about Aubrey. Better for her that Ulrich didn't pursue her.

CHAPTER THREE

"Can you come over?"

Aubrey's first call was to her friend, Eva.

"I wish I could, but I've got a shift tonight. Fucking desk duty thanks to the commander and chief."

The second was to Cherime.

"Can't do. Got a date with Mr. Big."

The third was to Trist.

"Sorry, but I have no one to watch the boys. Raff is on an overnight pack run. You could come here."

"I can't, Trist. Not in this weather." It was rainy, dark as the inside of an ant, and Aubrey's old Honda Civic was becoming more and more unreliable. It was time to replace the car, but she didn't have the credit to get a loan. "It's okay. Another time."

She hung up and glanced around her. Her apartment felt like a prison cell, claustrophobic and cloying. There was no one else to call except Honi, who was mate to Gideon, alpha of the Dominant Pack, but Aubrey didn't know her all that well.

And Leah, who she knew too well. She liked the little lunatic but had no way of getting hold of her. Leah didn't have a cell phone.

Who doesn't have a cell phone these days?

As if the universe read her mind, her cell rang. "Hello?"

"Hi!" It was Leah.

"Leah? Did you finally get a phone?" Aubrey knew it was a foolish question. Leah borrowed cell phones from unsuspecting people, she didn't have one of her own.

"I did... not. Can I come over? Nothing to do, no one to do it with."

Aubrey felt chagrined. "I'm not your first choice then?"

There was a rap on the door and Aubrey headed to it, peeking through the peephole to find the hallway empty.

"I'm not yours either, am I?"

She cautiously opened the door and discovered Leah leaning against the wall, phone pressed against her ear, a six-pack of Moosehead Lager in hand, and a playful grin on her face. "Leah!"

"Thought you might need some company." The little shifter was still talking into the phone.

Aubrey opened the door wider as she pressed the end button on the phone. "Come in."

"Did you just hang up on me?" Leah demanded, staring in disbelief at the phone.

"Leah...."

"You don't really have good social etiquette," Leah sniped as she walked past Aubrey into the apartment. She kicked off her runners and shed her wet jean jacket, dumping it on the floor. "The correct way to end a phone call is to say, *goodbye*."

Aubrey ignored the lecture. "You're soaking. Did you walk over here?"

Leah nodded as she glanced around the apartment. "No

one will let me borrow a car after the law took away my licence for stealing Gideon's truck." She headed towards the kitchen. "Also, and more importantly, I didn't want anyone to know where I was."

Aubrey wondered why as she followed Leah into the kitchen. "Are we drinking?"

"Yeah. I like it when you're drunk." Leah slammed open, rifled through, and banged closed the drawers in the kitchen. It was a quick search. There were only three drawers.

"What are you looking for?"

"Bottle opener."

Aubrey pulled one of the Moosehead bottles from the box and inspected the cap. "They're twist off."

Leah snatched the bottle from Aubrey's hand. "I knew that," she snapped.

Aubrey opened a beer for herself and put the remaining bottles in the fridge to keep them cold. She took a sip, then, when she noticed Leah eyeing Fake Goldie, the replacement goldfish for Goldie the First, said, "Hungry?"

Leah grinned widely as she headed to the couch and flopped on it. "Nope. Need a place to crash though. You okay with me sleeping over?"

"Of course." Weird request. Leah was super-independent, always around, but seemingly solitary. Her best friend was Trist, who was mated to the Lodge Pack's alpha and Aubrey knew that Raff's controlling nature with Trist strained the friendship. "The spare bed's made up."

"Thanks." She cast a critical eye around the open space. "Maybe I should move in."

No. No damn way!

Aubrey sat down on the other end of the couch, turning and crossing her legs so she was facing Leah. Instead of refusing outright, which was what she would have to do eventually, she said, "What's up?"

Leah flopped her head back and stared up at the ceiling. "Not much. Had a feeling you needed to talk, so here I am."

"Whose phone this time?"

"Alan Hawke's, that stupid fucking beta. His beer too." She rolled her head and stared at Aubrey. "I miss Varg." Leah belonged to the Dominant pack, aptly named because it was 60-strong, one of the largest shifter packs in existence. Varg used to be the beta but won a challenge with an alpha for a northern Albertan pack and took over. Gideon, the Dominant pack alpha, appointed Alan as beta. According to gossip, Alan was young, inexperienced, and kind of a jerk. Aubrey hadn't yet met him.

"You could visit Varg."

Leah sat up and took a draw of her beer. "How? Can't drive, can't shift, don't do busses. And besides, he's a grouch. And I don't think he likes me." She turned fully towards Aubrey and kicked her in the knee before crossing her legs yoga-style. "What's up with you?"

That was so Leah. She rarely talked about herself, always changing the topic. Underneath her seemingly impenetrable armour, Aubrey sensed a lost soul.

Takes one to know one.

"I'm prepping for the beginning of the school year. Starts next Wednesday."

"Wow. That's exciting." Leah rolled her eyes slightly.

"Sarcasm, right?"

Leah sat straighter as she gulped her beer. "No. I had a great time teaching your students last year."

Leah had caused chaos in the school by locking Aubrey out of her classroom for over an hour. It was a miracle that Aubrey still had a job. Well, that and they lived in Darkness Falls, a town that people left unless they were running, hiding, or shifters. "I'm sure you did."

37

"I don't know why you teachers complain about all the work you have to do. It was a breeze."

Aubrey tilted her head to the side. "I don't complain. I'm happy to have a job, but there's more to teaching than an hour in a classroom pretending to be a pirate."

Leah laughed, full-throated and uninhibited, something wonderful to behold. Something Aubrey never did. "I know." She switched topics. "Something's going on with you. Is it Ulrich?"

"What do you know about Ulrich?" Aubrey took a nervous gulp of the beer.

Leah leaned in and said in a conspiratorial tone, "I know he has a son that he had to kidnap back from his ex-wife. How's that make you feel?"

Leah knew stuff no one else did. She played the clown, but she was more sensitive and observant than most people or shifters. It was like she could read minds or divine the future. Of course, Ulrich having a son was pure gossip.

Aubrey didn't ask where Leah had heard the chatter – it was Darkness Falls after all, and gossip spread like a spring flood. But she also didn't address the question. Instead, she said, "He does. Tag's in my class this year."

Holy, Lean mouthed. "That's going to make things awkward since you and Ulrich are in the denial stage of your relationship."

"We're not in a relationship," Aubrey huffed.

"See? Denial."

Aubrey wasn't in denial. If she had her way, she and Ulrich would be getting to know each other, exploring the relationship. She felt a twinge below her waistline and veered away from the vision of exactly how she wanted explore Ulrich. She blew out a breath. "I need a friend, Leah."

Leah took a swallow of her beer as she speculatively eyed Aubrey. "I can be your friend. We're perfect for each other.

We're both short with brown hair, brown eyes, and lopsided boobs. Probably the same shoe and shirt size although my clothes actually fit my body. We both speak English and neither of us can shift."

And we're both at odds with the world, Aubrey thought but didn't say as she skimmed a hand over one of her breasts. They weren't actually lopsided, were they? "I need to trust you not to share my stuff with other people."

Leah bared her teeth at Aubrey. "What have I done to you or anyone else to suggest I can't be trusted."

Aubrey tilted her head. "You outed Eva's pregnancy."

Leah widened her eyes and nodded her head. "I did do that. But it wasn't a betrayal of trust. It was an unfortunate incident. Eva didn't tell me she was pregnant, so when I said so, I thought everyone knew."

"You still don't blurt out something like that when the pregnancy is so early."

"Cherime already said that, so I know better now. No more blurting out stuff. Got it." She crossed her arms and looked wounded. "Anything else?"

Aubrey shook her head, feeling uncomfortable about attacking Leah. If there was anyone in the world that she wished she was more like, it was Leah and her give-no-effs attitude. There wasn't much the little latent shifter wouldn't say or do. Heck, the night of Aubrey's drunken debacle, Leah took on Ren, the Mountain pack alpha. That took guts and a fair amount of stupidity. "You're right. I can trust you." She took a swallow of beer to give her time to think.

Leah aped her.

"Remember back in June when I got drunk at Becker's?"

Leah cackled. "How could I forget?"

Aubrey glanced down at the bottle of beer in her hand. "I kind of made a fool of myself when Ulrich dropped me off."

Leah grinned. "Did you guys...?"

"No! Ulrich wouldn't."

Leah threw back her head and laughed like a loon. "If he wouldn't, then what happened was you said, *let's* and he said, *no.*"

Aubrey grimaced. "Pretty much. His turning me down might have had something to do with me being slobbering drunk."

"No shit. Despite the local gossip, he's an upstanding guy."

Aubrey drew her lower lip between her teeth and nodded. "Yeah. So much so that he told me today that there could be nothing between us because he didn't want his son confused."

Leah blew out a breath. "Wow. He's dad of the year material. That makes me suspicious – he sounds too good to be true."

"Yeah." Aubrey swallowed the last of her beer and picked up Leah's empty bottle on the way to the kitchen. She dumped them into the recycle bin and grabbed a couple of fresh ones from the fridge. "His ex basically kidnapped Tag – that's the boy's name – and kept him hidden from Ulrich for over a year. But Ulrich has full custody." She used a dish towel to twist the caps off the bottles and returned to the couch.

"That doesn't even make sense," Leah said as she took the beer Aubrey offered. "Unless his old lady's human."

"Ex-old lady," Aubrey corrected testily. "Why doesn't it make sense? Sibyl's a shifter too."

"Thank god we're besties now," Leah said after she took a swallow of beer. "You don't know much about shifters, do you?"

Aubrey felt her face warm. Leah was right. Aubrey's knowledge of shifters was mostly learned through textbooks and a couple of side-trips to Wikipedia. She should have taken the time to study up on them, given that Darkness Falls had four packs that claimed territory around it.

"Enlighten me."

"Shifters don't recognize human law within packs. So two shifters getting married, unlikely. Even if they did, and human courts granted Ulrich full custody of the kid, shifter law wouldn't recognize it. Are they from the same pack?"

"I don't know." She didn't know much at all.

Leah launched another question at her. "Are they mated?"

"I don't know. Presumably."

"You know that shifters don't really un-mate – they break up, but if he marked her, the mating mark is for life."

Aubrey felt desolate at that. "So, he can never mate again?"

"Of course, he can. Her too. But the mating mark is something that's considered sacred, so it's not given lightly. It's a connection – a sacred bond between mates that tethers them together. What I don't get is if they weren't pair-bonded, why bother with a mating mark. I'll never under-stand why shifters do that."

"How do you know they're not pair-bonded?"

Leah rolled her eyes to the ceiling and shook her head. "Because, Nancy Drew, you and Ulrich are pair-bonded, hence he and any other woman in the world can't be."

Aubrey struggled to understand. "Uh, I don't think we're pair-bonded. We've known each other for a year now and he's barely spoken two words to me. And I'm human."

"So's Eva. Everyone has a pair-bond, including humans. Your kind just pretty it up by calling each other soul-mates and half the time you're fucking wrong because you're so out of touch with your instincts."

Aubrey scrunched her eyes together. "Why are we talking about this anyway?"

Leah shrugged as she picked at the label on her beer bottle. "I don't know. But in case momma wolf comes to visit,

I better keep an eye on you. You're right in the middle of a family feud."

Aubrey shook her head as her heart filled with regret. "No, I'm not. Ulrich won't give me the time of day."

CHAPTER FOUR

The first two weeks of school were relatively uneventful and not much of a hardship for Aubrey, teaching-wise. Her students were boisterous and unruly, but nothing she couldn't handle.

Tag had no problem fitting in. With his size, good looks, and confidence, he quickly rose in the ranks of the popular kids' clique. It didn't make everyone happy because he usurped previous leaders, which caused a ripple effect.

Not everyone liked him because of his swagger but he seemed not to care. He treated everyone the same, no matter his mood, and all the students responded similarly. If Tag was in a good mood, they worshipped him; if he felt indifferent, they tiptoed around him. He wasn't mean, but he also didn't back down from confrontation.

Aubrey wasn't sure that she liked how Tag ruled the classroom, but he did his homework, was engaged in all classroom activities, and treated her with respect, acknowledging her authority in class. He was smart, athletic, and positive. If she hadn't known better, she would've had trouble believing he'd been separated from his primary parent for over a year.

Unfortunately, the honeymoon didn't last.

The fight happened close to the end of lunch break. Aubrey was on playground duty, not her favourite part of the job, but she took the bad with the good. No job was perfect. She heard the shouting before she saw it. In fact, the commotion was out of her line of sight, blocked by a wing of the school, and she sprinted towards it as the argument escalated.

Of course, between the loud voices and the running teacher, it drew the curiosity of other students, who also raced towards the fight, most easily outpacing her because she was not by any means athletic. When she rounded the corner of the building, she encountered a mob of students, egging on the fighters, clapping, and yelling insults and encouragement. To add to the din, some of the girls were screaming at everyone to stop and a couple were even crying.

At the centre of it all were Taggart Calhoun and Reed Donnybrook, the irony of Reed's last name not lost on Aubrey as she shoved and elbowed her way to the front. She made it in time to see the boys land in a heap on the ground, rolling, grunting, and swearing as they tried to pummel each other.

Tag was bigger, stronger, more vicious in his assault and in no time, had the upper hand, managing to lay Reed flat out on his back. He started flailing on Reed as he straddled him, landing blows to his head, face, and chest, his face an ugly mask of fury.

"Stop!" Aubrey screamed, horrified at the violence. Both boys on the ground were taller than she was, likely weighed more, and she had no doubt were stronger. She glanced to her left, saw Allie Griffin, one of her quieter students, who was immobilized at the sight. "Get help!" Aubrey shouted at her.

It seemed to snap the girl out of her frozen state. She nodded once and sprinted away, followed by a couple of her friends.

Aubrey turned back to the disaster in the making. Reed was a bully, big, athletic, and tough. In any other fight, he'd have the upper hand, but not when he was up against a male shifter like Tag, a replica of his powerful father.

"I said stop!" she shrieked just as Tag's fist was about to crush Reed's already bloody nose. She threw every ounce of weight she had at Tag, grabbing him around the chest like a pro football tackler, and dragging him off Reed. She and Tag landed on the hard-packed dirt with so much force, the impact jarred her bones and teeth.

Tag twisted in her arms, freeing himself, his fist in the air, aimed at Aubrey. She flinched and thought about scrambling backwards, but she knew if she did that, she'd lose Tag's respect and that of the crowd of students who stood by in numbed shock at what she'd done.

Instead, her chest heaving, her heart pounding, she glared at Tag, held his hostile eyes. "Don't you dare." She gritted her teeth, refusing to drop her eyes.

His eyes, an icy amber tinging the dark blue irises, battled with hers for a few seconds, before common sense kicked in. "Fuck," he said as he sat back and spat some blood from his mouth.

You have that right, kid. "Language," she scolded as she scrambled on her hands and knees over to Reed, who was still lying on the ground, moaning for effect. The kid wasn't hurt all that badly and by the scrapes on his knuckles, gave almost as good as he got.

"I didn't start this," Tag immediately protested.

Aubrey glared at him as she brushed the hair off Reed's forehead to check for injury. "So what? How does that excuse you from beating up another student?"

She'd gone from horror, to fear, to downright anger. She realized that the summer dress she'd been wearing was tangled around her legs, well up her thighs. Her knees had been skinned and her hair had partially fallen from the bun she'd painstakingly fashioned this morning so that the curls brushed one side of her face.

And on top of it all, she was full-out shaking.

"The rest of you should be ashamed of yourselves!" she shouted at everyone as she looked around. She never shouted, yelled, raised her voice. In fact, it was her quiet manner and her simple interactions with the students that made them gravitate towards her.

She was the kind of teacher who not only believed in teamwork but exemplified it. One who led through example, would never humiliate a student, tried to create a welcoming, friendly, safe environment. Except today. Except right now.

"That you would all let this happen in your own school! That some of you would actually endorse this!" Tears stung her eyes as she hollered at the students. "I'm ashamed of you. Get out of here!"

Tag started to rise but froze as she transferred her fury to him. "Sit down! And you." She turned her attention to the still-groaning Reed. "Enough with the drama-queen crap. Sit up."

Reed opened one eye and pouted, splitting the cut on his lip wider. He sat up though, and then smirked at Tag, who growled. She was between them and for the first time since she'd come upon this disaster, she realized that if they turned on her, she'd have a hard time defending herself. However, they seemed to respect her authority, which empowered her and settled her thumping heart.

The principal's appearance eased it further. Mr. Blake was on heels as they rounded the corner of the building.

Mrs. Blake trailed behind them and covered her mouth with her fist and whimpered when she saw the scene. To her credit, and much to Aubrey's chagrin, she said, "Are you okay, Ms. Powell?"

Aubrey nodded as Mr. Blake looked behind him at Allie and her two friends, who were hovering in the background. "Thanks, girls, for getting us. Time for class." He turned to his wife. "Get all our students settled until we're back."

"Of course." Mrs. Blake's expression of adoration as she left made Aubrey's stomach squeeze. She wasn't sure if was nausea or jealousy.

"What happened!" Mr. Gaskill demanded using his serious principal's voice as he stared down at all three of them, all still sitting in the dirt. Aubrey felt like one of the students, felt her stomach quake, felt guilty, as though she'd been in the fight. Which technically, she guessed she had.

Tag, Reed and Aubrey started talking at once and Mr. Gaskill snapped, "One a time. Mrs. Powell, you first." He glanced down at her knees and the dress, still riding high on her thighs, his eyes narrowing in judgement.

Aubrey tugged the hem of the dress down, but her backend was resting on the bunched-up fabric, keeping it stubbornly in place. She'd have to stand to straighten it out, then she realized that she should be standing anyway. Not sitting in the dirt in such an undignified manner. Clearly, the fight had rattled her, and she wasn't thinking as straight as she should've been.

She climbed to her feet, sorting out her skirt and dusting herself off. The boys followed suit. Reed spat a glob of blood on the ground and Tag adopted a casual, defiant postured, crossing his arms and spreading his legs.

She looked at him – the kid would be formidable when he reached adulthood. Maybe that's why shifters hung onto the notion of packs – they needed tradition and strong ties to raise their young.

"Ms. Powell?" Mr. Gaskill invaded her thoughts.

"Sorry." She cleared her throat and swiped her unruly hair off her face. She felt like she was back in high school being grilled by Mrs. Colbert, the principal, who had been difficult and controlling. "I'm on playground duty today. I heard shouting and rushed over here to find the boys fighting." She indicated the boys with a right-left tilt of her head. I stepped in to break it up."

She stopped. What more was there to say other than to mention that Tag was wailing on Reed, which was why she got physical in the first place. But she didn't want to point out that Tag was the aggressor because it didn't seem fair. If Reed had gotten the upper hand, the same thing would've happened.

The superior Mr. Blake looked her up and down, lingering on her scraped knees and her dusty dress. "Looks like you did more than break it up."

Stupid jerk. She pinned him with a glare. "Sure. It looked like they were having so much fun, I jumped into the fray and started swinging." She immediately regretted her sarcasm as the boys snickered. "I'm sorry." She ran fingers through her hair, getting them knotted up in the curly tangled mess. "I'm a little shaken up. I tried to pry them apart and lost my balance."

Despite the entire student population witnessing her tackle Tag to the ground like she was a CFL line-backer, her version of the events would uphold unless Reed or Tag said something to the contrary.

"Reed?" Mr. Gaskill studied the bloodied boy. "Explain."

Reed stared at the principal and for a moment, Aubrey thought he was going to throw her under the bus. He crossed his arms and toed the ground, his eyes glued to the dust he kicked up. "It was nothing. We were messing around."

Tag furrowed his eyebrows as he turned to look at Reed. At first Aubrey didn't understand Tag's confusion, then realized that Tag hadn't been in a traditional school setting for a while. He didn't realize that Reed was applying the brotherhood rule – don't tell *the man* anything.

Mr. Gaskill sharpened his gaze as he turned his attention to Tag. "Lot of blood for horsing around."

Tag aggressively held the principal's gaze and Aubrey elbowed him. "Show some respect, Tag."

He turned his rage on her, but she held his eyes. Inside she was quaking, not because she was giving Tag the gears, but because she was choosing sides and Ulrich might resent her for it. Finally, he dropped his eyes to the ground and stuffed his hands in his pockets. "What Reed said," he mumbled.

Mr. Gaskill looked over at Mr. Blake, then back at Aubrey. "Your call. What do you want to do with these warmongers?"

Aubrey's heart skipped a beat. Why her call? Sure, she'd intervened, and the boys were in her class, but discipline related to fighting usually landed at the principal's feet. "They were fighting. Isn't that automatic expulsion?"

"Shit," Tag whispered under his breath, just loud enough for her to hear.

She turned to him in frustration. "You're in enough trouble, young man," she snapped, wishing she had a stronger, sharper voice. "You want to rub salt in it?" She was mixing metaphors, but who could blame her. She hated being judge and jury, and she had a bad feeling that she would also be the executioner.

"Sorry," he mumbled, not sounding the least bit sorry, which made Aubrey want to smack him. Smack a kid? Even if he deserved it, there were better ways to settle this.

She turned to the principal. "It's early in the school year, so perhaps we could give them a third strike warning—"

"That hardly seems enough." Mr. Blake used his snooty tone to interrupt her.

"I wasn't finished!" *Now that's more like it, Aubrey.* "Two-week's detention." She cursed silently as she said it. She was punishing herself too, but it was what it was. Part of the job. "Served after school in my classroom."

She snapped her eyes to Mr. Blake. "Unless you would like to oversee it, so the boys have a strong disciplinary hand."

Mr. Blake cocked his head to the side and narrowed his eyes. "It would be a good idea except that I have other commitments during the week."

"So do we," Reed whined. "Tuesdays and Thursdays are volleyball practice."

Aubrey slumped her shoulders. She couldn't win with this bunch. Stu Heron, the gym teacher and volleyball coach, would be all over her about taking two of his best out of practice, when the season began next week. "Ten days of detention. It doesn't have to be served concurrently, but you don't get to pick and choose either. Volleyball practice or a near-death experience are the only two reasons you don't stay after school."

"Their parents should be called," Mr. Blake interjected.

It was Mr. Gaskill's turn to glare. "I know my job, Mr. Blake. Perhaps it's time for you to get back to your classroom. It looks like Ms. Powell has things well in hand."

Mr. Blake gave a curt nod. "I imagine you'll be right behind me," he said to Aubrey.

"No." She softened her voice, retreating to the old Aubrey, the one who sounded like she needed to be rescued all the time. "Reed and Tag need to see the school nurse, so I'll escort them there. Please thank Mrs. Blake for agreeing to supervise a little longer."

"Of course." Mr. Blake gave a small officious bow and disappeared around the corner of the building.

"Have her look at your knees while you're there," Mr. Gaskill said to her. "They need to be cleaned up and bandaged."

He glanced at the two boys. "When you're done at the nurse's office, you will come directly to my office. Your parents will be called in and we'll be having a cozy meeting with them." He herded the boys towards the school as Aubrey kept pace at his side.

"Ms. Powell," he said quietly, so that he wouldn't be overheard. "In future, you do not get physical with the students. Do you understand me?"

She didn't, but she nodded anyway. "Yes." The tension of the past hour caught up with her and she felt tears threaten.

Never let them see you cry. It was Adrienne's oft-said cliché of an excuse for her hard, bitchy exterior. In that moment, Aubrey deeply missed her older sister.

CHAPTER FIVE

Ulrich and RCMP Darkness Falls detachment Commander Jackson Hayes, generally addressed as Chief though Jackson's official rank was Inspector, were having a lunch meeting at Ulrich's house when his phone rang. That they were chowing down on the double-protein cold-cut combo from a local deli, surrounded by gruesome crime scene photos, testified to both cops' hardened interiors. Their respective careers had knocked the queasiness out of them as they dug with relish into the foot-long subs Jackson had supplied.

"Yeah," Ulrich answered.

The voice on the other end identified himself as Jim Gaskill, principal of Darkness Falls Middle School, then in the next breath, confirmed to Ulrich what his gut was already telling him.

As anger flooded him, he stood up, knocking his chair back in the process. "He did what?" He was already almost shouting. This didn't bode well for the rest of the day.

"He and another student were fighting on school property,

during school hours, Mr. Calhoun," Gaskill repeated, his voice sounding world-weary.

Ulrich suppressed the urge to swear because he didn't want to reinforce any biases Gaskill might already have of shifters. He'd known this was going to be a difficult year for Tag and as he listened to Gaskill explaining the situation, for half a second, thought the kid would be better off with his mother's pack.

It was a fleeting momentary insanity because anything would be better than Tag having to endure another day in the grip of the anarchist shifters of Sibyl's pack. He sighed. "I'll come to the school."

Gaskill sounded like reasonable man. "Please do that. The other student's parents have also been called." He hesitated, then, "Sam Donnybrook, Reed's father, can be somewhat aggressive. It would be helpful if you didn't respond in kind."

Ulrich laughed without mirth. "What you choose to believe, Mr. Gaskill, is your problem. I have a good grip on my emotions."

Gaskill wasn't aware of who Ulrich was. In fact, other than Jackson, few people in Darkness Falls knew that he was a federal RCMP Inspector undercover in Darkness Falls to support the RCMP's investigation into the string of attacks and killings that had happened over the past year.

He sighed when he hung up. "I've been summoned to the principal's office. Tag was in a fight."

The Chief sat back and studied Ulrich. "With who?"

Ulrich shrugged as he swallowed the last of his sandwich. "Kid named Reed Donnybrook."

"Uh-oh." Jackson pursed his lips, his laid-back Texas-like manner hid his fast mind. "Sam Donnybrook is an asshole part of the time and a good ol' boy, the other half. You never know if he's going to slap you on the back or punch you in the face. Kid's just like him."

"Says the man with no children," Ulrich retorted, wondering why he was coming to the defence of the little shit who'd gotten into it with Tag. "Kid doesn't know whether he's coming or going either, with a dad like that. No power at home, takes it out on others."

Jackson's sleepy demeanour gave way to irritation as he stood and straightened his service belt. "Doesn't explain Tag's behaviour. Or does it?"

Ulrich almost laughed at Jackson's transparency. The Chief didn't like to be challenged. Controlling prick, but to give him credit, he had to be to run the Darkness Falls RCMP detachment. It was the only way to get the shifters to respect him, and they did, which earned him Ulrich's respect. Most of the time. "Tag's a shifter without a pack, been through the shit that is his mother, going through the change. Lot going on for him."

Jackson dropped the antagonism. "He's not dangerous, is he?"

If anyone else had asked that question about Tag, Ulrich would have punched their teeth through the back of their head, but coming from the chief, it was legit. "No. He's struggling, but he and I are working on his transition. He's a kid trying to make sense of his world. Like Reed Donnybrook."

Jackson nodded, but didn't look entirely convinced. "Sounds like this meeting is over."

Ulrich turned to look at the photos on his wall. "We gotta get this sorted, Hayes. I don't want to see another body."

Jackson nodded, following Ulrich's line of sight. "You and me both."

~

WHEN ULRICH STEPPED into the front office of Darkness Falls Middle School, he was greeted with chaos. Reed, he presumed, and Tag were sitting on a bench, several feet of space between them, while a tall, angry man was giving Jim Gaskill the gears.

Both of the boys looked like they'd been through the ginger-mill, with bruised faces, swollen knuckles, and down-cast expressions.

To his credit, Gaskill didn't cower, though Ulrich could sense his fear from where he stood.

"What's going on?" Ulrich growled as he stepped forward.

He heard a gasp from the bench, knew it hadn't come from Tag. He had that affect on almost all humans and shifters. His physical visage was intimidating.

Reed's father – what was his name again – oh yeah, Sam, blasted Ulrich with his heated anger. "You the little shit's father?"

Too stupid to be afraid, Ulrich guessed as he surveyed the man. Donnybrook was average everything except for the tattoos that covered most of his exposed skin except his face. Reed, a shorter facsimile of his father, would soon outgrow his old man in height, weight, and strength.

Ulrich steeled himself against the hostility, primarily because he was in a school, in front of two impressionable boys, but he didn't quite win the battle. "You the other fuck's father?"

He heard Tag snort.

"Don't you be clever with me you goddamn half-breed. Your kid was fucking with my kid. If you think I'm letting this go because you're a fucking shifter, you're wrong." Sam was inches from Ulrich's face, a menacing, nasty twisted face that was turning purple.

Ulrich hated the word half-breed. It was an ugly testament to the pervasive racism in Canada. "I'd venture you got more mutt in you than anyone else in this room."

"This is a school!" Gaskill intervened, which Ulrich thought was a good thing. Gaskill seemed braver now that Ulrich was there, and seemingly much more rational than either of the two fathers. "Let's go into the office to discuss this."

"Fuck that. I'm taking my kid and going home." Donnybrook turned to Reed, who was on his feet in an instant, but Ulrich held his hand in the air.

"I'd like to hear both sides of the story, if you don't mind, Mr. Donnybrook. Not just my son's." He risked a glance at Tag, who was wearing an angry frown. "Otherwise, neither of us will know what went down for sure."

Gaskill fanned the flames by saying, "It's school policy to discuss this with parents and explain the consequences of their children's action. If you don't sit down with us, I'll have no choice but to suspend Reed until you do."

Donnybrook's glare at the principal seemed somewhat conflicted.

Ulrich imagined him trying to decide whether to punch Gaskill in the face or back down.

The latter won. "Fine," he snarled. "Let's get this over with. Time is money and I gotta get back to work."

Typical of men like Donnybrook, prioritizing work and everything else over his kid, then wondering why the little shit was always in trouble. But Ulrich swallowed his bitchy retort, mostly because he was no parental paragon either. His first reaction to Gaskill's phone call had been irritation that his meeting with Jackson had been disrupted.

Instead, he decided to lower the temperature by extending an olive branch. "I'm with Donnybrook," he said to Gaskill. "This gets resolved fast. I have to get back to work too."

Gaskill offered a curt nod, then led them into his cramped

office. Ulrich almost groaned. Shifters had sensitive noses and being in a small room with four other males was going to be nauseating. His wolf buried its head under its paws and was whining like a wounded coyote.

He glanced at Tag as he tried to block the sweat, dirt, and body odour that were circling, but he was only half-successful. Tag seemed not to notice the garbage pile of odours.

Gaskill waved at a line of uncomfortable chairs, and Ulrich manhandled Tag into a chair to the far left, keeping the Donnybrooks to his right. He didn't like that Sam put Reed between them because the kid would be in the way if Ulrich decided to throw Sam through the window.

Just as they were settled, a woman came storming in the door. "What the hell are you doing to my boy?"

Fuck.

Ulrich dropped his chin to his chest in defeat. The woman was wearing a ton of make-up and heavily doused in stale perfume. "Mrs. Donnybrook, I presume," Ulrich choked out as the woman rushed over to hug Reed, much to the boy's embarrassment.

Ulrich heard Tag chuckle. He elbowed the kid in the ribs but kept his attention on the woman standing next to him. She was a fading beauty, probably his age, but life had been hard on her. She wore her weariness in the lines on her face, in her dull blue eyes, in the bottle bleached coarseness of her hair.

His mind shifted to Aubrey, who used beauty products subtly, in a way that perked up his wolf, not made it cower and gag. She was shy, but lively, a sparkle in her eye, a hidden streak of mischief. He didn't know why he was comparing Mrs. Donnybrook to Aubrey, but then he didn't know why he did anything Aubrey related. Well, he knew, but he couldn't make sense of it.

She turned to Ulrich and extended her hand. "I'm Shelby."

Ulrich took the surprisingly strong grip and shook it. He hoped she was the voice of reason in the Donnybrook family but was disabused of that notion at her next words.

"I think we can clear this up easily, as long as your son's apology is sincere."

Ulrich raised an eyebrow. "And why should my son be the only one to offer a *sincere* apology?"

She pulled a chair from the wall and positioned herself between Ulrich and Reed. "Because you're shifters. Shifters are thugs. Ergo."

Ergo? Did she even know what the fuck the word meant? "Some shifters are thugs, yeah." Ulrich was trying his best to keep his temper leashed. "So are some humans." He gazed past her to her husband, who was glaring at both of them.

"Cut it the fuck out, Shelby!" Donnybrook barked at his wife.

Ulrich groaned aloud as the Donnybrooks started bickering. Sam apparently was not sensitive enough to the boy, and Shelby coddled him like he was a fucking baby.

Yeah, Sam's words in front of the kid. Tag was enjoying the show too much, but Ulrich's glare wiped the smirk off his face.

Gaskill slammed his hand on the desk. "Enough!"

The Donnybrooks turned their ire on him. "Who the fuck do you think you are?" Shelby shouted.

"The principal of this school. I can't have parents shouting and swearing in my office. It sets a bad example for my students." His tone was both commanding and quiet, like his loss of temper never happened.

Ulrich admired the man for how quickly he reined it in, but Gaskill's heart was beating too hard in his chest. The man was not in his prime, a little too rotund, a little too soft.

Ulrich hoped he wouldn't have to deal with a heart attack on top of everything else.

Shelby pursed her lips but kept whatever she was thinking inside and Sam followed her lead, though it was clear he was pissed with his wife, the principal, Ulrich, and probably every other asshole in the universe.

Gaskill drew his attention. "Reed and Taggart—"

"Tag," Tag said.

Ulrich elbowed him again. "Shut it."

Tag objected. "Ow!"

Gaskill stared down father and son then started again. "Reed and Taggart," he repeated, glaring at Tag, daring him to open his mouth, "were fighting on school property during lunch break. Ms. Powell was on supervisory duty and intervened to break it up."

"Aubrey was there?" Ulrich blurted, his blood heating as it pulsed through his body. His wolf took notice too.

Tag shifted in his seat and this time elbowed his father. The increased speed of his heart wouldn't have been noticeable to anyone else in the room but his boy.

"Who the hell is Aubrey?" Sam sputtered.

"Ms. Powell is Reed and Tag's homeroom teacher." Gaskill turned back to Ulrich. "You two are on a first name basis?" His tone was glacial, and Ulrich didn't need to be a shifter to sense the undertone of suspicion.

"We've met each other socially a couple of times," he explained carefully. He didn't want to get Aubrey in hot water.

"Oh my god!" Shelby declared. "You're sleeping with Reed's teacher?"

"I'm not sleeping with Ms. Powell," he said through gritted teeth. "We're acquaintances, nothing more."

"But—" Tag started.

"Shut up, Tag. Don't you think you're in enough trouble already?"

The little shit had been thinking of throwing Ulrich under the bus. Thought he could out-clever his old man. He returned his attention to the principal. "You were saying?"

Gaskill was assessing Ulrich in a way that made him uncomfortable, but he let the topic of Aubrey go. "To stop the fight, Ms. Powell had to physically intervene."

Shelby's eyes grew bigger. "Are you telling me that a teacher hit my baby?"

Ulrich ignored her as he leaned towards the principal. "Did she get hurt?" His wolf was almost shaking at the idea of Aubrey being harmed.

That seemed to win back Gaskill's favour. "She neither hit the boys nor did they hit her." He pursed his lips as he steepled his fingers. "I was simply stating the fact that the boys had to be physically separated since neither responded to Ms. Powell's direction for them to stop fighting." He glared at Tag and Reed. "When asked, the boys refused to explain their behaviour."

Ulrich was aware that Gaskill hadn't really answered his question and had to restrain himself from racing down to her classroom and checking for himself. "What the hell?" he said instead as he turned to Tag. "Explain what's going on!"

Tag looked past Ulrich to Reed. They made eye contact briefly before Reed dropped his eyes. "Nothing's going on. Like we said before, we were playfighting."

Bullshit! Tag was lucky that Ulrich was the only one in the room that could hear the kid's heartbeat increase. Or unlucky.

"Reed?" Ulrich looked past Shelby to the kid, who was staring at his running shoes. "Care to elaborate?"

"Don't talk to my kid, shifter," Sam sneered as Shelby hugged Reed protectively. "Reed's no liar. If he says it was a playfight, then that's what it was." Tag was on the receiving end of Sam's glare and Ulrich clenched his hands to control himself.

A few more minutes breathing the same air as the Donnybrooks and Ulrich would bathe the walls in their blood. "You back off of my kid," he warned, fully aware he should grab Tag and get the fuck out of there.

Gaskill intervened. "Whether it was a playfight or not, the facts speak for themselves. The boys were punching each other, drew blood, didn't stop when they were told to by Ms. Powell, and forced her to get physical with them to prevent further injury."

Sam opened his mouth, but Gaskill shot him down. "I'm not defending Ms. Powell's actions – the school has a no-touch policy – but in this situation, her intervention was necessary."

"You're expelling them, then?" Shelby rasped, ready to go to battle for her undeserving son.

"No. They will be serving a ten-day detention from 3pm to 5pm under Ms. Powell's supervision." Gaskill glanced down at an open file in front of him. "They're permitted to attend volleyball practices on Tuesdays and Thursdays, which means it will take them a little more than three weeks to complete their punishment."

Shelby shook her head. "I'm not sure I'm comfortable with Reed being alone with that women."

Ulrich finally blew. "Have you even met Aubrey?" he shouted. "You didn't know who your kid's schoolteacher was until today and now you're casting judgement because she dared to intervene before your son got hurt. You should be fucking thanking her!"

Sam shot to his feet. "Back the hell off, you overgrown dalmatian. No one yells at my wife like that!"

Ulrich followed his lead, his hands clenched. "Except you,

I bet!" he snapped back, as Tag grabbed Ulrich's arm and shook it.

"Dad! Dad! Stop!"

Tag's touch snapped Ulrich out of his haze of fury. He dropped his chin to his chest and took a moment to recentre himself. What the fuck was he doing? "I'm sorry," he said as he reseated himself. "I had no right going off like that."

He did, but not in this setting and not in front of the boys. And he'd embarrassed Tag with his anger. What a role-model he was, blowing up at a woman, threatening a fight over the very reason they were there in the first place.

"We're done here!" Shelby snapped at Gaskill. "Reed'll show up for his detention, but if that woman lays a hand on him...."

"Jesus, your son outweighs her." Ulrich felt like dragging their stupid asses down to Aubrey's classroom so they could see how ridiculous their words were.

Gaskill quickly intervened. "I can assure you that Ms. Powell understands that under no circumstances should she touch a student."

The Donnybrooks left first, huffing out of the room with their noses figuratively out of joint, though Ulrich wished he could make it more literal. Once he was sure they were gone, he handed his keys to Tag. "Go get in the truck and wait for me. Lock the doors and don't say anything stupid to the Donnybrooks."

Tag glared at Ulrich as he snatched the keys and stomped out, slamming the door behind him.

Ulrich waited a heartbeat, then turned to the principal. "I'm not going to lie and tell you that I don't want to turn that motherfucking Donnybrook into dogfood, but my behaviour here was out of order. It won't happen again."

Gaskill slumped in his chair. "Don't threaten the parents of another student, Mr. Calhoun. I don't want to end up testifying against you in court if one or both goes missing." He paused as he rubbed at his generous forehead. "The Donnybrooks are... difficult." He was choosing his words carefully. "Reed is a good boy but can be a bully from what little I've observed. I thought he and Tag were getting along and even worried that they'd team up and terrorize the school."

Gaskill knew some of Tag's history, because Ulrich had informed the school of the no-contact order against his ex-wife, so he expected the principal to be a bit more forgiving in his assessment of his son. It seemed he was wrong. "Tag's not a bully," he said flatly.

Gaskill seemed exhausted. "According to the Donny-brooks, neither is Reed."

Touché.

As Ulrich made his way towards his truck, Sam Donny-brook accosted him. "You candyass shifter," he said, his voice low and dangerous. "Loser," he snarled. "You fucking apologize to my wife and kid for threatening them or I'm going to make your fucking useless life miserable."

Ulrich searched his mind for the words he'd said while the Donnybrooks were in the room. Sure, he'd made the stupid remark about dogfood to Gaskill when they were alone, and his behaviour hadn't been exemplary, but threatening them?

The man was either brave or stupid for taking on Ulrich. Either way, there was no fucking way he was going to say sorry to the asshole or his family. "I got nothing to say to you or your family. Stay the fuck away from my kid or you'll answer to me."

This was turning into a shitshow – exchanging threats in a school parking lot with a fucking human male who thought he was a tough guy. Gaskill was right – if something happened to Donnybrook, Ulrich would end up on the top of the suspect list.

"Dad!" Tag's voice jerked him out of his growing anger. "Let's go."

Ulrich glared at Donnybrook, letting his wolf's fury tinge his irises. Then he turned his back and stalked to his truck.

"Fucking animal!" Donnybrook shouted across the parking lot, but Ulrich didn't look back. He was too close to losing it.

He and Tag drove home in silence, Ulrich's rage fading to a slow burn as Gaskill's parting words played over and over in his head.

Tag's not a bully.

According to the Donnybrooks, neither is Reed.

Had he been overlooking Tag's behaviour because the kid had gone through some serious shit? Was he cutting him too much slack? Despite doing everything he could to get Tag back, he was still riddled with guilt about letting Sibyl take him, about how long it took to get him back. What parent wouldn't be?

He tripped over the thought as he laughed sardonically to himself. Sibyl, for one. And the fucking Donnybrooks. Both were prime examples of what parents shouldn't do. But then again, Ulrich was just as guilty, losing his temper in front of his boy, too proud to back off.

At home, he stopped Tag before he could run downstairs to his room. "Go get us a couple of Cokes and meet me in the living room. We're talking this through."

Ulrich seated himself on the couch, then pointed to the other end of it when Tag returned with the Cokes.

The can felt cool in his hand and even better as its contents slid over his tongue and down his throat. He wished it were a beer or a shot of scotch or bourbon, but he'd already lost ground in the parent-of-the-year contest. He didn't need to show Tag how grown-ups cope with problems.

"Tell me what happened today," he said after slamming the

Coke. He covered his mouth as he burped. "All of it. Not the play-fighting version."

Tag contemplated the can in his hands and for a moment, Ulrich thought the kid was going to clam up, but when he looked up, he met his father's gaze with a serious one of his own. "Reed broke into my locker and stole my lunch. When I found out it was him, I tracked him down. Guess he thought he was playing a joke on me, but I didn't like it and called him a pr.... uh, a name. Pissed him off, so he dumped my lunch on the ground and stomped on it in front of everyone."

Ulrich dropped his eyes to his hands, thinking about what he would have done in similar circumstances. Thinking about the pissing contest he'd had with Donnybrook in the school parking lot. "And?"

"Yelling led to pushing and shoving and then the punches started flying." He blew out a shuddering breath. "Reed's pretty strong."

"Not as strong as you and never will be." *Listen to yourself, you asshole. Might learn something.* "The good thing about shifter blood is that you can be who you want to be and no one but another shifter can stand in your way. But if you're living among humans, it comes with responsibility. Your superior strength means you have to learn how to manage your instincts, find a different way to diffuse a situation."

"Like you did with Mrs. Donnybrook?" The tone of Tag's voice was accusing Ulrich of hypocrisy.

The little shit had to go there. "Yes and no. Shifters are human and wolf. Lucky us to have the ancient blood coursing through our veins. Some shifters, like your mother's pack, justify their aggression by saying it's part of their heritage. It's a dangerous mentality. Militant, subversive – people and shifters will get hurt because of them."

"They say aggression in shifters is natural. That we shouldn't have to hide it. That it can't really be done."

"I'm proof that's a lie. If I followed my instincts, I might have destroyed your mother years ago. I wouldn't have let her repeatedly back into our lives. No one died when my team and I came to get you. I wanted to wipe out the entire pack, but instead, I suppressed the urge. We did it peacefully, at night when most of the pack was sleeping."

"Aragon will think you're a coward for doing that." Tag took a sip of his Coke.

Aragon was the alpha of Sibyl's pack, a mean sonofabitch who used his pack to further his interests. "Perhaps." Ulrich shrugged. "What he thinks isn't important to me. What you think is."

Tag's face wore the expression of a young boy who was unsure of his place in the world. "I don't think you're a coward."

"A coward uses violence to solve his problems. Incites it, dictates to the world. It's not just shifters who have to fight their instincts and aggression. Humans do it too." Ulrich struggled for the right words. "I lost my temper with the Donnybrooks today – that's a natural part of our makeup, whether we're shifters or humans. But what I did afterwards is more important."

"What you'd do?"

Ulrich almost rolled his eyes at Tag's obtuseness. A chip off the old block was what the kid was. "I apologized to diffuse the situation. I didn't want the shouting to turn into a fight, because you and I both know, if I wanted to, I could have taken out everyone in that room."

"Yeah." Tag nodded reluctantly.

"No more fighting."

Tag wasn't convinced. "What else could I do? I couldn't back down!"

Wasn't that what we were just talking about? Ulrich rubbed at his temple. "Why not?"

Tag looked at his father as if he were simple-minded. Maybe he was. "Because I'd lose respect."

"Of everyone? How many of your classmates lost respect of you today because you fought with Reed Donnybrook? What do you think some of them thought when a female had to physically intervene?"

Tag's face reddened. "Ms. Powell kind of lied to Mr. Gaskill about what happened."

Ulrich narrowed his eyes, his pulse becoming erratic at the mention of Aubrey. "What exactly did happen?"

Tag crushed the empty Coke can between his fingers. "She told us to stop, then when we didn't, she tackled me to the ground." His risked a quick glance at Ulrich, who was now struggling with the fact that Aubrey physically attacked his son.

"She tackled you? Not Reed?" He tried to keep his tone casual as he and his wolf got into it, both confused about which one they should feel protective over.

Tag caught his father's eyes. "It's not like what you're thinking. I was on top of Reed, punching him in the face, and she told me stop, but I couldn't." His eyes brightened with tears. "I heard her, I understood her, but I couldn't stop. Her making me stop was the only way."

Ulrich rubbed his face at the kid's confession. "Your wolf is struggling with you."

"I didn't feel anything," Tag argued. "Sometimes I think I don't have a wolf."

Ulrich sighed. "From the day you were born, you've had a wolf. You know that. But until you reach puberty, it's not a factor in your reactions. You're not far-off, so maybe your anger at Reed brought your wolf to the surface."

Tag slumped against the cushion of the sofa. "Well, that's just great." And because the universe had a sense of humour, his voice cracked.

Ulrich laughed, but sobered quickly. "Time to up the training, kid. You got your detention after school with Ms. Powell, and your volleyball, which I'll let you continue, providing you keep your nose clean. But the evenings and weekends are mine unless you have a game. For a month."

"A month!" Tag practically shouted. "C'mon, Dad!"

"You're lucky it's not more. And maybe it will be." Ulrich felt grumpy with his kid. "Depends on how seriously you take your training."

"Fine," Tag grumbled, getting to his feet and stalking out of the room. Ulrich didn't blame him for being surly. Lectures from parents sucked.

He relaxed against the back of the couch and thought about what Tag had told him. It irked him that Aubrey had involved herself, going so far as to lie about Tag's role in the fight to protect him.

He should be thankful, not annoyed, but he couldn't seem to shake his displeasure at the way she had handled the situation. Tag was simply doing what his instincts led him to do, which was to protect his territory, his placement in the so-called pack of school mates. Yeah, Ulrich would have to teach Tag how to manage his emotions, but what if the kid was being punished and picked on because Gaskill and Aubrey were humans and were applying their human prejudices to a shifter boy.

The other side of him argued that it was Aubrey's right to discipline Tag because Ulrich had chosen to raise him outside the pack. He and Tag were part of human society and thus had to adjust to fit in. There was no forgiveness for shifter aggression.

He wondered what Aubrey had been thinking when she tackled Tag. Or was she thinking at all? Maybe she panicked, thought Tag would kill the other kid if she didn't intervene.

What if Tag had turned on Aubrey? She had no defense again an angry male shifter, even if he was a 12-year-old boy.

He checked his cell phone, the tracking device he had on it telling him Aubrey was still at school. Time for the teacher to explain herself.

On his way out the door, he told Tag to order pizza and left his credit card on the kitchen table.

CHAPTER SIX

A ubrey's stomach growled and she paused, listening to it protest the fact that it was empty. When was the last time she'd eaten? She leaned back in her chair and tried to order her thoughts. It had to have been breakfast, because the day since then had been one poop-storm after another.

She didn't get to her lunch because she was on playground supervision, and the fight between Tag and Reed stole most of the afternoon. The stop at the nurse's office took an hour, while Santana Bosworth patched up the boys and sent them on their way to the principal's office.

After they'd gone, she turned to Aubrey. "You look worse than they do."

Aubrey felt worse too. She was only 24, but the energy she'd started the day with was sapped right out of her. "I believe it. God, what a day."

She and Santana got along well enough despite the school nurse being almost 10 years older than Aubrey. They were work friends, hanging out together in the teacher's lounge, sometimes lunching when their schedules synced, but never went out socially.

"C'mon." Santana motioned with her head. "Hop up on the table."

Aubrey complied, deciding it was easier than arguing.

After Santana tended to her skinned knees, she said, "You've got your choice of bandages." She went to her supply table and fumbled around before holding up three options. "Black with white skull bones, pink with white poodles, or white with bright yellow happy faces."

Aubrey groaned at the selection. "Don't you have normal?"

"Nope, I ran out of normal a few a years ago."

Aubrey snickered at the joke. "Fine, I don't do poodles and won't do skull bones, so I guess it's gotta be the smiley emojis."

Santana grinned as she affixed the happy face bandages over the worst of the scrapes, then cleaned up an abrasion on Aubrey's arm that hadn't hurt until Santana pointed it out.

After Aubrey was deemed healthy enough to return to work, she used the staff bathroom to wash off the remaining dirt and tidy her hair before returning to her class. By then it was almost 2:30 and there was no point in starting anything, so she gave her students license to read or talk quietly among themselves until the school day ended.

She hadn't thought about eating before, her stress levels dampening her appetite. Some people ate when they were anxious, others couldn't force the food past their lips. She was of the latter category, which was why she perennially looked underfed.

She sighed as she checked her phone for the time. It was almost 6 pm. No wonder her stomach sounded like she'd swallowed a shifter. She flushed as an image of Ulrich popped into her head. Swallowing a shifter held so much more meaning since she'd met the alpha shifter. She saw them together, him naked, his body a wonderland (yeah, she was that cheesy), her on her knees, between his open thighs, sucking him to orgasm. Now that was swallowing a shifter.

"Ms. Powell."

She looked up startled as the man of her fantasy, walked... no... swaggered into the room. He was so effing good looking in blue jeans and a T-shirt, a loose jacket covering his enormous bi-ceps.

"Mr. Calhoun," she exclaimed as she tried to get the circus in her stomach to dismount the trapeze. "I didn't expect to see you today."

He strode across the floor, stopping a foot from her, close enough that she was prevented from standing up without bumping him. He towered over her in such a way that she had to lean back against her chair and crane her neck to see his face. It forced her chest to jut out provocatively.

"Why wouldn't you expect me to drop by? You intervened in a fight, manhandled my son, then punished him for something he didn't start."

She couldn't tell from his expression if he was angry, but his choice of words didn't seem teasing.

She shook, but remarkably not from fear. He didn't evoke that emotion in her. No, the tremble coursing through her body was unadulterated desire. She huffed out a breath to steady her pulse but knew enough about shifters to know that he was fully aware of the affect he was having on her. Question was, how would he interpret it?

"I had to break up the fight." She was proud of herself for keeping the quiver out of her voice. "Tag wasn't listening to me."

"Tag's a shifter. He was in the middle of a brawl with another student." His eyes stroked her up and down. "And you thought you could stop it."

Aubrey's irritation mingled with the heated reaction her body was having to this giant. "I did stop it."

"By tackling my son."

The words were so blunt, so cold, that she struggled with their meaning. Was he accusing her of more than manhandling Tag? "Because he was the aggressor."

"He was defending himself against the little asshole who stole his lunch."

Aubrey's rein on her composure snapped. "If you've got something to say to me, then say it." Her voice had risen sharply and Ulrich's eyes, normally a light shade of blue, darkened.

Shit, now I've pissed him off. Belatedly, she thought to be cautious. What if he had no more control over his temper than Tag had?

As if to prove her point, Ulrich's hands curled into fist. "You don't understand shifter ways! How the hell can you be a schoolteacher to my son?"

Aubrey dropped her eyes to her hands, which were folded in her lap. She wished she were standing, though that wouldn't give her much height advantage. But still, to have this massive man towering over her, angry at her for reasons beyond her comprehension, made her want to get up in his face and shout back.

Except that she was in the school, in her classroom, late in the day, alone. Anything she said or did might rile him up further, and while she didn't exactly fear for her life, she was highly aware of the damage he could do to her if he lost control.

"I'm sorry," she said, trying to sound conciliatory, but her words fell flat, even to her ears.

She was shocked when he pulled her from her chair, his massive hands wrapping around her biceps. "You're not fucking sorry!" She was in the air suddenly, then thumped

73

down on top of her desk on her butt. That made her tall enough that she could see his mouth if she looked directly at him. He had a luscious mouth, lips full and pouty as they snarled at her.

Uh, Aubrey. Shouldn't you be outraged that he manhandled you?

Yes, right. Outraged. She blew out a breath to settle her racing pulse, then pushed her hands against his chest, the drumming of his heart beating against her palm. "Back up, Mr. Calhoun. I'm feeling threatened."

The words seemed to piss him off even more. "Because I'm a shifter. Like Tag?"

She tilted her chin so she could see his eyes. "Because you're considerably bigger and stronger than me."

He stepped back and raked a hand over the top of his head. "I would never hurt you." The wind had dropped from his sails and his eyes softened back to gorgeous watercolour blue.

The unbidden thought that they would make beautiful babies jumped into her mind. "Are you accusing me of manhandling Tag because he's a shifter?"

He paced away, his face red. Then, as if to justify his behaviour, he said. "My son is the most important person in the world. You fucked him over."

"Yes. I think we've determined that you think that's the case." Aubrey stayed seated on the top of her desk though she would have liked to pace around like he was. Still, it was better if she stayed more or less eye level with him than to walk out her discomfort. "I agree that I'm no expert on shifter behaviour, but in my defence, your son had another boy pinned to the ground and was punching the lights out of him. I'm not biased against your son and I resent the implication. I would have tackled whoever was on top if they refused to listen."

"The little shit was fucking with Taggart," Ulrich growled. "Shifters don't take shit like that lying down."

Aubrey couldn't tell if his words were meant to trap her into admitting she'd singled out Tag because he was a shift, which she hadn't. *Proceed carefully, girl.* "And nor should they."

Ulrich raised his eyebrows. "Really? So then tell me, Ms. Powell. How should have Tag handled it?"

Aubrey felt like she was lecturing a grown-up child. One who had huge powerful arms, sexy lips, and a butt so hard she was sure she could bounce a stick of chalk off it. "Violence should never be the first reaction to a situation. Taggart needs to learn to negotiate."

He stalked up to her, pushing up against her knees, his fists dropping to the desk on either side of her hips as he leaned in. "And yet, your first reaction was to tackle my boy."

Aubrey slanted her body backwards, flattening her hands on the desk to stay upright. Her pulse was racing again, and she willed it to settle. "I told him to stop. Twice."

"The kid stole Taggart's lunch." His words were decep-tively soft as he stared into her eyes. "Tag told him to give it back. Twice."

"I'm not biased!" she defended. "I was merely reacting to the situation."

"Then why wasn't the Reed punished for stealing Tag's lunch?"

"I didn't know about the fucking lunch until now!"

"Language, Ms. Powell, we're in a fucking school."

Was he playing with her, or serious? And why had he cursed? She tried never to do that.

She licked her lips as she tried to hold his intense gaze. It was impossible, but dropping her eyes to his lips was a big mistake. What were they talking about? Lunch. Right. He kind of had a point, but what if she hadn't intervened? What if she stood around like a Victorian woman, wringing her hands and screaming? She swallowed, thinking she should tell him that. Thinking she should tell him to back away and leave. Thinking nothing about this was right.

Then she thought to hell with it.

She grabbed the fabric of his shirt to leverage herself, then settled her lips on his. They were exactly as she imagined – full, soft, and just the right amount of dry as they took her kiss. At first, he didn't move, didn't reciprocate her boldness, but then she felt him press back, seeking more of the same.

Her right hand was all in as it snaked its way to the back of his neck. He didn't move, didn't touch her other than to return her kiss, pushing at the seam of her mouth, asking to be admitted inside. Aubrey opened to him with a soft release of breath, her tongue seeking his, tasting him.

It was so perfect, and she felt herself melting. She closed her eyes and let the sweetness of warm honey slide through her veins. Her nipples peaked, her sweet spot throbbed, and her body ached in a way she'd never felt before. She was drunk on the scent of sandalwood, high on the idea of him making love to her. He was every fantasy she'd ever had come to life. She couldn't resist him.

Apparently, that was not the case with Ulrich. He pulled himself out of her grip, the heat of his body, the press of his lips gone. Her eyes flew open to see him standing a few feet away, a curious set to his face. "Is that how you negotiate?" he said gruffly, sounding both heated and displeased.

She cleared her throat, realizing that she'd been less than professional. That was twice today. She'd manhandled a kid, and now she was kissing the kid's father. Schoolteachers were not supposed to kiss the parents of their students. She was not supposed to kiss Ulrich. It was also twice now that she'd thrown herself at him.

At least you're sober this time. Adrienne was probably looking down at her from heaven laughing at her prim younger sister making a fool of herself.

"I'm so sorry," she blurted breathlessly as she pressed her hands to her cheeks. "I shouldn't have done that." She hopped down from the desk and scurried towards the window. She needed air and space to settle her desire and get her head on straight. More than anything, though, she wished she could escape through the window, hide somewhere, and die of embarrassment.

She turned back to him. "I've never done that before. I promise you. I don't know what came over me." She wrung her hands together. "I… it's just…." She realized she was stammering and clamped her lips shut. What could she say to him that didn't sound insane?

Ulrich. "You need to stop kissing me, Aubrey."

Her face was burning. "I know."

He gave her a crooked grin as he headed for the door but when he turned back towards her, his face was serious again. "It's a bad idea and not just because you're Tag's teacher. Gossip is a hobby in Darkness Falls and your sister had a reputation."

She choked on his words. "That's not fair! The only one I've kissed is you!"

"That's good to know." His expression held both triumph and warning. "Keep it that way."

CHAPTER SEVEN

Ulrich's wolf was racing around inside him, pissed that Ulrich was such a cock blocker. Some days, Ulrich wished he could knock his wolf the fuck out so he could think clearly. But it wasn't his wolf, not really. It was all him, having regrets along with blue balls that he didn't lock that classroom door, bend her over her desk and take her like she was made for him.

Which she fucking was.

The mere thought of him inside her turned his blood molten and his dick into a painfully hard steel rod.

As he reached his truck, he slammed a fist down on the hood. "Fuck!" he shouted. Why did she have to kiss him? Again! It was his fault. He got up close and personal – goddamn, he'd practically assaulted her by yanking her out of her chair and sitting her on the top of her desk.

What he'd wanted to do was rip off her underwear, shove his way between her legs, and fuck her until she screamed his name. Everything about her made him come undone.

The second he stepped into the room, at the sight of her slight body sitting at her desk, head bent over some papers she was marking, he knew he should turnaround and leave.

She was exhausted. He heard it when she sighed, saw it in the slump of her shoulders. The roughness of her day lingered in the air: dirt and blood mingled with soap; the sweetness of her sweat, dried, but still enduring. And then she turned towards him, and he saw the bandages on her knees, white with bright yellow smiley faces and that's what almost did him in.

Almost made him slam the door behind him, turn the lock, and pull her into his arms.

Maybe it was because she'd been hurt in the fray, or maybe it was the goofy bandages giving him a peek into who she was. Maybe it was simply because she looked so vulnerable, hurt, rumpled, and tired. He heard her stomach growl, knew she hadn't eaten. That combined with her bruised body, the thrumming of her pulse as the beat of her heart increased, the clear scent of desire. Yeah, it was everything.

And then she'd kissed him, and he knew he had to leave before he completely savaged her. He'd held it together long enough to play with her before he bolted, to pretend he was unaffected by the kiss. It was the way it had to be. He didn't dare show her how crazy she was making him.

He climbed into his truck and waited as the sun set on the waning day. Tag was home, eating alone, vulnerable too, if his mother showed up, but he couldn't make himself leave until he knew Aubrey was safely in her car and heading home.

He should talk to her about her habits, staying late at school, being alone in the building. Ice crept up his spine when he thought how much of a target she could be. As a Special Units Inspector, he'd dealt with brutal crime scenes, too horrific for his mind to not swap Aubrey's body for another's in his imagination.

He almost went back into the school to tell her not to be

so relaxed about her safety but stopped himself. She was far too tempting and distracting, and he couldn't succumb to his primal urges, no matter what the universe decided. He needed to be focused on Tag, making sure he was emotionally okay, getting him ready for his shift.

And he needed to complete the job he came here for – find the shifter who'd been preying on women in Darkness Falls. Find him, arrest him, and get him locked up.

His train of thought slid back to Aubrey when she finally appeared, weighted down with a heavy backpack. The door slammed behind her and she turned towards it, testing the handle to make sure it had locked. He was tempted to teach her a lesson, grab her from behind and drag her into the shadows, but that was akin to burning a kid's hand to stop him from touching a hot stove. Better he talked to her or have someone do it for him.

His wolf prowled inside him as he watched her walk to her car, a rusty bucket of bolts that was barely road worthy. Another reason to worry. And she lived alone in a sketchy part of town in an apartment building without a locked lobby or buzzer system.

He could walk up those stairs anytime he wanted, kick in her door, and steal her away.

Fuck!

He shook his head to clear the panic.

Distance. That's what he needed from this woman. It wouldn't be easy since she was Tag's teacher. Parent-teacher interviews, volleyball games, and parents' meetings would ensure they shared the same orbit. Maybe he should ask Gaskill to move Tag into another classroom. He could use the excuse that he wanted to separate the kid from Reed Donnybrook.

Aubrey finally started her car and drove off in the direction of her apartment. He imagined her parking in the secluded lot, then walking into that seedy building without a care in the world until someone in the shadows grabbed her.

Nope, that wouldn't fucking happen on his watch. He started his truck, put it in gear and took a different route to her place so he could arrive ahead of her.

He parked in an unlit part of the lot and got out of his truck, making his way to the building, using the shadows of the trees and walls to conceal him. Then he waited while she pulled into her parking space, got out of her car, her hands so full that she'd be at a disadvantage if she were attacked. She walked to the front door and fumbled it open, unaware that he was feet from her.

Ulrich returned to his truck and waited until the light came on her apartment before he left.

CHAPTER EIGHT

Aubrey rolled over in bed and groaned as her cellphone alarm barked at her. She set it every night, though she didn't usually need it to wake up, but this morning as it yipped and yapped, she thought it odd that someone had brought a dog into the apartment building.

A few woofs later, and she sprang to full awareness, realizing that she'd overslept.

She muzzled the alarm, made her bed, then padded to the bathroom to take a shower and get ready for the day. Too late, she remembered her skinned knees as the spray of the nozzle hitting them became a stinging reminder of the previous day's events.

The happy face bandages didn't survive the blast from the shower, but she didn't think she needed to rebandage them. She dressed in pants to hide her knees, but also to be ready should she need to tackle another student to the ground.

As she turned on her coffee pot, she revisited her encounter with Ulrich the day before. He'd come to the school after-hours to scold her for her role in Tag's punishment. It was a strange encounter, not only because she'd kissed him—a-effing-gain—but also because of the crazy discussion they had. It was almost like he was accusing her for not going to bat for Tag.

She paused her thoughts as her body remembered every second of it, coming out the other end wetter, warmer, and weaker. Yep, the three-w's like she'd never experienced.

Where was she? Oh yeah, she should have told him that her solution was better than what could have happened. No expulsion on the kid's record. At least not yet.

The school day went smoothly, though Aubrey was dreading 3 o'clock. Maybe it wasn't a good idea that she be alone with these two boys, who appeared still antagonistic towards each other. If they got into another fight, she might not be able to stop it again.

Inevitably, the bell rung, school was out, and it was just the three of them: Tag, Reed, and herself.

They sat in the classroom like a scalene triangle with no sides or angles equal: she at her desk, which was crowded in the corner on the left side of the room, Tag sitting in a back row – yeah, she'd gone with rows, though planned to change it mid-way through the quarter—by the windows, and Reed parallel to him, but at the opposite side of the classroom by the back door.

It wouldn't do.

"C'mon up, boys." She pointed at two desks near the front that were separated by a row. Too soon to cozy them up next to each other.

Reed groaned but banged his way to one of the desks.

Tag didn't move.

Aubrey held his eyes. She wasn't an expert on shifters, but she understood enough to know he was issuing a challenge and she would lose him if she backed down.

The staring contest went on for at least 30 seconds, until Aubrey lost her patience. "Up front, Taggart." Yeah, she was that schoolteacher who used full names when the moment called for it. "Unless you want me to tack another week onto your detention.

"Fine," Taggart grumped as he grabbed his bag and made his way up front. He went to sit at a different desk than she indicated.

"No." She pointed her finger at the desk she wanted him in. Closer to her and Reed. "This desk, please."

He glared but followed her directions.

"Good," she said as she took in the two boys slumping in their seats. "This is a two-hour detention, which means like it or not, the three of us get to hang-out until five. Today, you're going to catch up on assignments you missed yesterday afternoon and then do you homework. Since it's Friday, the good news is that you'll be free and clear for the weekend."

"And the bad news?" Reed sneered.

She refrained from rolling her eyes. Twelve-year-old boys on the cusp of puberty were no fun at all. "I was going to say that the other good news is that starting Monday, you two are going to work a project together."

"What?" Reed said, disgust clear in the wrinkling of his nose.

"No effing way," Tag said at the same time, his upper lip curling.

Dammit Tag. "You're pushing your luck, Tag, and I can't quite figure out why, so we're going to discuss it at 4:30 today, after Reed leaves."

This time Taggart didn't even try to be civil. "He gets out early! That's not fair!"

Nothing in life is fair, kid. If it were, I'd have a date with your dad tonight instead of the remote control and a bowl of popcorn. "We'll add that to the list of discussion points for later."

"I have a few *discussion points* of my own," Tag shot back.

Aubrey acknowledged his snark with a bend of her head. "Perhaps you should start a list, too."

Everyone settled in and the next 90 minutes passed quickly. The alarm on her phone dinged quietly and she dismissed it, then looked up. Both boys had already packed up their books and were sitting at their desks, Tag's head resting on an arm laid out on the desk and Reed slouched in his seat, his legs kicking out from under the desk, one foot tapping on the floor.

He sat up when she caught his attention.

"Is your homework done?" she asked him.

"Yeah." Reed sounded like she'd insulted him with her question.

"Show me." She wanted to believe him without proof, but she also wanted him to understand that he needed to earn her trust.

He dragged his bag up to her desk and opened it, pulling out the sheets and scribbler. So old school, she thought as she looked at them. She needed to introduce more online work into her curriculum. Despite Reed's complicated homelife, he was intelligent and careful. It showed up in his work. "Looks good, Reed. Enjoy your weekend. See you Monday."

Reed smirked at Tag as he took off out of the classroom.

Tag pretended he didn't give a damn, his sleepy gaze pinning her. "Want to see my homework too?"

Aubrey nodded her head once. "Yes." She got up and walked to his desk, sitting down in the one across the aisle, fitting it as easily as any 12-year-old. She wished she were bigger, taller, rounder, everything that didn't make her look like she was one of the students.

He yanked his scribbler from his pack, opened the page, and handed it to her. She scanned the answers to the math problems. Tag's work was sloppy, like it was paired with an attitude, but it was complete.

"And the handout from yesterday?"

He shoved it at her. "Happy?" The edge to his voice was challenging and disrespectful.

She sighed as she handed him back his assignment. "No, Tag. I'm not happy."

His eyebrows shot up in surprise. "It's done! The answers are right. What more do you want?"

"You're angry with me," Aubrey said, drawing on the communication classes she'd taken as a requirement of her B.Ed. "But I don't understand why."

"Why do you think?" His attitude was still too belligerent, and she wondered if she should shut it down and try again on Monday, after he had a weekend to cool off. But if she did that, the unfinished business would ruin her weekend. This wasn't just any student. This was Ulrich's son, and she couldn't ignore the impossible need to get along with him, as if she had a future with his father.

"I don't know. That's why I'm asking. It can't be because you have detention because you were there for that conversation – the one where I asked Mr. Gaskill not to expel you and Reed. I don't think it's because I tackled you to the ground—"

"Which you lied about," Tag interrupted.

"I didn't lie," Aubrey protested, even though she had. "I omitted a detail that you could have included had you wanted to."

"Maybe I want to now."

Maybe I want to expel you now, you little bugger. "I'll walk with you down to the office, if you like." Aubrey wasn't about to be held hostage by a 12-year-old, Ulrich's son or not so she added, "But so you know, I'll have to explain why I tackled you."

"I think you hate shifters, that's why you tackled me."

Hate shifters? *Good grief.* "I don't hate anyone, Tag. Your father and I are friends." A little embellishment wouldn't hurt, would it?

"And that right there is why I'm mad!" Tag spat at her.

What? "Because I'm friends with your father?"

"Dad's gone all the freaking time. Like last night. I got beat up, so what'd he do? He tells me to order pizza for dinner, then he leaves. When he finally got home, he smelled like you."

Aubrey froze at the implication. Shifters had super-sensitive olfactory nodes so she shouldn't have been surprised. "He came to talk to me about what happened yesterday," she replied carefully.

Tag's brow furrowed in irritation. "I'm not some stupid kid that still believes in Santa Claus. I. Could. Smell. You. On. Him. You two were doing more than talking."

Aubrey felt her face heat. "We're friends," she said feebly. "I hugged him when he left."

Tag glanced at the clock over the door. It was almost 5 o'clock. "I don't want other kids knowing about you and Dad. It's embarrassing."

Aubrey shook her head. "There's nothing between me and your father." She almost added, I promise, but she couldn't make a promise she wasn't sure she could keep. At the same time, she understood where Tag was coming from. The kid had been through a lot in his short lifetime, and he didn't need to also have to deal with the mortification of his dad dating his teacher.

Tag picked up his bag as he stood. "Keep it that way. Leave my dad alone. My mom and dad will get back together when she comes to visit me. They always do. *Always*. And maybe this time, they'll make it work."

"Tag—"

"Can I go? It's 5 o'clock."

"Sure," Aubrey said, her heart full of empathy for the boy running full tilt out of her classroom.

After he'd gone, she folded her hands on the top of the desk and stared at them as she tried to get her emotions under control. She wasn't even sure why she felt so off-balance. She had no claim to Ulrich, no claim to his son, but as Tag talked about the relationship he had with his mother, she felt her heart break for herself, but also for Tag.

Is that what they did? An on-again, off-again relationship? It sounded almost toxic the way Tag represented it. If it were true, it would be toxic to Tag. She knew from experience. It wasn't a love-hate relationship that had messed with her, but a deadbeat father and an alcoholic mother who always sobered up long enough to get Aubrey and her sister out of the foster-care system, only to fall off the wagon again. It had been a destructive, damaging cycle that had long-term impacts for Aubrey and Adrienne. It was, Aubrey believed, a factor that led to her sister's death.

Remembering the hope that she used to harbour as a young girl, she didn't doubt that Tag believed every word of what he said. She used to think the same thing each time she was returned to her mother. This time the sobriety would stick. This time they'd be a normal family.

What she doubted was the veracity of Tag's claim. When Ulrich came to her after he'd enrolled Tag in school, when they talked about his wife, Sibyl, he didn't sound like a man in love or hate. He sounded like a parent, trying to do right by his kid.

She stood and stretched the muscles in her back, then gathered up her things and left the school. In her car, she felt paralyzed. She had thought her life good enough since she'd come to Darkness Falls. She had good friends who accepted her, a job with a good paycheck and benefits, and students that looked up to her.

She didn't draw male attention like some of her friends because she wasn't glamorous, or curvy, or particularly mouthy, but she was okay with that. While she enjoyed the company of others, she needed alone time to reset. She liked her quiet, her books, her singleness, perhaps because it was all she'd known in her life. Strangers had raised her.

Ulrich was a fantasy she needed to abandon for the sake of Tag. Or at least shelve for a few years. Besides, while he admitted they were fated to be together, he didn't seem interested. His control seemed shatter-proof.

This wasn't the first time in her life that she'd felt lonely, but tonight seemed different. She didn't want to go home to a dark empty apartment and eat popcorn for dinner. She wanted... no, needed to be with people, sit among strangers and be part of their world. She started her car and headed to Becker's. She'd have dinner, a glass of white wine, and let the energy of others give her strength. Maybe it would be enough to keep the past from haunting her.

CHAPTER NINE

I t was a few minutes past five and Tag was waiting in front when Ulrich swept into the school parking lot.

"What are you doing?" Tag asked as Ulrich picked him up, then found a sheltered parking spot. The kid seemed more irritable than usual, but Ulrich chalked it up to detention. He'd had a few – okay, more than a few – when he was Tag's age and remembered how unfair it seemed at the time.

"I was thinking I should go talk to Aub... Ms. Powell to make sure you and Reed behaved yourselves."

Tag rolled his eyes. "We were good, Dad. No fighting, no shouting. Ms. Powell didn't get to practice her chokehold."

He thinks he's funny. "I would expect you to take this a lot more seriously. At least she didn't expel you."

Tag slumped in the seat and changed the subject. "I'm bleeping hungry. Can we go home and make supper?"

"I was thinking of—" He stopped mid-sentence as Aubrey walked out of the school. His blood heated and moved south to his dick. Shit, this was the wrong place and time for him to get hard, but he couldn't seem to tear his attention off her.

Fortunately, he snapped out of the lust coma at the

pissed-off tone in Tag's words. "Geez Dad, she's not even that pretty."

"She is so pretty," Ulrich muttered, his eyes glued to the little schoolteacher. Inane comeback, but how could anyone not see her beauty? He took a few shallow breaths, then turned his attention to his son. "A man can admire a woman from afar. Nothing wrong with that."

Tag scowled. "Sure, that's what you were doing last night? Admiring her from afar?" His eyes flashed like a solar flare and Ulrich saw a younger version of himself – not as angry or defeated, but still, the fire simmering in his blood making him defiant.

He realized he'd been foolish for not showering when he got home before he joined Tag in the basement for cold pizza and a first-person shooter game, which he sorely lost. Too long since he had to worry about Tag knowing what he was up to. His last girlfriend had been four years ago. And yeah, maybe a weekend or two since, with a pretty woman who wasn't interested in commitment, but he'd made sure any notable traces were washed away before he came home to his son.

Now Tag was challenging him on his relationship with Aubrey. "We've already had this discussion. You're the priority in my life and you have my full attention until you don't need it anymore."

Tag shook his head. "I don't need it now. I hated mom's pack, I missed you, but no more than I miss mom when she isn't around." His face reddened as he tried to control his emotions.

Ulrich's heart twinged in his chest. "I'm sorry, but I can't trust your mother not to take off with you again."

"She misses you, Dad. You didn't even talk to her when you took me back."

Ulrich glanced out the window towards Aubrey's car as it

grumbled to life. The bucket of bolts needed to be retired or put out of its misery. He started his truck and backed out of his parking space, then put it in gear and trailed Aubrey.

"I couldn't, Tag. I wanted to kill her, and I might have if she started spewing her usual bullshit. The months without you were a nightmare for me. I could barely function. You were gone, living with a woman...." He groped for words that wouldn't completely vilify Sibyl. Tag needed to understand that she was a danger to him, but Ulrich didn't want to do it at the expense of his son's love for his mom.

Aubrey rolled to a stop at a red light and he followed suit three cars back.

Tag's heart was pumping, strong, steady, but far too fast. Ulrich glanced at him as the light turned green. Tag's hands were clenched on his thighs, his back stiff, and his gaze forward. He was waiting for Ulrich to finish his sentence.

"Your mother's unstable," he muttered as he rolled the truck forward.

Tag laughed harshly. "She's an addict, Dad, not unstable. I'm not a baby anymore. And she's clean. Stayed that way the entire time I was with her."

That's what Henry, his team-lead had said, but Ulrich had trouble believing it. "Doesn't matter. She violated the restraining order and kidnapped you under the law."

Aubrey turned left onto the main strip and Ulrich wondered where she was going. Not home. That was a right turn. Emotions swamped him – overwhelming fear that she was putting herself in danger, jealousy that she might be seeing someone else, and fury, for a reason he couldn't fathom.

"Human law," Ulrich dimly heard Tag snap.

"We don't have a pack, so yeah. Human law."

"I have a pack. I have two that I could choose from." Tag's declaration pulled Ulrich's attention away from Aubrey.

He focused on his son as he lost his temper. "You're 12 years old! I'm your father and my job is to protect, even from yourself!" He clutched the steering wheel so hard his fingers hurt. "You're not going back to your mother's pack – you don't want to anyway. And there's no fucking way you're going to my pack. You wouldn't last a minute there, because once the alpha realized you were my kid, he'd rip you to pieces! And just so I'm clear, we're talking about the guy who killed your grandfather!"

Yeah, he wasn't going to win father of the year, but goddamit, he also wasn't about to spend the next however many years having this conversation. The little shit was playing both ends. Or maybe he was as fucked up as his parents.

Tag blinked his eyes furiously, but to his credit, didn't cry. "I'm not saying I want to! I'm just saying I want you to give Mom a chance. She's had a hard time too and she's clean now!"

Ulrich drew in a deep steadying breath as he realized that he'd lost Aubrey's trail. His stomach somersaulted, his wolf roared, but his reason, yeah, fucking human reason won out over instinct. He modulated his voice as he returned his focus to Tag. "Your mother and I are never getting back together again."

Together they were toxic. It didn't matter what state Sibyl was in. They'd tried repeatedly, she returning to him clean, begging him to take her back, and he, letting her back into Tag's life and their home. But she couldn't sustain sobriety when they were together, because of him, because of who he was, how he was. There was no love left, only a bone-deep weariness that infected his and Tag's life.

"I don't understand why." Tag's voice broke alongside Ulrich's heart. "You always want her back."

It wasn't true. Each time she came back, he opened the

93

door for Tag's sake, but the kid didn't need that burden on his shoulders. "She crossed the line last time. Took you away from me." He paused to sort out his words, then added, "Us getting back together is like her falling off the wagon. I have to draw a line in the sand and say enough is enough." He saw Aubrey's car, sitting on the side of the highway, smoke billowing from the engine. "Shit," he muttered as he quickly changed lanes.

Tag was outraged as Ulrich pulled in behind Aubrey. "What are you doing?"

Ulrich didn't like the tone or the question. "Helping a friend. It's what we do, Tag. Help others in a crisis."

"She's not just a friend," Tag spat. "She's the reason you won't talk to Mom or let her see me."

That was utter bullshit and Tag knew it. Ulrich turned off his truck and stepped out. He'd deal with Tag's misunderstanding of his relationship with Aubrey later. "If you can't be nice to her, stay put. I'll deal with this, then we'll go home."

Tag slammed open his door and hopped out, then turned and snarled at his dad. "I'll walk home. You can waste your time, but I got better things to do."

Ulrich watched the little shit as he stormed off. Tag's attitude was starting to wear thin. He wondered briefly if he should hook him up with the Lodge Pack, ask the alpha, Lucien, to put him to work, involve him in pack activities.

The alpha in him roared. *No fucking way is that kid going to another pack. You'll find a way to sort through this without giving in.*

Sibyl was no longer welcome in his home for so many reasons, one of which included the woman opening her car door and stepping out onto the pavement, a soft, yielding gleam in her eyes.

CHAPTER TEN

A ubrey knew Ulrich was following her. Not just today, she'd seen his truck a few times, including the other night after she'd kissed him. When she'd come out of the school, she noted his truck, parked across the lot, somewhat hidden by a big birch tree. He followed her out of the lot, and as tempting as it was to meander around for a while, she followed her usual route to her home. At one point, to her disappointment, he disappeared, but then there he was, parked in the shadows of the apartment parking lot when she pulled in.

If he thought he was being circumspect, he wasn't giving her enough credit. She was a woman after all, and with her upbringing, she was fully aware of what could be lurking in the shadows. And then of course, she had a super-crush on him and could practically feel him when he was in her vicinity.

She knew as much as she could find out about him. Google, who was usually her partner in good gossip, seemed to blank out on the details of Ulrich Calhoun's life. She accepted it gracefully after much swearing and inciting both

Goldie the Second and Mr. Meow into a frenzy. They might have been hungry though, she thought, remembering how they settled down after she fed them.

What she couldn't find out from Mr. Google, she sought details out from her friends. The fact that she was usually the quietest one in the group, with the softest voice, added to her subtlety. Even Eva didn't question her interest. In fact, the Supercop was especially forthcoming because she had a loathe-on for Ulrich, so she didn't spare details, opining on anything and everything he said or did. All Aubrey had to do was introduce the topic.

And yes, she'd been dead drunk the night Ulrich took her home, but she knew the colour of his truck (black), the make (Dodge Ram), the yearish (didn't have to be exact). Eva had helped her pin down where he lived – a big two-story house in the burbs that got her imagination jumping to all sorts of scenarios that involved honeymoons and babies. It was easy to track down pictures of the interior by looking for past sales of the house. She knew what he paid for the house, the square footage, the number of bedrooms (four if you counted the finished basement) and bathrooms (three). The master bathroom was every woman's fantasy come true.

She knew his age, his shoe-size, and even the brand and type of underwear he preferred (based on an unreliable source – Leah, of course). The only thing she didn't know was what he did for a living. Clearly, he wasn't a criminal, or she figured she'd have found his arrest record. Maybe law enforcement because he hung out with Jackson Hayes. Or maybe the two were friends and nothing else.

If her teaching gig didn't work out, she could make a living as a stalker. She already had a clever name for her company. Aubrey Powell, Professional Lurker. Okay, it wasn't that ingenious, and she should probably call herself a private investigator so people didn't get the wrong idea about her nonexistent penchant for violence (if you didn't count the tackling of a 12-year-old shifter).

She acknowledged that none of it, other than the info about the truck, was relevant to how she knew when he was near. Her body acted like an early-warning-detection system – sort of like the DEW line, but it wasn't homed in to detect incoming Soviet bombers during the cold war. Nope. Her connection to Ulrich was much more sophisticated and instinctual. When he was near, the hair on the back of her neck stood up, goosebumps erupted over her arms, her nipples puckered, and contradictorily, her blood burned, sending heat downwards and firing up her lady bits.

When she left the school earlier, she'd known Tag was with him because that's why Ulrich was in the school parking lot in the first place. She wondered how Ulrich explained his tailing of the schoolteacher. Coincidence? Lesson in stalking? Pair-bond? She frowned as Tag's departing words replayed in her head.

Leave my dad alone.

The boy was clearly hurting and as Ulrich followed her when she made a left towards Becker's, she thought perhaps she should share the conversation between her and Tag. She didn't have to do it in a way that threw Tag under the bus. She could simply tell him that the kid fully expected that his parents would reconcile at some point in the future.

She rolled to stop at a red light ignoring the growling and clanking of her car's engine. It always had an opinion on what she was thinking. As it chugged away, she wondered if talking to Ulrich about Tag's fantasy would make her seem like she was seeking reassurance about his involvement with his ex-wife. She kind of was, but that was a secondary concern.

The light turned green and she pressed the gas. She'd just passed the RCMP station when the car started bucking. Steam, or smoke maybe, came pouring out of from under the hood and she had no choice but to pull to the side of the road.

She cursed as she slammed her hands on the steering wheel. "I need five more months out of you! Is that too much to ask? Five months and you can retire!" Neither the bank nor dealership would consider a loan until she had worked a full six months at the same job. She just needed to get to the end of February. Five more freaking months.

Cursing under her breath, she fumbled through her purse for a cell phone. The tow job would eat into the down-payment she was in process of saving for. No down-payment, no car because her current piece of junk wasn't worth more than a thousand bucks tops, or so said the salesman at the dealership.

A flash of movement in her rear-view mirror caught her attention and she looked up to see Ulrich's truck rolling to a stop behind her. Yes! She almost scrambled out to hug Ulrich in greeting, but Tag was with him and they were in a heated discussion as they both stepped out of the truck. A few more words were exchanged, then Tag turned and stalked off.

Ulrich banged his door shut and headed towards her. She was mesmerized by his long masculine strides, but she held herself back from doing anything but uttering a breathless, "Hi."

"What happened?"

She'd seen him yesterday – kissed him –and yet, it felt like the first time again.

C'mon, Aubrey, grow the heck up. This calls for adulting. "Is Tag okay?"

Ulrich stopped a foot from her and looked back at Tag's retreating figure. "Yeah – it's a case of boy meets adolescent drama."

She sensed there was more to it than that and maybe later, once she resolved the case of the smoking car, they could have a serious conversation. "The car," she explained and motioned towards it helplessly, "started bucking and then it started smoking. I pulled over to make sure it wasn't on fire and it quit."

Nature was cruising towards the end of September, and as the sun started to drop behind the mountains, she felt a chill in the air and shivered. Yeah, get the car fixed, get someplace warm – with Ulrich, of course – and have a good conversation. Probably should be public so she didn't accidentally kiss him again.

Ulrich skirted around her to the front of the car and unlatched the hood with his deft fingers. Aubrey tried not to swoon as he lifted it up and stared at all the parts. "I think it's the engine, not the radiator." He straightened up. "Think we better call for a tow."

No, not a tow. "Can't you fix it – get it running again so I can drive it home?"

He looked at her strangely. "Where did you get the idea that I was a mechanic?"

Oops. Reverse discrimination, but desperate times called for desperate anti-feminist measures. "You're a guy so I... uh... I figured you'd be able to know what's wrong."

"I'm a businessman. I don't know the first thing about your car's engine."

"Oh." Aubrey felt deflated and tried to come up with a solution that wouldn't involve a tow truck. "What if it's just the radiator? Even if it's leaking, if we fill it with water, I should be able to get the car home without having it towed." She took a few steps closer and reached to unscrew the radiator cap.

He caught her arm in his firm grip. "Don't touch that! It'll burn you!"

Pair-bonded or not, he didn't need to treat her like an idiot. "You said it wasn't the radiator!"

"I said I didn't think it was the radiator. But either way, it's still hot and you'll get burned."

"I know that!" she snapped, pinning him with her glare.

She didn't.

Then she became aware of the power in the hand that circled her forearm and lost the words she was going to say next. His touch seared through her like a... well... like an overheated radiator cap, making her legs wobbly and priming her for some lip-on-lip action. He shouldn't touch her. He should absolutely not touch her, but she couldn't bring herself to pull away.

His tone softened as he looked down at her looking up at him. "There's no point in towing it to your home. It needs fixing before you can drive it again."

"There's also no point in fixing it," she said, her eyes tracing the outline of his lips.

The hand that wasn't gripping her arm reached up and stroked the loose hair off her face. "It's not safe to drive. Sell it to the boneyard."

"The boneyard?" She studied the gentle blue of his eyes.

"Gin's Auto Parts, where all cars go when they die." He softly traced her jawline with the back of his knuckles.

"Still has to be towed there," she murmured as she grabbed his fingers and brought them to her mouth.

He caressed her lips as he loosened his grip on her arm and slid it upwards to her shoulders, pulling her so close to him, her breasts brushed his chest. "Why the resistance to having it towed?"

Aubrey stood up on her toes and took aim at his lips. He lowered his head to accept her.

"Hey! Can I help?"

They jumped apart like they'd been scalded with radiator steam.

Behind Ulrich's truck was a beat-up red tow truck with

Falls Towing emblazoned across the top of the windshield. The surprise and then anger on Ulrich's face suggested that the man approaching them was the last person he wanted to see.

The tow truck driver temporarily faltered as recognition lit his eyes. "Goddamn!" he said like he had marbles in his mouth, seeming to feel the same way about Ulrich.

"What the fuck are you doing here?" Ulrich snapped.

"My fucking job!" He switched his attention to Aubrey. "This asshole bothering you?"

Aubrey started to shake her head, but Ulrich stepped in front of her, blocking her from the tow truck driver's line of sight. "Get the fuck out of here, Donnybrook."

Aubrey popped out from behind Ulrich. "*The* Mr. Donnybrook? Reed's father?"

Donnybrook turned his ire on her. "Who the fuck are you?"

She withered under his glare, but only slightly. She'd encountered worse people in her past. "Reed's homeroom teacher."

Ulrich talked over her. "None of your fucking business."

Donnybrook's gaze was assessing. "Shifter-fucker," he swore at Aubrey, who gasped at his crudeness.

Ulrich shoved up against Donnybrook, his chest forcing the asshole to step back. "One more fucking word to her and it'll be your last."

Donnybrook tugged at his nose as he sneered. "I get it now. Sleeping with enemy, are you, teach? No one tell you that these fucking wolves are diseased."

Amber ringed Ulrich's eyes and Aubrey was afraid he was about to shift and rip the bigoted bastard to shreds. For a brief few seconds, she was fully on board with it, but like most of her bad ideas, it passed quickly.

She grabbed Ulrich's arm and shook it. "Don't," she said gently.

It seemed to bring him back as blue washed his irises. He glared at her, then turned his attention back to Donnybrook, picking him up by the fabric of his jacket and throwing him several feet towards the tow truck. "Get in your fucking truck and get out of here. I see you anywhere near Aubrey and I'll fuck you up so bad you'll have to eat your steak through a straw."

Donnybrook scrambled to his feet, his fists clenched, his face red with fury. "This isn't over, you sonofabitch." He stalked back to his truck, slammed the door, and kicked up dust and gravel as he spun his tires leaving.

Aubrey stepped backwards and coughed.

"You okay?"

Yes, she was okay even if her heart was throwing a hissy-fit. "What was that?"

"Met the asshole after Tag's fight. Has the fucking personality of a sewer pipe." Ulrich pulled his phone out and brought up a browser, then searched for Gin's Towing and Auto Repair. He called the dispatch and asked them to send a tow truck.

Aubrey crossed her arms, giving Ulrich her pissed-off teacher stare. No way was he going to get out of explaining himself, especially because, as Reed Donnybrook's teacher, she would have to deal with the aftermath.

He sighed. "Thought Gaskill would have told you about the bigoted bastard. We didn't see eye-to-eye over anything. No wonder Reed's a bully. Apple doesn't fall far from the tree, does it?"

"Reed's no more a bully than Tag is," she huffed. "They were both culpable."

"The little shit stole Tag's lunch!"

He was grappling with his temper and she appreciated

that he was trying to stay civil. Of course, her next words didn't calm him down. "Time to let it go, Ulrich. Tag needs a father, not a saviour."

He bared his teeth. "Don't tell me how to parent my son."

Cliché, but maybe he was right. She was Tag's teacher and shouldn't be getting overinvolved in family business. "Okay, I won't."

He scrubbed a hand over the top of his head. "Anything else you need to know about me and Donnybrook?"

"Is he dangerous?"

She felt exposed as Ulrich studied her face. "I think he's all bluster, but I'll do a background check."

A background check? That was a little weird given he was a businessman. For a moment, he sounded like a cop.

Fortunately, she was rescued from having to poke the bear further when another tow truck pulled up and a lanky man wearing blue coveralls popped out with a clipboard in hand.

He strode towards them, sticking his hand out towards Ulrich. "You called for a tow?" He nodded towards her car.

"Are you Gin?" Ulrich shook the man's hand.

"Yep." He glanced at Aubrey but didn't offer a handshake. "Shouldn't be letting your wife drive this beater. Doesn't look roadworthy."

"It's what I was telling her."

Aubrey was well aware that she was setting the women's rights movement back several decades, but she got fixated on the fact that Ulrich hadn't disabused Gin of the notion that she was his wife. She missed most of the back and forth, until Ulrich said to her, "Give Gin your keys."

She dumbly looked at the keys in her hand then curled her fist around them and pulled them to her chest. "Did you just sell my car?"

"No. Gin's going to tow it to his garage and take a look at

it." He sounded so patient... maybe too patient. Why the hell couldn't she snap out of this fog?

She found herself dutifully handing over the keys to Gin. "How much?" she asked as she reached into her car and pulled out her purse.

"Nothing right now. If I fix her, I won't charge for the tow, just the repair. If she can't be fixed, I'll take it off the $500 I figure she's worth for parts."

"$500! The car dealership said she... it was worth a thousand." The fog was lifting and with its disappearance came the awareness that she hated the way men feminized vehicles.

"That's 'cause those shysters get their money back on the cost of the new car." She was all but dismissed as he motioned with his chin towards Ulrich's truck. "You two head on home. I'll take it from here." He looked at Ulrich again. "Got a card or a phone number I can call you at?"

Ulrich opened his mouth to speak, but Aubrey stepped in front of him. "Excuse me. It's my car."

She fished in her purse for a pen and notebook, scrawled her name and phone number across the top piece of paper, ripped it off the pad with a flourish, and passed it to Gin.

"Thank you, ma'am." He tipped his cap as he caught Ulrich's eye with a raise of his eyebrows.

As Gin headed back to the tow truck, Ulrich turned to her. "C'mon. I'll give you a ride home."

"Thanks," Aubrey murmured, knowing how bad an idea it was to get in Ulrich's truck, especially since she almost kissed him again and he almost let her. However, it was still better than asking Gin for a ride.

She fished her backpack out of the car, then closed the door as she straightened up.

"Let me help you with that." Ulrich took the backpack from her.

"I can carry it," she said churlishly. She was getting tired of being inside Ira Levin's universe.

"I know," he said mildly, shutting down further discussion as he led her around the truck to the passenger side and held her door, waiting while she got into the vehicle.

The truck was high, like a lot of trucks around Darkness Falls, and as she inelegantly hoisted herself up on the seat, she wondered how she'd managed to get inside last June when she'd been falling down drunk.

After sorting herself out, she reached for her seatbelt, but Ulrich was faster. He gripped the seatbelt and pulled it across her, buckling it in place with a click. Then he leaned over her, his body heat making her gasp, and placed her backpack on the floor behind her seat.

Holy good grief and dog balls. She didn't know which was hotter. His body that close to her or the way he brushed her as he buckled her in. He buckled her in!

He threw a wave at Gin as he pulled back into traffic, then headed towards the east side, where her apartment was located. "Why do you live in such a shitty neighbourhood?" he growled as he focused on his driving.

"Uh...." She hadn't realized it was a *shitty* neighbourhood. "I kind of inherited the apartment from Eva Blakely and the rent's cheap."

"This is Darkness Falls, the rent's cheap everywhere." He seemed determined to be cranky.

Aubrey knew herself well enough to know she also wasn't above being cranky. "This is Darkness Falls. The rental options are somewhat limited." She crossed her arms and stared at the landscape as they passed by it. The deciduous trees stood proud, their colours in process of turning from green to varying shades of reds and yellows. She felt a pang as she thought of being alone over another long Northern BC winter.

As if Ulrich sensed her change in mood, and being a shifter, he very likely did, he said, "I worry about you."

Aubrey's heart took a leap. "There's no need to. I manage okay on my own."

Ulrich grunted as he turned right at a four-way stop without actually stopping. "I'd have thought you'd be more cautious, given what happened to your sister."

Wow, straight for the jugular. "I'm cautious enough," she said, adding an element of coolness to her voice to let him know he'd crossed a line.

He didn't seem to notice. "No, you're not. You work late at the school, are usually the last to leave, and then wander into the empty parking lot without a care in the world. What the hell is that about?"

A sardonic laugh escaped Aubrey's lips. "Because you're there, Ulrich. You've been following me, not all the time, but you're not subtle."

Ulrich glared at her. "I am so subtle. I know how to tail fucking people without being noticed."

Aubrey took a breath of courage. "I'm not just people, though, am I?"

"What the hell does that mean?"

She reached behind her and grabbed her pack. They were almost to her apartment, thank god. She needed some separation from the powerful, sexy, domineering man. Or else... well, she might lose control again. "Don't pretend you don't know. The minute you're near, I can sense your presence. I walk out of the school, and I know if you're there or not."

"But I'm not always there."

"I know."

"And yet you still work late and allow yourself to be vulnerable."

She felt like he was accusing her of committing a federal crime.

He turned into the car lot and parked in her parking space. Why not? Her rust bucket had one foot in the coffin. It wasn't likely coming back.

She reached to open the door, but he caught her wrist. "You didn't answer my question."

His touch seared through Aubrey and she tried to pull her hand away, but he tightened his grip.

"You need to stop touching me or I'll embarrass myself yet again."

He released her. "Answer my question."

"I forgot the question," she mumbled.

He narrowed his eyes. "Why do you stay so late at school?"

Tears blurred Aubrey's vision and she turned her head to stare out the window. "I prefer working at school, rather than coming home to an empty apartment." She blinked rapidly, then turned to him. "It's really that simple and I don't want to talk about it."

This time he let her open the door when she reached for it, but as she stepped out, so did he, quickly closing the distance between them.

"What are you doing?" *Don't you dare say you're coming with me.*

"It's getting dark and this place is a shit hole. I'm walking you to your door."

Hot and cold collided, Aubrey wanting him, but also irritated at his own game of ice and fire. "Why?" She held her ground, facing him, tilting her face up so she could glare at him. "You've already made it clear that you're not interested in a relationship other than you, as Tag's parent and me, as his teacher." She stepped back to gain some space from his heat. "Thanks for the help, Mr. Calhoun, and the ride, but you're not walking me to my door."

"I am walking you to your door, Aubrey." He stared down

at her, his gorgeous eyes flashing irritation. "Try and stop me." He reached for her arm and tightly gripped it in his huge paw.

"Let go!" Resistance appeared to be futile as she dug her heels into the pavement but was easily overpowered by his strength.

"No."

She folded like a pair of red threes. "Fine, walk me to my door. And then leave." This time, he let her pull herself from his grip.

She stalked ahead of him trying to maintain her anger, but was distracted by her awareness of him so close that she could feel the warmth of his body as it heated her back. His scent overpowered her. The raw masculinity of it made her wish for things she'd only ever read about. Her emotions were raw, and she knew she was a hair's-breadth away from making a fool of herself, again.

CHAPTER ELEVEN

U lrich wondered what the fuck he was doing as he followed Aubrey up three floors to her apartment door.

Playing with fire, and about time, his wolf panted.

The furball was right. Ulrich knew exactly what he was doing. On the side of the road, when they argued, when they almost kissed, it broke him. This fucking female was too much and most of it had nothing to do with the pair-bond. Aubrey was a woman in all the best ways. Beautiful, pure, sweet. Someone he could trust.

If there hadn't been a pair-bond, would he have noticed her?

In a heart-beat. She had no idea how perfect she was, and he wondered what negative tracks played in her head.

He knew enough about her background – okay, every fucking thing, because he couldn't stop himself. It helped him understand how solitary she seemed. It was a way of protecting herself, and though she had friends (crazy shifter females and the mouthy cop), she seemed to wear an invisible cloak to keep from being noticed.

It worked on others, but not him. Pair-bond or not, he was mesmerized by her big eyes, the colour changing from whiskey brown to smooth brandy whenever she looked his way; soft brown hair that made his fingers itch to run through the loose curls, to grip them, smell them, mess them up. Her quiet beauty, her small and compact body, the feminine sway to her hips as she walked—it all drew attention. His attention.

The idea of her singed his blood with heat, made his dick twitch, wanting relief. No, not just relief. He wanted to fucking be inside her and no one else – not ever again. By the time she unlocked her door and opened it, he knew he wasn't leaving.

She was on the verge of turning, the thank you dying on her lips as he grabbed her arms, propelling her into her suite, kicking the door shut behind him.

"Ulrich?" she breathed.

The smallness of her voice gave rise to a roar from the beast within. He crushed his lips against hers, taking the kiss she'd offered earlier and savaging it, possessing her, drinking her in as his tongue invaded her mouth. It was a storm of passion, a hurricane of lust.

Through the ache in his balls, his painful erection, the thrumming of his heart, he scented her response – female, needy, wanting, uniquely Aubrey. Perfect. Her heart was hammering too – with passion. As his hand slipped under her shirt and traced the silkiness of belly, as his body trembled with need, as his lips demanded her complete and utter surrender, he knew she would be his and he would be hers.

He pulled out of the kiss, cupping her face between his big hands with urgency. "Say yes, Aubrey. I need to hear it."

He saw a flicker of rejection in her eyes, felt it in her slight hesitation.

Say, yes, baby, because my control is about to snap, and it won't matter what you say.

Then, she whispered, "Yes."

He was faintly aware of her delicate hands clutching at the material of his jacket, the press of her body against his.

He held her tighter, knowing his grip was bruising, but couldn't seem to relax it. *Fuck her, you asshole. Don't break her.*

Filling his lungs with air scented with her natural perfume, he pulled back slightly, then picked her up, grabbing her ass to support her against his frame, shuddering with lust as she wrapped her legs around his waist and ground against his erection.

"Here," she huffed as he barrelled towards an open door. Her bedroom, neat, simple, perfect.

"I need you naked," he rasped as he dropped her on the bed and then fell on top of her, muscles straining to keep his weight from crushing her. What he needed was to bury himself inside her, what he needed was to take her, own her. Make her his.

His wolf roared as the blood pounded in his ears.

She was tugging at his clothes, her hands fumbling with the buttons, the zipper. It took all his will to let her go, but his clothes were a barrier to fusing with her. He stood and kicked off his boots, watching her watching him.

She was on her elbows, her chest heaving as he struggled out of his jacket, then yanked his T-shirt over his head.

"God," she breathed as her gaze stroked over his chest. Fear, desire, awe. He knew what she saw. He was a male shifter, bigger than average, his physique more muscled than most.

"Clothes off, baby, or I'll lose control and rip them off."

That seem to jar her out of her dream-state as she scrambled off the bed, taking off each stitch of clothing like it was an Olympic speed sport. Nothing sultry or teasing in the way she undressed, just a desperation so deep, like his. To be as close as they could get. To get lost in their mutual passion.

He pulled off the rest of his clothes as she struggled to pull her blouse over her head. It was the last of her clothing, except for her bra, which she unhooked with practiced hands, then turned to him, trembling.

When she saw all of him, her eyes widened, and the trembling turned to full-on shaking. The intake of her breath called to his beast and he pounced on her.

"Ulrich," she gasped as he pulled her onto the bed, flattening her onto her back and laying partially on her as he cradled her to his body.

"I won't hurt you," he lied. He knew he would. He was out of control, and it was taking every ounce of his will not to impale her with his dick and fill her with his seed. His hands stroked over her, cupping her small breasts, reveling in the hardness of the nipples, the silkiness of flesh under his fingertips, the wetness between her legs.

She cried out as he slipped through her heat, his fingers stroking over her clit, feeling it swell as he attacked it. "Ulrich." Her breath hissed out as she reached for his dick, but he denied her.

"I want inside you, now."

He was too far gone to wait for her to nod her head or give her permission. He spread her wider with his hands and his legs, settling between her thighs, his cock teasing her entrance.

She pushed at his chest. "We need a condom," she gasped as her pelvis surged towards him.

"We don't," Ulrich said, as he slid a finger inside her. She was slick, ready, but so fucking small. He wasn't sure he could hold himself back.

"I'm not on birth control." She bucked and let out a small cry as he worked another finger inside her.

"Trust me, okay? You won't get pregnant."

He saw her eyes cloud as a small frown slipped over her lips. Disappointment or something else, but he didn't care.

"Trust me," he urgently repeated.

"Okay," she relented, pulling him closer, running her lips over his jawline.

He kept thrusting with his fingers, then rubbed her clit with his thumb. He wanted to taste her, wanted to plant his face in her pussy and eat her until she was screaming his name. Next round, he promised, bringing the fingers wet with her desire to his mouth. Next round, he'd take care.

She tasted so sweet, so perfect he felt selfish. "Taste yourself." She opened her mouth as he slid his fingers past her lips, his other hand cupping her jaw to force her to suck them. She didn't need much persuasion.

"I need to fuck you, sweetheart. Right fucking now." He nudged his dick against her opening and she spread herself wider. So small under him, so fucking perfect.

He tangled his hand in her hair, holding her head still so he could see her pleasure as he filled her.

She moaned and closed her eyes, tilting her head back as she opened to let him in.

"Open your eyes, Aubrey." *Do as I say.*

Her eyelids slid up. "You're so...." Then she moaned as he pushed deeper, her long lashes fluttering against her cheekbones as her eyelids slid down.

"Eyes!" he commanded, and she raised her lids part-way.

"I'm going to come," she breathed. "I... god... oh god." Her sheathe tightened on him as she hit her peak, her entire body quaking as she pulsed. Her eyes rolled back in her head.

Ulrich held himself still. The mere push of his cock as he'd entered made her come and he wasn't in as deep as he could go, hadn't even started thrusting. He came perilously close to coming himself and it took a will of steel to not join her over the edge.

In her passion, she'd gripped his forearm, her fingernails digging in, the pain making him surge into her as deep as he could go. He stilled, closed his eyes, and savoured her. Better than he imagined, better than anything in the world. He slowly withdrew, then pushed in again, listening to her breaths, the drumming of her heart, the rapid pulse of her blood. Seeking a sign that he was hurting her.

"More," she uttered softly.

His control snapped. He thrust harder, his hand cradling her cheek, his eyes glued to hers, his body as close to hers as he could get without crushing her. She was gasping, her hands clutching his arms as he fucked her.

A small cry of protest escaped her lips as he pulled out but it didn't sway him from turning her to her side, so he could enter her from behind. It's what he needed to do, where he needed to be as he felt himself on the edge of losing control.

He slammed into her, his breath coming in gasps, hearing her moans, her mewls of pleasure.

He stroked her nipple, then pinched it, forcing a soft breathy cry from her lips that sent shockwaves through his body, making him lose his mind.

"Ulrich," she moaned and then shrieked as he angled his hips so he was pressing against the sweet spot inside her. His arm propped up her neck as he tangled his fingers into her hair, pulling her as close to him as he could. He drew the wetness of her desire to her clit and rubbed it until she was bucking her hips, seeking more, her cries getting louder.

"Wait for me, sweetheart," he whispered, his warm breath brushing her ear.

He slammed into her again and again. He was almost there, and he had a vision of pulling out, pushing her to her back and straddling her, fisting his dick until he exploded, his come spurting on her tits, her face, into her mouth.

"Fuck!" he roared as he lost control, clutching her bruisingly as she tightened around him, her breaths coming in harsh grasps, not able to do any thing but receive what he gave her because he held her so tight.

His come shot from him like a cannon, his body jerked, and his wolf roared. Then the tightness of her vagina as she came again, her body jerking under his, her cries lost in the fury of his groans.

His wolf banged at him from within. Take her! Mark her! She's yours!

In that moment, it was the only thing that made sense. The voice inside him, the one of reason, was too dim, too far away. His instincts overpowered him. This female was his, only his.

He felt the shift happening, the primacy of who he was surge from him. He held her to him, tighter than he should, wanting to be with her, in body, in spirit, in soul. It was the only thing. The only way.

Then his phone rang, Tag's shrill ring tone jerking him from his haze. The need to mark her was still there, still trying to dominate him, but he managed to pull himself back from the brink.

The reality of what he just did and what he had almost done, engulfed him.

CHAPTER TWELVE

Aubrey felt the exact moment that she lost him.

Ulrich's ringing phone invaded their intimacy and shattered the moment. The desperate way he held her was replaced by a rigidness. His cock, still stiff, slid from her as he pulled away. He flipped onto his back next to her, his eyes squeezed shut, his chest heaving.

The feeble light that spilled into her bedroom from the hall wasn't enough for her to see the expression on his face, but she didn't have to. She knew, could almost hear his thoughts. This shouldn't have happened. This wasn't right. Tag would be waiting for him.

The last thought made her feel guilty too, but she had no regrets and didn't believe anything they did had been wrong. Her body was still humming from the two, no three, orgasms he gave her. The press of his cock inside her, so big, so steely, against her g-spot, made her orgasm twice. A clitoral one, followed by the g-spot one barely a half minute later. She had still been quaking from the first when the second roared through her, both as amazing as the first one she'd had when he started to penetrate her.

It was hand's down the best sex she'd ever had. His bruising hold of her, the need and desire in his eyes as they stared into her soul. His lust so strong it bordered on desperation. His voice, his fingers, his scent. The commands, the pull of her hair, the heat of his breath brushing across her cheek, her neck.

Not yet sated, her body wanted more of him. No matter how often they made love, it would never be enough. She rolled so she could press her arms on his chest and look at him.

His eyes quickly shuttered.

Neither said a word for some time, her waiting for him to pull her back into his embrace. And him, holding her gaze as his breathing normalized.

She wanted to ask him to talk to her but knew he wouldn't. Whatever had happened between them was gone. As if to emphasize that truth, he gripped her wrists and gently moved her off him, then sat up on the edge of the mattress, and with his elbows on his thighs, scrubbed at his face with his huge hands.

She sat up on her knees, pulling the sheet around her to cover her nakedness, to hide the vulnerability seeping into her bones. "Ulrich?" The hollowness inside infused her voice. She wanted to touch him, and as if sensing her need, he stood abruptly.

He dressed quickly, concentrating on his clothes. He couldn't meet her eyes and she felt his discomfort, guilt, a thudding of rage.

"I have to go. Tag's waiting at home."

Her heart skipped a beat at how abrupt he sounded, but she was willing to forgive him because she couldn't bear the thought of being without him. "I understand. Next time we'll plan better." Her heart pounded in her chest so loudly she almost couldn't hear over it.

Almost.

"This can't happen again." Such blunt words, like they hadn't just been intimate.

She tried to school her face, tried not to show him how much his words hurt, but her mask cracked. How could it not? The way he'd touched her, held her, made love to her. It was with a desperation she hadn't thought possible.

"Why?" She could barely breathe out the word.

CHAPTER THIRTEEN

"*This can't happen again.*"

Ulrich watched as Aubrey's expression crumpled. She was expecting a different answer.

"Why?" The word trembled on her lips.

He shook his head. He couldn't tell her how close he came to marking her, but he knew that if they were intimate again, he'd lose control again. She was small and human, and he'd been almost too far gone to stop. He could've destroyed her in his passion.

"Tag," he muttered, knowing he was only partially lying. What if he'd marked her? She'd be his, and while he couldn't deny how badly he wanted her, marking her wasn't something he'd do to her without her fully aware of what was happening.

She sucked in her breath like she'd been punched and perhaps that's exactly what he'd done. "I'm not asking you to choose," Aubrey whispered. "Why can't it be both?"

Ulrich dropped his chin to his chest. It was a legitimate question, and no answer he gave her would make sense. Tag needed one sane parent right now, and what had almost happened in the passion of the moment was far from sane.

Aubrey made him feel out of control and none of them, he, Aubrey, or Tag, were ready for the consequences of his beast marking his territory.

So instead, he resorted to what he was best at – being a bastard. "Tag's gone through enough without having his dad fucking his teacher."

Her face reddened at his crudeness and he saw the glint of tears in her eyes. It brought out his protective beast, yet somehow, he managed to stay still, frozen in place.

"That's what this was to you? A fuck?" She lost her battle with her composure as wetness spilled down her cheeks.

Fuck, he was a prick. Such a fucking prick. "It was a mistake." Yep. He just won the jackass-of-the-year award - again.

"A mistake," she echoed hollowly. "Wow, first I'm a fuck and now I'm a mistake?" Her lower lip trembled as she closed her eyes. "You should leave," she whispered, clutching at her stomach as if she were in pain.

She was right. He should leave before he hurt her more than he already had. He took a step back. "This isn't about you, Aubrey. It's about Tag."

Lies that didn't work anyway.

She choked on a sob. "Oh my god. You think I'm some homewrecker who would come between you and your son." She slapped her hand against her forehead, and he saw her struggle between anger and desperation. Desperation won out. "I understand how much Tag needs you right now, but why can't we have both?"

Why? Why? Because he was a fucking savage who had no control. He stared at her small body, tiny and deflated. How could she survive his beast? What if he had marked her? Doing something like that without first discussing it was akin to rape. She was human; she wouldn't understand.

"Not now—"

"When? Tomorrow? Next week? Next year?" A sob broke loose. "I can't do that. I need you now, Ulrich. My heart...." She clutched at her chest. "I don't understand any of this, but I know I love you."

He struggled with the urge to take this woman in his arms and tell her everything would be alright, but if he did that, if he touched her, he would lose himself again. That's the one thing he couldn't do. Not to her and not to Tag. So instead of making any promises, he said, "You don't love me, Aubrey. And I don't love you."

Too much of a coward to watch her fall apart, he turned his back on her and left.

At home, he went immediately to the shower, washing all traces of her off his body. Then he threw his clothes into the washer and turned it on.

He felt like a cheating prick, the guilt over what he'd done, the fact that he chose to hide it from Tag.

The thought of his son steeled him. Aubrey was hurt and she had a right to be. Or did she? She was an adult woman, and not just any woman, she was also Tag's teacher. Why did she think this would end any other way? She knew his position with Tag. Had always known.

Fuck you and the jackass you rode in on, his wolf growled. The passion with her had been through the roof. The best sex of his life hands-down, even better than with Sibyl. His ex was wild and uninhibited - the kind of woman he thought he wanted.

Aubrey had proved him wrong.

His wolf was right. The moments he'd shared with Aubrey had nothing to do with sex and everything to do with passion, desire... love. He couldn't get close enough to her, couldn't be sated if they fucked a thousand times. Looking forward, he knew it was Aubrey or no one. He felt pain deep inside him as he made his decision. For now, he'd have to content himself with nothing. Maybe forever, if she wouldn't forgive him for being such a prick.

He stumbled down the stairs in a stupor but was still cognizant enough to note Tag scent the air from his position on the floor.

"Did you bring food home?" the kid said in way of greeting. "I'm starving." Apparently, Ulrich had passed the sniff test.

"Ms. Powell is fine, thanks for asking."

Tag rolled his eyes as he concentrated on his video game. "Glad to hear," he muttered.

Ulrich huffed out a breath of frustration as he pulled up the contact list on his phone. "Chinese?"

"Sure. Lots of it though. I'm—"

"Starving. Yeah, I know."

He hit dial and placed the order.

CHAPTER FOURTEEN

On Saturday, Ulrich almost broke down and called Aubrey. He needed to hear her voice, make sure that she was okay, beg her to understand his point of view. He needed her to forgive him, to tell him that she understood, that she'd give him time to sort through everything.

He'd had the phone open to her number, his thumb hovering over the dial button, when it rang. His first thought was that Aubrey was calling and he scrambled to answer it, not really registering that it was an unknown number on the display.

It was Sibyl.

"What do you want?" The ice in his tone warred with the hot rage coursing through his body. "And where'd you get my number?"

That she was crying came through loud and clear, the high tone, the shaky words. "I miss him, Ulrich. So much."

"How is that my problem?" He sounded tough, but inside, he felt pity for this woman. At one time he'd loved her and though she'd destroyed that, she was still the mother of his child.

"I know. I know it's not. It's just...," she sniffed. "I've been clean for almost three years. And—"

He didn't let her finish. "Which means you weren't under the influence when you decided to disappear with him."

"You have a right to hate me."

He detested when she said shit like that because he didn't hate her. She was toxic whether she was clean or not but hating her gave her far too much power. She was waiting for him to deny her words because that's what he always did, but she'd gone too far when she'd taken Tag and kept the boy from Ulrich for over a year. She didn't deserve an ounce of his forgiveness and he wasn't about to pander to her emotional games.

"You want to talk to Tag, is that it?" he said, his mind churning, the pros and cons of letting that happen.

"No," she replied softly, a practiced lilt to her voice that invited male attention. "I called to talk to you. To ask your permission to see my son."

A seduction technique that worked too often on Ulrich. Not this time – not ever again. "You've already been in contact with him." How else would she have Ulrich's phone number?

"He called me." She hesitated, then, "I wanted to give you space and time so I could prove to you I'm better."

"You took my son!" He shouted in the phone as fury pounded through him. "You fucking kept him from me for over a year! How the hell does that prove to me you're better?"

She was sobbing and he hardened his heart. She was why he couldn't be with Aubrey. She was the reason he had to stay away from the woman he should have had children with. The woman he should have worshipped.

When she got her crying under control, Sibyl said, "Can I come to Darkness Falls so we can talk? Just you and me, so I can explain. You don't have to like me or forgive me, but I need you to understand."

Ulrich squeezed his eyes shut as his temples pounded. If she came to Darkness Falls, he would have to let Tag see her. He wasn't going to lie to his kid about his mother being in town, and Tag would hound him about Sibyl until he gave up. Fucking kid though, calling his mother and letting her know where they were.

"Okay," he relented, frustrated, and trying to place himself in Tag's shoes. "But if you come, you come alone. I see any sign of your pack and I'll destroy them and you."

"Of course. I left the pack after what they did to you and Tag."

Sure she did. Same old Sibyl. Nothing was ever her fault. "I don't care what you've done, Sibyl. I'm telling you now. Only you. Anyone else and I'll fucking bury them."

"Thank you," she whispered.

After the call with Sibyl, he tracked down Tag and read him the riot act. "What the hell gives you the right to tell your mother where we're at?"

Tag was near tears. "I miss her, Dad. So I called her. No big deal."

"It is a big deal!" he raged. "This town," he pointed out a window, "is mine. No drama, no warring packs, nothing but good shifters who work hard to stay neutral."

"Geez, Dad. It's just a town."

Tag didn't get it, but what had Ulrich expected? Tag was young, his needs simple. Fill his belly, stroke his ego, be proud of him, give him a roof and two parents who loved him. But for Ulrich, Darkness Falls was a sanctuary, a place offering him a peace he'd never experienced in his life.

Even before he got Tag back, he'd been thinking about

staying in Darkness Falls. After the case was solved, maybe he'd dust off his law degree and hang up a shingle. It's why he'd rented a house on the outskirts of town where the backyard bled into the woods. He could run, hunt, settle. The current owner was willing to consider selling it if Ulrich made the right offer.

The fact that his fated mate was here underscored the draw he had to Darkness Falls. This was where he was meant to be. This was home. But how to explain that to Taggart, who was caught in the middle of a war between his parents, one he was too young and immature to understand.

Taggart withered under Ulrich's scrutiny, finally losing his battle with his composure. "I love my mom!" he cried, fat tears rolling down his cheeks. "I miss her." His lower lip trembled as he swiped at his face. "I'm sorry I called her! Okay! Are you happy now?"

Ulrich dropped his chin to his chest. "I wanted one place in this world where I had peace from her."

"Sorry!" Tag shouted as he swiped his runny nose with the back of his hand. "Sorry I ruined it for you. Maybe I should go back to the pack so you can get on with your life."

"No!" Ulrich couldn't temper the growl in his voice. "You're my fucking son! I don't want to hear another word from you about leaving!" His heart was beating wildly in that moment as the past months haunted him.

"Then what do you want?" Tag shouted back.

What did he want? He wanted Tag, he wanted peace, and he wanted Aubrey. Why was that too much to ask?

CHAPTER FIFTEEN

After the blow-up with Tag, Ulrich spent the remainder of the day in wolf form, running, hunting, howling. His wolf was his salve. Lonely sometimes, yearning for a pack to lead, but also content to be an outsider. The loneliness had scaled upwards since he and Aubrey hooked up, because his wolf yearned for his mate as much as he did.

His house butted up against several acres of forest not claimed by any shifter pack. Ulrich had thought about claiming it for himself and Tag, but two shifters, one not old enough to shift, did not a pack make, at least not one that could defend the territory. And he doubted the alphas of the nearby packs would be welcoming.

He stayed away for hours, letting his spirit blend with the gifts of the forest. Darkness Falls was a beacon for shifters, and he understood the attraction. The magnificent waterfall was a lodestone and while northern Canada and Alaska were home to many shifter packs, most were small and ragtag, living off the grid because it complemented their lifestyles.

But Darkness Falls somehow managed to marry the

human and shifter world, and while hostilities between the two often flared, the town and surrounding areas were proof that there could be harmony. Never perfect, of course, but then perfection wasn't something that could be applied to human beings.

Except for Aubrey, his wolf reminded him.

Except for Aubrey, he agreed.

As he wandered through trees that foretold the turning of seasons, drank from clean, cool streams, and napped in the warm afternoon sun, he reflected on the future. His future. One day, Tag would leave and then what? He was a shifter without a pack, which automatically made him suspicious in the eyes of both humans and other shifters.

Back when he was young and idealistic, living in a city was a means to an end. After he graduated high school, his plan had been to get his law degree so he could champion shifters, support, protect, and defend his marginalized people. Then Sibyl happened, followed by Tag. While he managed to finish his educational goals, he was forced off the trajectory he'd planned. Instead of following his heart, he joined the federal RCMP force and quickly moved up the ranks.

He could have made commissioner, but he no longer had the political aspirations he once did. He blamed Sibyl, whether it was fair or unfair. She stole his energy, his hope, his dreams.

And his son.

He veered away from the thought, not wanting to ruin his rare moment of peace by revisiting the ugliness of his life. There seemed to be no relief though, because if he wasn't thinking about Sibyl and Tag, he was thinking about the reason he was in Darkness Falls, the serial killer preying on women.

And inevitably, his mind sought out Aubrey. It seemed a cruel joke that she be his fated mate. He would have been attracted to her anyway, but his past experiences would have ensured his emotions didn't get tangled up in whatever relationship they might have had.

But she wasn't simply an attractive single woman. The other night he'd almost marked her, and that shook him up to no end. She, this thing between them, was messing with his head and he couldn't sort out what was right thinking. That had never happened to him before, not even when Sibyl disappeared with Tag. The separation from his son was hell, but his head was clear, his focus deadly.

He knew what he had to do to get Tag back and he worked patiently with his team until there was an opportunity.

But if someone took Aubrey.... He shuddered at the thought. There'd be no calmness, no ordered thoughts, nothing but white-hot anger and pain. He'd destroy everyone and everything that got in his way to get her back.

He stopped mid-stride, surrounded by the sympathetic forest, his wolf grieving over something that hadn't yet happened. Despite what she wanted, what he yearned for, she was far safer without him. At least until the killer was caught.

When he returned home, he half-expected Tag to ignore him, but the kid hovered while Ulrich dressed himself and put on some coffee.

Tag seemed to want to talk, but Ulrich didn't know how to start the conversation. He'd let his vulnerability slip and that's not what parents did. Kids needed the reassurance that their parents could conquer everything. They couldn't show weaknesses, shouldn't cry, or get drunk, or shoot heroin into their veins.

"Dad," Tag said after several long moments of weighted silence. He was clearly the one with the backbone in the family. "You knew that Mom would come to see me eventually."

Ulrich wasn't ready to listen to logic. "She kidnapped you. Under the law, she should be in jail."

"Human law. No one gets involved in fights between two shifters," half-kid, half-Yoda said.

"You should be thankful that human law applies to me. In the shifter world, I'd be justified in killing her." Thoughtless words that Ulrich regretted the moment he uttered them.

"Dad." Tag's voice cracked.

"Sorry." And he was. "I wouldn't kill your mother. I wouldn't do that to you." He needed to end the discussion before he said more stupid things. It was too hard to maintain composure when the subject was Sibyl.

"I miss her, Dad. And she misses me. I know you won't let me go to her and I understand that. I don't want to risk being taken by the pack again, but please, let her come."

Ulrich rolled his shoulders as the coffee pot gurgled to completion. He needed something stronger than caffeine and was tempted to open the cabinet over top of the fridge and grab his bottle of scotch. But not in front of the kid. Never in front in the kid. "Okay," he puffed out. "She can come see you."

Tag whooped and wrapped his arms around Ulrich, giving him a hard squeeze before letting go. "I'm gonna call her and tell her." He headed for the hall, but then stopped and turned back. "If that's alright with you."

Kid understood how to kiss ass. "Let me know what the plan is."

Sunday came and went with a good serving of the eggshell peace that typically followed a major blow-out. By the end of the weekend, Ulrich and Tag were once again relaxed around each other. Ulrich knew it wouldn't last, because Sibyl wasn't an argument, she was a dark destructive storm cloud that left a trail of debris in her wake.

At least he had a distraction, albeit an ugly one. Chief

Jackson Hayes had his own version of a frustrating weekend when one of Ascena Lacoste's pack members went missing. Ascena Lacoste was the de facto alpha of an all-female pack. She'd come to Darkness Falls for reasons that paralleled his own for wanting to stay. She'd sought out a haven for herself, a place she could hide from the world and live an ordinary life. And she offered the same sanctuary to other shifter females who'd been brutalized by their own packs.

The other three packs in the area tolerated Ascena's claim to a small piece of land, and Gideon and Lucien, alphas of the Dominant and Lodge packs respectively, gave her the protection she needed to shelter her females. It was another thing that made Darkness Falls unique. A female alpha wasn't a thing, but the leaders of the other packs acknowledged her authority over her claimed territory.

She was fiercely protective of her small pack of females, and when a young female shifter disappeared sometime Saturday night or early Sunday morning, she immediately called Jackson.

Jackson, in turn, called Ulrich. "Another woman's gone missing. Hope she's wandered off or is shacking up with some guy." There was a frustrated undercurrent to the Chief's voice.

Ulrich hadn't joined the official search but shifted and ran the woods behind his home. This time he didn't linger as every moment was crucial, but he came up empty-handed.

"Want coffee?" Ulrich asked Jackson when he greeted him at the front door of his house early Monday morning.

"Keg of it, please," Jackson grumbled as he followed Ulrich into the kitchen. The cop looked like he hadn't much sleep, which was most likely true.

"Anything to report?" Ulrich handed a steaming mug to Jackson, then pushed the carton of cream across the counter.

"No word, no sign," Jackson replied in disgust. "Macy

Kerrigan seems to have disappeared off the edge of the earth."

Not good news, and the fact that it was one of Ascena's made it even worse. The female was well known for her passionate and aggressive defence of her females. "How's Ascena?"

Jackson took a gulp of coffee. "Pissed. Emotional. Lying about something. Can't figure out what because she's out of her mind with worry."

"Then not her usual calm approach?" Even if it was a dark topic, sarcasm had its moment. It was wasted anyway because Jackson was too distracted.

"Never seen her so distraught." The cop headed down the hall to Ulrich's office, opening the folder he'd arrived with. He pulled out the picture of a young, attractive dark-haired female and waved it in the air.

Ulrich raised his eyebrows at the plump round face staring back at him. "How old is she? Surely not of age."

"Ascena says 18, but that's one of the things I think she's lying about. Eva thinks so too – she met the girl once. It's hard to tell though." He tacked the photo next to the line-up of other women, all dead or would-be victims of the same killer. "I'm getting old. Everyone under the age of 20 looks too young."

"And the search?"

"The minute Ascena raised the alarm, I got my staff and the other packs out searching." Jackson rubbed his temple. "It's fucked up, isn't it? The prick who grabbed her is prob- ably one of the search party."

Ulrich smiled grimly. The cop wasn't wrong. "She have a boyfriend?"

"Ascena says no. According to her, Macy rarely left the house. Too shy, too traumatized."

Ulrich closed his eyes for a minute, trying to fit the pieces together. Something was off. "Doesn't fit the MO. No boyfriend about to scratch her back; probably underage. I put her closer to 14 or 15."

"Yeah, that thought occurred to me too." Jackson's took a drink of coffee as he gazed at Macy's serious brown eyes staring back at him. "At her age, she'd be shifting, right? Even if she was 14 or 15?"

Ulrich nodded his agreement. "Probably, unless she's a late bloomer.

"I don't think Macy was playing hide the pickle with another shifter, but why would Ascena lie?"

"It's an unwritten rule that packs don't fuck with another pack's pups." He took a sip of his coffee. "If the other packs around town knew that Ascena had allowed a child into her pack, they'd come down on her hard because something like that could bring trouble to all the packs in the area."

Jackson sucked in a breath. "What kind of trouble?"

Ulrich almost laughed at the transparent horror in Jackson face. "We're not complete savages. Gideon and Lucien would have it out with Ascena, force her to send the female back to her original pack before that pack came sniffing around."

Jackson's expression turned to disgust as he curled his lip. "They'd force the kid to return to an abusive pack?"

Ulrich shrugged. "Look at wolf packs in the wild. They're so fucking organized and supportive of all members of the pack. Has to be that way to ensure their survival. But they don't go adopting another pack's pups."

Jackson looked like he wanted to argue his point further, but, consummate professional that he was, he let it go. "So Ascena's lying to protect the girl. It's the only way to get help from the surrounding packs without them turning on her."

"Yeah. If we operate under the assumption that Ascena

lied about Macy's age and if the female matured a little late, she might not yet be in control of her wolf."

Jackson pinched the bridge of his nose. "Meaning what?"

Ulrich sat in his office chair and took a swallow of coffee from his mug. "Shifters have two sides. The wolf side, which is ruled by instinct and the human side, which is ruled by reason."

Jackson barked out a sardonic laugh. "There is no such thing as a human ruled by reason."

Ulrich agreed. "Evolution met a fork in the road and one path held onto the shifter gene, the other didn't. Shifters blame their emotions on their wolf, but we both know it's not that compartmentalized." He pulled the thin file on Macy Kerrigan towards himself and flipped it open, scanning the missing persons report.

Jackson plunked himself down on the only other chair in the office. "Get to the point. Why does a wolf need training?"

"Wolves live here." He thumped a fist to his chest. "We're one and the same, but also not. Can't explain it any other way. You take a full-blooded wolf from the wild and decide to keep it as a pet, you're not going to take it home and let it play with the kids, are you?"

"Depends on the kids," Jackson muttered.

Ulrich chuckled. "You train the wolf to submit to you. Otherwise, it overwhelms you, takes over. Fights with you for supremacy." He leaned back as he thought about his wolf. "It's an evolutionary safety net. A shifter is human from the day he's born up until he hits puberty, when his wolf emerges. By that time, the shifter is in a better position to dominate his wolf. At the same time, if there are no guiding hands like a pack or parental figure to help with the transition, the wolf will emerge and take over."

Jackson toyed with a pen. "So, if the zookeepers aren't paying attention and leave the cage unlocked, once the animal is free, it takes over, supplanting the zookeepers' supposed control."

Ulrich grunted his laughter. "Never heard that analogy before, but yeah. If Macy hasn't been trained to control her wolf, and it emerges for the first time, it'll overwhelm her."

"And what happens then? She runs around town killing people?"

Ulrich shook his head. "Like any other wolf, she heads for the hills. She might be looking for a pack with a male alpha leader, she might go into hiding."

"Does her wolf take over completely?"

"Not in my experience. The wolf exhausts itself, and when that happens, the human side returns."

Jackson perked up. Hope tended to do that. "So it's possible that Macy lost control of her wolf and this has nothing to do with our killer."

Ulrich stared at the wall of horror. "Possible. You'll have to have a heart-to-heart with Ascena to know for sure."

Jackson drained his coffee cup and stood. "I'll track her down and talk to her."

Ulrich thought of the powerhouse who was Ascena and thought maybe Jackson needed a bodyguard, but kept his mouth shut on the topic. Instead, he said, "I should be helping with the search."

Jackson disagreed. "You're our ace, and I don't want your real reason for being here exposed over a simple case of wolf gone wild. I'll update you later today, maybe over a beer."

"Has to be after seven."

Jackson grinned sardonically. "No problem. My dance card is pretty fucking empty these days."

CHAPTER SIXTEEN

ubrey knew she looked like hell as she walked into her empty classroom room Monday morning. She abandoned her backpack on her desk and wandered to the window. August had been hot and the grass in the school ground was still a withered brown, reflecting her mood. She stood stiffly, her arms crossed over her chest, her stomach churning like it had all weekend, the hurt still bone-deep.

And yet, her traitorous heart, the one that had shattered, was still making excuses for Ulrich. He had a kid who was messed up because of the crap he'd gone through in life. She empathized with Tag; after all, she too was a child of addiction. And that of course, contributed to her understanding of Ulrich's behaviour. Except when her heart reminded her of what he'd said.

I don't love you. It was a mistake.

Those hurtful words had catapulted her back to her childhood, to the moments after the honeymoon period, when she and her sister were back with their mother. Each time she lost her fight with addiction, she became mean and accusing.

How many times had she and Adrienne been told that they were mistakes? That they were the reason their mother drank? That she hated being a mother?

Enough to plow a deep furrow in Aubrey's brain. Enough that the words had never fully been banished.

She blinked her eyes a few times to wipe off a few stray tears.

She was an adult now, not the little girl who'd cowered in a corner while her mother raged. And as an adult, she shouldn't be this hurt. The truth was, she barely knew Ulrich, despite feeling like she'd known him for several lifetimes. It was nonsense, a fanciful, romantic notion embraced by a needy woman.

She knew better than most people that there were no guarantees. Ulrich never made promises when their passion exploded. At the time, she didn't think he had to because he'd been so clear in his actions. The way he held her in his arms, not like a man taking advantage, but a man so deeply in love that he wanted to become one with her.

She turned at the sound of laughter in the hall. She should have taken the day off, gotten a sub, but that would simply be putting off the inevitable.

How the hell did she know anyway, about passion and love and how it made people feel? She'd never felt the same consuming need for another man. Before Ulrich, she'd never even had an orgasm during intercourse. With Ulrich, she had three, harder, longer, more powerful than anything she'd ever experienced.

She sighed as she made her way to her desk, pulling off her jacket as she went. It was disappointing. The bite of cold in the air, the dreariness of the cloud cover, the man Ulrich really was. The long, lonely weekend.

Saturday was supposed to be girls' night out, but she'd begged off, citing a headache. It was a heartache, but her litter of friends didn't know that, and she didn't want them to. They were bat-crap crazy, all of them in their own way, and the minute she joined them, they'd realize something was wrong. And Leah, who seemed to know everyone's secrets, would figure it out and forget to be discreet. Then they'd plot revenge on Ulrich, which would fail spectacularly, because all their schemes did.

And her private humiliation would become public, and she didn't want that. Any of it.

The warning bell sounded throughout the school and she steadied herself as she turned on her tablet. First roll-call, then a quick gab session. The morning would be full – math, then science. She wasn't on playground duty this week, thank god, and Phys ed was the first period after lunch, so she had an extended break while Mr. Heron took over.

Sure, that's what you need, Aubrey. More time to ruminate.

She plastered on a smile as students filtered into the room. The pleasant ones greeted her before sitting down, the cool ones ignored her as they stood in huddles talking over each other, and the surly ones dragged themselves in like they were being tortured.

Tag was in the second group; Reed had been bumped to the last group. Cliques were still alive and well and Aubrey wanted to give Tag a shake for being such a jerk.

"Bell's about to ring," she called over the din. "Let's get settled."

Tag glanced over at her with his father's eyes, except Tag's were filled with disdain. She wondered how much he knew of her and Ulrich's encounter. Nothing, she hoped. Because apparently it was nothing.

She broke the gaze by turning her back on him and picking up her tablet off the desk. It was an easy way to take attendance that eliminated the need for paperwork. It was also one of those rare Mondays when the entire class was present.

"Anything interesting happen this weekend?" That's how she started Mondays, a way to ease into the first day of the school week.

A few of the students offered up personal anecdotes, including Tag.

"My mom called this weekend," he said as he slumped in his seat, his long legs stretched out into the aisle, a pencil in hand, doodling in his scribbler. He didn't make eye contact.

Aubrey felt her throat close on her. "That's good to hear," she lied.

He lifted his head and held her gaze. "Yeah. Dad invited her to Darkness Falls so we could spend some time with her."

The wetness in her eyes and the hot flush to her face was the reaction Tag had been hoping for if his satisfied smile was any indication.

She crossed her arms over her chest. "That's super. I'm sure you've missed her." She somehow managed to keep the shake out of her voice.

He shrugged. "Guess so." He grinned at James, a buddy of his. "But Dad misses her more."

Tag was lying; he had to be. He was playing a game with her. She contemplated him for a few seconds, until he casually shrugged and dropped his eyes to paper that he'd been doodling on.

Let it go, Aubrey. Start the lesson. She opened her mouth to do exactly that, but what came out was, "When she gets here and settled in, I'd like to meet her."

"Sure. If she wants." The tone was dismissive, the blunt words, like his father's in tone, indicated the conversation was over.

Arrogant little bugger, but she let it go because what else could she do. It was time to move on.

The day was challenging – Mondays always were, but Aubrey appreciated the distraction. It helped her from dwelling on Tag's news, kept her from calling Ulrich to fact check.

By the time school was out, Aubrey wanted to go home, drink a bottle of white wine, crawl into bed and sleep for a month. But she couldn't because of course, Tag and Reed had detention.

"I thought we were working on a project," Reed said as he slumped in his desk, his Nike clad feet stretching out from under it.

"Yeah," Tag echoed. His attitude towards Aubrey had somewhat softened over the course of the day so that by the end of it, he was treating her like any other teacher.

She pulled a front row desk towards her a few feet and sat on the top of it, resting her feet on the seat. "Why were you guys fighting?"

Tag tilted his head and scowled. "He," he indicated Reed with a jerk of his head, "destroyed my lunch."

Aubrey nodded as she switched her attention towards Reed. "It started out as a practical joke, didn't it?"

"Yeah." Reed nodded sullenly as he ran a finger up the spine of his science textbook.

"Okay, so how did it escalate?"

Reed and Tag exchanged glances, neither seeming willing to go first.

"This stays between the three of us, I promise."

Reed drew in a breath. "Tag got pissed off and called me a... a...."

"Fucking prick," Tag filled in.

Aubrey's lips formed a silent 'O'. "Then Reed stomped on your lunch, and you threw the first punch."

Tag crossed his arms and slid further down in his desk. "So what?"

It was Aubrey's turn to shrug. "So you guys had a disagreement that escalated. Now you're no longer friends."

Tag curled his lip and glanced at Reed. "'bout sums it up."

She sighed as she stood up. "Get over it, both of you. I can't believe you're going to let a disagreement over a ruined lunch and some name calling destroy a friendship."

She walked to her desk, slumped down in her chair, and stretched her legs out in front of her.

"There are so many other bigger and better things to disagree on in this world." Her stomach was clenching as she thought of Ulrich, of what had happened between them. "Work together and find one incidence of a disagreement that had global consequences. Write me a report answering the big six: who, when, what, why, where, and how it ultimately was resolved. Was there a war, a loss of life, one of the parties snubbed on a global level? Someone get arrested, executed, fired? Or maybe the feuding partners worked it out. And if that happened, how were future relations impacted?" She took a breath. "Any questions?"

Reed raised his hand and she nodded. "How many pages?"

"Ten."

They both groaned. "Does it count for points?" Tag asked.

"Yeah." Reed this time. "What's it worth?"

She straightened up. "Tell you what. You write me a paper that exceeds expectations on the social studies performance scale, and I'll commute your detention."

Reed furrowed his eyebrows. "What do you mean, commute?"

Aubrey stood and walked over to the chalkboard, grabbed a piece of chalk, and wrote on the board. "Commute." She tapped the word with the chalk. "Look it up, boys. When you find the definition, write it on the board."

The boys glanced at each, but neither made a move.

Aubrey waved to the computer centre, which comprised a

long narrow table pressed against the back wall with chairs tucked under it and six Macs on top. "Off you go. By five today, I want the definition of commute and the topic of your paper."

Once the two were settled and talking quietly to each other, Aubrey closed her eyes. Five o'clock couldn't come soon enough.

CHAPTER SEVENTEEN

Ulrich rolled into the parking lot of Darkness Falls Middle School. He purposely arrived twenty minutes early so that he had a few moments to compose himself. A crazy weekend and a shit-filled Monday and here he was, sweating bullets over what he would say to Aubrey about his ex-wife.

Despite how they'd parted ways on Friday, he was compelled to let Aubrey know that Sibyl would be coming to Darkness Falls. He had to reassure her that his ex-wife wasn't a factor in why he had to stay away from her.

Chose to stay away from her.

It was fucked up reasoning, but the woman who held his heart seemed so fragile. Too easily broken and he'd already done enough damage.

And with the disappearance of Macy Kerrigan, his heart was thumping for a whole other reason. It was a reminder, not that he needed one, that there was a killer in Darkness Falls and Aubrey was an easy target, especially if word got out about their pair-bond. Sibyl could be a target too, and for Tag's sake, he had to make sure she was safe.

On top of trying to solve the case, he now had two women to worry about. One he was sure he loved, the other he didn't want anywhere near him or Tag.

It was a few minutes before 5 pm when he entered the school. The place was creepy when the halls were empty. There were soft voices in the office as he passed it – the school secretary and another woman, pausing their conversation as he passed. The secretary smiled and offered up a friendly wave.

Neither woman seemed intimidated by him and he wondered if he was losing his mojo. Most of his adult life, all he had to do to shut down a conversation was step into a room with a frown on his face.

Their soft laughter trailing after him didn't improve his mood.

Aubrey's classroom door stood open, and his stomach clenched when he heard her sweet voice. "This is a great start." Her words floated in the air like gossamer. "Thank you for taking this seriously."

"Anything to get this detention over with." Tag was speaking, his usual macho bravado to cover up his insecurities.

The other kid, Reed, added, "True that."

Whatever Aubrey was doing seemed to have some impact on the boys in terms of their relationship. They sounded relaxed with each other.

"See you both tomorrow and don't forget to read the Kipling assignment for English."

That was Ulrich's cue to make his presence known. He filled the doorway and Aubrey's smile died as she saw him. He couldn't interpret her expression, but he saw the flash of heat in the depth of her eyes. It had nothing to do with desire. He didn't blame her for being angry – he'd taken advantage of her and then left her high and dry. It was the most shameful thing he'd ever done.

"Mr. Calhoun," she said, the hostility in her voice apparent in the waver of her words.

"Ms. Powell." He nodded. "How'd everything go today?" He addressed them all, switching his attention to the boys.

Tag and Reed exchanged glances, then Reed hefted his backpack. "Gotta go," he mumbled. At least there was one person on this planet that he instilled a little fear in.

Ulrich watched him escape the room, then turned to Tag. "I need a few words alone with Ms. Powell." He tossed the truck keys and Tag deftly caught them. "I won't be more than a minute."

Tag shot Ulrich a scathing look, somewhere between betrayal and pure malice, but said nothing. He grabbed his book bag, murmured a polite goodbye to Aubrey, and left him alone with his woman.

No, you fucking idiot. She's not your woman and you have no claim to her.

As if reading his mind, she turned her back on him and walked to the chalkboard, picking up the eraser and furiously swiping at words, numbers, and nonsense drawings. "What do you want?" she asked coldly.

"I wanted to tell you—"

"Nothing!" She slammed the brush down on the ledge, raising a cloud of chalk dust that made her cough. Her spine was rigid as she gripped the ledge of the board, her gaze focused on her clenched fingers.

He saw the tremble in her body and stepped towards her until he realized that trying to comfort her would be a big mistake. His own body was a taut bow and touching her would make his will snap. "Aubrey, let me say what I need to say and then I'll go."

She whipped around, her eyes glinting with tears, her face red, her hands clenched. "Unless it involves Tag and is in relation to his schoolwork or his detention, we have nothing to say to each other."

"Aubrey." His voice came out too patient, too patronizing and he tried to swallow that fucking male side of him. "We need to be civil for Tag's sake."

"Wow. Does that work on your ex, too?"

His temper spiked at her snark. "This has nothing to do with Sibyl."

"Then don't talk to me like I'm your ex. Truth is, I never was. Never will be. You've made that abundantly clear." She pointed a finger at herself. "I'm Tag's teacher. Full stop. I know how to be professional." She held his eyes for a few long seconds. "So do you have something to say to me about Tag?"

The tension-filled air was thick, and her scent powered through the chalk dust, calling to his beast. He swallowed the urge to yank her to him and kiss the pissiness out of her. "Tag's mom is coming to Darkness Falls to see him."

Yep, that doused the flame inside him.

She held onto her stoic expression but betrayed herself as she crossed her arms and dug her fingernails into her palms. "What has that got to do with me?" If a tone could freeze, he'd be a solid block of ice.

"I didn't want you to think the wrong thing. Tag wants to see her, he misses her. I couldn't say no."

Her eyes dropped from his face to the floor, a study of his shoes. "The relationship you have with your wife—"

"Ex-wife. She's nothing to me but Tag's mother."

Aubrey sucked in a breath. "The relationship you have with Tag's mother is none of my business."

"I didn't want you to think—"

"What I think is none of your business." Her voice rose in volume, the frosty tone turning blazing hot. "You made it abundantly clear that we're nothing to each other." She swiped angrily at a rogue tear that had escaped down her cheek. "Unless this is about Tag, get out."

Fuck, he wanted to take her in his arms, make promises, make love. But he wasn't sure he could keep the promises. "I'll tell her not to come to the school."

"I don't care what you tell her." She stomped to her desk and grabbed her backpack, furiously stuffing it with random books. "I don't care what she does. I don't...." She stopped, staring at the math textbook in her grip, but not really seeing it. "I want you to leave."

Nothing he was saying was making any difference. He felt his temper rising at her immature refusal to have a civil discussion. Sure, he'd fucked up by sleeping with her knowing full well that he couldn't be with her, but she had been all in and neither of them made promises to each other. "I get it," he said bluntly. "You're pissed with me because I didn't offer you more than a fuck."

"Get out!" she shouted, her eyes blazing with anger. "I made the mistake, not you. I'm the stupid bitch that took everything too seriously. My fault for thinking that Friday was more than a fuck!" She swung the backpack around, her arms hugging it protectively to her front. "You're absolved of any wrongdoing, *Mr. Calhoun*." Her voice cracked. "So leave. Get out. Your son's waiting for you."

Ulrich raked a hand through his hair. "Goddamit, Aubrey! All I want is to have a mature conversation!" His frustration spilled into the tone of his voice.

"Then it's a good thing Sibyl's coming to town, isn't it?"

Her armour slipped and he was perversely pleased that he cracked it. "Aubrey," he pleaded.

She leaned against her desk. "You should go." The shake in her voice crossed the floor and punched him in the gut.

She was right. He needed to get out of there. He almost

reached the door before he turned back. "You heard about the missing girl?"

Aubrey narrowed her eyes at him. "Of course."

News travelled fast in Darkness Falls. "She hasn't been found yet." He stopped, trying to find words that wouldn't rile her up. "Be careful, Aubrey. I'm worried—"

"Shut up and leave. I don't need rescuing. And if I find you following me again, I'll report you to the police."

He banged his head lightly against the door frame. It was nothing less than what he deserved. She was the only woman in the world that mattered to him, and he was turning his back on her. He glanced up, but her eyes were glued to the floor. Even if he could fix things, it felt too late.

CHAPTER EIGHTEEN

Aubrey sensed when he was gone – the strength of his presence replaced by a hollowness that invaded the classroom and savaged her heart. She slid down the side of her desk until she was on the floor, her backpack clutched against her in a hug, her knees drawn up to her body.

The tears that she held back moments before waterfalled out of her and she hated herself for it. When she woke this morning, she'd told herself that she was done with the crying, that he wasn't worth it.

What the hell was he thinking coming into the school to talk to her? Why didn't he phone?

You'd have hung up on him.

Yeah, she would have. He seemed to have this need to tell her that Tag's mother meant nothing to him, despite her already knowing that. She wasn't above being jealous of another woman and despised Sibyl for hurting Tag, but the connection she felt with Ulrich, would always feel, helped her know that Sibyl was not a factor in his life, at least not romantically.

She buried her face in the top of her pack and cried until her tears ran out. Then she stayed that way for a few more minutes while she gathered the energy to go home. When she finally looked up, the sun had disappeared behind the mountain, the lights were too bright for her eyes, and Leah was sitting cross-legged on the floor, elbows on her knees, chin resting on her fists.

Her entire focus was on Aubrey, who yelped. "How long have you been here?" Her heart was racing, and she took a deep breath to settle it down.

Leah uncurled and stretched. "Not that long. I went to the apartment first, but you weren't there, so I fed the fish to the cat."

"You did what?" How the hell did Leah get inside her apartment?

She grinned widely. "I said I fed the fish and the cat. You're neglecting them. Their faces are gaunt."

Aubrey shakily inhaled as Leah crawled over, stopping in front of her, two feet of space between them.

"I got worried. Your car was missing, and you shirked girl's night out on Saturday."

"So you thought I'd still be here. It's...." She glanced up at the clock on the wall next to the door. "It's almost seven. I could've been out for dinner."

Leah shrugged. "Well, if you hadn't been here, then I would've checked Becker's next." She peered at Aubrey's face with curiosity. Aubrey knew what she saw – puffy eyes, tear-scored cheeks, a red nose. "What happened?"

Aubrey looked away in embarrassment. It had been so long since someone sincerely asked her that question. Maybe never. "Nothing," she mumbled, uncomfortable with the compassion Leah offered.

"Well, that's bullshit." The shifter sat back on her heels.

A small laugh escaped Aubrey's mouth. "I'm fine." She

lifted her eyes to Leah's face, then, when she saw the black and purple hand mark on her cheek, forgot about Ulrich and his baggage. There were bigger problems in the world.

"What happened to you?" Aubrey reached out to touch Leah's cheek.

Leah flinched backward. "Nothing."

"Well, nothing left a bruise."

Leah's mask of mischief slipped over the heartbeat of hurt as she smiled widely and jumped to her feet. She picked up a piece of chalk. "NOTHING," she shouted as she drew the letters in capitals on the board. "Can go FUCK itself!"

Aubrey laughed, not wild, crazy, or energetic, but for the first time since Friday night, it was genuine. "I'm hungry." And she was. It was well past feeding time.

"Me too." Leah offered her hand to Aubrey, who gripped it. "Where's your car?" the little shifter asked as she hauled Aubrey to her feet with hidden strength.

Aubrey reached for her coat. "Use your spidey senses."

Leah rolled her eyes. "I don't need spidey senses to know that the piece of shit is probably lying in a pit at the boneyard."

"Yep." Aubrey felt lighter as she shrugged into her jacket. "Clean that off." She nodded her head towards Leah's scrawl.

Leah huffed as she picked up the eraser. "Fine. But just so you know, it's rare I'm this prolific. Might never happen again."

They made their way out of the school, then stood in the empty parking lot. "Shall we order an Uber?" Aubrey asked.

"You should. I don't have a phone."

"Get one, Leah. Join the rest of us in the 21st century."

Leah shuddered. "No effing thanks."

Aubrey made the call and fifteen minutes later, they were at Becker's, seated at a table, white wine in front of Aubrey and a mug of beer for Leah. By unspoken consent, neither addressed the two elephants that they'd dragged in with them. Not yet anyway.

Leah ran through the girlfriend updates.

- Eva was still pregnant (human cop married to Aztec, former alpha to an Alaskan pack)
- Honi was now pregnant (Dominant alpha's red-headed mate)
- Cherime still hadn't conceived, despite the non-stop fucking with Ren.
- Mira, Cherime's sister, was simultaneously grieving her asshole dead husband and overjoyed at the birth of her little boy,

and

- Between Raff and their twins, Trist was exhausted, and Leah and Aubrey needed to take her to Las Vegas for some rest.

"I'm guessing you've never been to Vegas," Aubrey said drily.

"I've never strayed far from Darkness Falls."

That was surprising. "How come? There's this big, beautiful, amazing world out there to explore."

"This world is beautiful too." She waved hand in the air. "Besides, wolves stick close to their packs. Safety in numbers."

"You're more than a wolf, Leah."

"I'm barely a wolf." It was a matter-of-fact statement without bitterness or malice. Leah was unable to shift and too often, she was defined by others because of it. It was sad, because the latent shifter had so much to offer, albeit much of it was looney tunes.

Aubrey changed the subject. "What do you want to be when you grow up?"

Leah twisted her lips as she thought, then slowly said, "I think I'd like to be a teacher."

"I've heard that it's an honourable trade." Aubrey grinned waiting for Leah's punchline. When none was forthcoming, she added, "So go be one. You're young, single, smarter than the average bear."

Leah bared her teeth. "Even the dumbest shifter is smarter than the average bear."

Aubrey filed that tidbit away in the folder in her head that was labelled, *how to get under Leah's skin*. "If that's the case, go to school, get your education degree, come back to Darkness Falls and teach with me."

Leah shook her head. "Can't do that."

"Why not?"

"I'm a coward, Aubrey. Haven't you already figured that out?"

"You're not a coward," Aubrey scoffed, wishing this shifter female could see her own value. "I'm the coward," she added, knowing her words were as silly as Leah's.

Leah disagreed anyway. "You're the most courageous woman I know."

Aubrey snorted a laugh as she took a sip of her wine. "Clearly we have different definitions of courageous."

Leah leaned towards Aubrey, stabbing her index finger on the table. "Courageous is having a mother with an addiction problem and an absent father, spending years in and out of foster care, sticking it out in school, then going on to be a person who can help other kids like herself."

Aubrey wondered how Leah knew so much about her upbringing. She wracked her brain to think of when she would've shared such intimate details with Leah or any of the other women.

It didn't matter though because the little shifter across the table from her was wrong. "I simply walked through doors that someone else opened for me. Sometimes it takes more courage to stay, to find a way to make it work until the right door opens."

"I wasn't talking about you," Leah teased with a giant-sized grin on her face.

Aubrey mirrored Leah's smile. "Good, because I wasn't talking about you."

"Here you go." Lowry Pattison interrupted the Hallmark moment (thank god) as she approached the table with their meals in hand. "Chicken strips for the trouble-maker, and a burger and fries for Leah.

The three giggled. "You're in a good mood," Aubrey said.

Lowry glanced around the bar, then leaned closer, her voice lowered. "Did you know Jackson Hayes has a brother?" She tilted her head towards a corner booth, which was shared by two men deep in conversation.

Leah wrinkled her nose. "Yeah. The stink of Alan Hawke should have alerted me that they were in the building."

Aubrey didn't know Jackson Hayes had a brother, nor did she know who Alan Hawke was, but both were sizzling hot male specimens, she thought, when she followed the direction of Leah's glare. "Which is which?"

"You can't tell a shifter from a human?" Leah snarked, wrinkling her nose at the men.

"I can," Lowry said proudly.

"Sure you can." Leah almost sneered. "For the educated woman at the table, since Jackson is First Nations, it's clear that the one with the brown skin and black hair is the brother."

"Thanks, Sherlock," Aubrey said drily. "I try not to make assumptions."

154

Leah rolled her eyes towards Lowry. "Tell me, Miss Patti-son, which of those stinky boys catches your interest?"

Lowry blushed as she combed her hair behind her ear. "Either would do, but I'm kind of partial to Dexter."

"The brother," Aubrey observed as she bit down on a cherry tomato.

Leah gave her head a slow shake. "You're on fire tonight."

"Gotta go," Lowry said as a customer beckoned to her. "See you later."

Aubrey followed Lowry's retreat. "That woman needs a man."

Leah shoved two fries into her mouth and chewed. "Some women want men, but no woman needs a man."

Aubrey didn't want to agree even though Leah was mostly right. "Sometimes a woman needs a man," she said softly as she thought of Ulrich.

Leah swallowed and ran a napkin over her mouth before setting it back on the table. "A man did this." She pointed to Aubrey's puffy, red eyes. "A man did this." She pointed to her cheek. "Need and want are two different things."

Aubrey felt privileged that Leah had dropped her shields however briefly. The shifter usually went out of the way not to appear vulnerable.

"Why don't you leave, Leah?" she said softly, carefully.

Leah shrugged as she turned her attention to Jackson's brother and Alan Hawke. "I'm Gideon's Yoda. Dexter seems okay, but Alan Hawke is a dick. He's our pack's beta because stupid Varg left. Him leaving the pack weakened it. Gideon's weakened the pack further by giving Alan the beta role." She shuddered. "Worse, Alan is on the Integrated Crime Team Unit. The asshole represents my pack and try as I might, I can't sense a whisper of good in him."

Aubrey sucked in her breath. "You think he's the serial killer?"

Leah brought her attention back to Aubrey's face. "He's definitely a killer, but I don't think he's smart enough to be a serial killer."

That reminded Aubrey. "You know there's another woman missing?"

Leah nodded as she pushed her plate away. "I helped with the search. She's gone, Aubrey. Not a trace of her anywhere."

CHAPTER NINETEEN

UMP DAY!!!!

Someone had scrawled the words across the chalkboard and Aubrey was not impressed. Not only were they written over the previous day's lesson, but she also wasn't a big fan of so-called hump day. Everyone in Darkness Falls embraced it with the fervor of a cherished sports team, turning into it into something of epic proportions.

She didn't get it. It was Wednesday, another day in the week. Even the word was unattractive, filled with hard syllables and difficult to spell. It was Wednesday's fault, Aubrey decided, that the week had an odd number of days. Without Wednesday, the week would go so much smoother.

And this particular Wednesday was celebrated for more than the serendipitous fact that it landed precisely in the middle of the week. The harvest moon would be at its fullest and brightest tonight, an excuse for the school to celebrate replete with a corn maze event, pumpkin carving contest, and a lunch comprising root vegetables only made and served with clumsy care by the home ec class.

And of course, the full moon in and of itself was an excuse for the students to be ultra crazy.

By the time the last bell of the day rang, Aubrey was exhausted. A mad rush to the exit by students, teachers, principals, and custodian staff left the school deserted. They were off to celebrate the Harvest Moon with the rest of Darkness Falls. To top that sundae off with a nut, Reed had been absent from school, which meant she and Tag would be alone together for the next two hours.

The other implication of Reed's absence was that Aubrey's detention would be extended unless the two boys came up with a banging project.

And Tag was being particularly difficult as he loudly verbalized the unfairness of Reed's absence.

"You said that if we did a good job on the project, you would commute our detention." He was standing by Aubrey's desk looking down at her because she was slumped in her chair, the back supporting her head, hands folded across her stomach, eyes staring at the ceiling. At that moment, she didn't care if the project was handed in on toilet paper, she'd give it an A.

"Yeah," she said as she lolled her head towards him.

"Are you listening to me?"

She wasn't, not really, but she said, "Yeah," again.

"So how is it fair if Reed misses a day and then we both get our sentences commuted?"

"It isn't," she muttered. "Life isn't fair, Tag." If it were, she wouldn't be stuck in detention with the kid whose father she'd slept with and who subsequently rejected her because of said son.

Tag leaned in and peered at her. "Are you okay?"

Nice of him to ask. Aubrey straightened up. "I'm really tired. This day was crazy."

Tag laughed energetically. "You're telling me. Celebrating a full moon is so weird."

"True that," Aubrey grumbled. She realized that the two had something significant in common – it was the first full year at the Darkness Falls Middle School for both and they were stumbling along in unfamiliar territory. "It's not in the curriculum, so it must be something Darkness Falls does."

"Wonder why?" For the moment, Tag was distracted from Reed's absence and Aubrey was more than happy to postpone that conversation.

"Maybe because we live in a town surrounded by shifters."

"Yeah." He rolled his eyes as if Aubrey were clueless. "But we're not werewolves. We don't need a full moon to turn."

Nope, just a bucketful of hormones. She stood and headed to the computer centre. "Let's figure this out."

Tag followed her, then as she sat, he pulled up a chair next to her. Time flew by as they researched the fall harvest moon, building a premise for why Darkness Falls thought it was party-worthy. It became a blissful hour of connection with Tag that lightened Aubrey's heart, but also cracked it.

"I think," Tag said as he rocked his chair back on two legs, leaning it against the desk behind him. "That Darkness Falls uses it as an excuse to go wild."

"Well, some do believe that a full moon affects the behaviour of all living beings. It's symbolic of change, and the article on Wikipedia says that this time of year is a particularly active time for young shifters to go through their first transformation."

Tag's eyes lit up. "Wouldn't it be awesome if I shifted right now."

Aubrey felt her heart skip a beat. "No, it would not. You'd scare the heck out of me."

They both laughed, Tag loud and boisterous, which warmed Aubrey's heart until he threw his body back in the already unstable chair. His weight kicked the chair's back legs out and toppled him backwards, his head solidly banging against the edge of the desk behind him.

"Ow, ow, ow!" he yelped as he grabbed the back of his head and rolled on the floor, slamming his body into the surrounding desks.

"Oh my god!" Aubrey dropped to her knees. "Oh my god!" Her heart was pounding out of her chest as she tried to get Tag to stop writhing long enough to see the injury. "Tag, hold still and move your hands."

"I can't," he cried, holding his head tighter. "It hurts."

Aubrey took a deep breath to control the panic and gather her strength, then snatched Tag's hands and pulled them away from his head. Blood was seeping out of a large cut and seemed to spurt once it was uncovered.

Aubrey gagged and closed her eyes to the sight. "We have to get you to the hospital."

"Call my dad." He was a boy again, a young man on the cusp of puberty who needed his parent to reassure him.

Aubrey was already on her feet, grabbing several microfibre towels off the stack next to the Mac. "We'll call him on the way to the hospital." She shoved the towels to the back of his head, then yanked his hand to them. "Press on it."

"The hospital! How bad is it?" He was crying now, tears of fear and pain mingling together.

How bad? She couldn't tell through all the blood and didn't dare look at it again. The mere thought made her queasy. "Not too bad," she lied. "But you might need stitches and you hit the desk hard enough that you could have a concussion.

"I don't want a concussion!" he wailed. "I won't be able to play volleyball!"

She helped him sit up. "Are you okay to stand and walk? I

can call an ambulance, but I think it might be faster if we drive."

"Drive what?"

Damn! Aubrey closed her eyes. "Right. An ambulance it is."

"No!" Tag protested. "I don't want anyone to see me in an ambulance."

Aubrey almost rolled her eyes. Boys to men and nothing ever changed. "It's nothing to be embarrassed over."

"I'm not embarrassed," he insisted with a voice hashed by a grater. "I don't need an ambulance. Call my dad."

It wasn't wasted on Aubrey that the 12-year-old kid bleeding from the back of his head was thinking more clearly than she was. It's the blood, she consoled herself. "I'll get my phone. You stay there and don't try to stand."

She backed away, bumping into other desks, but unwilling to take her eyes off Tag. What if he had irreversible brain damage? What if he died? What if he bled out?

NO! Not on her watch! She fumbled her cell phone out of her purse and opened the screen.

"You have my dad's phone number?" Tag furrowed his brow together in a way that reminded her so much of Ulrich, it made her heart squeeze.

"Yes," she said as she scrolled through her contacts. "He asked me to be an emergency contact for him."

"Fuck," he muttered, and she glanced up in time to see the deep freeze settle between them. For a few precious moments, Tag had let his guard down and let her in. Now he was looking at her like she was the enemy.

"It's because he doesn't know many people in Darkness Falls. That's all," she mumbled, knowing he knew that she was full of crap.

She pressed Ulrich's cell number and waited as it rang. No

answer, but voicemail kicked in and her stomach twisted as Ulrich's deep rich voice invited her to leave a message.

"Ulrich, it's Aubrey... uh... Ms. Powell," she said quickly. "Tag's had a small accident and likely needs some stitches." She glanced at the clock on the wall. "It's just after 4pm. We're leaving for the hospital right now. Call me when you get this." She hesitated, then said a quick, "Bye," and ended the call.

"Of course, he's not picking up. Probably saw your number and ran for the hills." Tag was staring her down and she couldn't decide what to feel. Worry, fear, anxiety for him. Sadness that she couldn't build a bridge between them, Ulrich or no Ulrich. Or anger that he wasn't giving her a chance, that he was being a little bugger, and... and....

And also, he was bleeding out on the floor.

She opened her phone and ordered an Uber. "Let's go."

CHAPTER TWENTY

Wednesday afternoon, Jackson and Ulrich had a chance to get together again. They were both in solemn moods as they sat in the front seat of Jackson's parked jeep, which was facing the huge waterfall that the town of Darkness Falls was named after.

"Something going on with you?" Jackson asked as they sipped on cans of beers.

Yeah, it was illegal, but Jackson was an RCMP Inspector within E Division and Commanding officer in the Darkness Falls jurisdiction, he was wearing civvies, and in his personal vehicle. Ulrich was also an RCMP Inspector and an undercover cop with the National Headquarters assigned to assist in the murder enquiry in Darkness Falls. Getting pinched for having open liquor in a vehicle and drinking it on crown land was pretty fucking remote.

Ulrich sighed. No one would ever accuse him of being in touch with his soft side and talking with Jackson about the feels was a nonstarter. "Nope." He popped the P. "You?"

Jackson shrugged as he looked out the window at the

dying afternoon. "Macy Kerrigan's disappearance is fucking with me. Can't sleep." He took another swig of his beer.

Neither could Ulrich, not because of the girl who seemingly vanished without a trace, but because Sibyl was set to arrive on the weekend and Tag was so fucking excited about it. Ulrich already knew the outcome of the visit. Tag was going to be destroyed when Sibyl pulled a... well... pulled a Sibyl.

And then there was Aubrey.

She was on his mind every second of every day. His want of her. His need. But mostly his self-loathing at how he'd hurt her. Flogging was too light a sentence for the shit he piled on her.

He tried to turn his personal thoughts off so he could focus on the purpose of the meeting.

"How could she have disappeared without a trace?"

"You know why. Whoever the fuck is preying on women around here masks the scent."

Ulrich felt growly at the lack of progress they were making on the case. "I get that, but it doesn't make sense that the trail is so cold." It seemed impossible given how quickly her absence was discovered. "Every fucking shifter in this jurisdiction was involved in her search. How could none of them pick up a whiff. That's all it would take, one fucking whiff to give us a direction."

Jackson sighed as he leaned his head against the backrest and stared at the roof liner. "If I tell you something, can I trust you not to share it?"

Ulrich raised his eyebrows. "If you're about to confess, you know I'll have to arrest you." He was only half-joking because not even the cops were above suspicion.

Jackson grinned. "I'm not about to confess to anything but having open alcohol in a vehicle."

"Since I'm your partner in crime, I guess that infraction stays between us."

Jackson straightened up, drained his can, and pulled another from the six-pack and popped the top. "Ever hear of windwalkers?"

Windwalkers? Ulrich searched his memories. "Aren't they an aboriginal myth about dangerous creatures that manipulate the environment?"

"Yeah. Originated on the prairies." He stretched and tugged at the handle on the door. "Let's take a walk."

An icy frission of caution crawled slowly up Ulrich's spine. Something about the cast of shadows in an area many considered sacred ground, Jackson's strange mood, and the missing girl combined to set off warning bells. He stepped out of the truck, thinking he should shed his clothes, get ready to shift, but Jackson plunged into the trees and disappeared.

Ulrich swore under his breath as he quickly followed.

Jackson wasn't in sight, but a ruffle of leaves on a Sitka alder pointed Ulrich northwest. When he came out the other side of the dense bushes, he found himself alone again. He sniffed the air. Nothing.

What the fuck?

The one constant about the woods is that it never slept, never stopped, never stilled. "Jackson!" he called out, the silence unnerving him. "Where the fuck did you go?"

Shifters had their own lore, which was handed down from generation to generation. With a long oral history came superstitions and a belief in spirits unrelated to the god the Europeans had brought to Canada. Ulrich had little use for anyone's deities along with the accompanying mythology. That didn't mean he dismissed the spirt world completely.

"I'm here." Jackson's voice behind him had him nearly jumping out of his skin.

He twisted to face the cop, his heart beating far too fast. "How the fuck did you get behind me?"

Jackson shrugged and sat down on boulder. "I'm a windwalker." He said it simply like he was telling Ulrich the size of shoes.

Ulrich's fists clenched of their own accord. "Bullshit! There's no such thing."

"Being a windwalker is no stranger than being a shifter."

"So you're the evil fuck that's been killing the women?" Ulrich sneered, not believing it for a moment, but at the same time readying himself to let his wolf loose.

"No. I'm not an evil fuck." He stared past Ulrich. "Windwalkers are legends among many First Nations people. Maybe some Metis too. I don't know. I doubt there are many of us out there. I only know of a handful."

Ulrich crossed his arms and pinned Jackson with a glare. "What makes you so special?"

A dust devil kicked up next to Ulrich, then took a furious path directly towards Jackson, disappearing before it battered the cop. "With training, a windwalker can control the elements. Primarily air, which in turn controls water, earth, and fire."

Ulrich tried to shelve his skepticism and listen to what the cop was saying. "Are you trained?"

Jackson nodded. "Kind of. An old woman lives on my reserve. Don't know how old, but she's ancient enough to remember the days when more windwalkers existed."

Ulrich couldn't suppress a shudder. "Jesus, Hayes. If it's true, this has global implications."

Jackson barked out a laugh. "The truth is in the dust devil." One, then another, then three more little tornados of soil sprang up, then raced towards each and collided, forming a wind tunnel. The previous calm weather kicked more dirt into the air, growing in ferocity until Ulrich couldn't hear the roar of the nearby falls.

Then it stopped as abruptly as it started. "Cut it the fuck out!" Ulrich shouted as his wolf leapt around inside him, scrabbling to get out.

Jackson raised his hands in the air, an apology, and a promise to cut it the fuck out. "I don't know what a windwalker could do if he could control his full ability. I know what I can do."

Ulrich eyed him suspiciously. "And what exactly can you do besides perform circus tricks?"

"Up until last spring, I could make dust devils, ruffle trees, create a warm bubble around me and others if I was cold."

"What happened last spring?" Ulrich knew the answer but wanted confirmation from the cop.

He tilted his head towards the mighty falls, its roaring and churning an eerie backdrop to the conversation they were having. "When the body of Tia Gibbs was discovered in the cave behind the falls, I used my ability to control the falls so that my team could get in and out. Twice."

"That's no small feat."

Jackson agreed. "It took everything I had to get those falls to slow down. I was exhausted for a week, could barely drag myself to work, let alone get my head into it."

Ulrich shoved his hands into his pockets and hunched up his shoulders. "So you're suggesting our guy is a windwalker."

Jackson nodded. "It explains the lack of scent around the body, the lack of a trail to follow. Explains how Tia got into that cave."

Ulrich thought about the victims' bodies. Aubrey's sister, Adrienne had her throat torn out, a vicious mating mark on her back. "It doesn't make sense unless you can grow wolf-like claws and teeth."

Jackson chuckled grimly. "No. Can't do that, though I'll

admit, since this case started, I tried to." He laughed at himself. "I even went so far as to talk to the old woman about the possibility."

"And?"

"And she asked me if I was on drugs."

Ulrich chuckled. "So then there are two killers. A shifter and a windwalker who've teamed up." That made it both easier and harder to narrow for them to narrow down the list of suspects.

Jackson sobered. "She told me flat-out that I had no shifter blood and if I had, I would've known. There'd be a wolf inside me, guiding my actions." He paused, maybe for effect, maybe to gather his thoughts. "What she didn't deny was that a shifter could also be a windwalker. Both are genetic, so if a windwalker and a shifter had a baby...." He trailed off.

"Sounds like the punch-line to a bad joke."

Jackson stood. "Right now, we're operating under one huge unknown. Are we looking for a pair of killers or a genetic anomaly?"

As they returned to the jeep, Ulrich said, "Let's go with you being innocent—"

"I am innocent."

Ulrich knew that already. At least he thought he did. "Are windwalkers good liars?"

"No worse or better than anyone else, I guess."

"I don't sense you lying."

Jackson stared at him over the top of the roof of the jeep as he yanked open his door. "Thanks for the vote of confidence."

Ulrich joined him inside. "Who else, then?" Again, Ulrich knew who else, but he wanted Jackson to confirm it.

Jackson slid his key into the ignition and the engine roared to life. "Dexter. My brother."

Ulrich checked his phone on the return trip to town. A voicemail from Aubrey. "Shit," he exclaimed as he heard the recording of her panicked voice. "Tag's been hurt. Aubrey's taken him to emergency."

"Hang on," Jackson said as he made a fast U-turn in the middle of the highway and headed towards the hospital.

CHAPTER TWENTY-ONE

At the hospital, an attendant came out with a wheelchair and while Tag complained, Aubrey insisted he sit in it.

He was wheeled immediately into an examining room while a front desk nurse named Gillian, according to her name tag, stopped Aubrey from following. "I need a little information on your son."

Aubrey shook her head. "He's not my son. He's my student."

Gillian raised her eyebrows. "Oh. Where are his parents?"

Aubrey glanced down at her cell phone. "I've called his father. He's not picking up, but I've left a message."

"Okay." The nurse slowly tapped on the keyboard. "Surely there must be an emergency contact on the young man's school registration."

Aubrey's anxiety grew "Yes, there is. Me."

Gillian pursed her lips. "That would have been helpful information to start with."

Aubrey blinked away the sudden spurt of tears to her eyes.

"I'll try to remember that the next time I bring a boy who's bleeding from a head wound into emergency."

Gillian seemed startled by Aubrey's outburst. To be fair, Aubrey was a little surprised herself.

"I'm sorry," the nurse murmured.

"Me too." Aubrey felt heat rise to her face. "I'm a little shaken up. The blood...."

"Head wounds will do that to you. They look far worse than they usually are." Gillian looked at her monitor. "Let's start again. Name?"

"Aubrey Powell."

She typed it in. "And yours?"

"Aubrey Powell," she repeated.

The nurse hung her head and chuckled softly. "What's the boy's name?"

"Oh." Aubrey felt her face heat. "He's Taggart Calhoun. His father is Ulrich Calhoun. Single parent." She wasn't sure why she added that last tidbit of information.

"Oh wow!" a pretty nurse said as she sauntered up to the desk holding a tray of medications. "That guy is...." She fanned herself to make her point.

Back the eff off. Ulrich's mine! "I haven't noticed. We're friends." *Lies, all lies.*

Gillian raised her eyebrows as she peered down to her screen. "I need Tag's birthdate, health care number, home address, phone number."

Some emergency contact she was, but a soft baritone voice behind her saved her from having to show how little she knew about her *friend's* son.

"Are you Tag's mom?"

She turned to see a handsome man dressed casually in khakis and a light blue button-up shirt with the collar open. A white hospital coat hung open to mid-thigh and he was carrying a file. His short hair was sandy blonde, his eyes ocean blue, and his chiselled face and hard body the stuff of underwear models.

"No. His teacher. Uh...." She swallowed. "Friend of his father's."

For one precious moment she'd forgotten about Ulrich, about her heartache, her battered soul, and remembered she was a lonely woman. But her yearning for companionship was immediately supplanted by memories of Ulrich and all the emotions and baggage that tagged along.

She swallowed again and attempted a smile.

"I'm Dr. Cooper. Jared, though the world seems to think I like being called Coop." He offered his hand.

This time her smile was less forced. "Aubrey Powell."

His handshake was firm and warm. "Aubrey Powell. His expression tightened. "You're Adrienne Powell's...." He let it trail.

Aubrey filled in the blank. "Sister." She tried to lighten her tone. "Came for the ashes, stayed for the Harvest Moon."

He glanced down at the clipboard in his hand. "The best time of the year. You were smart to stay."

Time to get back on track. The hospital wasn't a dating site. "How's Tag?"

"She's his emergency contact," Gillian piped up. "Father's been notified."

"Ulrich Calhoun," Aubrey helpfully added.

Dr. Cooper tilted his head, his eyes unfocused. "Don't think I know him. Whose pack?"

Aubrey shook her head. "No pack." It felt wrong to tell this doctor information about Ulrich. Like a betrayal. "How's Tag? Can I see him?"

He gave her a clinical smile as he returned to his professional role. "Of course. This way."

Tag was seated on a table, his eyes shut as a nurse stood

behind him, swabbing his wound. He glanced at Aubrey as she entered. "Is Dad here?"

"On his way," she murmured, moving closer to him so he felt protected. It wasn't exactly a lie – Ulrich would be on his way as soon as he got her message. She turned to Dr. Cooper. "So, doctor, what's the verdict?"

"Ow!" Tag jerked in pain and clutched Aubrey's hand as the nurse dabbed some antiseptic on him.

Aubrey squeezed his fingers then loosened her grip, but he hung on.

"Well," Dr. Cooper said, talking to Tag. His bedside manner was another attractive quality of his. "Typically, I'd suggest sutures, but it is the back of your head, so if it scars, your hair will cover it. And with your shifter blood, you'll heal fast."

Tag released Aubrey's hand. "I can go then?"

Cooper shook his head. "Not so fast. Your dad will make the decision about the sutures and we need to make sure you don't have a concussion. I'd like to keep you overnight to monitor you."

Tag appeared torn. "Will I have to go to school tomorrow?"

Cooper grinned at Tag's transparency. "I think you should stay home for at least a day."

Aubrey almost rolled her eyes. "That'll even you out with Reed."

"What the hell happened?" Everyone jumped as Ulrich's booming voice invaded the quiet hospital. He stomped into the examining room, Jackson Hayes on his heels.

Aubrey glanced from Ulrich to Jackson. The police presence seemed like overkill. Was the Chief here to arrest her for negligence? She hoped not. She realized she hadn't followed protocol. Hadn't yet call the principal to report the incidence. Was that the problem?

Add to that the glare Ulrich shot her, and she lost her poise. "I... he... Tag."

"I tipped over my chair and banged my head against the desk behind me," Tag helped out. "No big deal."

Ulrich dismissed her like she was irrelevant. He turned to Dr. Cooper. "And, is he okay?"

Cooper nodded, his expression bland. "I was suggesting to Ms. Powell that he might need sutures, but it isn't entirely necessary since it's the back of his head, and it may scar but will be covered by his hair."

Ulrich lifted his chin at Tag. "Up to you."

Jackson had been curiously eyeing Aubrey and he offered her a friendly grin. "Shifters like their scars."

Ulrich glared at the cop like he was a bug to be squashed. "Not from something as trite as falling out of a chair."

Tag's face reddened and Aubrey jumped in to defend Tag. "It wasn't trite. There was a lot of blood."

Dr. Cooper smiled at her. "Lots of little vessels in the head." To Ulrich, he said, "I'd like to keep him overnight to make sure it's nothing more than a cut and a bump."

Ulrich glanced from Cooper to Tag until his cool gaze fell on Aubrey. "You can go."

"Yeah." Her throat tightened under his scrutiny, and she turned towards the door, happy to be dismissed.

"Uhm, Dad. She needs a ride home."

Thank you, Tag.

Dr. Cooper checked his watch. "I'm pretty much done for the day. I can give you a ride if you're willing to wait around for a few minutes while I make sure Tag is settled."

Aubrey loved the small-town vibe of Darkness Falls. She started to nod when Ulrich answered for her.

"Not a fucking chance!" His abrupt tone once again startled everyone in the examination room.

Dr. Cooper didn't seem overly intimidated. As a doctor,

he probably dealt with jackasses all the time. "Mr. Calhoun, is there a reason you feel compelled to tell Ms. Powell what she can or can not do?" His blue eyes tinged with amber.

What the hell? He was a shifter? How could she not have realized that?

Jackson, who had been largely forgotten, crossed his arms. "I'll give her a ride home."

"Good," Ulrich snarled. "You, I trust."

Aubrey finally found her voice. "Thank you, everyone, but I'll order an Uber." It was said softly without enough conviction, but at least she said it.

Ulrich dug in his pocket and pulled out a wad of bills. He flipped through them, then peeled off a 100-dollar bill and shoved it at Aubrey. "For the Uber."

She held his eyes for a few long moments, wondering who the hell he thought he was, offering money to her for helping his son. "Keep your money," she said coolly as she turned her back on everyone and left the hospital.

CHAPTER TWENTY-TWO

U lrich was surprised when Aubrey stalked out of the examination room, leaving him looking like a fool, his arm extended, money waving in his hand. What was wrong with offering to pay for her ride? Or maybe she was pissed that he'd said 'no' to Jared Cooper giving her a ride home.

Yeah, he knew he was a fucking idiot for protesting, sounding like he owned Aubrey and had a right to tell Cooper to back off. The stupid fuck would've sensed the pair-bond the minute Ulrich stepped into the room and should've known better than to make an offer like that.

He'd started out furious at Aubrey for letting Tag get hurt on her watch, but seeing her standing next to Tag, her face as pale as the kid's, brought out his protective side. Fucking pair-bonds caused a wild storm of emotions and took too goddamn much effort to control.

That's why he was being an ass.

That's why she'd refused his money and walked out on him like he was shit on her shoe.

Sure, blame it on the pair-bond, you fucking neanderthal.

It was a sad day indeed when his wolf was more civilized than his human veneer.

While the nursing staff were setting Tag up in a room, Jackson and Ulrich stood outside so they could talk.

"Little hard on Coop, weren't you?" Jackson said, a small smirk tipping his lips up. "Why not let him take her home?"

"I don't trust the guy. Never have."

Jackson snorted. "If that makes you sleep better at night."

Ulrich sighed as he squeezed the bridge of his nose with his fingers. "Why's he going home anyway? Tag's accident is the tip of the iceberg tonight. Even the humans are howling at the moon."

Jackson shrugged. "How would I know? His shift is over. He's got a hot date. He has plans to join in the harvest celebration. Fairly sure he'll get called in if a shifter shows up in a bad way, but that's not all that likely to happen. Most shifters will be with their packs, celebrating.

Jackson was right. Ulrich himself was feeling the pull of the Harvest Moon. Maybe that's why he was being so belligerent. He wanted to strip his clothes off, bay at the moon, join a pack of wolves and run with them. Of course, the latter was not an option. Wolves and shifters didn't get along. Ulrich thought it was because the wolves thought themselves too good for the shifters. They were probably right.

Besides, he needed to stay with Tag in case his wolf made an appearance. Bad night for the kid to end up in the hospital, but Ulrich wanted to make sure he wasn't seriously hurt. They'd both sleep over, Tag in the bed, Ulrich in the uncomfortable hospital chair that was too small for his frame. At least Cooper understood how the Harvest Moon might affect Tag, and told the nursing staff to set up a private room.

After Jackson left, Ulrich checked in on Tag. The kid was in a faded set of pajamas that the nursing staff had provided, in bed, the mattress adjusted so he was sitting up. Katie, a young nurse, was talking earnestly to him and Ulrich could see Tag's interest in the intensity of his eyes. If Tag didn't shift tonight, it wouldn't be much longer.

"How's the head?" he asked Katie as he loomed over Tag.

"It's good." She nervously glanced at him, then back to Tag, who seemed the more benign of the two choices. "I was about to get him a tray for dinner." She glanced at her watch. "Would you like me to bring you one too, Mr. Calhoun?"

Ulrich shook his head even as his stomach growled. "Thanks. I have to run a small errand, then I'll be back for the night."

"Where are you going?" Tag asked after Katie left.

Ulrich stuck his hands in his pockets as he considered his son. When he'd walked into the examination room, Tag and Aubrey looked thick as thieves, her standing next to him like a mother should. Even if he had been a belligerent ass, the sight hit him hard in the chest. They looked like they belonged together.

Maybe he could fix things with Aubrey; get Tag to come around.

Starting now. "I'm going to see Ms. Powell, to say thank you to her for what she did for you and apologize for being such as ass."

The shift in Tag's mood was palpable. "She's the reason I got hurt," he pouted. "Making me do computer work, trying to buddy up with me."

Ulrich didn't challenge Tag's version of the truth. The kid was hurt, needed to recover from a bad blow to the head. "Doesn't matter. I acted like an ass. We owe her a thank you for keeping a cool head and getting you to a hospital."

Tag shrugged, his bottom lip jutting out stubbornly. "That's her job, isn't it?"

"She could have called an ambulance and sent you off on

your own. Instead, she brought you here and stayed with you until I arrived."

"I didn't need her here," Tag protested. "I wasn't hurt that bad."

"Everyone needs someone," Ulrich said softly, his gut twisting at the thought of Aubrey so alone in the world.

"You offered her money and she turned it down." Tag grunted his displeasure, which forced Ulrich out of his musings.

"I offended her."

"Why?" Tag was clearly a chip off the old block. "If somebody offered me a hundred bucks, I sure as heck wouldn't say no."

"Maybe. But she helped you out the goodness of her heart. You don't repay kindness with money."

"Then how do you repay it?"

Good fucking question. "By saying thanks. Showing her that we're grateful. By not being asses."

Tag grinned. Of course, he'd be amused. He wanted to be like Ulrich, and he liked the idea that the two were asses. "I'll try not to be an ass, but since she didn't want the 100 bucks, can I have it?"

Ulrich chuckled at the audacity of his kid. "Not a chance. Do something to earn it." He moved towards the door.

"How long will you be gone?"

Ulrich checked his watch. "Not long." He was going to stop by Aubrey's to thank her and apologize for being a prick, then pick up some burgers and fries so Tag could have his second dinner and Ulrich could have his first. "How do you feel other than the head? Any sense that you might shift tonight?"

Tag's eyes brightened. "I hope so, but I don't feel anything."

"Okay. If the urge strikes while I'm gone, fight it."

The jut of Tag's lower lip betrayed his doubt. "Okay."

Ulrich shared his son's misgivings as he left the hospital. Tag was a strong kid, physically and mentally, which was why he wasn't more messed up. But the thump to his head and the pills Cooper had prescribed would weaken him. If his wolf made an appearance, Tag would have a hard time fighting it off.

On the bright side, his wolf would be as drugged up as Tag and in no condition to do anything but turn belly-up and ask the pretty nurse to scratch him.

He called Jackson for a ride to his truck, which was parked at the cop's house. It gave him the opportunity to revisit Jackson's big reveal, which he'd set aside when he got the call about Tag.

"A windwalker, hey?" Ulrich stood facing Jackson in the cop's driveway. "Think something like that would show up in DNA?"

"Maybe," Jackson muttered, seeming uncomfortable with the direction of the conversation. "I'm not offering up mine, if that's what you're thinking. I don't want my DNA in the system."

Ulrich understood Jackson's position. So much of the world was mired in a culture of blame and Jackson would become a target if word got out about his special abilities. "Is it an aboriginal thing?" He had to ask because shifters weren't limited to a specific race or geographical location, though there was speculation that they may have originated in Europe. Still, myths about wolves pervaded the oral history of almost every culture.

Jackson shrugged. "Don't know. My brother and I are the only two that I'm aware of. Dexter farts around with his abilities but doesn't apply himself."

Ulrich filed that away, but didn't say what he was thinking, which was that Jackson might not know the extent of his brother's abilities or training. "Is your mother?"

Jackson kicked at the dirt. "No. Came down through my dad's side, but I don't know if he's got the gene. He wasn't around much when I was a kid." He shrugged as he looked past Ulrich. "Shouldn't you be getting back to Tag?"

"Yeah," he said as he looked at his watch. Jackson was done with talking and the windwalker angle was something Ulrich could think about later, after he talked to Aubrey.

He said his goodbyes and headed directly to Aubrey's. Without her car, he couldn't be sure she was home, but a light from her bedroom window was on. He stood on the pavement for a couple of minutes settling his wolf who was agitated for some reason.

When he felt himself sufficiently in control, he lumbered up the stairs. At her apartment, he knocked softly on the door and waited for her. Her footsteps signalled her approach and he steeled himself for the flood of need that would hit him the moment she opened the door.

Except she didn't.

"Go away, Ulrich," her soft voice floated to him through the barrier.

He tried to temper his tone. "Open the door, Aubrey. I want to talk to you about earlier."

"So talk." There was no malice in her tone, and he wondered how she could be so forgiving given how much she'd had to overcome in her childhood. A lesser person would be bitter and angry, like Aubrey's sister had been, but Aubrey chose to let her inherent goodness guide her.

Ulrich thought he could learn a lot about forgiveness from her.

He pressed his forehead against the door as he thought about what to say to this woman. The pair-bond might have been what brought them together, but in his heart, he knew that she was who he yearned for. It wasn't spiritual, or magical. This small, gentle, fragile woman owned his heart for all the right reasons.

"Please. I can't do this through the door. I promise I'll stay on this side. I won't come in." It would kill him. His wolf was already yapping at him in disagreement, but he'd keep the promise.

He sensed her hesitation then the drawing of the bolt as she opened the door partway and peered at him. Her eyes were red, her face puffy. He'd made her cry again.

She tucked her bottom lip between her teeth. He couldn't discern her thoughts from her expression, and he couldn't sense anything except her exhaustion.

"How's Tag?" she asked.

He grinned as he thought about Tag's eyes brightening up when the pretty nurse carried in the food tray. "Good. He'll live."

She nodded. "Good."

Awkward was just the tip of the iceberg.

The door opened across the hall and the old woman stuck her head out. "Take it inside, you two." She eyeballed Aubrey. "I've about had enough of your revolving door."

Ulrich raised his eyebrows. "Revolving door?"

Aubrey shook her head and opened the door wider, stepping back to let him enter.

Go in, his wolf urged.

Don't go, his will ordered.

He stepped inside and closed the door but stayed near it. He didn't dare move towards her because his control was so shaky. He pressed his back against the wood and crossed his arms over his chest.

She was barefoot, wearing leggings and an over-sized long-sleeved tee. Her shoulder-length hair was in disarray. She was a waif, and it broke his heart again that she'd been crying because of him.

She kept a wary distance of about six feet between them and crossed her arms, waiting for him to say what he'd come to say.

He held her eyes because he wanted her to know he was sincere. "Thank you for looking after Tag. I'm sorry I was such an ass at the hospital."

"You were shaken up," she said softly, then her lips tipped upward slightly. "When I saw the blood, I almost fainted, so I understand how worried you must have been."

He didn't want her absolution. "That's no excuse for treating you like shit." He touched a fist to his heart. "You're a good, kind woman. You don't deserve the hell I've put you through."

Her face was conflicted as she hugged herself tighter. "I accept both your apology and your thanks." She hesitated, then, "You should go."

His wolf had been surprisingly behaved while they exchanged words but suggesting Ulrich leave provoked a resounding *hell no!*

This time he agreed with the beast. "I've been wrong, thinking I couldn't be with you because of Tag. I want us to be together. Tag likes you and he'll come around to the idea of us. After Sibyl comes to visit, when Tag fully understands that she and I will never reconcile, he'll understand." He struggled with what to say next, and then blurted out an unsatisfactory excuse for his son's behaviour. "He's confused right now, on the cusp of puberty. It's so much more complicated as a shifter."

Her composure crumpled and she wiped the tears off her cheeks. "I can't." Her voice broke.

Ulrich froze. Was she saying 'no'? Given that she was so into him, it hadn't occurred to him that she wouldn't come around. "What?" he asked, convinced he hadn't heard her right.

She sniffled and ran the sleeve of her shirt under her nose. "Adrienne and I used to have what we called cry-offs. When we were back with Mom or in a particularly bad foster home. It was a competition to see who could hold off crying the longest. We were both really good at it. One time, I went almost three months without crying. It was a new record." She tucked her bottom lip between her teeth and contemplated him.

He waited, not wanting to fuck up the fragility of the moment by saying something asinine.

"You know what broke me that time? The foster home I was in was a good one. We were fed regularly, helped with our homework. Maybe not loved, but at least nurtured." The drift of her eyes embraced the distant memory. "Then they gave us back to our mom. Adrienne was happy, but I wanted to stay with the family."

Ulrich's heart broke for the little girl she used to be, but he couldn't figure out why she was telling him. "I don't understand," he said carefully, a hollowness divining her next words.

"You make me cry, Ulrich." She shook her head and took a small step back, a physical symbol of the growing distance between them. "So much. Too much. Maybe I'm lucky that I was never really loved before because it hurts." She touched a hand to her heart. "You hurt me. The world can treat me like crap – that I can deal with. But you, no. You shatter me, break me so easily." She shook her head. "I can't be the woman I become when you're around. I can't be her, because she's weak and there is no room in my life for weakness." She dropped her chin to her chest and studied the carpet under her feet. "So, no."

She was trembling, her body shaking, her hands clenched

so hard her fingers were bloodless. And she wouldn't look up, wouldn't meet his eyes.

"Aubrey," Ulrich rasped, his emotions owning him. "I'll be better, I promise." He couldn't believe what she was saying to him, couldn't understand. They were pair-bonded; this was just another bump in the path towards each other.

"You should go," she said softly.

"Can't we talk about this?" He was panicking. His wolf was in full alpha mode. She didn't get to tell him 'no'.

This time she held his eyes, the dull sad brown piercing his soul. "Please leave, Ulrich. I want you to leave."

He stood for maybe a minute, maybe longer, waiting for her to say something else, but was met with nothing but her silence. He nodded once, then opened the door, and left.

CHAPTER TWENTY-THREE

Saturday morning, Aubrey woke to bright sunlight and a slight hangover. Nothing like drinking herself into a stupor. There was the old Aubrey before Ulrich, who'd never sought out alcohol or other mind-altering drugs to manage her emotions. Then there was this new Aubrey, one she didn't quite recognize. One she didn't like all that much. Not that the old Aubrey was much to celebrate.

She moaned as she rolled onto her back and shoved her pillow over her face to shield her eyes.

"About time you woke up."

Mr. Meow, her cat, jumped on the bed and for a few ridiculous seconds, Aubrey thought he was the one speaking.

Her heart hit overdrive and she bolted upright, then relief flooded her when she found Leah sitting cross-legged on the carpet, an open book on her lap. Aubrey's journal.

Aubrey sighed as her adrenaline settled. Leah had no understanding of social boundaries. "I'm not even going to ask," she muttered as she threw back her covers and got out of bed, yanking her journal out of Leah's hand on her way to the bathroom.

Leah leapt to her feet to follow, but Aubrey slammed and locked the door.

"That won't keep me out!" Leah called.

"Go feed the pets!" Aubrey muttered as she checked her journal. It wasn't really a record of feelings or a tale of woe, but almost every night, she jotted down the events of the day.

"That's not my job!" Leah sniped.

"You seem to be able to come and go at will, which leads me to think you've got a key to my apartment. And if you've got a key, that means you're a resident. Residents in my apartment are required to feed the pets and make coffee." Then as an afterthought, added, "And pay their share of the rent."

She didn't quite catch Leah's grumbled response, but it faded as the crazy one left the bedroom. Aubrey stared down at her journal. Effing Leah.

She did her business, washed up and dressed in holy jeans and a faded T-shirt with an A emblazoned across the front. It had belonged to her sister and it was one of a dozen things of Adrienne's that she couldn't bring herself to part with.

In the kitchen, Mr. Meow was sprawling on the sofa licking his paws, Fake Goldie appeared intact, and two steaming cups of coffee and an open jar of raspberry jam were on the coffee table in front of the couch. Leah was in the kitchen buttering toasts and humming a tune that sounded vaguely like *Eye of the Tiger*.

"Here you are!" Leah exclaimed as she carried the stack of toasts into the living room along with two plates, two butter knives, and a spoon for the jam, all of which she set up on the coffee table while shooing Mr. Meow to the floor.

"Wow! You're a domestic goddess," Aubrey teased as she sat down on the sofa.

Leah grinned and parachuted her herself onto the other end. "I know!"

Aubrey grabbed one of the toasts, spread jam on it and bit into it. "Yum. Best toast I've ever had, hand's down."

Leah grabbed a piece of toast and took a bite. "You know what would taste good with this toast." She slid her eyes to the fishbowl. "Sardines."

Aubrey laughed. She was suddenly glad to have opened her eyes to Leah sitting on the floor of her bedroom. It was the first time in a week that she'd woke up without spilling a few tears. "Thanks for coming over. It's nice to be looked after, although it does feel a little bit like stalking."

Leah nodded. "Which is why I dropped by."

"Makes sense. I thought you might be cheating on me, it's been so long."

Leah seemed not to notice Aubrey's teasing. "I have a bad feeling. I think I should be your bodyguard."

Aubrey considered the latent shifter, trying to decide if Leah was serious or toying with her. "You're pretty small for a bodyguard."

"But strong." Leah bent her elbows and showed off her admirable bi-ceps as crumbs from her toast scattered across the couch. "Reasonably fast too."

Aubrey decided to play along. "So tell me about these bad feelings of yours. When did you first notice them?" She took a sip of her coffee to hide the teasing smile.

"Monday when I found you crying on the floor of your classroom."

Aubrey groaned. "Thought we had an unspoken agreement that we weren't going there. Neither of us."

Leah ignored her. "And your diary confirmed what I already knew. You fucked Ulrich."

Aubrey hung her head in frustration. "Why does everyone refer to it as fucking? It's not what I did, Leah. Maybe Ulrich fucked me, but my heart was a participant in the event. Therefore, it wasn't fucking."

"Shagging, then."

"I'm not done. You have no business reading my journal. No one does!"

Leah seemed to think the trespass over. "Then why have one?"

Aubrey put the plate with her partly-eaten toast on the table so she could wave her hands in the air. "Because, if I need to look back in time for information about a particular day or event, I can."

Leah pretended to contemplate Aubrey's words. "Oh. Like if you need an alibi?"

"Sure," Aubrey muttered. "Let's go with that."

"Huh." Leah took on that kind of cross-eyed look that she got when she was about to say something that she thought was profound.

Aubrey braced herself.

"So, the shagging of you and Ulrich. That's something you'll forget?"

Aubrey sighed. The Chihuahua had a point. Everything about that day was burned into her memory. "No," she swallowed, her throat convulsing. "I won't forget." She shrugged, trying to appear nonchalant as she picked up her coffee. "The journal's a habit. A record of my life."

"I'm not saying it's a bad thing. If someone kills you, then the it offers up clues."

"Leah!" Aubrey gasped as she choked on her coffee. It was far too early in the morning to be talking about her imminent murder.

"I think Sibyl is good for it. Either her or the vapid Mrs. Blake. Or both, together." She jumped to her feet and paced the length of the living room, hands behind her back. "Why? Because they are both scorned women."

"I didn't scorn either of them!" Aubrey protested.

"Not yet, but ultimately, you will. Your nice little girl act eventually works on all men."

"It's not an act," Aubrey sputtered.

Leah stopped and narrowed her eyes at Aubrey. "You're not fooling anyone, you harlot."

She resumed her pacing as Aubrey rolled her eyes to the ceiling.

"They'll use each other as alibis, and their husbands will back them up."

"Stop. Leah, just stop." Aubrey was on her feet, her hands on her hips. "Sibyl is Ulrich's *ex-wife,* and they share a son! And Mr. Blake would have to be the last man on earth before—"

"Aha," Leah exclaimed, pointing her finger at Aubrey. "So you admit you find him attractive."

Aubrey dropped her head to her chest. "Exactly how long were you in my bedroom before I woke up?"

Leah shrugged as she returned to the couch. "Long enough to know you drool in your sleep."

Aubrey followed Leah's lead, picking up her now-cold coffee. "You don't understand boundaries, Leah."

Leah twisted her lips as she held Aubrey's gaze. "That's where you're wrong, Ms. Powell. I understand boundaries well enough. I don't respect them."

Aubrey slammed the last of her coffee, then flounced off the couch, grabbing Leah's coffee cup and taking it into the kitchen. "Why, Leah? It's not endearing."

"Why not? I don't kiss and tell."

"Yes, you do." Aubrey focused her attention on refilling the coffee cups. "You told everyone about Eva's pregnancy."

Leah raised her eyebrows. "I thought we already discussed that. And to be fair, I was merely stating a thought that came to me out of thin air. It was nothing concrete and if Eva hadn't overreacted, no one would've been the wiser."

Aubrey exhaled a heavy breath as she handed Leah her coffee and reseated herself. "So what's the benefit of reading my journal?"

"I wanted to know. If I don't know, how can I protect you?"

"Know what?" Aubrey huffed out a frustrated breath. "And I don't need you to protect me!"

Leah tilted her head, her brown eyes wide and piercing. "Yes, you do. I'm having one of those thoughts of mine."

"Maybe it's because the air in your head is so thin."

"Nice one!" Laughter spilled from Leah's lips.

Aubrey rolled her eyes and changed the subject. This was not how she envisioned her weekend starting.

AFTER LEAH LEFT, Aubrey cleaned up the breakfast dishes and settled down to grade papers. The short story assignment couldn't hold her attention as her mind kept wandering to Leah's assertion that she was in danger.

At least Leah hadn't mentioned the serial killer as a possible suspect. And Mrs. Blake was not even a remote possibility. Aubrey was small, but mighty and she was certain she could take Mrs. Blake if it came down to it. But Clayton Blake? Blech. He might be good looking but had the personality of a slug.

That left Sibyl, but Ulrich's ex-wife was barely a foot note in her journal.

Sibyl, ex-wife of UC is coming to town to see Tag.

No asides or editorializing. Aubrey didn't like sharing her feelings with anyone, not even a private journal. Well, not-so-private journal thanks to Leah. Just the facts so if she needed to, she could refer back.

She glanced at the last week of her journal.

Friday: *Car died. Ulrich drove me home. We made love and then he left. No promises.*

Sounded clinical. Sounded like it was just a fuck.

Saturday: *Got groceries. Confirmation that car can't be fixed. Skipped girl's night out at Becker's.*

Monday: *Okay day until Ulrich came by. TC's mother, Sibyl, will visit. Had dinner with Leah at Becker's. She had a bruise on her cheek.*

Aubrey wondered what Leah thought of that entry. Tuesday was mundane and Wednesday, while not glossed over, was brief. *Harvest Moon Celebrations in school. TC fell and hurt his head. Took him to hospital. Jared Cooper the attending physician. UC arrived along with RCMP Chief JH.*

Her journal was an observer's record of her life. Nothing more. Her feelings were safely hidden.

She closed the notebook, then hid it under a pile of scarves in a wicker basket on a high shelf in her bedroom closet. Leah would probably find it anyway, but at least Aubrey could say she made the effort.

Sibyl was coming in today. Flying in, according to Tag, who on Friday, when he returned to school, made it a point to let Aubrey know how excited he and his dad were over her impending visit.

You broke up with him, Aubrey. He stood there in your apartment offering you everything you wanted, and you turned him down.

Stupid, stupid woman.

But also, not. She hadn't lied to Ulrich. Only the very worst of things could make her cry, and he managed to do it without much effort. And not once, but multiple times. He wasn't good for her. They weren't good for each other.

The memory of Friday popped into her head. Of Tag by her desk, telling her about his mom. She should console herself with the fact that he was comfortable enough to talk to her, but she knew his motive was far less than noble.

He'd wanted to hammer home that Sibyl was his mother. Sibyl was coming to town to be with him and his dad.

Aubrey forgave him because Tag was so much like Aubrey when she had been his age. He was a kid battered by life, who had a survival instinct that he clumsily used to ensure his needs were met. Leah had said that women didn't need men, they wanted them. The same thing could be said about men needing woman, but it didn't apply to children. Tag needed his mother until he didn't. Until she let him down one too many times.

Which is why Aubrey's existence threatened him. He was making her the villain in the so-called triangle, even though she was certain that, deep down, he knew she had nothing to do with the breakdown of his parents' marriage.

She sighed as she checked the meets expectation box on the performance scale, then picked up the highlighter, stroking it across the performance statements. Her mind wandered to Sibyl as she stapled the scale to the essay and set it on the *complete* pile.

Ulrich's ex-wife was flying in today. The woman who had stolen his son and kept him for a year and a half. Yet Ulrich was still opening his door to her for Tag's sake. He was far more generous than she could ever be in the same circumstances.

Speaking of open doors, Aubrey wondered where Sibyl would be staying? At one of the two Motels in Darkness Falls? Or the Darkness Falls Inn, a big bed and breakfast on the outskirts of town?

Or Ulrich's?

She dismissed the Inn – it was situated across town from Ulrich's house and Darkness Falls was big enough that Sibyl staying there would be an inconvenience. Would she rent a car, or would Ulrich pick her up from the airport? Would he drive her around while she was here? And how long would she be staying?

Forget about her!

As if it were that easy. What if Sibyl lied to Ulrich and Tag about her sobriety? What if she broke Tag's heart again? The boy had been through enough, he didn't need more emotional trauma.

What if Sibyl and Ulrich reconciled?

"Argggh," she groaned as she threw down her pencil and grabbed fistfuls of her hair. What the hell was wrong with her? She shouldn't care, she didn't care. And she was a big fat liar too.

She blinked back tears as she walked to the window and stared out at the fall day. The sun had kicked in full-force, turning the bright sky a cerulean blue. It was like a bear fattening up before it was forced into hibernation. Soon, the gorgeous trees would drop their leaves, the snow would start falling, and the outdoors would become uninhabitable to humans for at least six months.

Get out of the house, Aubrey. Take a walk. Get some fresh air and perspective.

Wise words, she told herself as she shrugged into a light jacket and laced up her running shoes. As she emerged from her building, she slid on her sunglasses and strolled a few blocks to Paxton Park.

The park was an ode to Northern BC, with several acres of trees, broken up by hiking trails, surrounded a gorgeous freshwater lake. Little clearings that overlooked the water were set up with benches and the occasional picnic table. It was an idyllic place to walk, read, or fish.

It appeared that many of Darkness Fall's residences had the same idea as Aubrey. The trails were replete with walking groups, couples, parents with strollers and kids, solitary joggers, some fishers, and a whole bunch of dogs.

As she walked, some parents of her students recognized her and stopped to say hello. It felt right, felt good to be part of this community. For the first time in days, she found herself settled, felt that she could bounce back from her disappointment. That she could survive her heartbreak.

After a half hour walking, she came across an empty clearing several feet from the trail with a solitary bench that faced the lake. It was a perfect place to sit and meditate on the lovely fall day.

And she did, closing her eyes so she could better hear the rustle of leaves in the trees, the birds calling to each other, some querulous, some singing their praises. Distant voices, a child crying. Dogs barking. The gentle lap of water as it slapped the edge of the rock in front of her.

The scents helped to bring it all home. Pine on the breeze, damp earth and fallen leaves – mulch and loam. The slightly musty smell of the lake all meshing together into a harmonious celebration of the senses.

She reveled in the stroke of the breeze on her skin, ruffling her hair as it carried the cool dampness of the lake to her. The warmth of the sun, the powerful living earth beneath her shoes, the slimy feel of coldness against her hand—

Aubrey's eyes flew open as she snatched her hand to her chest to discover a big, panting husky, its tongue lolling out of one side of its mouth. And then its owner, she presumed, racing up behind her, breathless.

"Viggo!" he exclaimed. "I'm so sorry," he said to Aubrey as he came around the bench and grabbed the dog by the collar. "I don't know what's gotten into him."

Then he blinked in surprise. "It's you!"

"Dr. Cooper." Aubrey felt her stomach somersault, not because of the handsome man leashing his goofy dog, but also because of the handsome man leashing his goofy dog.

"Jared, please," he said as he sat down next to her.

She tried not to physically shudder when an unbidden feeling of aversion rippled through her.

"Do you mind?" he said, his warm eyes holding hers. "I can leave if you want me to."

Aubrey smiled to hide her discomfort. "No, it's fine." She paused. "I didn't get a chance to thank you for what you did for Tag this week."

He stared off across the lake as he scratched Viggo's ears. "It's my job. Besides, it gave me the opportunity to meet Tag's pretty schoolteacher." He caught her eye and grinned.

Aubrey felt herself blushing. "Are you flirting with me, Dr. Cooper?" She didn't know where her nerve came from or why she was doing this. Too soon. Too soon.

"Call me, Jared," he reminded her. "Please. I want one person in the world to use my real name." His eyes twinkled. "And maybe. Is it flirting when it's the truth?"

Smooth, very smooth.

"Tag was back in class yesterday, full of his usual exuberance." It was not too soon, she told herself as the image of Ulrich and Sibyl together floated to the front of her brain. Why should she mope around and feel sorry for herself while everyone went on with their lives?

"Good news," Jared said, then paused as if choosing his words carefully. "I had the sense that you and Ulrich Calhoun had some history."

She swivelled her head at him, shocked that he would get personal so fast. "I'd rather not talk about it," she said with frost edging her tone.

He raised his hands in the air. "My bad. I really would like to have coffee with you, but I don't want to step into the middle of something."

Out of practice or what, Aubrey? She attempted a sincere smile. "Our history is exactly that. History. In fact, there never was history." Did he know about the pair-bond?

Jared appeared relieved. "I'm glad to hear that. I'm not a big fan of Ulrich Calhoun. He's an outsider, gets overinvolved in stuff that's none of his business."

She wondered if Jared was jealous of Ulrich or if there was something more to it.

A thought popped into her head. At the hospital, Jared said he didn't know Ulrich. Something like that anyway, but maybe he simply hadn't recognized the name. Doctors were busy people with lots on their minds, so it was understandable to forget a name or a person. Except Ulrich was hard to forget under any context, and being an alpha shifter, Aubrey would have thought that other male shifters would be well aware of his presence in their town.

Her spine iced over at his lie. Settle Aubrey, he'll notice. Goddamn Leah for making her paranoid.

"You okay?" he asked. Yup. Definitely noticed.

Lie but don't lie. "Ulrich and I...." She stopped and shook her head. "You don't need to hear about that."

"It's okay. I get it. You have unresolved stuff."

"No, we don't," Aubrey protested. "We never had a thing."

The small frown tugging at Jared's lips made Aubrey think he didn't believe her. That was his problem. Despite his attractiveness, she already knew that Dr. Cooper was not her happy ever after for so many reasons.

He stood up, wrapping the dog's leash around his hand. "Gotta get the mutt home and head to the hospital."

Aubrey smiled as her stress level evened out. "A doctor's work is never done, is it?"

"Neither is a schoolteacher's, so I've heard." He scuffed his shoe in the dirt and focused on the little cloud of dust he kicked up. "Would you like to get a coffee with me sometime?"

Damn, her pulse was on a roller coaster, ramping up again.

She hoped she didn't burst a blood vessel in her eye. "Sure." She tried to feign interest. "That would be nice."

His smile lit up his eyes. "Great. I'll call you." He looked down at Viggo, who was straining at the leash. "Better go." He gave her a small wave before he headed off.

After he was out of sight, Aubrey pressed up against the back of the bench and took a deep breath. What a weird encounter. Weird that Jared had showed up in the park, weird that the dog had invaded her little clearing. Weird that Jared had lied about knowing Ulrich.

Weird that she was overreacting, that she could admire Jared's sexiness, but felt uneasy around him. Maybe the Harvest Moon was affecting her too.

She needed someone to talk to who wasn't Leah.

CHAPTER TWENTY-FOUR

Aubrey was seated in an oversized stuffed chair in Eva's rustic log cabin, which was one of many that the Lodge pack owned.

Eva had been Aubrey's official first friend when she'd rolled into town to pick up her sister's cremated remains. The day that she had walked into the Darkness Falls RCMP precinct, she had no idea of how important Eva would become in her life.

That day, all she saw was a tall blond, who stood proudly and smiled warmly. Aubrey was immediately intimated by the woman dressed in a uniform, including an equipment belt that held a firearm. Eva was blonde, beautiful, confident, and strong – everything Aubrey was not.

And then Jackson Hayes entered the room, a god in his own right, and Aubrey worried that she had accidentally stepped into another dimension where all the people were perfect except for her.

That day was also the first day she met Ulrich. Actually, it was the first day that she'd ever laid on eyes on a shifter. Grief over her sister's death disappeared as endorphins flooded her body. She wanted to faint, fan herself, and drop to her knees and worship him. Her heart didn't return to normal until well after he left the room.

"How's the fish?" Eva startled Aubrey from her thoughts as she carried two mugs of tea into the small living room.

Aubrey took a sip of the Earl Grey that Eva handed her and sighed in satisfaction. This was exactly what she needed, a chat with her human friend who was whip smart and only half the nutter that Leah was. "Fake Goldie's fine, although this morning Leah threatened to turn her into a sardine."

Eva snickered as she sat down at the end of the couch nearest Aubrey. "What will you name Goldfish number three if Fake Goldie ends up as an appetizer?"

"If Leah eats fake Goldie, the fishbowl will go up for sale. Fish are too high maintenance."

Aubrey glanced around the cabin Eva shared with her mate and husband, Aztec. They lived on the perimeter of the Lodge pack territory. It had been a compromise for Aztec, a place he could maintain his privacy and independence, but contribute to the pack by policing the northeastern border.

The cabin itself was on the small size, a single-story unit that had three rooms: a bedroom, a bathroom, and the main living area which encompassed the kitchen, dining room and living room. It was cozy and warm, and Eva's small touches had turned it to a home.

"You're going to need more space when the little one comes," Aubrey observed.

Eva's eyes sparkled. "Yeah. Aztec and I keep talking about what we're going to do – well I talk, he listens and then goes outside and chops wood."

Aubrey giggled. Aztec was a man of few words, but what he did say held meaning. "Manly stuff."

"He's excited, but we're both overwhelmed at the idea of being parents. I think we'll sort out our living situation over the winter, and then implement it in the spring." She waved her hand around. "This place is big enough for the three of us for a while, especially since one is a little baby."

Dread teased Aubrey's mood. "You won't leave, will you?"

"Darkness Falls? No. We've discussed buying some property and moving closer though."

"Leave the pack?" Aubrey was surprised.

"It's not really Aztec's pack. Neither was the Mountain pack." She grinned like her life was perfect. "It doesn't matter where we live as long as we're together."

Aubrey's heart ached a little at Eva's happiness. "Just don't leave Darkness Falls." She took a sip of tea to give her time to get her emotions under control. "Selfish reasons of course."

Eva settled her eyes on Aubrey's face. "I heard a rumor about you and a shifter."

"Did you now?" Internally, Aubrey slapped her forehead and cursed Leah. "What exactly did you hear?"

"Apparently you and Ulrich Calhoun are an item." Eva's tone was far from teasing and Aubrey knew why. There was no love lost between her fated mate and her human friend.

"We're not," she said too quickly, and Eva raised her eyebrows.

"Not, no more?"

"Never were."

"Leah says that you're pair-bonded."

Aubrey felt a flair of irritation. "Leah says a lot of things. I saw him, I liked what I saw. I had that same reaction when I saw Jackson Hayes for the first time." *Liar.*

"Really?" It didn't seem like Eva was buying it.

"Yes! And Dr. Cooper and the bartender, what's his name,"

"Harris Palmer," Eva said helpfully.

"Yeah him."

Eva shifted her body as she laid her hand on her barely

protruding stomach. "Okay. I can buy that. Young, pretty, red-blooded schoolteacher in her mid-twenties. You clearly need some male attention."

Perfect segue. "Jared Cooper seems to think so. He's invited me out for coffee."

Eva studied Aubrey over the rim of her cup as she took a sip of her tea. "Interesting."

Aubrey went to her insecure place first, the one where Eva was implying that Dr. Cooper was out of her league. "Why, interesting?"

Eva shrugged. "Just is. Coop is interesting – has the doctor vibe. Cool, professional, but Cherime says he's an animal in the sack."

Aubrey wrinkled her nose. "Is there anyone in Darkness Falls she hasn't slept with?" Their friend, Cherime was legendary for her exploits with the opposite sex, or at least had been until Ren, alpha of the Mountain pack, laid claim to her.

"Ulrich for one."

The conversation was right back where'd they started. Eva had some mad interviewing techniques. Good thing she was a cop and not a medieval inquisitor.

Aubrey set her teacup down and scrubbed at the sides of her face. "Yes. Okay. Ulrich and I are pair-bonded, but it isn't going to work long-term because of his son."

Eva rolled her eyes. "I don't like him because he's an overbearing, misogynist asshole, but then we've only had a couple of encounters, so maybe he makes a shitty first impression."

"It doesn't matter what he's like. There's no relationship because Ulrich won't let me in for fear that I damage his son."

Eva snorted. "And how would you do that? Stomp on the kid's head?"

"Are you sure you're ready to be a mother?" Aubrey asked,

completely serious, her ears slightly burning at the memory of tackling Tag to the ground.

She waved a dismissive hand. "Okay, noted. Mom's shouldn't make jokes about violence against kids."

"No. They really shouldn't."

"I want more. How're you going to hurt the kid?"

Aubrey wondered how much she wanted to tell Eva. All of it, she decided. After all, wasn't that why she paid a fortune for an Uber to get her out to the absolute edge of the world? "I'm Tag's homeroom teacher."

"Ah, well that's a bit of a wrinkle, isn't it? Fairly sure Tag would be embarrassed if word got out that his dad was banging the teacher."

"Nice," Aubrey said, frowning at Eva's bluntness. "Tag's had it rough these last couple of years and he needs attention, especially because he's a shifter on the verge of puberty."

"Sounds like Ulrich is using Tag as an excuse to be a MAN."

Time to change the subject. "Putting that aside for a moment, I want to ask you something about Jared Cooper."

"You want dirt, talk to Cherime." Eva waggled her eyebrows.

"I want to know how well Jared and Ulrich know each other."

Eva's eyes lit up in understanding. "You don't want it to get awkward if you and Coop become a thang. I get it."

"No, that's not it," Aubrey denied. "I get the feeling that Jared doesn't like Ulrich much, especially after Ulrich barrelled into the hospital ordering everyone around."

Eva mouthed the word *Wow*. "Need more info, Aubrey. I'm not connecting the dots."

Aubrey stared down at her feet as she thought about how to broach the absurd subject. "Last week, Tag had an accident after school. Wednesday. Everyone was out celebrating the Harvest Moon, but Tag had detention and I was supervising."

She paused to wet her throat with a sip of tea.

"More?" Eva asked as she nodded at Aubrey's cup.

Aubrey shook her head. "I'm good right now. Anyway, there was no one around and I couldn't get hold of Ulrich, so I took Tag to the hospital. Dr. Cooper was the attending physician."

"Okay," Eva prompted.

"When I told him that Tag was Ulrich's son, Jared said he hadn't yet met Ulrich."

Eva sat back. "There you have it then. They don't know each other."

"Yeah, okay. But this morning, Jared and I crossed paths at Paxton Park and when we talked, he kind of made it sound like he did know Ulrich."

Eva raised her eyebrows. "Interesting. Wonder why he'd lie?"

"He might not have lied." Aubrey jumped to Jared's defense. "I could've misunderstood."

Eva narrowed her eyes at Aubrey. "Contrary to the negative self-talk that parties in your head, you're a smart, good-looking woman with a lot to offer. If you have a weird feeling about Coop, then say what you're thinking."

Aubrey threw a chagrined smile at Eva. The cop was one of the most confident women she knew, and had always been supportive, even offering Aubrey a place to stay the first day she arrived in town.

"Okay." She shuddered. Intuition was making her imagination run away with her. "Until last week, I'd never met Jared Cooper. Then we got introduced at the hospital."

"With you so far," Eva said as she picked up the teapot and refilled the cups. "Unless you want a drink? If I weren't pregnant, we'd be polishing off a second bottle of wine by now."

"Tea's fine." Aubrey took a sip of the over-steeped brew and tried not to grimace. "I feel like I'm crying wolf."

Eva snorted a laugh. "Good one. I'll have to use that on Aztec." She leaned forward and dumped a spoonful of sugar into her tea. "You can tell me anything, Aubrey. Anything. And if something's bothering you, then you should tell me. Even if it's just for the sake of good gossip."

Aubrey felt a rush of affection for Eva. It was good to have girlfriends that cared enough to listen to her, invade her privacy, and yes, even read her journal. It was like it was all meant to be, that her being in Darkness Falls wasn't a coincidence but an alignment of stars. That made her think of Ulrich. Yeah, it was meant to be. All of this was meant to be. She swallowed thinking of Adrienne's murder.

How could that be meant to be?

That last thought spurred her on. "Like I said before, I only met Jared on Wednesday, then this morning, when I was sitting on a remote bench in the park, he showed up."

Eva scowled and Aubrey quickly amended to avoid the safety lecture. "Easy to see from the trail but you have to walk into the clearing a little way to get to the bench. I had my back turned to the trail, looking at the lake when this dog runs up and slobbers on me. Turns out the dog belongs to Jared."

"I didn't know Coop owned a dog."

Aubrey shrugged. "I don't know anything about him. But isn't it weird that I ran across him twice in a week? The hospital I get, but the park...." She wrinkled her nose.

Eva pursed her lips. "Maybe he liked you and made a point of seeking you out. We all get a little stalkerish when we get crushes."

Aubrey thought about how she'd relentlessly googled

Ulrich and how he followed her home after school. But Dr. Cooper, she wasn't quite buying it. "Yeah, maybe. But how would he know where I lived? How could he have known I'd be in the park unless he followed me? I hardly ever go there."

"Bad feeling," Eva said.

"Creepy feeling," Aubrey supplied. "With that young shifter girl disappearing, I know we're all a little spooked, but his lie about knowing and not knowing Ulrich weirds me out."

Eva stood and grabbed the teacup out of Aubrey's hand. "Let's go find the Chief and talk to him about this."

"Uh." Aubrey felt herself flush. It was one thing talking to Eva about her overactive imagination, but Jackson Hayes?

"We've all been knocking our heads against the wall trying to find something, anything that will lead us to this fucking serial killer. Anything helps, and maybe it's nothing, but what if it's not?"

That made so much sense. Eva's energy was contagious. "Okay. Let's go then!"

Outside, Eva skipped over to Aztec, who had been splitting logs, his shirt off, the sweat on his body gleaming under the bright autumn sun. Eva hit the jackpot with that one, Aubrey thought. They both had. How wonderful it was when soul-mates found each other.

Eva stepped into Aztec, wrapped her arms around his torso and leaned back to see his face. Aztec pulled Eva in and nodded before kissing her lips, gently at first, then deeper, more sensual. This time, Aubrey did fan herself and didn't stop as Eva returned to her.

"He's hot, isn't he?" Eva said as glanced back her husband.

Aubrey felt lighter as she nodded. Something about the two of them together gave Aubrey hope that she too could find her way to love.

CHAPTER TWENTY-FIVE

Jackson hadn't started the day cranky, but by noon, he was ready to go Ozzy Osbourne on the world. Thank god he didn't have any chickens.

Ascena's phone call interrupted his shower and normally he'd welcome the silkiness of her voice, his imagination filling in the rest for him. However, this morning, her tone was hard and expectant.

"Why haven't you called me?" she demanded. "I'm going out of my mind waiting for some news!"

Ascena was a lot of woman to handle on a good day, but when she was raging, everyone in her path ducked and covered.

Unfortunately for Jackson, that wasn't an option. "Because," he said as he dried himself off, "there's nothing to tell."

"So what! Would it have killed you to touch base with me anyway?"

Screw that bull shit! "This is an ongoing investigation, Ascena," he all but shouted. "And your relationship to Macy Kerrigan, while admirable, is nothing more than an acquaintance." He was being unprofessional, but the woman was infuriating.

"I'm far more than her acquaintance," she said hotly.

"Then what are you? Her sister? Her guardian?" and because he was feeling particularly prickish, added, "Her mother?"

He heard Ascena's intake of breath and imagined the outrage on her face. Ascena was a siren. There was no other way to describe her. Breathtakingly beautiful, she knew it and used it to her advantage to get what she wanted. But she was at most 30 years old, which made her old enough to be sensitive about her age, but not old enough to be Macy's mother.

"She is my friend." Ascena bit the words off, the volume of her voice dropping to medium. "Someone I care a great deal about."

Better, Jackson thought, but knew there was far more Ascena wasn't saying. "Friend, huh? Tell you what. When you're ready to tell me the truth about Macy, I'll provide you with regular updates. Morning, noon, and night. Hell, I'll call you at 2am if you want. But right now, your vague explanation of your relationship with her makes you as much of a suspect in her disappearance as any other of her friends or acquaintances. Maybe even more so."

"You can't be fucking serious." Shouting again and he held the phone from his ear.

I am fucking serious, he thought, then hung-up. Too fucking early for Ascena in a mood.

The next phone call was from Ulrich. "Can't meet today. Don't want to leave her alone with Tag."

Jackson knew who *her* was. When Ulrich had returned to Darkness Falls at the end of summer with his son in tow, he'd made it a point to sit down with Jackson and share his life story. "Is she using?" he asked.

"Don't think so," Ulrich replied. "But that doesn't make

her any less difficult." Jackson heard the frustration in Ulrich's tone.

"Tomorrow then?"

"I'll try." It was the only commitment Ulrich seemed to be willing to make.

Jackson spent the rest of the morning in his home-office, which he'd dubbed the murder room after the slaying of Adrienne Powell last fall. It had been a year, he mused. A fucked-up anniversary that kept him awake too many nights.

He stared numbly at the pictures of the dead women, the bruised body parts, and the mutilations. None of it moved him like it should have, like it did when he first joined the force. He hated that he was becoming desensitized to the gruesomeness of crime scenes.

Each day that they didn't find the killer meant one more day for the killer to strike again. No wonder Ascena was out of her mind over the disappearance of Macy. If the bastard had the young girl, the next time any of them saw her, she'd be on a coroner's table. The chances of her surviving at this point were practically nil.

They had no concrete clues to her whereabouts, no solid suspect.

His thoughts spurred him to revisit the evidence and notes again. He'd done it so many times before it was insanity. Nothing new jumped out at him. Nothing would.

Mid-afternoon his phone rang. It was Eva.

"I'm on my way in," she said breathlessly. "Your house, not the precinct. I think we might have a break in the case."

Jackson felt his adrenaline spike. She didn't have to say what case, she didn't have to explain why she was coming to his house. Everything in her tone told him that this might be the one. The big one.

CHAPTER TWENTY-SIX

Ulrich released a breath.

Today was the day Sibyl was blowing into town. Not surprisingly, she flew. She'd always been like that. A destination person. She chased highs no matter the consequences; everything she did in life was a means to an end.

He was sitting in his truck in the parking lot of the Darkness Falls Airport. Tag was inside waiting for his mother to arrive. Ulrich didn't think Sibyl would do anything underhanded in the airport and he had no interest in witnessing the mother-son reunion.

It was hard though, waiting in his truck, seeing into the future. Already knowing how it was going to play out. Sibyl crashed and burned when she was with him, maybe because of him. Every time their relationship hit the rocks, she would accuse him of being overbearing, controlling, and unwilling to compromise.

Which he was, and yet, over the 15 years they'd know each other, all the times she left him, she'd still come crawling, begging him to take her back.

The first two years they'd been together were good, but as her behaviour got more erratic, she became harder to live with. It was crazy combined with drugs, a dysfunctional cycle on repeat. And now that Tag was old enough, he was contributing to the conflict and Ulrich, trying to give Tag what he needed, was letting him.

He sighed as he tapped his fingers on the steering wheel. This time was different though, even if it resulted in the same fallout. This time he couldn't take her back, wouldn't. Not for anyone's sake.

Like he'd done every minute since the night of Tag's accident, his mind turned to Aubrey. He walked himself through their last conversation again. Could he have said something different, done something to make her change her mind?

Together or not, she was the difference this time.

In the past, Ulrich gave in to Sibyl because of Tag, because there was no other woman in the picture. Even if Aubrey wasn't currently in his life, she was in his heart. Because of her, he understood what it was like to know a woman. Her depths, her heart, her everything. The love he'd shared with Sibyl paled in comparison to how he felt about Aubrey.

Guilt filtered through him as he thought of Aubrey. There he was, picking up his ex-wife at the airport and not once since Aubrey threw him out did he check in on her to make sure she was okay. He should have, but coward that he was, he couldn't bear her rejection.

He'd blown it spectacularly because he was a giant-sized dick. It killed him when she told him he was the reason for her tears. That no one else in the world could hurt her like he could.

He wasn't wrong that Tag needed his attention, given everything that had happened and was about to happen in his life, but Ulrich knew that he gave his boy too much power.

He should have had a man-to-man talk with Tag long before now about his relationship with Aubrey, his love for her.

And they should have talked about Sibyl, about the fact that Ulrich would always support Tag in his relationship with his mother providing it was a healthy one, but there would never be a reconciliation. He needed to put his foot down. He needed Tag not just to understand, but to accept that when Ulrich saw the future, he saw Aubrey by his side. It was her or no one.

The kid had been so excited this morning, talking non-stop about the things they could do while Sibyl was there. As a family.

Ulrich didn't want to rain on his parade, but he carefully explained on the way to the airport that Sibyl was coming to see Tag. That Ulrich's role was to facilitate that.

He hated that she was going to be staying with them, but what else could he do? A hotel was the obvious alternative, but there was no fucking way he was going to let Tag out of his sight when she was with him. At least in his home, he could keep an eye on her, make sure she wasn't secretly using or saying shit to Tag that would fuck with him.

If Aubrey found out, she'd be hurt. He'd tried to explain on Wednesday, but she wouldn't listen to him. In his mind, he saw her again, falling apart over him. Because of him. Because he was such an ass.

And Tag, young as he was, understood the power of manipulation. The kid would've made sure that Aubrey knew Sibyl was coming to town and he'd do in a way that implied there was more to it. Ulrich asking him not to stir that particular pot would only make it worse, because it would give the little shit more ammunition to use.

And the white-haired witch currently walking towards his truck, her arm around Tag's shoulders, looking as giddy as the kid, would always be a shadowy backdrop to any future relationship he and Tag had with Aubrey.

Belatedly, he thought he should call Aubrey, explain the living arrangements. She'd pretend she didn't care, and he'd let her. Maybe she didn't, but he didn't want to take that chance. He didn't want to hurt her more than he had already. He'd call her as soon as he got home.

"Dad!" Tag shouted boisterously as he and Sibyl approached the truck. "She's here!"

Master of the obvious was what that kid was.

He reached across the seat and flicked open the back door of the crew cab. He didn't want Sibyl up front, didn't want her near him. "Put the suitcase in the bed," he told Tag, who was already hefting it over the side.

Like father like son.

Sibyl slid into the truck, still smiling, her mood buoyant. "Hi Ulrich," she said breathlessly. "You look great."

Not a single sign of embarrassment or guilt in her face. That was typical. Even though she'd taken Tag from him for 18 months, she thought they would slip back into the same old dysfunctional pattern of behaviour. Why the hell had he given into his son's pressure? Tag would be better off if he'd never laid eyes on Sibyl again.

Fifteen years ago, he was a first-year student at the University of Alberta and almost fell over when Sibyl walked into the political science classroom. Her long, naturally blond hair was parted on the side and hung in magnificent waves down her back. One side of her face was partly obscured by her hair, which added to her mystique.

Everything about her was exotic from her almond-shaped blue eyes, her milky skin, her pouty lips. She was tall, perfectly shaped, wearing faded jeans and long-sleeved black T-shirt that clung to her perfect tits. She was perfection.

The buzz in the lecture hall died as she paused a moment

and looked around the space. Her eyes locked onto Ulrich and she gave him a bright, happy smile. She headed straight for him like they were already lovers, which they were by the end of the day.

The first two years together were fantastic, but their relationship was a secret that they didn't share with either of their packs. They wanted to finish their degrees, then they'd officially mate and return to his pack.

The plan was for him to take over for his father, the alpha, after Ulrich obtained his degree. He planned to bring Sibyl home with him, but everything unravelled. They'd slipped up and Sibyl got pregnant with Tag, which forced her to admit to her own pack that she was having a relationship with an outsider.

Her pack went sideways, demanding Sibyl break up with Ulrich and return to the pack. Of course, it would be over Ulrich's dead body that she'd take his baby from him. He turned to his pack for support, which spurred one of the younger power-hungry males to throw down a challenge for alpha. His dad lost the challenge and his life, and the new alpha put a price on Ulrich's head should he try to return to the pack.

That was a dark period of his life because he couldn't avenge his father's death, didn't dare return and fight for his rightful place. If it had been just him, he'd have fought to his death to reclaim his family's honour, but with a pregnant Sibyl, he had more to consider than a hostile pack.

He and Sibyl made the decision to give up their packs for the sake and safety of their unborn child. They wed under human law.

Sibyl's struggles were understandable: she'd dropped out of University, lost the support of her parents, and after Tag was born, had severe post-partum depression. Ulrich added to the pressure by entering law school. Their marriage fell apart under the pressure of new responsibilities that neither were prepared for.

Sibyl's breakdown came a few months after Tag was born. She packed a suitcase and disappeared, leaving Tag alone in his crib for hours.

Ulrich came home to a screaming, wet, hungry, and traumatized baby and a note on the table from Sibyl, crinkled from tears that had dried. He had tried to find her, bring her home, but she kept herself well-hidden. He thought he'd never see her again, and then several weeks later, she waltzed into their home, unpacked her suitcase, and declared herself returned.

And Ulrich let her in because she was Tag's mother and because he loved her, or so he told himself. The problem was that she hadn't returned empty-handed, she'd come home with an addiction problem. At the time, Ulrich thought that with enough love and support, she'd overcome it.

He was wrong.

Over the next couple of years, Sibyl used their apartment as a revolving door. She'd leave for a few weeks, then return when she needed money or a place to crash, always begging Ulrich to take her back, promising that it wouldn't happen again.

And idiot that he was, he let her back in because she was Tag's mother, because she seemed so fragile and alone, because he thought they could fix things. The biggest issue, the one he chose to ignore over every other problem, was that she had little interest in Tag. As Tag became a demanding toddler, it drove her away as much as her addiction did.

The final straw happened when she took off for a few weeks, then returned home high.

Ulrich had been in class the day she returned home to find the apartment empty. She knew that their neighbour,

Patricia, looked after Tag, so she had forced her way in, accused Patricia of stealing her son and beaten her up. Patricia was human and no match for Sibyl.

Much later in the day, Patricia's husband, Gene, returned home and found his wife unconscious, his house a disaster zone, and Tag missing.

He notified Ulrich immediately after calling 9-1-1. When Ulrich got home, he found Tag in the apartment running around, his diaper full, his face scored from crying. Sibyl was there too, passed out in Ulrich's bed.

Sibyl was arrested for assault and Ulrich was granted full custody of Taggart after the divorce. She'd been handed down a three-month prison sentence. Once released, she petitioned the court for supervised visitation of her son.

It was granted on the condition that she stay clean and because she was Tag's mother, because Ulrich once loved her, because he was alone, he let her live in his house and in the early days, in his bed. It worked until it didn't. Until the fights got too frequent, the words got too hostile, then she'd relapse and take off.

Around the time Tag was eight, she'd convinced the courts that she was clean and was granted regular unsupervised visits with Tag. She had a social worker who inspected her home regularly, visited when Tag was with Sibyl, and made sure Sibyl stayed clean.

It was a relief for Ulrich. Tag got to spend time with his mother and Ulrich had separation and some alone time to move on with his life.

Tag was old enough to be aware of his parents' dysfunction, but still young enough to tell Ulrich everything. Which was nothing much. She was still the same mother to Tag that she'd always been. Uninterested in his life, letting the television or video games parent him when he was visiting. It wasn't Tag she wanted; she seemed fixated on reconciling with Ulrich. Or maybe it was the concept of family. She spread her ugliness by playing head games with Tag, talking about when the three of them were a family again, raising his expectations, casting her as the victim and Ulrich as the villain.

At some point, she reconciled with her pack, but they wanted Tag too.

Which brought him to his present hell, parked at the airport, his ex-wife sitting in his truck, greeting him like she always did. Like time hadn't passed, nothing had happened. Like they were still a couple.

He watched as she moved over so Tag could sit with her in the back. As he headed into town, he thought of the quote by Simon Bolivar, the 19th century Venezuelan military and political leader.

Judgement comes from experience and experience comes from bad judgement.

CHAPTER TWENTY-SEVEN

Aubrey feared for her life as Eva drove like a maniac. Generally, the drive from the Lodge pack territory was 20 to 25 minutes, but Eva seemed determined to set a new record. By the time they arrived at Jackson's house, Aubrey was ready to crawl out of the car and kiss the pavement.

Jackson was standing outside when they pulled up, and after a brief exchange of greetings, he ushered them into the house.

His home was set back into the trees, and the yard was carved into the rock, giving the impression that the house had been built to fit the land it was on.

They had to pass through a galley kitchen to make their way into the living area, which was L-shaped. The dining room and a cozy sitting area that was attached to a sunroom made up the long side of the L, while the short side appeared to be a media room. A huge deck with everything a man could want on it stood sentinel beyond a set of sliding glass doors.

Aubrey paused on the way to the sitting area to appreciate

the lived-in domesticity of it all. Something deep inside her was wistful and she wondered how often Jackson invited friends over for barbecues. She longed for an invitation, longed to be among people she could laugh and joke with. Bring a salad and some beer, maybe drink a little too much so that she was tipsy and flirty, and of course, at the end of the party, have Ulrich take her home.

She caught Jackson's gaze on her as she turned, his expression understanding as if he knew what she wanted because it was what he wanted too. Someone to share all the good moments of his life. Someone to love.

He waved to the overstuffed sectional in the sitting area, and Aubrey sat down on one end, sinking into the plush cushions that made up the back, the seat too wide for her legs. She felt like she was 10 years old and struggled to regain some semblance of dignity.

Eva kicked off her running shoes and tucked her legs under her as she sat on the other end of the sectional in the familiar manner of someone at ease in the current environment.

"Don't be polite," Eva said as she waved at Aubrey's feet.

"Yeah, make yourself at home," Jackson reiterated.

Aubrey followed Eva's lead as Jackson passed a bottle of water to his colleague and a glass of beer to Aubrey, who gratefully accepted. Despite the relaxed, inviting setting, the intensity rolling off Eva and Jackson fed into her own heightened emotions. A little beer would settle her down.

"Tell him what you told me," Eva said after she took a swallow of water.

Jackson sat in a comfortable leather armchair that faced the sectional with a notebook and pen in hand.

She banded her fingers around the beer glass and repeated what she'd told Eva.

Now and again, Jackson interrupted with a question,

made a note, and then nodded for her to continue. After she finished talking, she took a long swallow of the beer. It was refreshing despite her propensity towards white wine.

Jackson and Eva seemed to forget Aubrey was there as they fired questions and answers at each other.

"We checked Coop's alibi for the two vics," Jackson said, then flushed when he remembered that the sister of one of the *vics* was sharing his air space. "Sorry. Adrienne and Tia."

"Yeah," Eva said with a quick glance at Aubrey. "Both times he was out of town."

"Convenient. Check again, be sure that there are witnesses who can attest to his whereabouts."

Eva pulled a notebook out of her purse and wrote in it. "No forensic evidence because—"

"—he's a doctor. He knows how to sanitize a scene."

"Doesn't explain—"

"—the lack of scents."

"Nothing explains the lack of scent," Eva grumbled.

"I have a theory about that," Jackson muttered, then veered off the topic. "How long has Coop been in Darkness Fall? I thought he was always part of the Dominant Pack."

"I'll ask Gideon."

"Subtly. Tell him we're asking about the background of all male shifters in the area." Jackson glanced at Aubrey, then back to Eva. "Why the interest in Aubrey?"

Eva was writing in her notebook. "Beautiful, single, unmarked, he knows Ulrich's been sniffing around."

Heat rose to Aubrey's face at how casually Eva was discussing her. "Jared, Ulrich, and I were in the same room for barely a minute. I can't imagine how he'd be aware of the non-existent relationship Ulrich and I have."

"He's a shifter, Aubrey. He'll know about the pair-bond."

Jackson's head shot up. "Pair-bond?"

Aubrey felt herself flushing and rolled her eyes to

compensate. "Means nothing. My connection with Ulrich is through his son."

A heavy silence descended on them, then Jackson threw his notepad on the coffee table in disgust. "Psychofucking-path!" He ran his hand over his mouth and down his chin. "He didn't even have to insert himself into the investigation. We invited the bastard."

Eva threw her head back on the sofa and stared at the ceiling. "Why didn't we look at him harder?"

The conversation seemed like an avalanche that Aubrey was responsible for starting. She imagined the public tarring and feathering that might happen before Jared got his day in court. "What if it's not him?"

"We find out if it's him or not." Jackson looked at Aubrey with an intensity that made her shrink. "You can't go home," he declared.

"She has to," Eva countered. "This might be it!" She jumped to her feet and paced excitedly. "We'll keep an eye on you," she said to Aubrey. "Go for coffee with him."

"No!" Jackson put a hand in the air.

Eva whirled on him. "Yes! She's safe in a public coffee shop."

Jackson stood too. "The coffee invite is bullshit. It might be the lure to get her to leave the house, but he won't meet her publicly if he intends to kill her."

Aubrey sucked in a breath, tried to interrupt, but the two cops were standing nose to nose.

"That's how we'll know if it's him," Eva argued. "If he shows up at the coffee shop to meet her, then it's unlikely."

Jackson stared past her, his eyes unfocused. "Okay." He paused as his attention settled on Aubrey, then returned to Eva. "Even if he shows for coffee, it's still abort mission. Aubrey goes no where with him."

"Of course," Eva agreed. "If we can make this happen fast, we might get him in time to save Macy."

"If it's him," Jackson cautioned.

"It's him." Eva tapped her chest with her fist. "I feel it."

"Yeah, and we both know how much prosecutors love feelings as evidence." He gave Eva a hard look. "Everything has to be by the book. If it's him, I want him prosecuted under federal law. I don't care if he's a shifter, he killed a human woman."

"I'm with you," Eva agreed. "Now we have to get him to move on the coffee date."

"I could call him," Aubrey interjected.

"No." Jackson took a swig of his beer. "The killer's profile suggests that he needs to be in charge, be the aggressor. If you call him, it'll seem too forward. He won't like it and might even back off."

Eva nodded her agreement. "I think so too." Her agitation was obvious as she bounced one of her legs. "All I can think about right now is that Macy Kerrigan is out there. Time is something we don't have."

Jackson studied his shoes. "Maybe it would help if Ulrich sniffed around her apartment."

Aubrey shook her head, but Eva spoke for her.

"His wife's—"

"Ex." Aubrey finally got a word in edgewise.

"Ex-wife," Eva amended, "is in town."

"I know," Jackson said.

That stopped the conversation as Eva shot him a suspicious glance. "How do you know?'

Jackson gave an I'll-explain-later look. "It doesn't matter. No way Ulrich will let Aubrey meet Cooper."

"Excuse me?" Eva was outraged on both women's behalf.

"Not now, Eva," Jackson said in a voice that sounded a little too patronizing to Aubrey.

She stood and faced down Jackson. "How about me? Am I allowed to be insulted because you think Ulrich's opinion has any influence on my decisions?" She was out of her comfort zone in a huge way, but she wasn't about to let Jackson dismiss Eva even if he was the Chief, or proceed forward with the notion that she gave a flying leprechaun what Ulrich thought.

Jackson turned his annoyance on Aubrey. "You and I both know Ulrich will go ballistic if he finds out you're messing around with a possible killer." Clearly, Jackson was a stubborn man and despite his position, somewhat obtuse. Aubrey's thought was underscored when he added, "Cooper doesn't even have to be a suspect for Ulrich to go apeshit. All he has to is be male and show a little interest in you."

All feelings of nervousness disappeared and Aubrey channelled Leah. "Let me explain the way the world outside of Darkness Falls works. If Ulrich and I had a relationship—"

"You have a relationship," Jackson protested.

"We surely do not. There isn't one, hasn't been one, and when I look into the future, don't see one." It broke her heart all over again to think of a life without Ulrich, but that was for another time and place when she was alone with a bottle of wine. "I'll do whatever I want to do, no matter what you and Ulrich say." She glanced at Eva for moral support and the blonde nodded her approval. "You can either keep me safe or not." She didn't really want to meet Jared Cooper for coffee, but it was too late to back down. "It's coffee for god's sake, in a public place with other people around. I'm not a big fan of getting murdered so I'll try to keep my Nancy Drew tendencies suppressed."

Jackson hung his head. "I'm sorry." His glance touched each of them. "I guess I'm hanging around with male shifters too much."

"Like Ulrich," Eva murmured.

"Yeah," Aubrey echoed. It dawned on her that Ulrich knew Jackson better than he let on.

It was like Eva read her mind. "I think Aubrey has a right to know what the deal is with you and Ulrich. I didn't realize you knew him so well."

Jackson glared at Eva. "I need a word with you. Alone."

Eva seemed to seek Aubrey's permission.

"I'm okay," Aubrey said, returning to her seat and taking a sip of the tepid beer. Ugh.

The two cops stepped outside on the deck, Jackson closing the sliding door to keep their discussion private. It worked at first, the conversation too muted for Aubrey to hear much of anything, but then the volume increased as their tempers flared.

"I had a right to know!" Eva's words were mixed with outrage. "You shouldn't have kept this from the ITCU."

"There are fucking shifters on the ITCU!" Jackson sounded frustrated. "I didn't want any of them to have a heads up."

"Does Ivan know?" Eva's voice was cool, but the fury behind the question seemed explosive to Aubrey's ears.

Ivan? Aubrey remembered the letter she'd received from the man about Adrienne's remains. He was a forensic specialist with the Darkness Falls RCMP.

"Yes," Jackson said, steel in his voice. "He's the sergeant."

"Fuck you, Jackson. He's the acting sergeant because you haven't posted your old position yet. What are you waiting for? Me to go into labour so I'm distracted from applying?"

Aubrey scrubbed at her face as the two on the deck seemed to forget to be discreet. She should go out there and tell them to lower their voices. She stood up and took a step, then stopped. No, this was none of her business. But Eva's tone suggested she needed someone to prop her up, keep her calm before she said something career-ending. That's what friends did, didn't they?

Jackson's voice was a barely contained volcano. "Not that I have to explain a goddamned thing to you, but I was talking about Ivan's forensic experience, not the fact that he's acting staff-sergeant. I needed a second opinion."

"My opinion used to be good enough for you."

Aubrey sucked in her breath as Jackson replied. "It used to be, Eva. But you've changed since Rusty attacked you and even more so, after you and Aztec hooked up."

Whoa! Mentioning the attack by a deranged shifter that left Eva permanently disfigured was low. And if not for Aztec, Eva might have drowned in a pool of depression.

Eva didn't seem phased. "We didn't hook up, you asshole. We're married. And maybe you're the one who's changed. What's wrong? Pissed off that you didn't make a move on me or that Aztec's a better man than you, hands down?"

That was Aubrey's cue. Eva was about to crack, and Jackson appeared to be about as sensitive as a frostbitten toe. She rushed to the door and pulled it open. "Stop," she ordered in the voice she used on her students. "Get inside, both of you. This is not the place to air your problems for the entire neighbourhood to hear."

Jackson narrowed his eyes at Aubrey but turned and stalked inside. Eva's glared at Jackson's back as she followed him inside. "Fucker," she muttered under her breath as she passed by Aubrey.

Aubrey closed the door behind her, leaned against it for a few brief seconds, then squared her shoulders and marched back into the living room. "I think I should go. Eva, I need a ride."

"No," Jackson objected, his emotions seemingly back under control. "I'm sorry you had to overhear that. Not very professional of us."

"Eva's my friend, Jackson. Friendship supersedes the job. I don't expect her to be professional around me. I expect her to be supportive."

She didn't glance at Eva for fear she'd see a smirk on the cop's face. The jab was as much directed at Eva as it was at Jackson. Whatever was going on was ruining the friendship the friendship between the two and Eva was at a disadvantage because Jackson used his rank as a weapon. At least that's the leap of thinking Aubrey took after overhearing their argument.

Jackson didn't seem to like being lectured. "Nevertheless, on duty or not, I expect my team to maintain a certain level of professionalism." He glanced at the phone in his hand. "I'm going to put a tail on Cooper. And I think we should get Ulrich over here."

Aubrey shook her head. "He's—"

"I know!" Jackson scrolled his contact list, pressed a button, and then turned his back and walked towards the kitchen, but not far enough that he couldn't be overheard.

Aubrey glanced at Eva who was pale and tense. "You should sit down and have some water."

"Yeah," Eva rasped, taking a long drink from the bottle after she seated herself. She patted the cushion next to her and Aubrey sank down beside her. There was safety in numbers, and they borrowed strength from each other.

Jackson's voice floated to them. "I need you over at my place."

He waited for Ulrich to respond, then, "I know. Bring them with you."

No, don't bring them with you! Audrey's stomach turned over a half-dozen times.

Another moment, then Jackson said, "Aubrey's here—"

He was interrupted.

"Eva brought her over. I want you to hear what she has to say about Cooper."

"I don't want to deal with Ulrich," Aubrey whispered to Eva. "I don't want to meet his ex-wife."

Eva gripped Aubrey's hand. None of her friends were touchy-feely except maybe Trist. Aubrey wasn't either, but Eva's touch was reassuring. Sisters in solidarity. "This is a safe place to meet the ex. I'm here, Jackson's here. He'll use his charm on the ex and offend her too. The three of us will form a sisterhood."

Aubrey didn't respond to Eva. Knowing Ulrich's history with Sibyl made it impossible for Aubrey to want anything to do with the woman. Aubrey knew about addiction, had been caught in the wreckage throughout her childhood. Tag didn't deserve what his mother put him through. And Sibyl? She didn't deserve Tag.

Jackson returned to the living room, narrowing his eyes at the two women huddled together like they were grieving Italian wives. "He's on his way, but he's bringing Sibyl and Tag with him. Doesn't want Tag left alone with his mother." His eyes met Aubrey's. "I hope that won't upset you."

Aubrey almost rolled her eyes. "Why would it upset me? There's nothing between me and Ulrich. I don't know how many other ways to say it."

Which was a lie that slapped her upside the head when Ulrich arrived with Sibyl and Tag in tow.

As he stepped into the living room, his gaze landed on Aubrey and she felt the familiar pull at her heartstrings. She heard Sibyl behind him, a soft, sweet lilting voice that seemed both pure and evocative. But it was the vision that greeted her that left her almost gasping for air.

The woman, Ulrich's ex, Sibyl, was ethereal. So beautiful it almost hurt to look at her. Tall and shapely with long, almost white hair that flowed down her back in exquisite waves, she was stunning. She was dressed in jeans and a T-shirt under an open plaid jacket, minimal makeup on her face. The simplicity in how she presented herself added to her grace and sensuality.

Eva's grip on Aubrey's hand tightened and she glanced at her friend. Eva's mouth was slightly open, her expression of surprise seemed frozen.

Aubrey sensed Ulrich's attention on her, but she dropped her head to avoid meeting his eyes. No wonder he welcomed Sibyl back each time she returned to him and Tag. Everything felt like a lie to Aubrey and though she knew it was unfair to be angry at Ulrich, it didn't stop the pain in her heart or the sudden sting of tears in her eyes.

Sibyl glanced around the living room with a smile on her lips. It seemed genuine, nothing in it that suggested she was hostile or uncomfortable. Her gaze lingered on Jackson for a few long seconds, before moving over to Aubrey and Eva.

Then Tag popped in-between his parents. "Ms. Powell," he said excitedly, like the boy he was and deserved to be. "Meet my mom." He dragged Sibyl over to Aubrey by the hand.

Sibyl laughed as she let herself be maneuvered. Even the smile was perfect. Aubrey blinked her eyes rapidly to banish the tears but knew she was fooling no one. Anyone who looked at her would know she was battling with her emotions.

"Hi!" Sibyl said as she stuck her hand out.

Aubrey released Eva's hand and reluctantly shook Sibyl's. Her heart was beating too fast, but for once it wasn't because of Ulrich. In fact, other than feeling deceived, she barely registered his presence she was so caught up with his ex-wife. "Hello," she said, relieved at how professional she sounded. "I'm Tag's teacher."

"I know. Tag and Ulrich told me about you. I was hoping we'd get to meet and here we are already."

"Must be fate," Aubrey murmured as she forced a smile. She glanced past Sibyl to Ulrich.

He was watching her, his mouth set in a grim line, his rage seemed barely leashed. She shivered, not sure if she was the target of it or not.

"I don't believe in fate," Sibyl replied dismissively. "Tag's told me so much about you."

Okay, Aubrey. Use your manners. She offered a quick smile at Tag, who was grinning so proudly it hurt her heart. "Good things, I hope."

"Well, you are Tag's teacher," Sibyl teased. "So he's had a few complaints." She wrapped her arm around Tag's shoulders and possessively tugged him into her. "He doesn't like detention for some reason."

"Yes. I'm aware," Aubrey dryly replied as she glanced at the boy. His eyes held a triumph that Aubrey wanted to wipe off his face, but she reminded herself that Tag was a kid, she wasn't a violent person, Sibyl was a shifter, and she was in a roomful of cops.

Eva seemed to sense that the conversation was taking a turn for the worse. "I'm Eva." She stuck out her hand towards Sibyl.

"Lovely to meet you, Eva." Sibyl crossed all the t's and dotted all the i's. She was too perfect to be real.

"Same." Eva turned towards Tag and stuck her hand out towards him. "And you're Tag. Ms. Powell has talked a lot about you."

The gesture unsettled young Tag, but he clasped her hand as he glanced nervously at Aubrey.

Aubrey smiled. "Constable Blakely-Reeves is messing with you, Tag. I respect the privacy of my students."

Tag seemed relieved. "I figured," he mumbled.

Jackson broke up the meet and greet by stepping up and offering his hand. "I'm Jackson Hayes."

"My boss," Eva said bluntly. Clearly, she hadn't yet forgiven Jackson for his trespasses. "Darkness Falls RCMP Chief of Police."

"I'm honoured," Sibyl said as she shook Jackson's hands. Her eyes swept over him slowly, taking him in the way most women did. "My plane has barely landed and I'm already in such esteemed company." She returned her attention to Aubrey and held her eyes as she smiled.

All at once, Aubrey felt herself responding to this woman, her lips curving up to mirror Sibyl's. The woman's words should have been offensive and coming from anyone else they would've been. But Sibyl's tone held no hostility or veiled insult. She seemed open, genuine, guileless.

Eva stood and made her way over to Ulrich, offering her hand, almost daring him to refuse. "We've met, Mr. Calhoun, and both Aubrey and Jackson have told me a lot about you."

Ulrich took her hand as everyone watched. "I need you to do me a favour, constable," he said in that deep, rich voice that made Aubrey's nipples stand at attention.

Eva remained impassive, but Aubrey knew inside she was a pressure cooker about to explode. "What favour would that be, Mr. Calhoun? And please call me Eva. No need to be so formal."

"I need you to take my son and his mother to my place and stay with them until I'm through here."

That startled Eva and she turned to Jackson. "Seriously?"

Jackson nodded, but kept his tone friendly, not superior. Maybe he wasn't so obtuse after all. "I know you're not on-duty, but Ulrich needs to hear what Aubrey has to say. And because it's related to the case.... You know."

Sibyl's composure cracked as a pout formed on her lips. "Can't this wait until tomorrow?" she appealed to Ulrich. "I only just got here and wanted to spend time with you and Tag as a family." Her voice held neither anger nor resentment. She came across as a reasonable woman with a reasonable request.

Aubrey checked the other faces in the room and was surprised to find that no one was buying Sibyl's disingenuous façade except, of course, Tag. No wonder the kid was messed up.

"It can't wait," Ulrich said flatly as he glanced at his son. "You're here to visit Tag, not me."

"But—"

"No buts, Sibyl. You can't be alone with Tag unsupervised."

"Geez, Dad," Tag hissed as his face turned crimson.

Sibyl dropped her head as if she too were embarrassed by the airing of dirty laundry, but Aubrey knew embarrassment, was intimately acquainted with the hot blush that bloomed every time she felt uncomfortable. And Sibyl was not embarrassed. It was an act.

Ulrich was about to respond when Eva took a step towards the door. "I'm happy to help," she lied. Eva would never choose babysitting duty over being in the middle of the drama, but she seemed to understand why it had to be the way it was. "Tag, grab your mom's suitcase from your dad's truck and we'll head out."

"Nice to meet you," Sibyl murmured as she turned and headed towards the door.

As she brushed past Ulrich, he caught her by the arm and said something to her that was too quiet for Aubrey to overhear.

Nodding, Sibyl's lips curled upward as she held Ulrich's eyes a few seconds too long.

"I'll behave for now." This time there was no hiding the seductive tone. It was meant for everyone's ears. Sibyl waved a friendly goodbye as she followed Tag out the door.

Blind rage roared through Aubrey, at Ulrich touching his ex-wife, at his whispered words, at her teasing response. Fuck her! Fuck him! Fuck them all!

Eva rolled her eyes, not at Aubrey, but at Ulrich as she walked past him. "Aubrey will need a ride home."

Nope! Not in this fucking life-time.

Before Eva was out the door, Ulrich stopped her, touching her too for fuck's sake. "Call Aztec and get him to join you. Sibyl's a handful, and I know you are too, but she's a shifter."

Eva didn't respond to the veiled insult. Instead, she nodded at Ulrich, which surprised both Aubrey and judging by the expression on his face, Jackson. "I'll do that before we leave."

Thanks, Eva," Jackson called after her, but the banging of the door was all he got for his efforts.

CHAPTER TWENTY-EIGHT

After Eva left with Sibyl and Tag, Ulrich felt like a weight had been lifted from his shoulders. It was setting out to be a long fucking week, but at least he was in the same room as Aubrey.

He sensed his mate's anger rolling from her in waves, her heartbeat elevated, her blood pumping too hard through her veins. He was gratified by her mood. It would have been a knife to his heart if she'd been unemotional about Sibyl's presence. But there was nothing neutral about how she was feeling and that meant he still mattered to her.

The problem, of course, was that Sibyl knew it too.

Jackson retreated to the kitchen and an awkward silence descended between him and Aubrey. "How are you?" he said softly. Stupid, useless words.

Aubrey shrugged carelessly, her demeanor contradicting the battle she was having with her emotions. "Sibyl seems nice."

Lying to me doesn't work, sweetheart. "It's a fucking act. She's far from nice."

He sat at the other end of the sectional, the middle cushions acting as a chaperone. If Jackson hadn't been there, he would have had no qualms about dropping down next to her, pulling her into his arms, and overcoming her protests with kisses. He knew, could tell by her anger, that her rejection of him a few nights ago had passed. She was back to wanting him with fury.

Jackson returned with three bottles of beer, handing one to Ulrich and swapping the partly full glass of beer on the coffee table in front of Aubrey with a fresh one.

He guzzled the rest of Aubrey's beer and Ulrich thought he should break the fucking cop's neck for doing something that intimate with his woman.

Jackson grinned at Ulrich's pissy look and wiped his mouth with the back of his hand. "No point in wasting good beer." He seated himself and leaned forward. "Ulrich, you need to tell Aubrey who you are." He shifted his eyes to Aubrey. "And Aubrey, you need to tell Ulrich what you told me."

Ulrich scowled at Jackson. The cop sounded like a fucking marriage counsellor.

"What happened?" He turned to Aubrey, his heart thudding like it did when Jackson had called him and told him Aubrey was at his house.

"You first," Aubrey said softly as her mood settled. Her voice lacked its usual lustre, though.

He took a moment to study her. There were small lines around her eyes, which were tinged with red. A puffiness under them, that seemed almost blue against her fair skin. Her shoulders were slumped, and the rest of her body seemed lifeless.

She was tired, he realized. And defeated, sad. Whatever kind of day he was having, Aubrey seemed to be having a worse one.

"I'm a field inspector with the federal RCMP agency.

Means I lend a hand in communities where there are unsolved crimes. I'm in Darkness Falls to help track down the killer."

Her face registered confusion. "The serial killer? The one who killed my sister?"

He nodded, holding her gaze. "Yeah. Someone with a similar MO was active in the lower mainland for a while, then there was a lapse of about a year. Then another murder near Prince George. I followed the trail here."

Aubrey dropped her face into her hands and stayed there for a moment. Long enough for Ulrich to shift over next to her and touch her hair. He felt the familiar sizzle of attraction and desire, but it was so much more. This woman gentled him, and he liked that about her. She made the world more tolerable, less ugly.

Finally, she looked into his face. "I'm not sure what to feel right now. I understand that you don't want the real reason you're here known, but I'm not just anyone. I'm Adrienne's sister and your... your...."

He cupped her cheek. "My what?" He wanted to hear her say it.

She pushed his hand away, but the pulsing in her body and the scent of her desire was palpable to him. "You know," she whispered.

A moment passed as she closed her eyes, then she snapped her eyes to his. "Unless that's all a lie. Unless getting close to me was part of your cover."

On any other day, he would have found her accusation insulting. If that's what he had been doing he didn't deserve his salary. "I was a perfect gentleman at all times. You were the one that couldn't keep your hands to yourself."

Her face turned scarlet as she risked a quick glance towards Jackson. "Shut up," she hissed, but it seemed to be enough to lead her away from her line of reasoning.

"We're... us... that's personal," he said, taking her hand and drawing his lips across her knuckles. "And we're barely off the ground. What I do to earn a paycheck has nothing to do with what we are to each other."

She pulled her hand from his grip but made no move to put more space between them. "Right. Sure. Whatever." Her eyebrows knitted as she sputtered to a stop. She gave her head a small shake, then locked eyes with him. "What now?"

Jackson sat forward, the bottle of beer he'd been sucking back dangling loosely between his fingers. "Aubrey's turn."

Ulrich listened as Aubrey told him about Cooper, about his inconsistencies, her feelings. About running into him in the park and the suggested coffee date. As she spoke, his beast roared with fury and fear. Fury at her for engaging with another man, fear for her life. And the cop in him was buoyant that they might finally have a break.

He said nothing to her about any of it. That would come later when he took her home. His place. No fucking way was she going back to her apartment while Cooper was stalking her. Instead, he turned his attention to Jackson. "You've had more time to process. What do you think?"

"I think she should meet him for coffee."

Ulrich took a breath so he wouldn't leap across the room and savage the goddamn cop. "Are you out of your fucking mind!"

"I agreed," Aubrey said as she peered at the cuticles on one of her hands.

"No! No fucking way is that happening."

Jackson grinned behind the rim of the beer bottle as he brought it to his lips.

"What's so fucking funny." Ulrich was doing his best not to raise his voice.

Jackson took a swallow of the beer, then still grinning like a jackass, said, "That's what I said you'd say." He turned his smile on Aubrey. "Eva and Aubrey made it pretty fucking clear that you don't make decisions for your little mate."

Ulrich turned towards Aubrey, his wolf urging him to throw her over his shoulder, carry her back to her apartment and show her exactly who was boss in this relationship. But his words died on his lips when he caught the darkness in her eyes, like she was the devil readying to pitchfork him.

"I don't know what the hell is going on between us, Ulrich, but it doesn't matter." The anger was back in the rapid pulsing of her blood. "It wouldn't matter if we were married with six kids and two dogs. It's my decision to make. And this isn't about who you are or what misguided sense of propriety you have. This is about my sister, who died because some shifter thought it was okay to kill her."

Ulrich took a deep breath to steady his rage. "That's the point. The same asshole who killed her might be interested in making you his next victim."

Aubrey shrugged as she took a nervous drink of her beer. "Yeah, lucky us if you think about it. We can stop him now before he kills again."

"Maybe we can stop him before he kills Macy Kerrigan," Jackson added, a grim expression replacing his previous good humour.

CHAPTER TWENTY-NINE

Aubrey had been on an emotional roller-coaster since Ulrich arrived. She wavered between anger, sadness, anxiety, despair, and hope depending on the topic. None had to do with anyone else but Ulrich, who blocked her every time she made a point.

He was relentless, but so was she.

Ulrich pounded his fist on his chest as he made one more valiant attempt to change Aubrey's mind. "Do you know how hard my heart is beating? If something happened to you—"

"You'd carry on like you were planning to, anyway." They were mean words but needed saying.

"That's bullshit!" Ulrich threw up his hands in defeat and looked to Jackson, who had stayed silent through it all. "What're you going to do to keep her safe?"

"Assign a car to her 24-7. Unmarked so it blends. She gets the call from Cooper, agrees to meet him."

"No letting him pick you up." Ulrich, naturally.

"Yeah," Jackson agreed. To Aubrey, he said. "He calls you, you call us."

"Okay." Now that they were somewhat settled, her

growing awareness of Ulrich's sexy body was making it hard to think. She wished he would give her a little space, but of course, didn't want to say. "You'll come to the café?"

"Yes," Ulrich said.

At the same time, Jackson said, "No."

Ulrich narrowed his eyes at Jackson, but the Chief didn't back down.

"If Cooper's the guy, it would raise his suspicions. I'll have someone else on the inside. A less familiar face."

Ulrich nodded as if he was finally granting permission for this to happen. "Don't touch him, don't tell him anything personal," he rasped at Aubrey.

"It might not even happen," she replied. "And I won't touch him if you don't touch Sibyl." Yeah, she went there, but she was pretty much over his bossy-butt attitude.

Ulrich stood abruptly. "We should go. We have things to talk about that Jackson isn't part of."

Aubrey stood and filled her hands with empty beer bottles and glasses, dropping them on the counter on her way through the kitchen. Ulrich and Jackson were still talking, but she tuned them out. Well, not so much tuned them out as got stuck in her head. She and Ulrich were going to be alone together for the first time since she told him they were over.

If she had a wolf, she imagined it would be pacing, excited, and all-in at the prospect of another round with Ulrich. Was she, though? Time and space since their last conversation had helped her put things in perspective. Her heart yearned for him, her body lusted after him, but was it enough for her to have just a physical relationship with Ulrich without letting it spill over into their respective lives? Could she wait until he sorted out his family drama? Was she secure enough to watch from the sidelines while Sibyl played games and used Tag to get close to Ulrich?

She stepped outside and drew the crisp autumn air into her lungs. It helped clear her head.

The answer was 'no' to all of the above, which left her with two options. She could walk away from Ulrich and find someone else to share her life with. The thought left a hollowness in the pit of her stomach. Whoever she ultimately replaced Ulrich with would always live in his shadow.

She glanced back at Jackson who was waving a hand in the air to emphasize a point he was making. The Chief had it going on in every conceivable way. He was masculine, sexy, successful, wanting what Aubrey wanted, and yet, she had no interest in him. If she didn't want someone like him, then the alternative would be to spend the rest of her life alone.

The idea of it broke her heart.

The other option was to lay down the law. If Ulrich wanted a relationship, and he made that clear the night of Tag's accident, then it would be on her terms. She wasn't demanding or bossy or manipulative. She was who she was: roughed up by life, which toughened her up to deal with all the bad stuff without needing to ask for help. But it was a lonely life and she wanted more than a secret relationship with the man she loved. She wanted it all, needed it all. Leah was a wrong. Aubrey *needed* Ulrich, all of him, good and bad.

She glanced at the men again in time to catch Ulrich's scrutiny of her. He nodded once to Jackson then joined her on the concrete walk that split the front yard. "Let's go," he muttered as he gripped her elbow and steered her towards the truck.

Aubrey let him manhandle her, let him help her inside the truck. Even let him do up her seatbelt. She'd throw him a few bones because the rest of the conversation was unlikely to roll out the way he envisioned.

She waved at Jackson as Ulrich backed out of the

driveway and pointed his truck in the direction of her apartment.

"I don't want to go home," she said softly, keeping her eyes down because she didn't dare look at the man beside her. She needed to keep her emotions under control and his eyes were hypnotic, overpowering her will to do anything but jump his bones.

"Where do you want to go?" Ulrich eased off the gas to give her time to tell him.

Where did she want to go? "Someplace where it's just the two of us. Neutral. Not my apartment."

"I can't do that. Sibyl's alone with Tag."

This was the mountain she was climbing, but if she didn't start somewhere, there'd be nowhere to go. "Then take me home. Drop me off and go."

"Aubrey—" he started.

"Make your choice, Ulrich. Make it right now." Less than a minute with him and she was on the verge of crying again. She gazed out the window so he couldn't see her face.

"I can't—"

"Then take me home."

"Fuck." Ulrich slammed his foot on the gas pedal and the truck shot forward. He made a right turn too fast, but Aubrey barely noticed. He was doing what she told him to do. He was taking her home. She wanted to die she was so disappointed and hurt, but the spark of anger inside fanned the flames.

If silence had a voice, it would be thunderous, angry, frustrated. Aubrey bit her lip, dug her nails into the palms of hand, tried to think of something funny to keep from screaming at him.

As he neared her apartment, he slammed on the brakes, hard enough for Aubrey to have to clutch at the dashboard to keep from chin-planting. He glared at her as he spun the truck around and headed in the opposite direction.

The drumming of Aubrey's heart was almost too loud for her to hear him say, "We talk, then we go home. To my place where you'll be safe."

She released a breath she hadn't realized she'd been holding. He was driving too fast, his face etched in a scowl, his breathing rapid. Darkness Falls flashed past in a blur and less than 30 minutes later, after a long, bumpy drive down a barely-there path through unending stands of coniferous trees, they emerged at an overlook. He slowed his truck, then put it in park a few feet from a wooden fenced barrier that had seen one too many winters.

The view was spectacular. Darkness Falls kicked up white water as it thundered in the near distance, a determined and potent symbol of subjugation. It would win because it was allmighty. Aubrey shivered as its power reached for her over the distance, both promising and threatening.

She sensed the heavy blanket of Ulrich's gaze and turned to face him, drawing on the power from the falls to give her the mental strength to take him on. "Where's Sibyl staying while she's in town?"

Ulrich's silence was damning.

She released her seatbelt and moved her body so she was directly facing him. *No cowering or softness, Aubrey. Say what you need to say.* "Darkness Falls is my first real home. I've never known the support of friends or family. I've never had a man love me like I want to be loved. I've never been first in anyone's life."

Ulrich sucked in a breath as he faced forward, his hands clenching the steering wheel.

"The first time I saw you was the last time I looked at another man with interest. I met my soul mate, and that part of me that was empty, disappeared." Her voice cracked and she swallowed. "You aren't the only one with baggage. The difference is that you can't see mine."

She paused to regain her composure, then looked across the chasm to the falls. "I was alone from the day I was born. I got good grades, put myself though university." She lost the battle with her tears. "Buried my sister."

She swiped at her face and Ulrich reached out to touch her, but she flinched back.

Hurt marred the grim lines of his face as he withdrew his hand.

"We feel each other, don't we, Ulrich? I don't have to read your mind or see you in action or even talk to you, to know who you are inside where it counts." She thumped a fist to her heart. "You're a good man, hurt like me over a past you didn't ask for. The difference is that you try to control it, shape it to fit in your world. Me, I float along with my past, letting it control me."

"I'm not—"

"I need to finish." Aubrey couldn't let him speak or she wouldn't get out what she needed to say. "Please let me finish."

He nodded, his shoulders bunched, the tension of staying silent clearly mocking him.

On a shaky breath, she said, "I don't want to be alone anymore, but I won't be second either." Time to draw the hard lines in the sand. She pushed her back against the door and brought her feet up to the seat as she turned towards him, hugging her knees like a Kevlar vest. "You can see right into me to see the kind of woman I am. I would never hurt Tag. I would never come between you and him. And maybe if you let me in, together, we could give him the support and stability he needs to grow up into a good man. You love him; let me love him too."

She stopped, licked her lips, gave him the space to say something. A minute passed and the only sound between them was their shallow breaths. Finally, he turned his head to look at her. "How do I do that, Aubrey? I don't know how to do that."

Aubrey lifted the corners of her lips in a slight smile. "You don't do it. We do it together."

"How then?'

It was about to get real. She laced her fingers together and hung on hard. "You don't put Tag first, you put us as a family first. You kick his butt when he plays the guilt card. You let me kick his butt. You tell him the truth about you and Sibyl."

He ran a hand over the top of his head. "I've tried."

"Sure, you've told him, but you don't show him. Every time Sibyl knocks you let her in." He opened his mouth to respond but she quickly shook her head. "I'm not done. You have some misguided idea that you're the one coming between Sibyl and Tag. You're not. She is. She's done this to herself and to Tag."

"I've had a role in it too," he muttered, a jut to his chin.

"He's not the first boy to have only one parent. Or to witness his parents' marriage breakdown. You treat him with kid-gloves, and he takes advantage. It's a learned pattern of behaviour and he probably isn't even aware of what he's doing."

Ulrich's glare told her she'd pushed it too far. "What the fuck do you know about anything, Aubrey? You're Cinderella, wandering through life, hoping that one day your prince will come."

Okay, so it was going to be like that. She slammed her way out of the truck and stomped over to a dry, bare patch of earth. He stalked after her, stopping a few of feet from her, his expression as dark as storm clouds. She wasn't afraid because *she knew him*. Trusted him. He'd never hurt her. And he knew her too, but he was a stubborn ass.

She pointed her canvas-covered toe and literally drew a four-foot line in the dirt. "You want concrete? I'll give you concrete. If Sibyl spends a single night in your house, we're done. That's non-negotiable. Next, you and I tell Tag that we're together. You let me into your life. All of it. No more second chances or do-overs, Ulrich. I won't be second, but I'd love to share the front of the line with Tag."

Ulrich stood on the other side of the line, arms crossed, his eyes considering.

"It should be simple, you ass!" she snarled at him as she clenched her hands to the point of pain. "You shouldn't even have to think about it."

Her anger fed Ulrich's. "See that right there tells me you don't really get it. You're holding me hostage too, Aubrey."

Stupid, effing man. Were they all like that? "Let's flip this around. What if my ex- blew into town and I invited him to stay with me because my kid wanted nothing in the world but for his parents to reconcile."

"It's not the same."

So feeble. "Answer me, goddammit! The truth!"

She saw the moment he deflated. "I'd kill him, lock you up, and make the kid face facts."

Aubrey blinked at the spurt of tears. "And yet you expect me to be understanding."

Ulrich stood motionless on his side, eye's pinning her. "I love you, Aubrey. Only you. There's nothing between Sibyl and me but hostility."

The line she'd drawn had become an obstacle. Maybe insurmountable.

"Love and reassurances aren't enough."

He studied his shoes. "I don't know how to do this. Tag's been my only concern for so many years. I don't know how to make us happen."

Dammit. Now she wanted to cross the line. She took a step towards it but made herself stop. "How it happens is easy. You let me into your lives, show Tag what a loving, functional relationship looks like."

He snorted with derision. "Our relationship is functional?"

Ouch. "We don't have a relationship. We have to build one, nurture it along, work out the bumps together. And you have to let me into Tag's life."

"But I can't cut Sibyl out of his life."

She hated Sibyl's name on his lips. "I would. She poisons your relationship with Tag."

"Are you sure that's why you would?"

Aubrey let out a snarky laugh. "You mean, am I jealous of her? Of course, I am! Your beautiful ex-wife is staying in your house. She's a manipulative woman who will play all her cards to get what she wants."

"She doesn't manipulate me, Aubrey. She's sick."

Aubrey yanked on her hair as she took a step back. "You're so damned obtuse! She's been manipulating you for years. Sure, she's an addict, but you, mister, are her enabler." She paused because it felt like they were spinning their wheels. "I'm sorry I'm judging you," she said softly. "I can't know what hell you've been through with her." Exhaustion, disappointment, sadness washed over her, and she sank down to the ground, cross-legged, her face buried in her hands.

A minute, maybe two passed, then she felt his shadow as it blocked the sun. She looked up to see him dropping to his knees in front of her. He'd crossed her barrier, but he didn't reach out to touch her.

"I'm sorry," Ulrich said softly. "I need you like I need air. You're right, I do know you. You're beautiful inside and out. When we're not together, I feel like part of me is missing."

She nodded to acknowledge his words but couldn't bring herself to speak for fear she'd say something to break the fragile thread between them.

"You're the best thing that's happened to Tag too. You understand his pain more than anyone else. You're kind, nurturing, and strong." He dropped his eyes. "I'm an ass."

He was. "No, you're not. You're a father who's trying to do best for his son. You're struggling to find the right path for Tag." She wanted to say more, but then it would sound like fawning and he might think she was backing down.

"We'll go to my place, I'll take Sibyl to a hotel. You'll stay and we'll talk to Tag."

No. "You'll take me to my apartment, then you'll go home and move Sibyl into a hotel. You'll talk to Tag about why it's not okay with you that his mother be in your house. You'll be honest. No sugar-coating it."

"I don't want you going back to your apartment. It's not safe."

Her apartment didn't feel safe anymore, but Jackson would make sure someone was watching her and there was no way she'd walk into Ulrich's home while Sibyl was there. "You'll take me home."

She saw the struggle in his face and then the moment he let go. "Can I kiss you?" he asked her.

Her heart jumped into her throat as her blood heated. "I'd like that."

He grinned as he shuffled himself closer. "You really do like me, don't you?"

"Yeah," she said as he half-pulled and she half-crawled into his lap.

His big arms blanketed her, and she sank into his embrace like they were built for each other. A moment passed as he rocked her, which was wonderful, but according to her lady bits, not enough.

"Are you going to kiss me?" She glanced up into his face as he looked down.

"Yeah."

He cradled her head in his hands as he touched his mouth gently to hers, barely a whisper, but enough to send Aubrey's body into overdrive.

She paused to savour the warmth of his breath before grabbing his head like he was gripping hers and pressing her lips to his. The kiss was a tender exploration, and Ulrich opened to her, letting her taste him.

What a bounty she'd found.

CHAPTER THIRTY

The one thing Ulrich couldn't do, he wanted desperately to do. All the blood in his brain was pooling south, making him reckless with lust. He was the alpha, she was his female. He would take and she would submit. It was nature at its basest.

But fuck his primitive urges. Aubrey was a treasure, a fragile miracle, a symbol of rightness. The sappy shit helped him settle. Instead of ripping off her clothes, he willed his dick to stand down, and told his wolf to fuck off.

The peace between them was precarious, the moment easily shattered if he asked for too much too soon.

He was a stubborn prick, a jackass who hated being wrong.

But he had been.

It had been only a matter of days, but it seemed a long hard road to bring them to this point. He wouldn't let anything ruin their reconciliation, including his big stubborn fucked-up ego and the alpha call to possess this woman's body.

He let Aubrey take the lead, enduring her soft kisses and

the gentle way she explored his mouth with her tongue. Her caresses were tentative, the slide of lips along his jaw, unsure. Was she waiting for him to take over or was she simply being herself, a gentle woman who was seeking that in return?

It was torture though and his fingers itched to grab her hair, force her under him, taste her, lick her, make her wild with need. "You're killing me, baby," he breathed into her ear.

She pushed herself off him, putting enough space between them that he felt the air cool the moment of passion.

Stupid fucking ass. Why do you always open your mouth and ruin the moment?

"I really want to know you, Ulrich."

That sounded like she wanted to take this somewhere. He nodded, not daring to speak in case he fucked it up again.

"All of you." She climbed to her feet and took a few steps back. They were still on her side of the line, but their movements had blurred it. "I want to meet your wolf. I want to see you shift."

This time he couldn't respond because his heart squeezed the breath from him. He wanted that too, but deep down he was panicking. She was human, he was not, and his wolf was a beast. It was too soon to do this. He'd scare her away.

"Please." She stood in front of him, looking down, letting him see her vulnerability in the softness of her eyes and the way she clasped her hands together. "I want to know all of you. Please let me in, Ulrich."

He finally found his voice. "You don't know what you're asking." He climbed to his feet and stepped back across the line, this time to gain some distance. His wolf felt his tension, but the excitement he expected was muted. The wolf was curious, intrigued. It wanted what she wanted.

"I know I don't," she said,

Shit, he hadn't expected her to agree with him. "My wolf

is ...." His wolf was what? "He's not gentle," he finished lamely.

She tipped up the side of her mouth. "One day we'll mate, won't we? You'll have to show me then."

If the moment hadn't been so tense, he would have laughed. His beautiful woman knew sooner and better than he did what they were to each other. She'd been the one to kiss him first, the one who opened the door to them, and now she was the one talking of mating.

"Yeah." Clearly, he was no Cyrano de Bergerac even if the nose fit. The intensity of her gaze was too much for him to bear and he looked past her to the falls. The beautiful, mighty, enduring falls. "I'm not sure I trust my wolf around you."

The moment the words fell from his mouth, he wanted to deny them. He was his wolf, and his wolf was him. And he would never hurt Aubrey, so by logic, neither would his wolf. And yet, he remained doubtful. His wolf had been hard to tame, was still hard to control.

He already struggled with his savageness when he was with Aubrey, how could he trust himself in wolf form?

The disappointment in Aubrey's eyes was the catalyst.

"Okay." He backed away several feet then pulled his T-shirt over his head and dropped it to the ground.

Her gaze travelled across his broad chest, lingering here and there as it slid to his stomach. A small upturning of her lips and the glint in her eyes had him grinning. "You're a little beast, yourself," he said.

His reward was a toothy smile. "Don't think you can use your perfect body to distract me from what I want."

He kicked off his boots, then shucked the rest of his clothes, noting that the flush to her chest and face grew as each article of clothes landed on the ground.

He was hard, achingly so and he pulled at his dick as he

watched the colour of her eyes become smokier. "It's only fair that you be naked too."

She moved her attention to his face, the smile still teasing her lips. "I'll get naked after you show me your wolf."

He felt urgency from his wolf, not aggression, but the need to be freed from his bodily constraints. "He's big. Angry. You gentle me, Aubrey, but I'm not sure about my wolf."

She blinked like he'd surprised her with an unwanted gift. "But you are your wolf, aren't you? It's not separate."

"Yeah, but—"

"I'm not afraid."

Not afraid?

He grabbed onto the miracle of the air, the thunder of the falls, the magic of the earth and shifted. It was not painful like so much of fiction portrayed, but a spiritual release, an orgasm of liberty.

Aubrey's gasp was amplified by his wolf's sharp hearing. She took a step back, then another and he almost leapt at her because she was too close to the rickety wood barrier that separated the hard packed earth from the danger of the cliff.

He sat instead. His heart was beating the drum of a beast as her emotions rippled over him. Her rapid pulse made him hunger for her; the need to mark her pushed at his edges. She was there, a few feet from him, fixated on him. He sensed everything she was feeling—awe, acceptance, love, anxiety. But she hadn't lied. She wasn't afraid.

Still, he waited for her to come to him.

The uncertainty on her face turned to resolve. She took a step, then another until she was next to him, still standing, peering down at him. She reached out a hand, waving it under his nose as if he were a dog and she was acquainting him with her scent.

He felt joy and laughter bubble up at her innocence.

"Can I touch you?" she asked as her hand wavered tentatively over his head.

Please touch me. He dropped to his belly and stretched out, placing his snout on his paws, trying to appear as nonthreatening as possible. It was astounding to him that his wolf was so calm, so settled. Never in his life had he felt this serene and trusting.

She sank to her knees next to him and ran her fingers over his coat again and again. "You're so beautiful," she whispered as she buried her face in the fur on his back. A few minutes passed, then she fell on him, wrapping her arms around his neck in a passionate embrace as she curled up half on the ground, half on top of him.

Her body shook as her arms tightened and she let out a soft sob. She was crying.

CHAPTER THIRTY-ONE

Like a typical woman obsessed, once she'd had Ulrich in her sights, Aubrey read as much as she could find on shifters—who they were, how they operated, how they mated. None of it had prepared her for Ulrich's shift.

One second he was standing in front of her, his perfect body making her forget what she'd asked of him, and the next second, he was a wolf. Beautiful, proud, gracious. In his element, his soft blue eyes staring at her like she was precious.

She gasped and took a couple of steps back. She needed a little more space to see all of him.

He was nature and nature was him. And he was hers. In that moment, she wished she could shift so she could be with him in a world they couldn't otherwise share. She desperately wanted to run with him, hunt with him, bay at the moon with him.

She wanted everything that was him. The pull between them was so strong that she had no choice but to go to him. He didn't meet her half-way, but she hadn't really expected him to. He was alpha, she was his mate; she would come to him and he would wait for her.

At his side, when she touched him, he lay down, giving himself to her, letting her know him.

She was overwhelmed as she fell to her knees and embraced him as hard as she could. She wanted to be one with him, next to him for the rest of her life. Her tears started falling and she let them. No hiding now, he gave her all of him, and she was returning the gift.

A minute passed, then another, his wolf's body wrapped around hers, warming her, protecting her. Then he shifted again, and she was in his arms.

"Are you okay?" he said softly.

She nodded, trying to find the right words to express how she was feeling. "I love you so much."

He grinned as he wrapped her hair in his hand and pulled her face to his. "I love you, too. You were right. I needed to do this. I needed to know how I'd be around you as my wolf."

"We can mate?"

He chuckled. "Get naked, baby."

She pushed off him onto her knees. "Not now, though. We have to plan this."

She could see his blue eyes cloud. Something about her words bothered him, but he simply agreed with her. "Not now. Not until Sibyl is gone and Tag understands that we're committed to each other."

She grinned as she tugged her shirt over her head. "In the meantime, let's practice."

He bolted to his feet and picked her up. "I'm not fucking you in the dirt." He carried her to the bed of his truck, pulling the tailgate down and setting her on it.

"We're not fucking," she said as he fought with the hooks on her bra until she finally brushed his hands away and undid it herself. "We're loving each other."

His eyes fixated on her chest. "I don't know why you wear a bra. Your tits are perfect. Pert, soft." He bent down and licked a nipple. "Delicious."

She gasped as he drew the nipple into his mouth, nibbling, sucking, licking. She grabbed his head and used it as an anchor as she burned inside. "God, Ulrich. I'm going to come before we get started."

He grunted as he dropped his face in the hollow between her breasts. "I'd like to see that." His voice was muted as he inhaled her.

Me too, she thought but didn't say. Orgasms were elusive for her and the fact that Ulrich barely had to touch her to bring her to the edge spoke loudly to how hot he was, how hot she was for him.

He stood. "Don't move."

Aubrey watched over her shoulder as he opened the door on the crew cab and fumbled around. He grinned as he returned to her with a blanket. "Here we go." He folded it into a pad, placed it next to her, then lifted her on it.

"Thanks," she said as she reached for him.

He evaded her touch. "We get you naked first." He pulled her canvas shoes from her feet, then bent over and kissed the arch of one.

It tickled and she kicked out slightly, enough to get his attention. "Behave, woman." He didn't need help getting her out of her jeans, and a half-minute later she was naked, her legs spread open, her calves resting on his shoulders as he dropped to his knees and nuzzled his face between her thighs.

One long lick of her sweet spot sent her over the edge. She tried to hold back to no avail. Premature orgasm. Good thing she was a woman.

Ulrich turned his face up, watching her expression as she came. "I could come watching you," he said on a ragged breath.

He returned to her pussy, opening her wider and forcing her backwards on her elbows. He feasted on her, licking her, sucking her, nipping her. He plunged a finger inside her, and she felt herself wrapping it in her warmth. She threw her head back and moaned. He fucked her that way for a moment as her hips thrust towards him.

A second finger found her G-spot and she almost shot off the bed of the truck when he scrubbed at it.

"Ulrich," she cried. "Oh my god." She wanted him to stop and not stop. She wanted him inside her. She wanted... shit, didn't matter. Her body jerked hard as pleasure raced down her legs to her toes, leaving a trail of smouldering embers in its wake.

"I can feel you," Ulrich murmured around her clit, his warm breath bringing her up.

She jerked and moaned. She could feel him too. And his masculine scent settled around her like a possessive windstorm, there to swallow her up, and at the same time, keep her safe.

"Like that, do you?" He blew on her clit, staggering the length of each exhale.

Yep, apparently, she did like that. "Inside me, please. I need you."

He stood and pulled her into his arms, his mouth crashing down on hers. She could taste herself as he sucked her tongue. She wanted more and tried to lick his lips, but before she had the chance, she was in the air.

He slid her slowly down his body as his cock inched into her.

Her walls accepted him in a welcoming stretch and hugged him greedily as her pelvis ached to take him. "Ulrich," she cried as she wrapped her legs around his hips, her arms around his shoulders, burying her face in his neck. Her mouth was moving though, kissing him, licking him, biting him. She couldn't stop any more than he could stop thrusting up into her.

He carried her weight easily, his legs sturdy, his breathing growing more laboured with each passing thrust. "Fuck. Aubrey," he rasped her name, his voice heavy with passion. "I can't get enough of you. I'll never get enough of you."

He swung around and seated himself on the blanket as she brought her knees down on the cold biting steel of the truck bed so she was straddling him. Her brain dimly registered the discomfort before her body took over again. The new position, the way she was seated put him deep inside her, but she couldn't take him all. He knew it, gathering his arms around her waist helping her taking him to her limits.

This time his face was buried in her shoulder, his hot laboured breath warming her. "Aubrey," he groaned. "Aubrey." It was a passionate plea, needy, possessive, promising.

She felt herself coming and she grabbed his face, forcing it to hers, holding his gaze as she spasmed around him.

It was the tipping point for him. His arms tightened, his groans grew louder, and his thrusts increased in intensity. He shouted her name as he let go and it seemed to wrap around the roar of the falls, the cool breeze staking a claim, the rustle of the trees opening to her. She became part of the world that Ulrich belonged to for a few precious moments.

CHAPTER THIRTY-TWO

Ulrich stepped inside the house and headed directly to his bedroom. The murmur of voices told him that everyone was in the basement. He reached to pull his T-shirt over his head, then stopped. Why was he showering? There was no reason to hide what he and Aubrey had been doing. They were together; he loved her.

The world and especially Tag and Sibyl needed to know.

Before he retraced his steps, he scented the air. Sibyl had been in his bedroom, and he felt relief that Aubrey refused to come home with him. Aubrey couldn't have scented Sibyl, but she would've known, just like he knew that at that moment, she was safe.

He opened a window to freshen the air, then headed to the basement.

Everyone turned as he entered, and he almost smirked at the quizzical looks the three shifters in the room shot him, but it was Eva's knowing grin that gave him pause. He was surprised that she supported Aubrey's relationship with him.

"You should shower," Sibyl said in that sweet tone she

used to fool everyone around her into thinking she was a fawning wife.

He ignored her as his instinct pulled his attention to Aztec, the other male shifter in the room. Another alpha without a pack.

He waited for his wolf to roar and try to tear out of Ulrich's chest, but nothing happened. His wolf was belly-up, tongue lolling, eyes in two different directions. It may as well have been wearing sunglasses and sipping a pina-colada on a beach in Mexico for all the interest it showed the invading alpha.

Ulrich did what his wolf was too mellow to do. He held Aztec's eyes, tensing up in case the alpha thought to challenge him, but the shifter stood, nodded at Ulrich, then glanced at his watch.

Eva popped up too. "That was one long conversation you and Jackson had."

"Aubrey and I talked after."

Eva grinned again with a quick raise of her eyebrows. "I guessed. He called to check up on me and to make sure the kids were behaving themselves."

The kids. Ulrich glanced at Tag and Sibyl, both of whom were watching with intense expressions. "And did they?"

Eva held out her hand. "Like angels. That'll be 100 bucks please."

He grunted a laugh, which died on his lips when Eva stared at him expectantly. "You're serious?"

"It was my day off. I was going to knit some booties for the kid." She caressed her stomach. "And I need feeding." She glanced past Ulrich to Aztec, her expression softening. "So does my man."

He dug in his pockets. "You don't seem the knitting type," he mumbled as pulled a $100 from the cash he had folded in his pocket.

She snatched it from his hand. "And you don't seem like the type of man who would take advantage of my friend." She leaned a little closer. "So don't."

He met her eyes as his lips quirked.

Then Aztec was at her side, his hands on her shoulders, moving her towards the stairs. "Time to go, Eva."

Ulrich knew that tone. It was one he called the alpha tone. The one he used when Aubrey got too close to another male. It didn't move Eva anymore than it moved Aubrey. "Just a sec." She peeked around Aztec's body, grinning at Tag. "You shouldn't have made the bet, Tag. I told you I was good, really good."

They disappeared up the stairs and as the door banged shut behind them, Ulrich turned to Tag. "What bet?"

Tag pretended to pout. "I told her about you offering Ms. Powell $100 in the hospital and when she said no, how you wouldn't give it to me."

Ulrich winced. Not one of his finer moments.

"She bet Tag that she could get a $100 from you," Sibyl interjected with a small frown. "And she did, at my expense."

"And so easy." Tag grinned, not understanding why or maybe not realizing that Sibyl was embarrassed. "Eva's pretty cool, Dad."

"Says you. She didn't run off with your money."

Tag checked behind Ulrich, his mood darkening. "Is Aubrey here?"

"No. I took her home."

He seemed relieved. "Eva's right, you took a long time to get home. I'm hungry."

Ulrich's eyes flicked to Sibyl, who watched him expectantly. Most moms would feed their kids – hell, they'd make dinner for everyone in the house, but Sibyl didn't understand her role in Tag's life. For her, mothering didn't come naturally.

No excuse, he decided as he scowled. "Hot dogs in the fridge. Microwave a couple."

Tag didn't like the response. "I figured since Mom was here, we could go out to eat."

The fight with Aubrey had been liberating; it made him see everything in a new light and he finally, fully understood what she'd been talking about. "No. Your mom and I have some catching up to do, so we're going to take a drive and you're going to stay here moaning about how neglected you are."

Tag tilted his head and shot Ulrich a confused glare as he headed for the stairs. "Should I make enough for everyone or are you leaving right now?"

Even Tag had more domestic instincts than his mother. "We're leaving right now."

Sibyl shook her head at him. "Not until you shower. You stink like her."

"Like Aubrey?" He breathed the lingering fragrance of his woman in. "It's perfume, Sibyl. The sweetest smelling scent I've ever inhaled."

He watched as Sibyl's expression changed from scorned woman to understanding and then, longsuffering ex-wife. "I'm happy for you, Ulrich. You've found someone." Such a soft accepting voice as if the shit coming out of her mouth was sincere.

He jerked his head towards the stairs. "Let's go."

Tag was already part-way up the stairs. "When will you be back?"

Ulrich shrugged. "Don't know. An hour, maybe longer. Be in bed by 10."

"C'mon, Dad. It's Saturday."

"Yeah, and last I checked, you were still grounded."

"Fiiine!" Tag's voice faded as he stomped up the rest of the steps and disappeared.

Sibyl turned to Ulrich. "He's such a great kid. You have no idea how much I miss him."

That statement exemplified Sibyl. Self-involved and unable to empathize. "I kind of do," he snarled. "You kept him from me for 18 months."

Sibyl pulled her lips into a delicate frown. "I haven't apologized for that, but I am sorry. I take full responsibility."

Ulrich sighed and headed upstairs, walking outside, and letting the cooling air settle him. That was Sibyl in a nutshell – always taking full responsibility for anything that happened, as if she were throwing herself under the bus for the sake of her team. Except she didn't have a team, she had a pack. The pack was guilty of hiding Tag, but Sibyl was the one who walked away with him.

His wolf fed into the direction his thoughts had gone, waking with an appetite for vengeance.

Not tonight, Satan. "Let's go," he snapped when he sensed Sibyl's presence behind him, so close he could feel her heat. Once it might have turned him on, but now, it made his gut hurt. It had taken one small, human woman to show him what really mattered. And Sibyl didn't. Not anymore.

He held the truck door as she seated herself, then slammed it a little too hard behind her. As he climbed in behind the steering wheel, he was grateful there was a big-ass console in the centre of the seats. It prevented Sibyl from moving closer to him and it prevented him from savaging her.

He drove aimlessly through Darkness Falls, the silence between them helping him sort his thoughts and formulate his words. He needed to focus on his argument with Aubrey and use it to anchor his certainty.

As he crept through the industrial section of town, his attention was drawn to the warehouse where Simon Flannagan had been killed. They were no closer to solving the murder of the mentally ill man than they were at solving the serial killer murders. Simon's death had almost certainly been committed by a human.

Sibyl forced her way into his thoughts. "Are we going to drive around for the rest of the day or are we going to talk? I'm hungry too. Why don't we get something to eat somewhere?"

For the same reasons he was having this talk. "No. We're not going to be seen in public. It would get the rumour mill started and it would hurt Aubrey."

"I see." Sibyl's petulant tone implied she didn't see at all. "She does seem like the jealous type."

He wasn't about to get into it over Aubrey. "This isn't about her. It's about you and Tag." He drove out of the industrial section and made a left turn on the main road leading him south out of town.

"What about me and Tag?"

He pulled air in his lungs to steady himself. "I've booked a hotel for you – you'll be staying there tonight."

Sibyl furrowed her brow. "That doesn't make much sense. How will I spend time with Tag if I'm in a hotel?"

"Figure it out, Sibyl. You were smart enough to kidnap Tag, I'm sure you can negotiate with me to set up supervised times."

"So generous of you," Sibyl muttered. "This is about her, isn't it? That frail human female who doesn't look strong enough to bench press a bag of marshmallows."

"Yes." Then, "No."

Sibyl scowled. "Since when are you so wishy-washy?"

Despite his wolf's urging, Ulrich refused to let her goad him. "I love that frail human female. Besides Tag, she's the most important person in the world to me and I won't do anything to hurt her."

Sibyl rolled her eyes and started to say something, but Ulrich talked over her.

"And you staying at my house will hurt her, even if I chained you in the basement."

Ulrich saw the moment Sibyl snapped; her eyes edged with rage and her face flushed scarlet. "You're putting that goddamned woman before Tag."

"You hypocrite," Ulrich seethed breaking his vow to stay calm. "Don't you fucking tell me what I'm doing where Tag is concerned!"

Sibyl turned so she was fully facing him. "He hates her! He told me how she pushed him over when he injured his head!"

Ulrich didn't know who was lying – Sibyl or Tag, but it wasn't Aubrey. "He doesn't hate her! He has a fantasy that we're getting back together, a fantasy you feed, and he sees Aubrey as a threat to that happening."

"She is a threat! To Tag's safety and well-being, but you're too busy fucking her to get your head out of your ass." She wrinkled her nose. "You're so fucking disgusting coming home smelling like sex and her."

"My home, Sibyl. Not yours so don't pretend it is!"

If Ulrich hadn't been so angry, if he and Sibyl weren't ripping each other to pieces, he might have seen the vehicle behind in enough time to avoid the collision. As it was, he was pulling out of a steep curve, driving too fast and reckless.

Too late he saw the tow truck in his review mirror, too late to swerve to avoid the impact as the driver careened into him. He had no time to dwell on the deliberateness of the action as his truck fish-tailed out of control.

Ulrich tried to stay on the road, but to no avail. The truck slid off the edge of the pavement and plummeted down a steep, rocky slope. Sibyl's scream was abruptly cut off as the truck side-swiped a huge boulder, which caused the air bags to engage and blocked Ulrich's view and ability to steer the vehicle to a stop. The truck flipped over several times as gravity claimed it, then shuddered to its final resting place in a ravine at least a hundred feet from the road.

As consciousness faded, Ulrich thought of Aubrey, of what would never be.

CHAPTER THIRTY-THREE

Jackson woke to pounding on his front door. What the hell could be so important at... he checked his phone... 6:30 in the morning? Groaning, he rolled out of bed and made his way downstairs. "I'm coming! Stop the fucking knocking!"

He pulled open the door and his heart fell to his toes as Ascena stood before him. The female alpha was a mess. Her hair was tangled and uncombed, her face was makeup-free, and she was wearing an old, faded T-shirt and ripped jeans.

He'd never in his life seen Ascena so undone.

His dick jerked at the vulnerable wildness of the beauty who stood before him. He wanted more of that and less of the made-up, perfect woman she presented to the world.

"What's wrong?"

She launched her trembling body at him and hugged him to her, wet tears falling on his bare shoulder. Fuck, he'd jerked off to this moment far too many times, and it didn't seem fair that when it finally happened, he'd have to be a gentleman. "I'm sorry," she mumbled into his neck. "I should have called."

Jackson reluctantly let the lust go and channelled the cop instead. He untangled himself from the beautiful woman and guided her into the living room, his hand firmly around hers. His cock played peek-a-boo in his boxer briefs and he drew on his windwalker heritage to cover his desire. He needed to get himself the fuck under control.

He helped her sit, then sat on the coffee table so he was directly in front of her, not next to her. The darkness of the room and the space between them somewhat helped. "Tell me what's going on."

"It's Macy." she sniffed.

He reached behind him and offered her a tissue box as chills tracked up his spine. "What about her?"

She shook as she dabbed at her eyes, then her nose. "We found her clothes in a hollowed-out tree." Ascena was rocking, clutching her stomach. "Shredded. Blood on them. Too much blood."

Jackson still couldn't figure out what Ascena's relationship to Macy was, but it wasn't the time to press the distraught woman about that. "Where?"

"Near the Falls. Neutral ground but it borders the Lodge Pack territory."

That wasn't good news. Ascena's territory was adjacent to the Dominant pack's and they had primarily concentrated their initial search for Macy on the two areas, leaving the Lodge pack's alpha, Lucien to organize a search of his territory and the boundaries beyond.

Lucien would have made sure the search was thorough, but his pack had found nothing.

Jackson wondered if the area where the clothes were found had been missed the first time through or if this new evidence surfaced after that fact. He'd have to get the alpha out of bed.

"Who found the clothes?"

Ascena sucked in a jagged breath. "Some of us went on a pack run."

Her eyes didn't meet Jackson's and he wondered why she was lying. "At night?"

"Yes. Just some of us," she said in a tiny voice. "The ones that were ready to venture beyond my territory."

Overexplaining the wrong details. Also an indication that she was lying.

"At night," he repeated.

Her chin quivered. "We've been looking for Macy. Later at night when it's safer."

"From other packs if you happen to cross into their territory." The cop in him wanted to yell at her for her recklessness; the man wanted to draw her into his arms and protect her from herself.

He gave her an encouraging nod instead.

"We went to Darkness Falls. We were running the perimeter when we found the clothes." She ran her fingers through her hair, then grabbed a handful and tugged. "Why aren't you doing something?"

"I am," he said gently. "I'm getting the information straight so that we don't go off on a wild goose chase."

Ascena looked like she wanted to argue, but then a shiver wracked her. "I think she's dead."

Against his better judgment, Jackson ran his hands up and down her arms, trying to comfort her. "We can't know that. This is good news, Ascena. We have a location, we have her clothes, hopefully the blood on them isn't just hers." He felt like puzzle pieces were starting to click.

Then his mind turned to the conversation he'd had with Aubrey the day before. Shit – he'd have to call off the tails he had on Aubrey and Cooper. Macy was the immediate priority for obvious reasons, and he needed all his men and women on hand to organize a wider search party.

The information on Cooper was too thin to even put him on the suspect list, he justified to himself. And a hunch was secondary to finding Macy safe and sound.

To Ascena, he said, "I'm going to get dressed, then pull a search party together."

He made several phone calls on his way to the precinct, one to Ulrich, who wasn't picking up. Because Ascena was with him, he didn't leave a message. She couldn't be privy to confidential details.

CHAPTER THIRTY-FOUR

Aubrey woke up early Sunday morning with a black cloud hanging over her head. Ulrich had said he'd call her last night, but he hadn't.

As a result, she'd barely slept.

When she did drift off, she'd had nightmares. She couldn't remember any of them except the last one; the one that jarred her into full awareness. In the dream, it was dark, foggy, and cold. She was alone, bare feet, always bare feet in her dreams, calling out to Ulrich, but she couldn't find him, couldn't see him.

She heard his voice, muted, hollow, pained, calling out too. At first, she'd thought he was replying to her, and she tried to run towards the sound, but then she heard the name he was calling. Sibyl. Repeatedly.

She had been terrified and angry at the same time, but the nightmare felt wrong, like it was real but not real.

She sighed as she threw off the covers, deciding that even if she were able to go back to sleep, she didn't want to revisit the horrible dream.

Darn insecurities, she decided as she fed her coffee

brewer some beans and water and then opened a cabinet and sorted through various over-the-counter medications until she found the pain pills. She dry-swallowed one, then gave Mr. Meow a scratch as he wove around her calves, crying out for his breakfast.

She topped up his bowl, then sprinkled some fish food into Fake Goldie's bowl. By then, the brewer gurgled its completion, and she filled a mug. The first sip led to a protest in her stomach and she set the cup down with a bang, watching as coffee splashed over the sides and pooled on the countertop.

She waited for the nausea to pass, then reached for a towel. The phone rang just as she sopped up the last of the spill.

"Dammit," she mumbled as she clutched at her chest, trying to control the beating of her heart. What savage called so early in the morning? The sun was barely cresting the mountains.

She pulled the phone towards her, but the number came up unknown. Maybe it was Ulrich on a different phone. Maybe it was Sibyl or Tag trying to call her. Maybe Ulrich was hurt.

Or maybe you should answer the damn phone.

"Hello?"

"Hey, Aubrey, it's Jared."

Chills raced through her and her churning stomach forced bile up her throat. "Hi." It was all she could say for some reason. She was rattled by everything. The dream, Ulrich's silence, and now, Dr. Cooper calling her so early.

"I know it's early, but I wanted to catch you before you made plans. I didn't wake you, did I?"

"No," she said. "I was up. Making coffee."

"That's why I'm calling. I have rounds at the hospital midmorning and then a shift in the ER. I was hoping we could meet for coffee before that."

Aubrey hesitated. "Uh...." Yep, she was that clever.

"I know. Short notice, but next week's ridiculous for me, and after that, I'm out of town. And you're working, so I don't see another chance to get together until after Thanksgiving."

"I guess we could meet." She ran a finger over the cool countertop. "When were you thinking?"

The relief in his voice was palpable. "How about an hour? We could meet at Rozi's Café. You know where that is?"

"Yeah." She sort of did, but the Uber driver would know for sure.

As if he read her mind, he said, "Wait, you don't have a ride. Why don't I pick you up?"

Aubrey looked at her phone to give herself time to think. The answer was clearly, *no effing way am I getting in a car with you,* but that might raise his suspicions. "No. It's out of your way and I need to pick up a couple of things."

Fist bump, girl, for thinking on your feet without caffeine.

"I don't mind."

Dammit, no means no, Dr. Cooper. "I know, but...." But what? Her stomach clenched as if it had an answer. And it did! "It's embarrassing. That time of the month for me and I... you know... I have to stock up."

His chuckle sounded so normal. "Okay. I get it." He didn't even pull the no-need-to-be-embarrassed-I'm-a-doctor card.

After a few more polite exchanges, Aubrey ended the call, swallowed her pride, and immediately dialled Ulrich. His phone rang several times before it booted her to voice mail. She hung up, her heart and head pounding in tandem. Where was he and what was he doing? She stomped on the small insecurity that tried to apply an ugly answer. After yesterday, after what happened between them, she knew, really knew, that if he were able to take her call, he would have.

A chill invaded her body as she conjured up all kinds of horrible scenarios.

She dialled again, waited until the voice mail answered, and said, "Ulrich, it's Aubrey." She blinked back a spurt of rogue tears. "Call me when you get this. I'm meeting Jared Cooper for coffee at Rozi's in an hour and...." She faltered. "Just call me."

She hung up then pulled up the contact list again and connected with Jackson. After a couple of rings, his phone went to voice mail. What the heck?

She left a message for him like the one she'd left for Ulrich.

Mr. Meow jumped on the counter in front of her and did a little sensual waltz through her arms. Not now, feline, she thought as she shooed him away.

Maybe Eva would pick up. Aubrey hesitated though. Eva had spent the day before dealing with Aubrey's issues and it didn't seem fair to drag her into something like this, especially when it was going to turn out to be nothing.

She'd wait, she decided, until after she was dressed. If Ulrich or Jackson hadn't reached out by then, she'd give Eva a call.

Her coffee forgotten, she took the world's shortest shower and dressed quickly in clean blue jeans and a nice pink sweater. She glanced in the mirror and decided she needed to wear a little make-up to hide the dark circles under her eyes.

After she was done, she stepped back and examined herself. Her outfit screamed ambivalence. She looked like a woman who was already thinking of friend-zoning the guy she was about to meet. It would have to do. She wasn't a seductress and never would be.

She glanced at the clock on her phone. It was time to go

and she hadn't yet heard back from Ulrich or Jackson. She was getting worried. Her shoulders were aching, and unlike the gratifying pull of muscles from Ulrich's recent attention to her, this was more flu-like.

Damn.

That left her with one option.

She called Eva and then cursed at herself when Eva's groggy voice greeted her.

"Eva, it's Aubrey. Sorry to bother you, but I can't get hold of Ulrich or Jackson."

Blankets rustled in the background. "What's going on?" All traces of sleep from Eva's voice had disappeared."

Aubrey vomited the words. "Jared Cooper called and asked to meet for coffee. I said yes. I shouldn't have agreed, but he said if we didn't do it now, we wouldn't get another chance until after Thanksgiving and I couldn't think of a good reason not to." She paused to drag some air into her lungs. "I need to leave now to be on time."

"Where?"

"Rozi's Café."

Eva was jostling the cell phone like she was getting dressed, murmuring to Aztec, and talking to Aubrey all at once. "Jackson said he was going to put a tail on you and Cooper. Not sure who, but I'll call into the precinct to find out and have them dispatch me through. I'll get someone to track down Jackson and – just a sec, I have someone on the other line."

Aubrey shrugged into her fleece jacket as she waited for Eva to get back to her. It was taking too long, and she needed to order an Uber.

She scribbled a note and left it next to Fake Goldie's bowl in case Leah showed up. If the little shifter was serious about being Aubrey's bodyguard, she needed to up her game.

Eva came back on the line just as Aubrey closed and

locked her door behind her. "We have a break in the Macy Kerrigan case. I have to go. Stay home, Aubrey. You don't need to take the risk."

Eva was wrong. There was no solid evidence that Jared was anything but an interested man, and she needed to know one way or another. For Adrienne's sake. "I'm going to meet him," Aubrey said.

"Not a good idea."

Aubrey felt irritation at Eva. She loved the woman, but Eva was bossy and sometimes too much of a know-it-all. Too often she used her career as a cop to legitimatize her opinion.

"I'm going." Aubrey's heart was in her throat. "We don't know it's him to start with, but if he killed my sister, I want to know." She paused as she justified what she was doing in her head. They would be in a public place with people around them, having coffee. It was not much of a risk.

"Aubrey—" Eva started.

"It's fine. Go do your job and we'll connect later." She hung up.

She trudged down the stairs thinking that this was how all the women in the serial killer movies got killed. They downplayed the risk and overestimated their ability to handle the danger.

At least she still had her tail.

She stepped outside and glanced around the parking lot, looking for a sign of the cop who was supposed to be following her. There was none, but maybe that was the point.

Twenty minutes later, she was standing on the sidewalk outside Rozi's Cafe. The parking lot was empty and the café itself had an air of abandonment. It was Sunday though, and the few times she'd been out and about this early on the holy day, it was like walking through a ghost town. Sundays were for sleeping in, going to church, eating roast beef, and lazing around. Unlike Wednesday, Sunday was a day she could definitely get behind.

Dizziness swamped her as she took a few steps towards the door; her airway felt constricted like she was having an allergic reaction to something. Whatever had been ailing her earlier seemed to be worsening.

She leaned against the wall of the cafe and tried to take a gulp of the fresh morning air. Some got through, but not much.

As she gasped, she spotted Jared striding towards her through the small empty parking space. He waved as he approached. Where was his car?

"Are you okay?" he asked as he neared.

No, she wasn't. "I can't catch my breath," she wheezed as she rubbed both hands on her chest.

He reached past her to the door and yanked on it. "Shit," he swore. "They're not open yet."

She tried to take another breath and this time, nothing got through at all. "Help me," she squeaked as her knees started to buckle.

Jared caught her. "This way." He pulled her into a hug and steered her towards the side of the building.

As they rounded it, he pressed the key fob he was holding at a car, and Aubrey heard the doors unlock. Her head was swimming, dots floated in her vision, and no matter how hard she tried, no air was getting into her lungs.

Jared yanked open the back door and helped her sit.

"You need to call me an ambulance," she slurred.

He crouched in front of her. "You don't need an ambulance. I'm a doctor, Aubrey. I'll make it better."

She blinked at him, tried to focus on his face, but her oxygen-starved brain was shutting down. She was about to black out.

CHAPTER THIRTY-FIVE

"What the fuck are you doing, pounding on that door so early in the morning!"

Tag turned to see an old woman, too big for her frayed, washed-out blue bathrobe, glaring at him.

It was only kind of early. Just barely 8 am and Tag didn't think old people slept in anyway. He was about to apologize and explain the problem when a female emerged from the stairwell.

For a single second, Tag was flooded with relief, but then realized that while the woman had some resemblance to Aubrey, it wasn't her.

It could have been Aubrey's sister though, except this one was a shifter. He knew without a doubt.

She strode directly up to him, her fingers fisted. "I'm Leah," she said as she grabbed his hand and bumped it with her own.

If he hadn't been so rattled, he would have told her that fist-bumps were not a thing anymore, but the old woman turned her ire on Leah. "Another one of you! What is it with that teacher? Is she running a whore house on the side?"

Tag felt his face heat, but Leah seemed unaffected as she turned her attention towards the old woman. "Hey! That hooker is my friend! And who might you be?"

"None of your business," was the snarled reply.

"You should go inside." Leah pointed at the woman's door with her chin. "All your loud talk is going to wake the neighbours. And so early in the morning." She shook her head and tsked. "Shameful."

Leah's eyes travelled over the women, not in any particular order, but jumping from her thighs to her bi-ceps, then down to her calves and then up to her shoulders. Tag found it unsettling and apparently, so did the woman, who chuffed out a breath, then fled inside her apartment, closing the door too loudly. The slide of the bolt declared the end of the argument.

Dismissing the grouchy old lady, Leah turned her attention to Tag. "I'm guessing you're Ulrich's kid. What 'cha doing here?"

"My dad and mom went for a drive last night and didn't come home."

"Blimey," Leah said as she produced a keyring from her pocket and unbolted Aubrey's door. "So you hurried over here because Aubrey is big and strong with the nose of a bloodhound."

She pushed open the door to the shadowy apartment and stepped inside like she lived there.

Tag trailed behind, feeling defensive. "She's the only one I know who can help me find Dad."

Leah seemed to bop as she walked through the apartment, checking the rooms as she went. A cat snuck through Tag's legs and he made a futile grab to stop it from escaping.

"Don't bother," Leah said as she came to a halt in front of a fishbowl and stirred the water with her finger. "Cats are the devil's nursemaids. Aubrey's better off without it."

Tag didn't know what to say to this strange female, who had stopped moving, her back towards him. He waited, his blood pumping with adrenaline, then he decided to leave.

"Stop," Leah commanded before he moved, her back still to him. "You didn't tell me why you thought Aubrey could help."

Tag huffed out a breath. "I don't really have time for this."

She turned then, her brown eyes measuring him. "But you have time to run around town without a car, looking for a human female you don't know well enough to know where she'd be on a Sunday morning at 8 am, all because you think she can find your father?"

Tag sighed his impatience. "No, but you're not helping."

"Why?" Leah asked.

He flung his hands in the air. "I don't know why you're not helping!"

She grinned like she appreciated his response. "Why do you think Aubrey can help you find your dad?"

Fine. She wanted him to say it, he'd say it. "They're pair-bonded!" he exclaimed. "She'll know where to go."

Leah was still smirking as she approached him. "See, that wasn't so hard, was it?" She bopped into the hall, then waved for him to join her.

"Do have your driver's licence?" she asked as she locked Aubrey's apartment door.

Tag wrinkled his nose. "I'm only twelve."

She turned towards him, clearly confused. "I asked if you had a driver's licence, not how old you were."

He tracked her as she headed down the stairs. "No. I don't have a driver's licence." He couldn't believe he was following the crazy female.

She grimaced. "Damn it. The bleeding cops took my licence, so I'm not supposed to be driving either."

Tag blinked at the bright day as he exited the building,

then followed Leah over to a monster of a truck. It was a four-wheel drive Dodge Ram, so big it dwarfed both of them.

"Since neither of us have licences, I guess we'll have to share the driving."

Tag was losing his patience. "I. Can't. Drive. I don't know how!" He raised his voice deciding that crazy was Leah's first language, not English.

OH! Leah mouthed, her expression one of exaggerated understanding. "Why didn't you say so? I guess I'll have to drive." She unlocked the truck with the fob. "Get in," she motioned with her head, then heaved herself up behind the steering wheel.

Tag skirted the truck and got in the passenger side, doing up his seatbelt as he looked over at the woman whose feet barely reached the gas pedal. "This is your truck?" he asked as she started it up.

Leah shook her head. "Nope. Don't own one. Borrowed it."

"From who?"

She looked over at him. "Ever been handcuffed, kid?" She shoved the truck into gear.

"No." Tag grimaced and grabbed at the dashboard as the truck lurched forward.

"Then better you don't know the details." She ground the gears again and the truck bucked like a wild horse before it shuddered and stalled.

"Tabernacle!"

Tag closed his eyes and searched for his patience. "I know French swearwords."

"Mothertrucker! I don't like to swear in front of children." Leah twisted the key to restart the truck.

"I'm not a child!" He hated when people called him that. He was twelve going on thirteen. He wasn't a kid anymore.

"Then why can't you drive?" Leah countered as she slipped

to the edge of the seat so her foot could better touch the pedal.

"Why can't *you* drive?"

She slumped her shoulders and looked over at him. "Because I am a child." She waved her hand over herself. "Look at me, Peter Pan. I never grew up."

Tag took a long look at her, trying to decide if she was lying. She had boobs, kind of small, but that didn't matter to him. Boobs were boobs. He liked them all. She was definitely older than he was by a long-shot. Kids didn't talk the way she did, especially to old people like the granny back at the apartment.

He decided to change the subject, moving his attention to her right hand, which was tightly curled around the gear stick. "Do you even know how to drive a standard?"

She shoved the stick into second and let the truck roll forward. "Not really. Why do you think I wanted you to drive?"

Tag rolled his eyes as he reached for the door handle. "Maybe I should walk."

"Walk where? You don't know where you're going."

Finally, the truck was in motion. She ground the gears as she shoved it into third, aiming for the parking lot's exit. When she reached it, she squealed the tires into a right turn, fish-tailing before she straightened out.

"And you do?" Tag clung to the dash thankful that it was Sunday and still too early for there to be much traffic.

"Yep. She at Rozi's Cafe having coffee."

Tag's jaw dropped. "How do you know that?"

"Heyzues, you ask a lot of questions."

The truck chugged along the road at about 30 kilometres an hour, which would have been okay had it been a school day and had they been in a school zone. As it was, the few cars that passed them were going double the speed.

Tag rolled his eyes. "Tell me how you know."

She returned the gesture, then braked slightly and made another hard fast right. "She left a note next to the sushi bowl." She dug a crumpled piece of paper from her pocket and handed it to Tag.

He smoothed it out.

Leah,

Gone for coffee at Rozi's with Jared Cooper. Can't get hold of Ulrich and Jackson's not picking up either. Need somebody.

Aubrey.

Tag furrowed his eyebrows. "Why is she having coffee with Dr. Cooper?"

Leah grinned smugly, like she had a secret she wasn't sharing. "You sound jealous, kid."

He wasn't jealous! "My dad likes her. She shouldn't be messing around on him."

"Thought your mom and dad were together."

Tag thumped his back against the seat. "They're not. Not really." Tears started in his eyes and he tried to hold on to them. He didn't want Leah to think he was a baby.

"Listen." Her voice softened, and for a moment, she almost sounded like a real adult. "Let's shelve your dad and mom for a moment. I clucked up and let Aubrey out of my sight. Look at the note again. *She needs somebody*."

"You?"

"Us."

Another couple of pant-peeing turns and they were finally at the café. Leah tried to stop the truck, but it rolled past the building, finally coming to a rest when it bounced off a curb. It bucked once, then died. Leah puffed out a relieved breath. "Next time I steal a trucking truck, remind me to get one that's an automatic."

Her confession barely registered with Tag. "There she is," he yelled as he scrambled out of his seat-belt.

Aubrey was in an isolated part of the lot, sitting in the back seat of a car, legs outside, her head hanging down as Dr. Cooper crouched in front of her.

She looked like she wasn't able to catch her breath, and that scared him worse than his dad and mom being missing.

Leah zipped by him, barrelling towards the car. "Aubrey!" she shouted.

Dr. Cooper startled, then stood as Leah elbowed her way in, dropping to her knees in front of Aubrey.

"What's wrong with her?" Tag asked as he ran up.

Leah grabbed Aubrey's bicep's and peered into her face. "Breathe, you two-bit hooker. C'mon!"

"Jesus, Leah," Dr. Cooper snapped. "What's wrong with you? I'm the fucking doctor here."

Aubrey sharply inhaled, then took another deep gulp as Leah glared at Dr. Cooper. "Watch your language around the kid."

Tag was irritated by being called a kid, but he was more worried about Aubrey. "Is she okay?"

Aubrey coughed and pushed Leah off her. "I'm okay," she choked.

Relief rippled through Tag. "Why are you having coffee with Dr. Cooper?" Maybe he was wrong about his teacher and his dad. Maybe it was just his dad interested.

"It's what grown-ups do, Tag." Leah widened her eyes at him as if to tell him to shut it.

He widened his eyes back at her. *You shut it.* "What's wrong with her?"

"Panic attack," Dr. Cooper diagnosed. "We were about to go inside when she started to feel faint. I got her over here and was trying to get her to breathe."

"Why're you having a panic attack?" Leah addressed Aubrey directly.

Tag knew why and, in that moment, he felt like he was

going to barf. "Because something bad's happened to my mom and dad."

He spun around so his back was to the adults while he tried not to cry.

"Hey, Tag." It was Aubrey, on her feet, her hands on his shoulders, comforting him. "You might be right. My stomach's been churning all morning."

CHAPTER THIRTY-SIX

Aubrey had thought her interspersed moments of nausea had more to do with having coffee with Jared and all the related possibilities, but now realized what Tag already knew. Ulrich was in trouble.

The panic attack made far more sense in that context. It had to be the pair-bond because she'd never in her life had a panic attack and there'd been plenty in her past to panic over.

She stood for a moment with her hands on Tag's shoulders, lightly squeezing him. It was clear he was trying to hold it together and failing. "How long have they been gone?"

He turned towards her, his eyes seeking hers, a narrow pinprick of a bubble, everything else fading. "Since last night. After he left you, he came home and told Mom that they needed to talk." His voice cracked and his eyes hooded. "I fell asleep and when I woke up, they weren't home yet."

Leah stepped into the circle. "Not your fault, kid. You've got plenty enough to feel guilty about, so don't focus on the wrong thing."

Aubrey glanced at Leah not sure whether to be irritated at

Leah's approach or grateful that she was sensitive enough to reach out to Tag. "Walk us through it, Tag."

He scuffed at the gravel under his feet. "Dad came home and said that he and Mom were going to take a drive."

"Okay." Aubrey felt Jared's heat at her back as he shuffled closer. Between his presence and Ulrich's disappearance, it took all the effort she had not to freak out. "What time did they leave?"

Tag scrunched up his face. "I guess it was around seven. He got home, paid Eva, and then told me that he and Mom needed some alone time."

"He paid Eva?" Leah, of course. "What'd she do? Give him a lap dance?"

Aubrey flicked her hand at Leah like she was shooing away a pesky mosquito. "So they left. When did your dad say they'd be back?"

"He said he'd be an hour, maybe longer. I waited, then I fell asleep playing video games." He lost his battle with his composure and swiped impatiently at the tears on his cheeks.

Aubrey wanted to share Tag's misery but had to hold it together for his sake. Even so, she felt herself splintering. What if the talk had gone sideways? What if Sibyl had lost her mind? An image of blood spurting from the aorta artery in Ulrich's neck made her stomach somersault and she took a few quick steps away from the huddle in case she vomited.

"Easy, big guy. We'll call the police." Jared moved next to Aubrey and rubbed small circles on her back. Terror and revulsion invaded her body.

Intended or serendipitous, relief washed over Aubrey when Tag inserted himself between the two, forcing Jared away from her. "We can't wait for them. We gotta go now!"

Leah nodded her head as she addressed Aubrey. "Better we do this ourselves. We'll find him faster than the cops because you two are pair-bonded."

Aubrey agreed but for difference reasons. The cops were otherwise occupied and even though Jackson knew about Ulrich and Sibyl's troubled relationship, Macy's disappearance trumped a divorced couple who weren't yet missing 24-hours.

"It's true." Tag threw a quick glance at Leah before returning his attention to Aubrey. "And I'm his kid. I'll know when he's nearby. If you call the cops, they'll get in our way and won't let you get involved."

"Okay," Aubrey said. "That makes sense, but I don't know where to start. Where do we start, Tag?"

"I know my dad, where he'll go. Darkness falls. He loves it out there."

Aubrey felt her back go up. "And that's where he'd take your mother?"

She could almost see Tag's thoughts bouncing around inside his skull. "Maybe. No. I don't know. He finds it peaceful out there, it helps him when he gets pissed off." He held Aubrey's eyes. "It's not romantic."

If the situation hadn't been so dire, she would have laughed out loud. It was certainly romantic yesterday afternoon. "Okay, let's go." Then she cursed. Yup, the F-bomb and in front of a student. She could almost here Mr. Blake saying, *Have you no shame, Ms. Powell?*

"Sorry," she said to Tag.

He didn't seem fazed by her potty mouth. "What's wrong?"

She turned to Leah. "How'd you get here?"

Leah threw a thumb over her shoulder to a huge 4-wheel drive truck haphazardly parked next to the curb. "Can't take that unless you can drive a stick."

Jared cleared his throat. "I'll drive."

Aubrey didn't want him to, didn't want any of them to get into the car with him. "You have rounds."

"Don't be ridiculous," Leah said as she slipped into the

back seat of Jared's car. "This is more important than senior citizens who can't poop." She motioned with her hand for Tag to join her in the back. To Aubrey she said, "You ride shotgun so you can direct Coop."

It seemed odd that Leah didn't sense danger around Jared. That and the fact that Tag and Leah were already in the back-seat, doors closed, seat belts on, waiting expectedly, helped make up her mind. "Thanks for doing this," she murmured to Jared as he opened the door for her. "It might be nothing at all."

"Let's hope it is," he said, a grim set to his lips. "But if he and his wife are hurt, I'll be there to help."

"Ex-wife," Aubrey muttered as she slid into the passenger seat.

Jared started the car and backed out of the parking lot, putting it in drive and heading north towards the falls.

It was the wrong way. Aubrey didn't know how she knew it, beyond the almost physical pull she had. "The other way," she said.

She twisted in her seat to look at Tag, who nodded.

Jared turned the car around and made his way to the main highway leading south out of Darkness Falls.

Aubrey closed her eyes to concentrate. Dread grew like a storm in the pit of her stomach every kilometre they passed until tears fell from her eyes.

"What's wrong?" Jared said when he saw her crying.

"It's bad," Leah replied from the backseat. She shuddered, then reached for Tag's hand. "When we get there," she said to him, "you'll need to hold it together. No hysterics."

Twenty minutes passed in silence. All Aubrey could hear was their collective breathing; all she could see was a haze of pain behind her eyelids. All she could feel was a growing pit of despair.

"Here," she gasped as her eyes flew open. Her stomach

dropped when she saw where they were. The road curved sharply and there was a steep drop-off to the right. Tire marks marred the pavement, pointing the way to the bank where a vehicle had gone over.

Jared braked quickly and swerved the car over to the side of the road.

Aubrey's tears dried up as she scrambled out of the car and headed down the steep slope, Tag and Leah on her heels. She could see Ulrich's truck laying at the bottom of the ravine, a twisted mass of broken steel.

"Slow down!" Jared called from above, standing next to the open trunk of his car. "If they're alive, then a few more minutes won't kill them." He didn't say the if-they're-dead part, and Aubrey felt grateful for it.

Against her instincts and panic, she forced herself to descend more carefully. "He's right," she said to Tag who trotted by her. "Dr. Cooper will have his hands full without having to fix us up too."

Leah was on Tag's heels and righted Aubrey when she almost tripped. Her face was pale, the lines of her lips grim. "He's okay," she said. "You'd know if he wasn't."

Aubrey's felt the twist in her gut as she watched Tag scramble ahead of her. "But what if she's not? We shouldn't have let Tag come with us."

"Too late, now," Leah mumbled then moved ahead of Aubrey. "We're shifters. Nimbler than you. I'll catch up to the kid and slow him down."

It took Aubrey 10 minutes to pick her way to the bottom. By the time the ground evened out, she was panicking. Ulrich's truck was nothing but a twisted mass of metal. The windshield was broken, and the airbags prevented her from seeing inside.

She didn't have to, though because the bodies weren't in the truck. Sibyl was huddled on the ground several feet from the truck, Jared already next to her while his hands roved over her. Tag was kneeling by Ulrich's prone body, which was next to the truck, tears scoring his face.

Aubrey's heart skipped a beat. He couldn't be dead. Please don't let him be dead. She scrambled over to Ulrich as he lay on his back, his blue eyes open, staring at the matching blue sky.

"No!" she cried as she dropped to her knees. "Ulrich, no!"

"He's okay," Tag said as shuffled closer and folded an arm around her shoulders. "Look." He pointed to Ulrich's chest. "He's breathing."

She was touched by Tag's overture but didn't have the mental strength to process it. She reached out and tentatively touched her lover's chest. "Ulrich?"

His gaze slid to her face and his hand found hers. He squeezed it. "Can't move," he said, almost too quiet for her to hear. "Where's Sibyl?"

"Dr. Cooper's helping her," Tag explained.

Ulrich narrowed his eyes. "Cooper's here?" He tightened his grip as his eyes tinged with amber. "What the fuck are you doing with him?"

"It's okay, Dad." Tag ran interference. "We needed a ride, and he was there."

Leah's shadow fell on Aubrey. "Mom's okay. Eyes open, talking to Coop. She's asking for you, kid."

"Thanks," Tag said as he scrambled away.

Leah crouched down next to Ulrich and laid her hand on his forehead. "Something else is going on in Darkness Falls. The cops are busy." She glanced at the wreckage. "Coop already called for ambulances and a rescue team." She held Ulrich's eyes as she talked. "You were with your ex-wife so you have no right to be pissed about Cooper.

Aubrey exchanged glances with Ulrich. He hadn't been

jealous, he was afraid for her, but Leah didn't know that. "It's okay," she said to him. "I promise."

Leah removed her hand from Ulrich's forehead and sat on the ground. "That cut on your forehead is going to ugly up your pretty face, but you'll live."

Aubrey furrowed her forehead. Leah was talking and acting stranger than usual. "How do you know?"

Leah flicked a pebble at Aubrey. "Go check on the kid. I need a word with your old man."

What the hell? "Why?"

Leah glared at Aubrey. "Shoo." She jerked her head towards Tag, who was sitting several feet away from Dr. Cooper and Sibyl, his head resting on his knees, hiding his face in his arms.

Sirens peeled in the distance and Aubrey felt a rush of relief. "Okay," she said softly as she stood. "But only this once." She felt lighter knowing that Ulrich was okay, then chided herself for falling victim to Leah's nonsense.

As she advanced on Jared and Sibyl, a cold breeze kicked up, tossing leaves and other forest debris into the air. She noted Jared leaning over Sibyl, his eyes glued to hers, his body tense, his expression shocked. He wasn't working on her, not doing doctorly things like checking her pulse or listening to her heart.

Aubrey watched with fascination as Sibyl slowly reached up to cup Jared's face. "What are you?" the woman whispered.

CHAPTER THIRTY-SEVEN

Jared insisted that Ulrich and Sibyl stay in the hospital overnight.

Considering the shape the truck was in, Sibyl was relatively intact. Broken ribs, a concussion, and some serious lacerations, one of which required surgery to fix a small tear in an artery.

Ulrich fared better coming out of the crash with bruised ribs, lacerations, and a concussion.

"It's the shifter blood," Jared told Aubrey as she walked with him out of Ulrich's private hospital room. "A human would have died, but a shifter heals faster, which kept Sibyl from bleeding out before we got there."

"How long will she be in the hospital?" Aubrey was too thankful over Ulrich's and Sibyl's survival to be anything but grateful to Jared. She knew Sibyl would likely have to return to Ulrich's to recover, but she'd already decided how to deal with the situation.

Ulrich didn't know it yet, but Aubrey was moving in.

"A couple of days," Jared answered, no longer looking at her like they had a future. Something had happened out there at the accident scene, something with Sibyl. She worried that Tag's mother was now in Jared's line of sight, but her thoughts about it were interrupted by Tag's approach.

He stopped next to her, not saying anything. His presence kicked up an awkwardness that quickly got under Jared's skin.

"Uh... I'll see you later," the doctor said, then retreated hastily.

The moment they were alone, Aubrey turned her attention to Tag.

"Are you okay?" She smoothed his hair, which was standing in a half-dozen different directions.

"Sure," he mumbled, shoving his hands into the pockets of his jeans. "Hungry."

Of course, he was. It was almost 4 pm and neither of them had eaten that day. "I am too. Let's go feed ourselves.

They walked in silence to the cafeteria, then placed as much food as they could on two trays. Aubrey's credit card would take a beating, but she'd worry about that when the statement came in. Tag was a 12-year-old boy who needed nourishment and Aubrey wasn't above buying his affection.

As they settled, Aubrey took a cheesecake slice and forked a piece into her mouth.

Tag raised his eyebrows as he swallowed down half the hot dog he was holding. "Dessert first?" He sounded almost scolding.

Aubrey grinned at him. "Dessert is a concept, like mealtime. It only exists because we choose for it to exist."

Tag rolled his eyes as he polished off the rest of his hot dog and reached for a second one. But he also grinned, which warmed Aubrey's heart.

"How are you doing, Tag?" she said, hoping she didn't mess with the fragile peace between them.

He shrugged, sucked down half his Coke, then let out a

burp. Not too loud and he held his fist in front of his mouth, so she forgave him for being a little savage.

"I'm okay," he replied. "Everything is weird, though. Isn't it?"

Aubrey couldn't disagree. Sibyl's words to Jared echoed in her head. *What are you?* "Like what?"

He focused on the trays of food, then grabbed the slice of chocolate cake and set it in front of him. Aubrey twisted her mouth to the side. She should have called dibs.

"Do you think Mom forced Dad to drive off the road?"

Aubrey stopped in mid-bite of her egg salad sandwich as ice swept through her. She'd been so sidetracked by Ulrich's injuries, that she hadn't thought about the cause of the accident. Based on what she knew of Sibyl, Aubrey thought that it wasn't beyond the realm of possibility. "No, I don't think that."

What was a little lie between table-mates? "And quit answering my questions with questions. Tell me what you're thinking." She used her teacher voice assuming it could double for a mom voice if necessary.

Yeah, she went there because she fully intended to go there eventually.

He stalled by opening a bag of Lay's potato chips and dumping it into Aubrey's discarded sandwich container.

"Plain's my favourite," Aubrey said as she took a chip.

"Mine too," Tag replied, then leaned over the table, his body language inviting her in for a huddle.

She shoved herself forward so their heads were bent together. "When I went over to check on mom, she and Dr. Cooper were whispering to each other like they were friends."

That was weird, Aubrey thought.

"And she barely looked at me when I knelt down beside her. She didn't even ask how Dad was." He blinked away the shine in his eyes. "Like she didn't care if he died." He slumped back in his seat. "I don't get it. She always tells me how much she loves Dad and then when he's hurt, nothing." His face reddened. "She crawled away from the truck, but she didn't help Dad."

Aubrey hated that she was about to defend Sibyl. "Your mom was in a serious car crash, Tag. She was probably in shock."

Tag's chin jutted stubbornly. "No. I know what I saw and heard."

So did Aubrey. *What are you?*

"When she and your dad are better, we can all discuss it. Sort it out."

Tag's tears abated but not the flush to his face. "You're with him, aren't you? Like forever."

"Yeah." Aubrey sat back in her chair. "Yeah, we are."

"Great," Tag mumbled, but he was being ironic.

"What are you afraid of, Tag? That I'll make your dad not love you anymore? Or that you won't be able to see your mom because of me?"

Tag deftly changed the subject. "I'm not sure you should trust that friend of yours, Leah."

That startled Aubrey. "Why not?"

"You couldn't hear them talk because you weren't close enough, but I'm a shifter." He tapped his ear. "Easy to hear stuff."

Aubrey was curious but not worried. Leah was complicated, more so than anyone she'd ever met and despite her penchant for 'borrowing' other people's belonging, the woman was also honest. Deep down, Aubrey knew Leah. Almost like she knew Ulrich. "Okay. So what did you overhear?"

Tag stabbed at a congealed slice of pizza with a plastic fork. "She told Dad not to worry. She'd be back."

Aubrey shrugged. That was Leah to a fault, cryptic and unfiltered, but Aubrey didn't see the problem. "And?" she prompted.

"She lied and said you didn't have a panic attack."

Aubrey raised her eyebrows. That was weird, even for Leah. Tag and Jared witnessed the panic attack, so why would Leah lie about something so easy to disprove? "Strange woman."

"Yeah." He took a bite of the pizza, grimaced and tossed it back on the paper plate.

Aubrey peeled a piece of pepperoni off the discarded slice and popped it into her mouth, savouring the peppery saltiness of it. "Leah's the kind of woman you want on your side," she told Tag as she wiped her fingers on her napkin. "She's complicated and hard on the head, but she's loyal. She had a reason for saying what she did and it's easy enough to find out what it was."

"It is?"

Aubrey grinned at him. "Yeah. We ask your dad."

Tag appeared sceptical. "If Dad doesn't want to talk about it, he won't."

Aubrey swallowed the cold dredges of coffee that had been almost undrinkable when it was fresh. "We ask anyway. It's the hardest thing to do sometimes, but it's the most direct. If you want an answer, ask the question."

"Is that what you do?"

Aubrey nodded. "Almost always." She stopped to think. "Unless it gets me into trouble. Then I try a workaround."

Tag appeared to think this over. "Okay, but what if he won't tell us?"

"He'll tell us, because I'll insist on it." Aubrey stood, picking up her purse and swinging the strap over her shoulder. "Let's go see how's he doing, then check in on your mom."

Tag stood too. "You're not mad at her?"

Aubrey pursed her lips, thinking about how to play this. He'd asked a question and she'd be a hypocrite not to give him an honest answer. "Yes and no. We don't know what happened to cause the accident, so I can hardly blame your mom for that. I'm not angry at her for wanting to stay with you and your dad. I'm kind of angrier with your dad for letting her."

"Why?" Clearly Tag was on his way to joining the ranks of insensitive male.

"Because it makes me uncomfortable and because what she did was unforgiveable."

Tag furrowed his brow. "I don't get it."

"She took you from your dad and hid you from him for over a year. I know she has an addiction problem, but that doesn't excuse her actions."

They walked side-by-side down the hall of the hospital. "You didn't even know Dad when that happened."

"Doesn't matter and it's not actually about your dad anyway. It's about you. She had access to you before she took you and yet she took you anyway." She paused to formulate her words. "I know Tag, what it's like to miss someone. To hope the next time is the time that works. I know how it feels in here—" She gave her stomach a light punch. "When it all falls apart. She loves you. I'm sure of that, but what's she done to you is unforgiveable."

Tag's face reflected the emotional roller-coaster he was on. "I don't get it. Why does Dad let her see me then?"

"For your sake." Aubrey laughed to dispel the tension. "Believe it or not, kids don't come with an instruction manual and neither do parents. No parent is perfect and so many of them aren't even any good. To be a good parent you can't put yourself first. Not ever. It has to be about the kids until they grow up and can look after themselves."

"How do you know all this? You're not a parent." His hand brushed hers, a casual gesture, but it spoke volumes to Aubrey because it wasn't accidental.

She choked up at his innocent question. "No. But I was a kid once."

CHAPTER THIRTY-EIGHT

Ulrich hated hospitals, despised being sick, loathed the fucking sunlight that was streaming through his west-facing window.

And he was also quickly coming to detest the cop standing next to his bed, writing in his notebook. "I drove off the road. Is that so fucking hard to understand?"

Jackson's bland expression told him that it was that fucking hard to understand. "Perfect day, no rain or snow. Not even a frost warning. Sure, you were going around a tight curve, but you're a shifter. Your reflexes are razor sharp."

"I can't remember what happened," Ulrich lied. He pointed to his head with the only fucking finger that didn't hurt. "Concussion."

"Are you protecting your ex-wife? Did she cause the accident?"

It was the first time he couldn't blame Sibyl for fucking with his life, but he decided to throw her under the bus anyway. "Yeah. We were fighting, she got physical at the wrong time. I lost control, broke through the barrier, and you know the rest."

Jackson jotted a couple of notes. "Victim is spewing bull-shit," he read aloud.

Ulrich gritted his teeth and ignored Jackson's sarcasm. "This makes it shifter business, so thanks for caring, but this is between me and Sibyl."

"We used provincial resources to attend the scene; the emergency team risked their lives to get you extracted from the ravine. You live in Darkness Falls as an Independent. And also, you're full of shit."

Ulrich sighed. He *was* full of shit, but he wanted to deal with Sam Donnybrook on his own. If Jackson got involved, Donnybrook would be arrested for reckless driving and leaving the scene of an accident at the very least. Attempted murder was more likely the charge because Donnybrook very deliberately rammed him with his tow truck. It was likely unplanned, and an unfortunate coincidence that they were on the same road at the same time. That didn't matter though. Donnybrook made a bad decision that could have had deadly consequences.

Ulrich wasn't being noble by not wanting to turn the asshole in. He wanted to deal with it himself in a way that Donnybrook understood. Either he became a stand-up guy or Ulrich would bury his body somewhere he would never be found.

Why the second chance? Same reason he kept giving Sibyl access to Tag. He was a motherfucking bleeding heart who didn't want Donnybrook's kid to have to grow up without a dad.

It was fucked up and what he really needed was Aubrey to help him think things through. Instead, he had the Chief of Police standing next to his bed calling him a liar. "Did you forget you were Chief, you asshole?" Best defence was a good offence. "The union's going to kick your ass for doing your subordinate's job."

Jackson quirked an eyebrow as he made another note. "Victim appears to be hostile," he read, then snapped the notebook shut as he smirked. "If you'll excuse me, I'm going to go see if Sibyl shares the same account of the events."

"Do that. And while you're at it, tell Cooper to count the drugs."

The grin dropped from Jackson's face. "Macy Kerrigan's bloody clothes were discovered just beyond the Lodge pack territory, so we're combing the area."

Ulrich groaned as he pressed his head into the pillow. "That's pretty fucking sloppy for our killer."

Jackson nodded his head. "Cooper was—" He clamped his mouth shut as Aubrey entered the room.

Ulrich panicked that she was alone. "Where's Tag?" he barked, then softened his voice when his wolf smacked him upside the head. "Is he okay?"

"Yeah, he's fine. He stopped to talk to that pretty nurse who looked after him when he broke his head." She glanced at Jackson. "How's the search going?"

The Chief tilted his head. "How do you know about the search?"

She rounded the bed so she was facing Jackson across the mattress. "I was talking to Eva when you called her. Cooper wanted me to meet for coffee and neither you nor Ulrich were picking up." She said all this in a hushed voice as she slid her fingers around Ulrich's hand and squeezed. "I needed someone to tell me what to do."

If Ulrich hadn't been so broken, he would have leapt from the bed. "She told you to meet him!"

Aubrey shook her head, her eyes pleading for him to settle down. "No. That was my decision and turns out it was the right one."

That didn't settle Ulrich or his wolf. Shifter's generally didn't die from heart attacks, but in that moment his chest hurt like it was about to explode. "Nothing's right about you having coffee with that fuck!"

"Take us through what happened from the moment he called," Jackson interrupted as he pulled his notebook from his pocket.

Aubrey tossed a tidy little grin Jackson's way and Ulrich gripped her hand harder. "Look at me, babe," he said through clenched teeth. "Don't be smiling at that jackass."

"You're a bad patient," Aubrey scolded, then tuned back into Jackson, going over the events earlier in the day. She reached the part about the café without interruption. "The Uber dropped me off and I didn't see Jared, so I walked up to the building, but it was still closed. Sunday, I guess. We were too early."

"What time was it?"

She shrugged. "Around 8 am."

"And Cooper wasn't there?"

She shook her head. "No, although I think he was. I just couldn't see his car because of where he parked it."

"Where did he park it?" Ulrich asked.

Aubrey frowned. "I don't know why, but he parked it around the side of the building. Not really visible from the front."

Ulrich sensed her heartbeat increase. "What happened then?" He already knew.

"I had this sense of dread all morning, but I didn't realize it was because of you. I guess I panicked when I saw Jared. I couldn't breathe. I felt light-headed. Jared helped me to his car and seated me in the back. He said it was a panic attack."

Ulrich exchanged glances with Jackson. "You have them often?" Jackson asked.

Aubrey shook her head. "Never." She stopped, seemingly to gather her thoughts. "I guess it was everything at once.

That sense of dread. Being alone with Cooper. Thank god Leah and Tag showed up."

"Why?" Jackson asked, then clarified, "I mean good that they showed up, but how did they help?"

Aubrey gave her shoulders a little shrug. "I guess their presence calmed me down, because I snapped out of it."

"Aubrey," Jackson said, a grim edge to his voice. "Did Cooper say anything to you before Leah and Tag arrived?"

Aubrey nodded. "He told me I was a having a panic attack and he would help me."

"Is that what he said?"

"Yeah. Something like that."

Jackson pushed her. "It's important. What were his exact words?"

Aubrey closed her eyes and Ulrich held his breath. Jackson's excitement was palpable and if he hadn't been drugged up, Ulrich expected that his heart would be racing too.

"I told him I needed an ambulance," she said slowly. "And he said..." She popped her eyes open. "*You don't need an ambulance. I'm a doctor. I'll make it better.*"

A chill swept through Ulrich as he and Jackson exchanged knowing looks.

She dropped her eyes to the hand she had wrapped around Ulrich's. "Tag said he overheard Leah tell you that it wasn't a panic attack." She flicked her gaze to his. "Why would she say that?"

Ulrich glanced at Jackson who raised his eyebrows slightly. "Leah's right, baby. You don't have a history of panic attacks and it stopped the moment she and Tag arrived on the scene."

Aubrey furrowed her forehead. "Then what?"

There was a bang in the hall that splintered the tension in the room. Jackson checked behind him, then he said in a low, careful voice. "We need to shut this conversation down right now. Who knows who might be listening."

THANK THE HUMANS FOR AIRBAGS. Ulrich felt like a train had hit him, but it could have been so much worse.

Despite it all, he ignored Cooper's advice and checked himself out of the hospital at around 11 pm. Well, his version of checking out, which was shifting, and sneaking down the hall to the stairs. His body hurt like hell, human or wolf form, but in wolf form, he could withstand the discomfort enough to get himself home.

Shortly after their conversation with Jackson, Aubrey left with Tag. Before she left, Ulrich had asked her to stay with Tag at his house until he was home. "Bolt the doors behind you and push a chair under the knobs."

As an added measure of security, Jackson put a man on Aubrey, though she was unaware.

None of that stopped him from slipping inside the house. He knew how to bypass his own security and in wolf form, he did it easily. He padded down the stairs and checked in on Tag, who was sprawled across his bed in his underwear, sleeping soundly.

The memory of the moments after the crash made his heart pound. Lying at the bottom of the ravine, his body too battered to move, drifting in and out of consciousness, led to some serious soul-searching. The thought of never seeing his son again made him vow to be a better father.

He raised his snout and breathed in Tag before turning and heading upstairs. Aubrey had been his oasis out there in the dark. Her simple beautiful truth guided him to peace. He was nothing without her, and if he hadn't realized it before, he knew it now. Tag was what made him a good man, Aubrey was what made him whole.

He followed the perfume of her scent. She was everywhere – in the basement, in Tag's room. Upstairs in the kitchen, the living room, in and out of the spare bedrooms, including the one designated for Sibyl, but he found her where he expected her to be. In his bedroom, in his bed.

She was breathing softly, asleep, but not deeply, her hair a tangled mess on the pillow, her body clad in one of his T-shirts. Even through his pain he felt his lust growing.

He shifted and approached the bed. "Aubrey," he said softly as tried to slip between the sheets without groaning.

"Ulrich?" Her sleepy voice reached out to him as she turned onto her back. "What are doing out of the hospital?"

He drew her close to him once he was settled. "Missed you."

She snuggled into him, her eyes closing again. "Missed you, too."

CHAPTER THIRTY-NINE

In the morning, Aubrey woke to Ulrich snoring softly next to her and Tag standing in the doorway of the bedroom, already dressed for school. "What time is it?" she mumbled.

"Almost eight," Tag replied softly. "When did Dad come home?"

Shoot. She was going to be late for school. "Last night sometime. Guess he missed us."

"How am I gonna get to school?"

Aubrey sat up and brushed the hair out of her face. "How do you usually get to school?"

"Dad drives me."

"You don't have a bike?"

Tag nodded. "Yeah."

It appeared that was all the explanation Aubrey was going to get. She scrutinized Tag. The kid's hair was in disarray, she knew he hadn't showered, and there were dark circles under his eyes.

"Tell you what," she said as she threw the blankets back

and slid out of bed. "I think we have a legitimate reason for taking the day off."

Tag's eyes brightened. "Really?"

"Yeah." She casually looked down at herself to make sure she wasn't flashing her future stepson. The T-shirt hung almost to her knees and billowed around her. *Nothing provocative to see here.* "I'll call it in."

After the awkward conversation she had with the school secretary about Tag's absence and her need for a substitute teacher, she made her way to the kitchen and put on a pot of coffee. She dusted off her unused domestic goddess hat and pulled some eggs and bacon out of the fridge, and a loaf of bread from the freezer.

She wasn't much of a cook and never really wanted to waste her time learning. The supermarket offered everything she needed. Or used to need, she thought as she looked around her new kitchen. It seemed like it was well-equipped with all the necessary doo-dads to whip up a turkey dinner.

Ulrich could cook, she decided. He'd know how.

The smell of frying bacon drew Tag from his lair. "Are you making breakfast?" he asked as he entered the kitchen.

"That depends," she said, moving the cooked bacon onto a paper towel for degreasing. "Are you eating breakfast?"

Tag grinned as he pulled out a chair and sat down. "I could eat."

She decided she would wait on him just this once and placed a plate of food in front of him. "After you're done, you need to shower."

Tag stopped shovelling eggs into his face long enough to nod, then resumed.

Aubrey cradled the cup of coffee in her hand and watched him while he inhaled his breakfast. She wanted a baby-sized one of him, maybe a couple, and wondered how he'd feel about it. Not a question to ask now though. Best she let

Ulrich know she'd moved in before she started discussing the expansion of the family.

"Thanks," Tag said, his mouth still full of toast as he picked up his plate and carried it into the kitchen. "That was good. Dad hardly ever makes bacon and eggs for breakfast."

"I do. All the time," she lied.

"Awesome." He punched the air and took off out of the room.

"Don't forget to shower," she called after him.

"On it," he called back.

She took another sip of coffee as she contemplated the mess in the kitchen with a frown.

Time to check on Ulrich.

He was awake, on his back, his eye focused on the ceiling. "Close the door and lock it," he said as she entered the room.

She did as he asked. "How are you?"

"Tag still home?"

"Yeah. We're both taking the day off."

"Naughty," he rumbled.

Yes. I've been a naughty girl. She carefully crawled onto the bed and sat on her knees near him, but not touching him. "Do you need some water? Coffee?" Did he have pills for the pain?

"I need you, baby."

Good answer. She shuffled closer then slipped down until her body was pressed to his side. "How's this?"

He anchored her to him with his arm. "I can barely move this morning. Stiff everywhere."

Her fingers twitched as she rested them on his belly, then she slid her hand below the sheet until she brushed his hard cock. "Yes, you are."

He breathed in deeply as she toyed with the silky knob, her thumb swiping through his precum. "Aubrey." His voice held warning.

"Can I help with your stiffness?" she teased, wrapping her fingers around the cock's width, not coming close to encasing it with her hand. It was a wonder he fit inside her.

"We should wait."

She shimmied down the bed, taking the sheet with her until she was eye level with his monster cock. "Will it hurt if you come?" She was sliding her hand up and down his shaft, then knelt up so she could use her other hand.

He was breathing hard as he met her eyes. "In the best possible way."

She bent her head down and licked the tip of it, her tongue lingering on the precum that was beading. It tasted interesting, bland, not terrible. And it excited her to have him at her mercy. She slid her lips over his knob and held it in her mouth, her tongue mapping it slowly, circling the small crevice where the length of him started.

He sucked in a lungful of air each time she mouthed him. She slowly pushed past his head to pull more of his shaft in her mouth. His fingers tangled in her hair, swiping it off her face so he could watch his cock buried in her mouth. She turned her head slightly and caught his eyes. They held hers, the blue irises, the tinge of amber and then, as her teeth gently raked him, slowly closed as he hissed and dropped his head back on the pillow.

What to do next? His balls were there for the taking and she gently squeezed them, one a time before dipping her tongue downwards and licking them, tasting them, tracing the seam.

Her desire pooled between her legs and as much as she didn't want to let go of his cock, she needed some stimulation. She maintained a solid grip with one of her hands while she drew the other into her panties, pulling her desire up so she could rub her clit.

"Mmm," she moaned as she closed her eyes.

"Let me help," Ulrich said, his voice strangled as he tried to pull her around.

"No," she mumbled and returned her attention to his shaft, alternating between sucking and licking. "Tell me what you want."

He groaned as she tried to take him deeper. "Touch yourself. It's so hot to watch you."

No problem there. She grinned around his penis as her fingers tap-danced on her clit. It was hot, so hot. She was already close to coming and knew that him watching her would take her orgasm to the next level.

So concentrated on pleasuring herself, she almost forgot she was sucking on Ulrich's cock until he surged into her mouth and she choked. She didn't have a ton of experience in the blowjob department, but she knew enough to know that men liked it deep. She tried again, tried to take as much as she could and hold it there. She choked, fought for control, then felt Ulrich's grip on her hair pulling her off him. "Don't do that to yourself."

"I want to make you come," she said, sounding a little petulant.

"Not that way. Lick and suck near the base of my dick, on the underside near my balls."

Her body jerked as she grazed her clit, his hot words pushing her limits.

She did as he said, and he groaned. "So good, baby. Now up to the top. Take it in your mouth, suck on it like a lollipop."

She slipped a finger into her vagina, then a second one. She wanted to take off her panties, but also didn't want to stop. She was hot, she was high, she was close to exploding.

And so was Ulrich if the way he surged into her mouth was any indication. His hands tangled in her hair as he controlled the tempo, his hips jerking, the pace building.

"I'm coming, Aubrey," he gasped. "Where?"

Where? That seemed obvious. She felt the spark of fire that lit her fuse, the dynamite trail from her sweet spot down her legs, and up her body just before she exploded. She lost pace and rhythm as she came, and she gasped for air as Ulrich wrapped his hand around hers and moved it up and down his shaft. "Fuck, Aubrey," he choked as he released.

He spurted into her mouth and then yanked her by the hair, forcing her face up, his come still spurting from him, painting the T-shirt she was wearing, some landing on her face. His groans were loud, and she knew he was trying to temper them.

When they both stopped pulsing, she moved carefully up his body until she was near his mouth.

He brought his hand to the back of her head and forced her lips to his. He owned the kiss, deeply tasting her, licking her face where some of his cum landed. "We taste good together, baby."

She nodded, her body getting all warm again. "How long do you think before we can... uh...?"

"Tonight," he said as he closed his eyes and rested his head on the pillow. "I can't wait longer."

CHAPTER FORTY

U lrich felt like ground beef. His back hurt like hell, his ribs rained hellfire on him, and Aubrey had just given him the best blowjob he'd ever experienced. Everything was amplified with her. How she sucked him, licked him, took him. And her fucking hands in her panties as she squirmed. It was mesmerizing, a little like an erotic, teasing peep show that he knew he would be rerunning in his head until he got to see it again.

He didn't need to see her naked – in fact, the mystery of what she was doing to herself brought him to the brink of coming more than once.

And then when he did, his world narrowed to that single moment in time, just the two of them together. It made him forget everything else – Donnybrook, Sibyl, Cooper. It was a perfect moment and he selfishly let himself have it.

"I think you need more time to heal," Aubrey said doubtfully. She sat up on her knees next to him and pulled the sheet and blanket up to his stomach.

He pointed at an armchair that sat next to his dresser. "If

I do, then tonight, I want you there, naked, making yourself come."

The flush that spread across her face contradicted her behaviour moments before. "That's a little pervy."

He loved it. Loved that she retreated to shyness after being so bold.

He grinned through the pain that hammered at him. "Yeah. That's how I roll." The words came out gruff enough for Aubrey to notice.

"Did you bring any medication home with you last night?"

"I shifted to get home, so no." He thought he should shift again, let his wolf take over for a while. He felt less pain in wolf form.

"I'll call the hospital for a prescription and pick up some for you."

He hated that the real world was intruding on them. "How are you doing?" He brushed her silky hair away from her face and watched as she went from an easy smile to a conflicted frown.

"I've moved in," she announced.

Laughter bubbled up from his chest. "Moved in here?"

She nodded. "I'm not compromising on that. We already know our future, so why wait? I'll feel safer here, we'll be together, and Tag will be okay with it."

Ulrich couldn't help but tease. "He'll hear us, Aubrey. I don't know how to be quiet with you."

She flushed. "We'll have to work that out."

He picked up a strand of her hair and rubbed it between his fingers. "Tag okay?"

"He's confused about a lot of things, especially where Sibyl's concerned." She twisted her lips as she gazed past him, her eyes unfocused. "I don't want her here, but she'll need a place to recover."

"No," Ulrich started, because he didn't want Aubrey having to compromise where Sibyl was concerned.

"It's okay. She's a shifter. She'll recover fast and then we'll run her out of town." She grinned brightly. "I think the hardware store has a sale on pitchforks this week."

His lips twitched. "We'll see." The pain in his ribs flared up and kicked his ass. "I hate being helpless like this," he groaned as he rearranged his torso to find some comfort. "I want to be able to deal with Sibyl, talk to Tag man-to-man, move you in."

She grinned. "I don't like you being like this either." The sound of footsteps in the hall forced Aubrey to her feet. "I'm going to shower and then go home to pick up some stuff." She tugged his soiled T-shirt down to her knees so that it modestly covered her thighs.

His cock jerked at how perfectly dirty she was. "I don't like the idea of you alone." Again, the sense of helplessness washed over him.

"I'll take Tag. We have to drop by the hospital anyway to pick up some pain pills for you. We'll check on Sibyl to see how she's doing. Tag will want to, anyway."

The light rap on the door ended the conversation. Aubrey gathered up her clothes, then unlocked and opened the door. "Your dad's awake," she said as she scurried into the ensuite.

Tag wandered into the bedroom and stood over Ulrich. "Ms. Powell said it was okay for me stay home."

"Sit," Ulrich said as he patted the mattress. "We gotta talk."

Tag nodded and climbed onto the bed, sitting cross-legged a couple of feet from Ulrich. "Are you okay?"

Ulrich heard the vulnerability in Tag's voice and felt guilt. What if he'd died out there? He had nothing in place to support Tag through his death. Sibyl's pack would force him to return to them and Tag would grow up having a miserable life. "I'm great," he said with as much energy as he could muster. He shoved himself somewhat upright to prove his point.

Tag nodded doubtfully. "What's going to happen now, Dad? I know Mom caused the accident."

Ulrich raised his eyebrows. "Your mom didn't cause the accident."

Tag gazed at Ulrich through half-closed lids. "Then how else did it happen?"

Maybe Sibyl deserved to be tarred and feathered but not over something she didn't do. "Some other vehicle passed us and accidentally bumped into the truck. I was going too fast on a curve and lost control."

"And they didn't stop?" Tag was outraged.

"They might not have even realized what they did." What were a few lies between father and son?

Tag seemed sceptical, but let it go. "What's going to happen with Mom?"

Ulrich wondered why both Tag and Aubrey seemed to feel they were responsible for Sibyl. "Your mom's a grown-up. She'll figure it out for herself."

"Aren't you going to let her come back here?"

"No," he said, sounding frustrated. "Maybe. Depends on Aubrey."

"Why?"

"She's moving...." He stopped remembering how Aubrey had phrased it. "She's moved in, Tag. She's part of our family now and I need to... we both need to... respect her feelings."

Tag's face reddened. "So I can't see Mom anymore, because of her?" His volume and tone were quickly climbing.

Ulrich knew he had no one to blame but himself for the dysfunction. "Aubrey has nothing to do with whether you can see your mom or not. You know that. But your mom can't stay here with us. I should have put a stop to that years ago."

CHAPTER FORTY-ONE

s Aubrey stepped out of the shower, the rumbled conversation between Tag and Ulrich reached her ears.

"Did Ms. Powell ask you about Leah?"

"What about Leah?" Ulrich's sexy voice made her heart jump.

She rolled her eyes at herself as she towelled off.

"I heard what she said, Dad. That she had to leave, but she'd be back. And she lied about the panic attack. Aubrey did so have one. I saw."

Right, Leah – Tag was right. What the hell was going on with Leah?

She slid into yesterday's clothes hating that they were brushing up against her clean body. First thing, she was going home to change. She paused her thought. Not home anymore. A soon-to-be-empty apartment.

She stepped from the bathroom to find Ulrich propped up awkwardly against a stack of pillows, the hard headboard of the bed offering begrudging support. Tag was sitting cross-legged near her pillow a couple of feet from him. They stopped talking and looked at her when she entered.

"Where did Leah go?" she asked Ulrich.

His slight shrug was followed by a slight grimace. "She said she'd be gone a few days and to tell you not to worry."

"Now, I'm worried." And she was.

Leah was a strange mix of bravado and reticence. For her to leave Darkness Falls alone was at the very least strange if not downright absurd. The town and her pack were her safety net, and the idea of her travelling beyond it was impossible for Aubrey to wrap her head around.

Unless she left with someone.

Ulrich patted the mattress next to him and Aubrey climbed onto the bed, sitting near his hip, cross-legged like Tag. It was a weird kind of family meeting, an equilateral meeting of minds – if they were a triangle.

The warm clasp of Ulrich's fingers as he linked them with hers forced a rush of warmth to her face.

"I don't know why Leah said what she did," he said to both of them. "It sounds like you had a panic attack and Cooper said it happened. Obviously, he'd know what he was talking about."

Aubrey and Tag exchanged glances.

"You're lying, Dad."

Ulrich glared, his fallback reaction. "Why would I lie?"

He was keeping something from them, but Cooper was a suspect in the serial murders, and it was likely that whatever he was hiding, was confidential.

Aubrey decided to help him out by changing the subject. "Did your dad tell you I moved in?" she said to Tag. Yep, that did the trick.

"Aubrey," Ulrich said, the tone of his voice warning.

At the same time, Tag replied, "Dad told me." He shuttered his expression. "What're you going to say to everyone at school?"

Tag's response indicated his acceptance, and Aubrey felt relieved that his biggest concern was how this was going to impact him.

"You'll be fine." Evidently, Ulrich's injuries were not helping him get in touch with his sensitive side.

"Tag, this is not the first time in the history of education that a student and teacher had a connection to each other outside of school."

"I know." He reddened. "But they'll all know that you and Dad will be...." He scrunched up his face, then covered it with his hands.

Ulrich's rumbled laughter was cut off by a groan as his body took exception to the humour he found in Tag's discomfort.

"Yeah," Aubrey said ignoring Ulrich. "And you'll know how to manage it. You're the new kid and yet, you have all the other students eating out of your hand. Why do you think Reed got into it with you?"

Tag shrugged and Ulrich started to say something, but Aubrey squeezed his hand hard enough that he groaned.

"You're as insensitive as your Dad."

Tag grinned at that and exchanged a happy glance with Ulrich. "So?" he said to underscore Aubrey's point.

"So Reed used to be top of the pyramid and now you are. And because of the fight the two of you had, his classmates are rejecting him in favour of you."

Tag grinned like that was a good thing, then masked it when he caught Aubrey's glare.

"Put yourself in his place, Tag. How would you feel?"

Tag dropped his head and plucked at the blankets. "Okay, I get it." He glared at his dad like it was Ulrich's fault he was getting lectured.

"You're a leader in the class. How you choose to lead is up to you – you can be a little fascist or you can be inclusive and understanding."

"Whoa," Ulrich interjected on Tag's behalf. "That's a little harsh."

"What's a fascist?"

Aubrey tilted her head at him.

Tag sighed. "I know. Look it up."

"My point is that the other students in the class are more likely to give me the gears than you. And you, my friend, have the power to make it easier or harder for me at school."

"I do?"

Aubrey nodded. "But now that I'm living here, I have the power to make your life a living hell at home."

Tag's eyes widened. "Dad!"

Ulrich laughed, groaned, then laughed again. "Leave me out of this."

"But she's not my mom."

Aubrey bit her tongue, so she didn't say all the means things about Sibyl that were threatening to spill out of her mouth. "I'm not trying to replace your mom." Did that sound okay? She caught Ulrich's slight nod like he read her mind. "There's room for me in your life just as there's room for you in mine. Not just our lives, Tag. Our hearts."

He wrinkled her nose at her attempt at a hallmark card moment. "You're different than at school. I need time to get used to you."

Aubrey nodded once. It was a win. "Me too. I've never lived with a kid before."

"Not a kid," he reminded her. "I'll be 13 next month."

"Okay. I'll refrain from calling you a kid." She turned to Ulrich. "Are you okay alone for awhile? Tag and I are going to go to my place and then to the hospital to check on Sibyl."

"Yeah. I'm fine." His grip on her fingers loosened. "I need a little help to get to the bathroom."

Aubrey looked to Tag. "Maybe I can help him out while you order an Uber?"

"'kay," Tag replied eagerly as he climbed off the bed and headed out of the bedroom. Give a kid... uhm... teenager an adult task and they'll always be more than happy to agree to it.

"Dammit," Ulrich muttered as he moved his feet to the floor. "I don't even have a fucking truck for you to drive."

Aubrey shrugged. "One thing at a time, Ulrich. First, we get you better and Sibyl sorted out."

"And you moved in." He was standing now, the sheet fallen away to show off every inch of his perfect body.

She wrapped her arm gently around his waist, tucking her itchy fingers into fists so she didn't touch him inappropriately... well, inappropriately in that context. "Yeah."

They both knew if he lost his footing, she'd be no help whatsoever, but his leaning on her was symbolic. Anything he needed from her, she would give him.

CHAPTER FORTY-TWO

The apartment felt strangely deserted when Aubrey and Tag entered it. It was shades of shadow, light, and disuse, even though she'd been gone only one night.

Tag stood a foot inside the door with his hands in his pockets. "Do you want me to do anything?"

Aubrey was heading towards her bedroom eager to get out of yesterday's clothes. "Check on Fake Goldie. If she's alive, feed her. If she's dead, flush her."

"Okay." Tag headed towards the fishbowl as Aubrey stopped, looking around.

"Mr. Meow's not here," she said.

Tag's eyes widened in a classic look of *guilty*. "The cat got out of the apartment when Leah and I were here yesterday."

"You were here?" Despite everything that had happened yesterday, not once did Aubrey question why Tag and Leah showed up at Rozi's Café together.

"Yeah. When Mom and Dad still weren't home yesterday morning, I came to see if you knew where they were."

Aubrey took a long look at the boy in her apartment. He

was so resilient; much like her when she was his age. His world had been imploding and he had the common sense to reach out for help. She wanted to tell him how grateful she was that he thought of her, how much she appreciated him, how good it would be for both of them to have each other. Instead of all that, she said, "And Mr. Meow ran off."

"Yeah." He tucked his hands in his pockets as he dropped his eyes. "Sorry."

Aubrey shrugged. "Nothing to be sorry about. He probably spent the night lurking the halls waiting for me to get home."

"Maybe that old lady across the hall has him."

Aubrey's lips twitched. "If that's the case, we might have to rename him Stew."

Tag furrowed his forehead. "That's lame, Ms. Powell."

So it was. "Let's see if he comes back on his own before we go knocking on doors." She paused, then said, "You should call me Aubrey when we're not in school."

"Really?" The grin on Tag's face reminded of her Leah at her most annoying.

"Don't make me regret it," she muttered as she entered her bedroom.

It took less than 10 minutes for Aubrey to change and pack a suitcase with the clothes she'd need over the next few days. Tag looked up when she emerged from the bedroom. He was placing Mr. Meow's bag of kibble by the front door, next to Fake Goldie's fishbowl.

"FG was still alive, and MM arrived a few minutes ago."

She glanced over at *MM* who was next to his bowl of kibble chowing down. "We'll have to come back for the zoo. We can't take them to the hospital." She set her bag next to FG's bowl. "Guess we can grab my stuff on the way back, too."

Tag hesitated when she motioned him out the door with

her head. "Won't Mr. Meow eat the fish?" he asked.

"Well, he hasn't so far. I think he's a little afraid of Fake Goldie."

On the way to the hospital, Tag asked why the fish's name was Fake Goldie, provided a lengthy explanation about why there was a mutual dislike between shifters and cats, and worried he'd get in trouble if someone from school saw him at the hospital.

As Aubrey paid the Uber driver, she told herself that Tag's non-stop talking was a good sign. Her ears and her brain weren't quite in agreement.

They by-passed the front desk and went directly to Sibyl's room. It was empty and not as in, the-patient-was-in-the-bathroom empty, but cleaned-up, bed-stripped, patient-was-gone empty.

"Where's Mom?" Tag said, a tremor to the words. He was on the verge of crying.

"Maybe they released her, Tag," Aubrey said gently. "Maybe we crossed paths and she's already at your house."

"No. She left again. She always does that!" Tag glared at Aubrey and she braced herself for his wrath. "Did you know she was gone already?"

Aubrey shushed him. "If I knew she'd left already, I would have told you." She grabbed his arm and pulled him towards the nurses' station. "This is easy to solve without waking up the entire hospital."

The familiar face of Gillian, one of the attending nurses the day of Tag's accident, smiled at them. "How's your dad?" she said to Tag. "I was told he checked himself out last night."

"He's fine," Tag muttered, his eyes cast down.

Aubrey butted in. "He left without his prescription for pain tablets, so we'd like to pick that up. But we're also here to check on Tag's mom. Sibyl...?" She glanced at Tag for help.

"Calhoun," he muttered.

Aubrey's stomach kicked up an angry storm of honey-bees. The blasted woman was still using Ulrich's name even though they'd been divorced for a decade. The heat in her face and Gillian's raised eyebrows signalled to Aubrey that she was not keeping her jealousy well-hidden. She told the bees to settle down. *Time and place, you little buzzers. Time and place.*

"Calhoun," she repeated.

"Your family's a stubborn bunch," she said to Tag. "Mrs. Calhoun checked out this morning." She tapped on the keyboard as she studied her monitor. "Dr. Cooper cleared her to go after she insisted on leaving."

The abating storm in Aubrey's stomach reformed into a howling tornado. "Who'd she leave with?" She could barely hear herself over the thump of her heart.

"Dr. Cooper offered her a ride to the airport. She said she was going home."

"Without saying goodbye to me?" Tag's outraged voice barely registered with Aubrey.

So stupid, all of them, not to see it coming. "How long ago?"

Gillian gave Aubrey a quizzical look. "An hour, I guess. She waited until he was done with his rounds."

"Excuse me," Aubrey said, then strode off, leaving Tag at the nurses' station, his face red, his eyes shiny.

She pulled up Ulrich's number, which went to voice mail, because of course his phone was missing. "Shit, shit, shit," she muttered trying to get her shaking hands to work.

"What's wrong?" Tag came up behind her and she didn't have to be a shifter to know that he was sharing her panic.

"I don't know yet," Aubrey lied. "I want to check on something." She finally found Jackson's number and called him.

Jackson picked up after one ring. "Aubrey," he said. "How are you? How's Ulrich?"

Aubrey had no time for pleasantries. "Sibyl checked out of the hospital this morning." She glanced at Tag, who was visibly shaking. He knew. *He knew.* "Dr. Cooper offered to drive her to the airport."

"Fuck," Jackson said as the scrape of a chair on the other end told her he was already in motion. "Gotta go. I'll check back later."

"Wait! Her suitcase is at Ulrich's so they might go by there. Ulrich's in no shape to defend himself."

"Ulrich's home?"

"What's going on?" Tag demanded and Aubrey waved her hand to tell him to wait.

"He came home last night."

"Tag in school?"

"No. He's with me." She glanced at Tag, his rigid body standing a foot from her. "We're at the hospital."

Jackson's voice became muted as he barked orders. "Eva, get over to Ulrich Calhoun's and check on him. Take Adam with you. Dagmar, track down Jared Cooper. Put an APB out on his car. Ivan, you're with me." To Aubrey, he said, "Stay at the hospital. Don't leave until you hear from me."

He ended the call and Aubrey turned to Tag, feeling like he looked. He was pale, pupil's blown, lips tight. With his shifter hearing, he'd heard every word that was exchanged.

"I'm going home," Tag said as he tried to run past Aubrey.

"Tag, wait!" She grabbed him by the arm, but he wrenched out of her grip with a strength that belied his skinny 12-year-old body.

"I don't understand what's going on, but Dad's in danger again, isn't he?" He glared at her. "I'm going home."

Aubrey pulled the phone from her purse and ordered an Uber. "I'm going with you."

CHAPTER FORTY-THREE

Ulrich's body was slowly working the kinks out. He checked the time on the microwave as he poured himself a coffee. Aubrey had only been gone an hour and he already missed her. It didn't help settle him that she and Tag were out there alone, vulnerable and unprotected.

He hadn't been thinking straight when he let the two of them leave. Until it was established that Cooper was not a threat, Aubrey wasn't safe. He didn't have a phone to call Jackson, couldn't take a call from Aubrey if she needed him. He was in too much pain to try to get to her, even in wolf form.

He was like an abandoned baby, forced to sit helplessly until someone came to rescue him.

A knock on the front door drew his attention and he set his coffee cup down.

"Ulrich!"

It was Eva Blakely's voice. His heart leapt into his throat as his imagination ran amok.

What the fuck would a cop be doing knocking on his

door unless it was bad news? His ribs protested as he limped quickly towards the door, flinging it open. "What's wrong?" he demanded.

"You okay?" Eva asked, looking past him to the interior. Constable Adam Cole was standing slightly behind her.

"I'm fine! Are Aubrey and Tag okay?"

Eva let out a soft breath she'd been holding. "They're at the hospital. Can we come in so I can update you?"

Ulrich stepped back and opened the door wider, then closed it once Eva and Adam filed past him.

"You're in," he said tersely, his body blocking them from moving further into the house. He wasn't intentionally being difficult, but at the same time, he wasn't going to serve them tea and crumpets while he waited for Eva to explain.

"Aubrey called Jackson from the hospital. Sibyl checked out. Apparently, her plan was to leave Darkness Falls and Jared Cooper offered to drive her to the airport."

Ulrich dragged a hand through his hair. "Shit!" The implication of the news bowled him over. "So why're you here?"

"It's possible that they would have gone here first, to pick up Sibyl's belongings. You were vulnerable."

He raised his eyebrows and bent his head towards Eva. "Do I look vulnerable to you?" His beast was roaring at these keystone cops. "Why aren't you at the hospital making sure Aubrey and Tag are safe?"

Eva raised her hands in the air. "We're following Jackson's orders. He told Aubrey to stay put at the hospital until he called."

The door banged open and Tag and Aubrey fell over each other getting inside. "Are you okay?" Aubrey asked as she inspected his body.

"What are you doing here?" Eva said, unmistakeable authority in her voice. "You're supposed to be at the hospital!"

Tag lost his composure and started crying. "Mom left, Dad! Again! She just left."

It was clear Tag was furious and hurt.

"It's okay, Tag." Aubrey tried to comfort him, but he brushed her off.

"I am so over all of this." He glared at Eva, then pointed a finger at Ulrich. "You're all lying to me. I'm her kid. I have a right to know!"

"There's nothing to know!" Ulrich's temper was strung tautly. He was in pain, Aubrey had ignored Jackson's orders to stay put, and the devil was shoving hot pokers into his back and ribs. "I need you to go downstairs, Tag, until I sort this out."

Tag reacted like Ulrich had slapped him. "What the hell, Dad!"

"Now, Tag!" Ulrich roared.

Tag bared his teeth and glared at Ulrich. Amber tinged his irises.

Aubrey saw too. "Ulrich," she gasped.

"Get it together, Tag. Now's not the time for you to lose your shit!" Ulrich decided he would feel guilty later for embarrassing Tag in front of everyone. He held Tag's eyes, willing him to back down. It was the equivalent of a western stand-off.

Finally, Tag blinked, then his shoulders slumped. "Sure. Fine. Whatever!" He shoved his way past Aubrey and stomped down the stairs. The slamming of his bedroom door put the cherry on top of the fucked-up cake.

Ulrich turned to Aubrey. "Why are you here! Jackson told you to stay put!" He was still yelling, but he couldn't contain himself. If something had happened to her or Tag. "You're responsible for my son!"

Aubrey's face turned a spectrum of colours as she shook under his rage.

"Hold on!" Eva tried to interject.

"Shut it, Corporal." He kept his eyes on Aubrey, waiting for her to answer, already feeling like a jackass for taking his fear out on her.

She held his eyes. "Tag planned to leave the hospital, with or without me. I couldn't convince him to stay, so I chose to come with him." The coolness to her voice didn't disguise the hurt she was feeling.

Why not tackle him and sit on him? Ulrich had the good sense not to say. He rubbed a hand over his face as he stared at her. Then he did the only thing he could do. He reached for her and yanked her into his arms, gripping her tightly as his beating heart slowed. "I'm terrified," he whispered to her. "I don't what I'd do if something happened to you two."

"Same," she said softly. "We were scared too." She pressed her head against his chest, wrapped her arms around his waist.

He turned his attention to Eva, whose lips were tight, eyes narrow. "Call your Chief and get an update on Sibyl. I got a kid in the basement freaking out and I don't want to have to tell him his mother's missing."

CHAPTER FORTY-FOUR

J ackson and Ivan converged on the airport although Jackson wasn't sure that made any sense at all. If Sibyl and Cooper were here, then there was no call for alarm. If they weren't, then they were in the wrong place. Still, he had to do his duty and check.

Darkness Falls Airport was a small local airport with two daily flights, one in and one out. The gate for the departing flight was already closed and Jackson was flashing his credentials to people who already knew he was a cop.

"I want you to delay the flight," he barked, then, from the corner of his eye, saw Jared Cooper stroll by, his head down as he scrolled through his phone.

Unaware how hard his heart had previously been beating, he noticed it slow as he took a deep lungful of air. He turned his back to Cooper and sent a quick text to Ivan, who was talking to the airline boarding attendant.

He's here.

Cooper kept walking, concentrating on his phone, and Jackson forced himself not to approach. So much had happened in the past few days and he hadn't pulled the team together to formally discuss the details. Not the Integrated Crime Unit, which comprised Shifters and Cops. With Cooper as a suspect, he had to handle the fallout with kid gloves. Gideon, Cooper's alpha, would go apeshit and Jackson didn't have time for that. He and his team had to develop a plan before another woman got killed.

He thought of Macy Kerrigan. Maybe he was too fucking late. Maybe Cooper already figured out he was a suspect. Maybe his good-doctor act was meant to throw the suspicion off him. Or maybe they were sniffing up the wrong tree. The guy who left the airport was walking like he had not a single care in the world.

Maybe Aubrey had a panic attack after all.

Ivan jogged up to him. "The airline confirmed that Sibyl Calhoun boarded the airplane. Everything is as it should be."

Jackson nodded. "Call off the APB, but let's get a tail on him."

"No problem, boss," said the burly, bearded cop. He strolled out of hearing range as he talked into his phone.

Jackson dialled Eva and gave her an update.

CHAPTER FORTY-FIVE

The news from Jackson drew a collective sigh from everyone in Ulrich's house, except for Tag, who was in his bedroom playing his music so loud that Ulrich, Aubrey, Eva, and Adam had to step outside to talk.

"Still sucks that she took off without saying goodbye to Tag," Eva said, glaring at Ulrich as if it were his fault.

Ulrich wanted to tell her to stay the hell out of his business. "He's used to it."

"Doesn't make it easier on him," Eva countered.

"I can't wait until your kid turns your hair gray."

Eva patted her belly and grinned. "Me either."

Constable Cole looked up from his phone. "The chief wants us back at the precinct to debrief."

Eva nodded, then turned to Aubrey. "You need anything, you call." She glanced at Ulrich as she twisted her lips. "Anything."

"Thanks," Aubrey murmured, then gave Eva a hug. "I'm fine. This is fine. It's all fine."

Ulrich tugged Aubrey into him as the cops pulled away. "Sorry, I lost it in there," he muttered.

Aubrey tightly embraced him, her head resting on his chest, her ear pressed against his heart. "The last couple of days would break anyone."

"It didn't break you."

A tremor rippled through her as she tilted her head up. "Yeah, it did." They stayed that way for a moment, then she started crying.

"Aubrey," he whispered as he rocked her. "I love you so much."

She sniffled, laughed softly, then disentangled herself from him. "Let's get you drugged up so you're mellow when you talk to Tag." They held hands as he led her inside.

Later, after Ulrich talked Tag off the cliff, he took more pain pills, returned to bed and passed out. His shifter body was healing fast and already he could feel the pain fading. As he dropped off, he made up his mind. There was one way to make sure Aubrey was safe. One, irrevocable way.

When Aubrey woke him later, to feed and water him, he told her his plan.

CHAPTER FORTY-SIX

Eva and Ulrich agreed to take Tag overnight. Tag didn't complain all that much because he got to miss another day of school. So did Aubrey, who took the rest of the week off.

Ulrich was shirtless, but Aubrey was so distracted by his nervous pacing that she couldn't focus on his lust-inducing physique.

"It's okay," she said softly from her perch on the mattress. "I trust you."

He ran his hand through his hair. "That's nice, Aubrey, but trust doesn't change the fact that I might hurt you."

She tucked her knees under her and knelt up. "You won't, Ulrich. Please. It's what I want. Your instincts will guide you like they did last time."

He stopped pacing and turned to her. "What do you mean, last time?"

She shrugged, not really wanting to bring his ex-wife into their intimate conversation, but if it helped him get over his stage fright, she'd do it. "You know. When you marked Sibyl."

He climbed on the bed and circled her bi-ceps with his large hands. "Who told you I marked Sibyl?"

"No one." She held his serious gaze. "I assumed—"

"No." He shook his head. "We were married in a civil ceremony by a justice of the peace. I never marked her and she didn't want to be marked."

Aubrey's jaw dropped. "What?" And then because she was a needy woman, added, "Why?"

He ran his finger down her cheek, over her jawline, then traced her lips. "We talked about it, but it never happened. There was no pull with her like there is with you."

More, tell me more. It was the sweetest thing she'd ever heard, the aphrodisiac that sent her love for him into orbit. She was his first. He had no idea how much that meant to her.

She parted her lips and drew his lingering finger inside her mouth, pretending it was his cock.

"Aubrey," he groaned when she teased her hands down his chest until she was at the open button on his jeans. She cupped the press of his erection through the material.

He pulled out of her mouth and grasped the sides of her head, pulling her in for a hard kiss. His tongue replaced his finger, but it was more elusive as it led their sweet dance. She let him take over. It was the only way she was going to keep him out of his head.

He yanked off the lacy camisole she'd chosen to wear for the occasion, then folded her breasts into his hands, squeezing the mounds, thumbing the nipples.

His own nipples peaked as she slid her fingers down his sides, the feather-soft touch making him shiver.

"How do I drive you wild?" she whispered as she lowered her head and nipped him on his pec.

His body jerked and before she could react, she was under

him, his body over hers, held rigid by his strong arms. "Keep doing shit like that, baby."

"Okay." She grabbed his ass and squeezed, wishing he were out of his pants. When her wish didn't come true, she said, "You should get naked."

He climbed down her, hitching his thumbs in the sides of her lacy panties and hauling them down her legs. He held them to his nose and inhaled, then tossed them to the floor. In seconds, his jeans and underwear were pooled next to them. His eyes held hers as he knelt on the mattress between her legs, then he lowered himself, his face inches from her pussy.

"So wet," he murmured as he ran his fingers through her desire, using it to polish her needy little button, but only a little as he replaced in with his mouth. He drank her in like she was the elixir that gave him life.

"Oh god," she moaned as she arched her back. "It's too much, Ulrich. I want you inside me when I come."

"Do you?" He looked up past her stomach and chest to capture her eyes. "Why not be greedy? Why not have everything?"

She sat up and grabbed his head, pulling him upwards until their lips met. It was soft pillowy kiss, but so sensual she felt it to her toes. "Not tonight. I only want you tonight. Us. Together. I don't want to take more than you."

CHAPTER FORTY-SEVEN

"Not tonight. I only want you tonight. Us. Together. I don't want to take more than you."

Ulrich's painful erection didn't want to argue, and neither did his wolf, who was pacing inside him, grim, determined, pressing at his chest.

He pushed against Aubrey's legs, forcing her knees to bend so the fronts of her calves rested against his chest.

Arms rigid, carefully holding himself over her, he held her gaze. He wanted to see every moment of this sacred ritual. This irreversible joining of their bond.

Her soft moans echoed in the room like whispering willows in the breeze. As he inched inside her, she grabbed his shoulders, her nails digging into his flesh, deeper each time he flexed his hips.

Her body welcomed him, and he savoured the tightness of her walls as he rocked inside of her. In her position, she couldn't do much more than let him fuck her, but that's what he wanted. Needed, instinctually. She was his mate, submitting to him, opening to him.

Their breaths deepened and synced as he thrust gently.

No words were needed. Ulrich almost wept when he felt the moment of unity, when they were no longer separate, but an entity of their own. They would never be alone again, even when they were apart.

"It's time," he whispered as his wolf pressed against him.

"It is," she agreed as she drew in a breath. "I'm ready."

He slipped from her and turned her over, then pressed his chest against her back. He guided himself into her, holding her tightly to him. His thrusts were faster, his breathing jagged as his need to dominate her grew.

He felt the tightening of her walls around his cock, her strangled cry as she came. The spasms seared through her body and into his. It was the wildness of the beast, the roar of the falls, the warmth of the sun, the lightness of air. It was everything.

"Aubrey!" he roared as the force of nature swept through him, seizing him, cradling him. Catching him as he fell. His semen spurted from him and he knew. He knew. This was their joining but also the moment of conception.

He knew.

CHAPTER FORTY-EIGHT

Aubrey came first, barely a second before Ulrich gripped her bruisingly, one hand holding her throat, pushing the back of her head against his chest, the other wrapped under her thighs, forcing her knees almost to her chin. His orgasm shuddered through him and he roared her name.

It was magic. And heart wrenching. And safe. The lonely girl who'd wandered through life seeking an elusive sanctuary disappeared. In her place was a woman who was loved, wanted, cherished, full. It overwhelmed her and the emotions building inside her sought an outlet.

She pressed her face into the pillow as tears slid from her eyes. She could feel everything he was feeling, knew what this moment was for him. She felt his heart, knew his joy, scented his urgency.

He slid from her and moved her gently to her stomach. She felt the charge in the air as he shifted. He was there as his wolf, nuzzling her neck, licking the tears on her face as his animal eyes reached inside her to her soul. Then he was gone, replaced by a searing pain that took her breath away.

She squeezed her eyes shut trying to move past the agony to borrow Ulrich's strength, and then, like a herald, he howled long and joyous and, in that moment, she found him.

She lay there, overwhelmed with emotion as he licked her back, each stroke of his tongue helping the pain fade. And when he was done, he shifted again. The mattress bounced gently as he reclined, sliding his arms around her waist and gently cradling her.

"You're going to have my baby," he whispered.

CHAPTER FORTY-NINE

Two days later and Ulrich was still riding high from his unity with Aubrey.

The first time he'd seen her, at the cop shop, was a day he would always celebrate. That moment led to all their moments together, both the good and the bad. It had been a necessary journey to get them to where they were now, which was looking forward to all the future love and happiness they had yet to share.

Sappy, yeah, but he forgave himself. After all, he was the luckiest man in the world.

He walked out of the Ford dealership with the keys for his brand spanking new Super Duty F-450 XL

in hand. Aubrey was right – there was something to this retail therapy concept. He'd wanted to buy her a new car, but she refused. It almost turned into an argument because he couldn't understand her point of view.

Stubborn waif that she was, she distracted him by swallowing his dick.

He grinned at the memory as he steered down a service road that took him to Falls Towing. A parking spot was open close to the front door and Ulrich pulled the truck in, reveling in the purr of the new motor before turning it off.

A middle-aged woman watched from behind a front desk littered in paper as he approached. "Where's Donnybrook?" he rumbled.

She furrowed her brow, clearly not liking his tone. "He's in his office. Name?"

"Back there?" He gestured to a hall.

She made a move to stand as if she were going to block him. He didn't give her a chance to take her life in her hands. His shifter swiftness had him down the hall before she was upright. There were three doors, and while he wasn't a genius, he figured the door marked office was his best bet. He flipped it open.

Donnybrook was seated behind a desk, talking on the phone. His eyes widened when he saw Ulrich. "Gotta go," he muttered into the phone, then ended the call. "What the fuck do you want?" he sneered with all the bravado of someone about to shit his pants.

Ulrich plopped into a chair on the other side of the desk as his bottle-blonde receptionist finally caught up to him. She paused in the doorway, looking helplessly at Donnybrook. "I'm sorry, he—"

"Close the door and leave." Donnybrook probably bullied her too.

He held himself steady under Ulrich's glare, but his heart was beating too fast, the stink of fear rolling off him. "I don't know what—"

"Don't talk, you bigoted fucker," Ulrich said. "Not a fucking single word." He shoved a few files off the desk for effect. "The cops don't know that you ran me off the road."

Donnybrook tried to look dumb, which wasn't really that hard. "I don't—"

"—want to interrupt me again." He said it with a cool

malice that had the other man swallowing his tongue. "This is between you and me." Still, he maintained a deadly calm to his voice, his posture suggesting this was a friendly chat. "I wasn't alone in that truck. My kid's mother was there too."

Donnybrook pressed his lips together, but he had the decency to look shocked.

"Could have been Tag with me, you sonofabitch. You could've killed someone." He sat up, dropping his feet to the floor with a bang. "Now, I could decide to go the biblical route – eye for an eye, destroy your family like you tried to destroy mine, but unlike you, I'm not that fucked up."

"They had nothing—"

"Shut your fucking mouth!" Ulrich bellowed.

The blood drained from Donnybrook's face as he cowered in his chair.

"I'm usually a zero strikes kind of guy. You fuck with me and mine, you don't get to see the sunrise ever again. But I'm giving you a break because my kid's friends with your kid. And my *mate* is your kid's teacher."

Donnybrook blanched at Ulrich's last tidbit of information.

"You don't look at them, talk to them, go anywhere near them and I'll let you live. But you do anything to fuck with me or my family ever again, and I'll rip your fucking head off and plant it on the flagpole at the cop shop while I smear the parking lot with your entrails."

Donnybrook was shaking. His mouth was gaping like Fake Goldie's. "I—"

"—will never speak of this to anyone." He stood, swiped the desk clean of remaining papers then slammed his fist down in the centre of it with so much force that it broke in two.

Donnybrook shrieked and scrambled backwards, falling out of his chair and crawling towards the corner.

Ulrich stared at him, holding his face as neutral as possible as his body locked up on him. Too much jarring of the body so soon after the accident made him feel like someone had tasered him, the shock of agony jarring all the injured parts of his body.

Fuck, that fucking hurt.

He wanted a last word but was afraid anything he said would come out soprano, so once he was sure he wouldn't collapse, he turned his back and exited with as much stoicism as he could muster.

In his truck, he fumbled in his pocket with his left hand, yanked out the bottle of pills, then struggled to open it. The lid came off with force and the little white tablets flew everywhere. He managed to extract three from the cup holders on the console, which he dry-swallowed.

His next stop was Jackson's house, where he was meeting Jackson and Ivan Polski, who doubled as the precinct's staff sergeant and forensic specialist. They needed to talk a few things over.

Ivan was sucking on a beer when Ulrich arrived, and greeted him jovially. "Glad I didn't have to haul you out of that crevice. My back couldn't handle it." Ivan was Russian and spoke decent English, but his accent was unmistakeable.

"Let's get down to it," Jackson said as he handed Ulrich a beer and sat down.

Ulrich stood against the wall, not wanting to force his body to bend. He took a long swallow of the beer, holding it gingerly in his throbbing right hand. It was a small consolation that his fingers could still grip. "Where're we at?"

Ivan flipped open a file that had been laying in front of him on the coffee table. "The clothes found just beyond the Lodge pack's territory consisted of a plaid button up shirt and a pair of jean shorts. No underwear or footwear. No jewelry or anything else. Ascena confirmed they belonged to Macy

Kerrigan and provided a photograph of Macy wearing the top." He took a swallow of his beer, giving Jackson and Ulrich a moment to ask questions.

Neither did.

"An analysis of the blood on the clothes confirmed that it belonged to a shifter and that it came from a single source. Judging by the saturation on the clothes, I'd say the blood loss was somewhere between a half and one full litre."

"That's what? One to two pints?" Ulrich interjected.

Ivan nodded. "Ascena puts Macy's body weight at 45-48 kilograms."

"Shit," Jackson said. "That's a lot of blood loss for a 100-pound woman."

Ivan tugged his beard. "I assume you're using the term 'woman' loosely."

Ulrich looked to Jackson. "Did you get Ascena to admit the girl's age?"

Jackson shook his head. "It's irrelevant anyway. We still have a missing person."

"It's not irrelevant. It's the difference between our killer having her or not."

Jackson didn't like being told he was wrong. "There's blood on her clothes. A lot of blood. Something obviously happened to her."

"I know." Ulrich didn't like being told he was wrong either. "But if she's a kid, she's outside the killer's MO."

"How do you know that? Maybe she had a boyfriend she was sneaking around with." Jackson tapped the picture in the file. "She might not be 18, but she's also not a child."

Ulrich had trouble believing that the killer would even be aware of Macy, boyfriend or not. "Doubtful she had a boyfriend, not if she was sheltering in Ascena's pack."

Jackson switched topics, returning his attention to Ivan.

"Have you determined that the blood actually belongs to her?"

"I don't know. I need something to compare the DNA in the blood to and Ascena claims that she has nothing of that nature of Macy's."

Ulrich glanced down at Macy's photo. "Seems like she'd need a hairbrush to keep that mane neat." Heavy rich auburn hair framed the girl's face and fell in front of her shoulders down to her waist.

"Yep. Said the same thing to Ascena," Ivan replied. "I don't think the woman likes me."

"It's your fucking beard, Ivan." Jackson gathered the empties and took them to the kitchen, returning with a fresh round.

Ulrich tugged at his own beard. "Hasn't hurt me."

"Jackson's jealous because he can't grow one," Ivan grumbled. "One more thing on the Kerrigan file. However the blood came to be, it didn't happen at the site where the clothes were found."

"Shit," Ulrich cursed but he wasn't all that surprised. The killer was a clever fuck – another reason to look at Cooper as a suspect. Doctors had to have sharp intellects to get through their medical training.

Jackson twisted the beer in his hands. "Lucien said the same thing when we asked him how come his pack missed the clothes when they swept their territory. They weren't there the first time round."

"The blood on the clothes wasn't fresh, though there's no way to determine how old it is unless we send it out for analysis." Ivan took a gulp of beer and let out a soft belch. "I don't think that's necessary though. I'm thinking the blood spilled on the same day she disappeared."

"Ten days ago," Jackson supplied.

Ivan nodded. "Yep. Then placed where they'd be found."

Ulrich gave his back a small stretch to work out the stiffness that was setting in. "The killer's jacking us around," he rumbled.

Jackson met Ulrich's eyes. "Pretty fucking convenient that we were distracted while Cooper was making a playdate with Aubrey."

"Maybe it was a good thing I crashed my truck." Shivers racked his body.

He closed his eyes, saw his mate's face, and said a silent *thank you* to the universe.

CHAPTER FIFTY

"I'm worried about, Leah," Aubrey said to Eva.

"Me too." Something rustled in the background and then the slide of the handle on a toaster reached across the airwaves.

"Toast?" Aubrey stated the obvious.

"It's weird, but I can't stop eating it. All I can think about is toast and butter with crab-apple jelly.

Aubrey wandered into the kitchen. The talk of toast was making her hungry. "I've never heard of crab-apple jelly."

"Me neither. Not until Aztec's mom sent some. She sent us all sorts of canned stuff that she grew. I want to eat it all at once."

Aubrey's mouth watered as she envisioned jars full of various colours and flavours. Sweet, tart, zingy. "Stop talking about food."

"Okay." A crunch followed and then Eva mumbled around something that made Aubrey wish the conversation was face-to-face. "Where do you think she went?"

"I don't know. She's only been gone two days and she'd

never leave Darkness Falls alone. Maybe she's hiding from her asshole father."

Aubrey bit her lip. "What if Jared got to her?"

"Coop? I doubt this has to do with him. After all she told Ulrich she was leaving."

Aubrey wrinkled her nose. "It's so weird that she'd tell Ulrich and not me."

"Yeah, it is." Another loud crunch sounded.

"What are you eating?" Aubrey exclaimed, pressing a hand against her belly.

"A dill pickle. I wasn't supposed to open the jar yet. Apparently, they should sit for a few weeks after being canned, but I couldn't resist."

"Wish I was there." Aubrey flipped open the door on the fridge and peered at the mostly barren shelves.

Eva snorted. "Because you think I'd share my food with you?"

Aubrey grinned as she moved an almost empty orange juice bottle on the top shelf over a few inches. Behind it was the saddest looking green pepper she'd ever seen and also, the only vegetable in the fridge. "I did think that, but guess I'm wrong, huh?"

"As long you didn't bring Ulrich with you."

"I don't think your mate would approve if Ulrich came with me to visit."

Eva changed the subject. "How's your back?"

Her back? "Amazing." And it was. The pain of rent skin and muscle, the shrinking of the wound each time Ulrich shifted and cleaned it – it was a surreal, astonishing experience that she clung to. They'd only just mated, but she wanted her mark to sing to her forever.

Sappy, sure, but Ulrich brought it out in her.

Eva snorted. "That's not the way I remember it."

"You know what I mean."

"Yeah." Eva's voice softened. "I do."

The bang of the door drew Aubrey's attention to the hall and her pulse sped up as Ulrich walked past her with grocery bags in his hand, dumping them on the counter. "I gotta go." Aubrey ended the call before Eva had a chance to say goodbye.

She knew she was smiling too widely; knew he would sense how much she wanted him. She couldn't help it. Maybe it was the honeymoon stage, maybe it would pass, and things would get real, or maybe she'd feel this bliss for the rest of her life.

"I love you," she said, in case he'd forgotten.

He finished stuffing some frozen meals into the freezer and straightened up. His eyes were softly blue but glittering like the sun on the ocean. "How's our little one?" He glanced at her belly.

She almost melted at his question. Our little one. It was too soon to tell the world that she was pregnant, though she wanted to shout it from a mountain top. "Our little one is snug as a bug."

Ulrich's grin conveyed his proud papa status. "Where's Tag?"

"Basement."

"Want to sneak out and go for a ride? I got the new truck."

Aubrey wanted nothing more in the world than to take a ride in Ulrich's new truck. "What if he catches us?"

"We'll lie." He pulled her to him. "The way I see it, we go to our spot, christen the truck, then, while we're naked, I'll shift and clean the mark."

She giggled as she settled against his chest. "I like the sound of all of that. Except lying to Tag."

"Nothing less than he'd do to us."

He jerked as she tried to take his hand.

"What the heck?" she said, staring in horror. His right hand was twice the size of his left, red and angry looking. "What did you do?"

"Broke a desk," he mumbled.

He broke a desk? "You broke a desk?"

"Long story." He changed the subject by kissing her soundly. "Let's go, before we lose the new truck smell."

CHAPTER FIFTY-ONE

Tag took the stairs two at a time, then watched out the window as his dad and Aubrey took off in his dad's new Ford.

He'd heard Dad come in but didn't want to come up right away. He had to admit that even if he was a little pissed that they'd taken off with out him, he was happy that he didn't have to hang around them.

The lovey-dovey crap was really getting to him.

Just this morning, he'd watched his dad and Aubrey as they sat across from each other at the kitchen table, their hands linked, their heads bent together while they whispered. It was funny, he thought, that they bothered trying to hide from him. He was a shifter, he sensed their hearts beating the same rhythm, overheard the sappy exchanges, scented how much they wanted each other. All that mushy stuff disgusted Tag.

He understood that they were newly mated, that they were having sex, and as long as he didn't picture what that looked like, he could deal. What he couldn't handle was the idea of being mated.

He shivered. He liked girls... a lot, but not enough to be with one forever.

Of course, his dad was old, and it was probably time for him to settle down. He knew they'd have some kids of their own and it didn't really bother him. As long as he didn't have to share his room, he could handle a brother or sister. Brother, he decided. He didn't want a screaming girl messing with his stuff.

Aubrey was a girl, yeah, but she was different. Tag didn't mind that Dad chose Aubrey. Not anymore. In fact, as each day passed, he appreciated her more. She was the girl-version of his dad, except she really got what Tag was about, talked to him like he was an adult. Mostly treated him like that too. It's probably why the kid's at school liked her so much.

He felt guilty because she was nothing like his mom and that's what was most appealing. He missed Sibyl, but he was still pissed at her for not caring how he felt after the accident.

His face heated as he thought about how she'd left town without even saying goodbye. That was so typical, and he couldn't figure out why he still loved her.

The weekend had opened his eyes enough to see how messed up his mom was. Aubrey, Eva, and even that weirdo, Leah, were so different than his mom. They talked straight, goofed around. Aubrey especially fussed over him. Even more than his dad.

He swiped at the sudden wetness in his eyes.

It was going to suck to have her as his teacher, because he wouldn't be able to get away with anything like how much homework he had or if he got in trouble.

He felt a sudden sense of urgency that this year be over. Not only because he'd move out of her class, but because by then, he'd be a full-fledged shifter. Each day the urge was getting stronger. His dad knew it too. He promised Tag that they would start the training in earnest. He was so looking forward to that.

He turned from the window and headed into the kitchen. Bags of groceries were sitting on the counter, and he grinned that his dad, who was usually so neat, left them out and took off with Aubrey. That was awesome.

He rifled through the bags, found a box of Ritz crackers, which he shoved under his armpit as he grabbed the peanut butter and a glass from the cabinets, and the new jug of milk, which was still sitting on the counter. That would be a good start, he thought, then spotted the bag of chips and tucked it between his fingers.

His stomach growled as he headed downstairs.

Damn, he was hungry.

EPILOGUE

Leah stood at the edge of the forest and took a deep breath as she stepped across the unseen barrier. She froze for a moment, motionless, expectant, fearful.

Nothing but the usual songs of the universe noticed her trespass into the Lodge pack's territory. It bolstered her resolve. She could do this. She had to do this. The only other person she trusted to share her burden with was Aubrey. She choked up at how lucky she was that Aubrey came to Darkness Falls.

The breeze tapped a reminder on her face that she had more pressing matters than counting her cloverleafs. She looked at the stands of trees before her and swallowed down her panic. She could do this. In and out and no one would be the wiser.

She tucked the blanket she was holding between her knees so she could transfer her backpack to her shoulders. It wasn't all that heavy – a couple of bottles of water, an extra pair of running shoes, a dog collar and leash, and some protein bars. If she could've shifted, she wouldn't have needed the bars. Rabbits had plenty of protein.

Her wolf was there, curled up inside her like a Siamese twin. It refused to come out. Refused to be independent. Lazy sod, Leah thought, but didn't dwell on it. After all, she'd made it 21 years without shifting. What were another 50 or 60 more?

She grabbed the blanket and tossed it around her neck like a scarf and then plunged into the trees. Nothing would happen to her, she reassured herself. Nothing she couldn't handle.

If she got caught, she would channel goofy Leah. Lucien would be pissed that she had trespassed into his pack's territory. So would Gideon when he found out. But the alpha brothers could go to hell, both of them. She was on a mission and she wouldn't stop until it was accomplished.

An hour later, Leah sat down on a fallen log to reorient herself. She had all the qualities of a shifter – better hearing, keener sight, superior strength, but that was in comparison to humans. And frankly, her strength was relative because she had been the runt of the litter, one of a set of triplets, the only female.

Turned out her older brothers were bastards before they were even born, denying her the nutrition in the womb to grow. It was a shitshow after the birth too, her parents always fighting over the boys, about what the needed, how to raise them. It was always about the boys. Leah was nothing to them but an inconvenience that they would marry off as soon as they could.

Over time, the fights escalated and eventually become physical. It was rare the violence was directed at Leah and her siblings, but they all learned to stay out of the way. At least her brothers did. They went out of the way to make her the scapegoat too often.

It wasn't much past her 9th birthday when her mom took off with her brothers. Everyone knew where they'd gone – to her pack, but her dad was too weak to go and get them. Good riddance, he'd say, then look at her. "Why the fuck are you still here?"

Nice words from her old man, but Leah was scrappy, had to be to survive in Gideon's pack.

What the hell, Leah?

Why was she going on about shit she couldn't change? She had more important things to do. She stood, closed her eyes, and let her senses take over. The dream that woke her each morning for the past week, floated to her. The scene was the forest, the light mist forming a pathway, pointing a direction.

She turned her body slowly, then stopped. When she opened her eyes, she saw the misty trail. If anyone were with her, they would think she was nuts, but she wouldn't tell them that she could see what they could not. She'd simply say something confusing, then head off in that direction.

But alone was better, no one to distract from her rescue mission.

There was too much going on in Darkness Falls, and it was starting to take its toll on her, but she had to prioritize. First this, then she'd go to Aubrey.

Aubrey would know what to do about Sibyl.

THE END

THANK YOU!

Dear Reader,

Thank you for reading Primal Heat (Shifters of Darkness Falls Book 5). I hope you loved reading it as much as I loved writing it.

Please consider leaving a review - it only takes a moment of your time, but it helps me promote the book and helps readers decide whether to read it.

Love Jasmin Quinn

FORBIDDEN

Shifters of Darkness Falls Book 6

Leah's story is coming!!!! I'm so excited to write this book. Leah is dear to our hearts and my most treasured heroine. I plan to give her a love story without messing with the core of who she is.

~

Leah is a shifter who can't shift, an omega who doesn't act like one, a loner who dances to her own drummer. She also mixes her metaphors.

Lucien is an Alpha living his life as nature intended until he catches Leah in his territory, alone and hurt.

She shouldn't have been there. She should've run when she saw him.

Because Lucien's not supposed to have her.

She's forbidden.

But it's too late.

She belongs to him now.

Available August, 2021

ALSO BY JASMIN QUINN

Available at the following booksellers

Available at these Book Sellers!

Running with the Devil

- The Darkest Hour (Book 1)
- Secrets inside Her (Book 2)
- Black Knight (formerly Black Surrender) (Book 3)
- Without Mercy (Book 4)
- Hard Lessons (Book 5)
- Courting Trouble (Book 6)
- Shattered (Book 7)
- Past Sins (Book 8)
- Wild Card (Book 9)
- Fallen Angel (Book 10)
- Duplicity (Book 11)
- House of Shadows (Book 12)
- Boxset: Books 1-4
- Boxset: Books 5-8
- Boxset: Books 9-12

Shifters of Darkness Falls

- Basic Instinct (Book 1)
- Fierce Intentions (Book 2)
- Alpha's Prey (Book 3)
- Savage Hearts (Book 4)

- Primal Heat (Book 5) (February 26, 2021)
- Boxset: Books 1- 4

After Dark

In collaboration with Nikita Slater

- Collared: A Dark Captive Romance
- Safeword: A Dark Romance
- Chained: A Forced Mafia Marriage Romance
- Good Girl: A Captive BDSM Romance
- Hostile Takeover: An Enemies to Lovers Romance

Standalone Books

- First Blood Moon
- Unleashed

ABOUT JASMIN QUINN

Jasmin Quinn is an international best-selling author of contemporary steamy romance novels with strong male and female characters. Anything goes in her world as long as there's lots of hugs, kisses, and sex.

Jasmin tries not to take herself too seriously, but some things matter to her – like good manners, compassion for humans and animals alike, and Canadian maple syrup on vanilla ice cream. She stays in shape by exercising her rights to her opinion.

Jasmin lives in beautiful British Columbia, Canada with her husband.

STAY CONNECTED WITH JASMIN

Be the first to hear from Jasmin as she shares the latest news and updates about her books.

When Jasmin isn't writing about sex and romance, she's blogging about it.

This is where she lets her hair down, releases pent-up passions, and embraces her naughty side. Sometimes she interviews her book boyfriends, other times she harasses authors she loves (and their books), and even occasionally writes public letters to Mr. Big (Face–book, not Chris Noth).

- Check out her blog at: www.jasminquinn.com
- For updates, bonus material, and freebies, join Jasmin's Dark Side: https://www.facebook.com/groups/509374932806476/
- Like Jasmin's Facebook Page: https://facebook.com/jasminquinnwritesromance/

Primal. Savage. Untamed.

DARKNESS FALLS

I have fallen back in love with shifter books because of Jasmin Quinn. Aztec and Eva's story is just amazing. Its touching with a side of omg hot! After all Aztec is a tall, sexy, wolf shifter! Yum! I highly recommend it! Keep the Darkness Falls series going!

5-star Amazon Review

A nail biting story from start to finish. Lots of action, suspense, intrigue and a whole lot of hot shifter sex! Raft and Trist were made for each other. Such amazing characters. Their chemistry is smouldering and intensely hot! With so many panty melting moments!

5-star Amazon review

RUNNING WITH THE DEVIL

This is an awesome series. It doesn't have to be read in order, although that adds another dimension. Shattered is my favorite; when I finished it I reread it within the week

5-star Goodreads Review.

★★★★★

Every book Jasmin writes is a well written, scintillating tale of perfect tension and plot twists that always reels me in and keeps me engaged.

5-Star Amazon Review

★★★★★

Your books are so detailed, the drama and suspense and all the excitement and the hard love.The characters are awesome. And you are an AWESOME writer!.

5-Star Amazon Review

★★★★★

It's so good to be bad!

UNLEASHED

This is a book of full emotional range - from fear to relief, from sadness to joy. I loved every minute of the read.

5-star Amazon review

It had me captivated and entertained throughout. Highly recommend.

5-star Amazon review

This is not a short book, so don't start it too late in the day or you will be up all night. Read wisely.

5-star Amazon review

Printed in Great Britain
by Amazon

61707391R00220